*He stare: moment, long enough for Laura to see his enjoyment in sparring with her turn to something else. Something hot. Something sexual.*

"I have another idea what the stakes could be," he said finally. "But I've got a feeling you're not going to like it."

Laura knew at once what those stakes were. She'd seen it in his eyes the very first time he had looked at her, felt it the other night when he had almost kissed her. That he would even suggest such a thing infuriated her. It also made her stomach tighten, her skin heat. "You're right. I don't like it. And despite what you might think, going to bed with you isn't my idea of a prize."

He laughed. "That's a pretty big assumption you've made."

Laura could feel the colour rush to her cheeks. "All right. So what *did* you have in mind?"

"Forget my idea," he said, his amusement

"Forget my idea", he said, his amusement fading. He inched a step closer. "That dark and hungry look was back in his eyes". "I like your idea better".

# Spencer's Forbidden Passion
## by Brenda Jackson

ᗡᘖᗢ

## *He couldn't deny he wanted her.*

Never before had he been so aroused by a woman. And Chardonnay had been fully conscious of the sexual attraction between them, even though in the midst of a business battle they'd attempted to downplay it.

As a plan formed in his mind, Spencer called his lawyer. "Find out which bank plans to loan her the money and let me know immediately."

He'd have her – one way or another. Chardonnay Russell would be his.

"Yes," he said through a smug smile. A marriage for love was out of the question for Spencer. But he'd certainly entertain the idea of a marriage for lust…

# Available in June 2009
# from Mills & Boon® Desire™

*What the Millionaire Wants…*
by Metsy Hingle
&
*Spencer's Forbidden Passion*
by Brenda Jackson

ꙮ ✿ ꙮ

*Seduced by the Enemy*
by Sara Orwig
&
*Baby on the Billionaire's Doorstep*
by Emily McKay

ꙮ ✿ ꙮ

*The King's Convenient Bride*
&
*The Illegitimate Prince's Baby*
by Michelle Celmer

# What the Millionaire Wants...
## METSY HINGLE

# Spencer's Forbidden Passion
## BRENDA JACKSON

MILLS & BOON
Pure reading pleasure

*First published in Great Britain 2009
by Harlequin Mills & Boon Limited,
Eton House, 18-24 Paradise Road, Richmond, Surrey TW9 1SR*

The publisher acknowledges the copyright holders of the individual works as follows:

What the Millionaire Wants... © Metsy Hingle 2008
Spencer's Forbidden Passion © Brenda Streater Jackson 2007

*ISBN: 978 0 263 87101 2*

*51-0609*

*Printed and bound in Spain
by Litografia Rosés S.A., Barcelona*

# WHAT THE MILLIONAIRE WANTS...

by
**Metsy Hingle**

Dear Reader,

What is it about those tall, dark and dangerously sexy men that fascinates us? You know the ones I mean. He's the guy who walks into a room and seems to stand a little taller, the one who has a bit of a swagger in his step. He's the one with the mischievous smile and a gleam in his eye that says he knows everything there is to know about pleasing a woman and that he'd be happy to show you. You also know that getting mixed up with such a man would be asking for trouble.

Ever wonder what type of woman is brave enough to tangle with Mr Tall, Dark and Dangerously Sexy? Or what type of woman it will take to steal his heart and make him a one-woman man? I did. That's how I came up with my new book for Desire. I had a wonderful time creating Jackson Hawke and Laura Spencer's story. I hope you have fun watching them tangle in the boardroom and bedroom on their way to falling in love.

For a commemorative bookmark or to learn about the next book I'm working on, write to: Metsy Hingle, PO Box 3224, Covington, LA 70434, USA or visit me on the web at www.metsyhingle.com.

Happy reading!

Until next time,

*Metsy Hingle*

## *METSY HINGLE*

is an award-winning, bestselling author of series and single-title romantic suspense novels. Metsy is known for creating powerful and passionate stories, and her own life reads like a romance novel – from her early years in a New Orleans orphanage and foster care, to her long, happy marriage to her husband, Jim, and the rearing of their four children. She recently traded in her business suits and fast-paced life in the hotel and public-relations arena to pursue writing full-time. Metsy loves hearing from readers. For a free bookmark, write to Metsy at PO Box 3224, Covington, LA 70433, USA or visit her website at www.metsyhingle.com.

For the City of New Orleans and its people
who continue to inspire me

# One

"I am not for sale, Mr. Hawke."

Jackson Hawke bit back a smile as he stared at the woman across the desk. "I'm not trying to buy you, Ms. Spencer. I'm merely offering to employ you."

"I already have a job," she informed him with the cool disdain of a true Southern belle. "I'm the general manager of the Contessa Hotel."

He had to give her points for moxie, Jack thought. He had expected any number of reactions to the news that he had acquired the defaulted bank loan on the small New Orleans hotel. He had made a career of taking over financially troubled companies, revamping them and turning the once-failing operations into profit centers. In each case, his presence was seldom welcome. More often than not his arrival was met with trepidation or anger, and in some cases both. He had expected no less from the owners of the Contessa Hotel. What he hadn't anticipated was defiance. And *defiant* was the only way to describe the woman seated across from him. Unfortunately for Ms. Laura Jordan Spencer, her defiance didn't change the fact that he now owned her family's hotel. "True. But given the circumstances, your position here could prove to be temporary," he countered.

"There is nothing temporary about my position here, Mr. Hawke," she advised him, a hint of temper coloring her voice. "My great grandfather built this hotel nearly a hundred years ago and it's been owned by the Jordan family ever since. I'm sorry if you were led to believe that we would consider selling the property. But I can assure you, the Contessa is *not* for sale."

"I have a receipt for fifteen million dollars that says otherwise," he told her.

"Which I'm sure the bank will refund you once I've straightened out this…this misunderstanding."

He leaned forward, met her gaze. "Take another look at those documents, Ms. Spencer," he said, motioning toward the packet of legal papers he'd presented her, which outlined his acquisition of the hotel via her mother's defaulted bank loan. "There *is* no misunderstanding. Hawke Industries now owns this hotel."

Anger flared in her green eyes. "I don't care what those papers say. I'm telling you there's been a mistake," she insisted and punched the button on the intercom. "Penny, try Mr. Benton at the bank again."

"You're wasting your time," he told her. He already

knew from his meeting with the bank chairman the previous afternoon that the man had left town that morning.

"The only one wasting my time, Mr. Hawke, is you," she fired back.

While she waited for her assistant to place the call, Jack used the opportunity to study her more closely. He noted the almond-shaped eyes, the stubborn chin, the smooth skin and lush mouth. She wasn't classically beautiful or slap-you-in-the-face sexy. But there was something about her, a sensuality that simmered beneath the all-business exterior. Judging by the quelling look she shot him, his appraisal hadn't gone unnoticed. Nor had it been appreciated.

At the buzz of the intercom, she grabbed the phone. "Yes. I see," she said. "Thank you, Penny."

"Still not available, I take it," he remarked when she hung up the phone.

"He and his family have left for the Thanksgiving holiday. His office is trying to reach him. When they do, I'll get this mess straightened out."

"Talking with Benton isn't going to change the facts, Ms. Spencer. Your mother pledged this hotel as collateral on a loan and Hawke Industries purchased that note, along with several others, from the bank. Since your mother defaulted on that loan, the Contessa Hotel now belongs to Hawke Industries."

"I'm telling you, you're wrong," she insisted. "There is no way my mother would have ever pledged the Contessa."

Tiring of her refusal to accept the obvious, Jack snatched the stack of legal documents, pulled out the collateral mortgage note signed by her mother and slapped it in front of her. "Look at it," he commanded. "That's a promissory note signed by your mother, pledging her stock in the Contessa as guarantee on the loan. Are you going to deny that's her signature?"

Something flickered in her eyes as she stared at the damning document. For the first time since he'd arrived and introduced himself to her as the hotel's new owner, the lady looked uncertain. Just as quickly it was gone and the defiance was back. "I don't care what that says. Even if my mother had wanted to use the hotel as collateral for a loan, she couldn't have."

"And why is that?"

"Because my sister and I each own ten percent of the hotel's stock. And neither of us would ever consent to her using the hotel."

"She wouldn't have needed your consent—not to pledge her own stock. Which is exactly what she did," he pointed out.

"My mother would never do such a thing. Not without telling me first."

There was something in her voice, a hint of uncertainty. There was also a flicker of fear in her eyes. It was that fear that stirred something inside him. "Didn't you say your mother was out of the country on business?"

She nodded. "She and her husband are opening a night-club in France."

"Well, maybe she meant to tell you, but just never got around to it," he offered, surprising himself with this sudden surge of empathy. He frowned. Emotion was something he never allowed to enter into his business dealings. It was his own cardinal rule. In the dozens of takeovers he'd engineered, no amount of tears, pleas or offers of sexual favors had deterred him from his course.

"She *has* been busy getting ready for the grand opening."

But he could tell from the lack of conviction in Laura's voice that she didn't believe that telling her about the loan had slipped her mother's mind any more than he did. He had learned firsthand that when it came to money and sex—blood was no thicker than water. Apparently, Deirdre Jordan Spencer Vincenzo Spencer Baxter Arnaud had sold her daughter's legacy and hadn't bothered to inform her of what she'd done.

"At any rate, if, and I'm not saying that she did, but if my mother did pledge her shares of the Contessa as collateral on a loan, I'm sure she didn't understand exactly what that entailed," she told him.

Her stubborn denial sobered him. Shaking off his uncharacteristic spurt of compassion, Jack reminded himself that this was business. Sentiment had no place in business. He didn't intend to let a pretty face, a great pair of legs and a mountain of attitude deter him from his plan. "Or perhaps your mother understood exactly what pledging the hotel as collateral meant."

She stiffened. "Just what is it you're implying, Mr. Hawke?"

"I'm not implying anything, Ms. Spencer. I'm simply pointing out that if your mother had wanted to sell the hotel, but knew you would be opposed to it, using it as collateral on a loan and then defaulting on that loan would be a means of accomplishing her goal."

"How dare you!"

"Why don't we skip the outrage, Ms. Spencer. You strike me as a smart woman. Don't tell me it hasn't crossed your mind. Your mother isn't interested in this place. Why else would she have dumped it in your lap and left the country?

Not that I blame her. The hotel was barely breaking even when your grandfather was alive. Since his death, it's been losing money steadily."

She narrowed her eyes suspiciously. "I won't waste my breath asking where you got your information." Temper laced her voice causing the trace of a Southern accent she bore to be more pronounced. "But apparently your source doesn't have all the facts. If he or she did, they would have informed you that the hotel has shown a steady improvement over the past four months. Whatever difficulties the Contessa may have had in the past, they're over. The hotel is doing just fine now."

"Showing a slim profit on last month's financial statement is a long way from being fine."

"I—"

Jack held up his hand. "I'm aware of what you've done since you took over the management six months ago. But you and I both know that this hotel is in need of major upgrades. I intend to see that it not only survives, but that it dominates the small luxury hotel market in this area." He paused, then pressed his point home, saying, "Since you own ten percent of the hotel's stock and are familiar with its operations, I'm willing to allow you to be a part of those plans. Or not. It's your choice. Either way, I'm prepared to make you and your sister both a fair offer for your stock."

"I'm not interested in selling my stock. And neither is my sister."

"Don't be too hasty, Ms. Spencer. After all, you haven't heard my offer yet. And neither has your sister."

"I don't need to hear it. I don't—"

"I'll give you and your sister each two million dollars for your stock. And—"

"I'm not interested."

"Please, do allow me to finish," he said pointedly and noted the angry color flooding her cheeks. "In addition, I'm willing to offer you a management contract with the Contessa at a substantial increase in salary. A salary, which, I might add, is far greater than the one you earned when you were working for the Stratton Hotel group or the Windsor," he added, mentioning the two hotels where his research revealed she had held positions previously.

She hiked up her chin a notch. "Perhaps you should have your hearing checked, Mr. Hawke. As I've already told you, I'm not for sale and neither is the Contessa."

But before he could point out that he already owned the majority of the hotel's stock, there was a tap at the door. "I'm sorry to interrupt, Laura," the perky brunette assistant who had ushered him into the office earlier said from the doorway.

"It's okay, Penny. What is it?"

"You're needed downstairs." She looked over at him, then back at her boss. "You know, for that meeting you scheduled with the kitchen staff."

"Thank you, Penny. Tell them I'm on my way."

Jack didn't miss the look that passed between the two women before her assistant retreated. He suspected it wasn't a meeting that required Laura Spencer's immediate presence. More than likely it was another crisis, one of the many that had plagued the hotel in recent years. As beautiful as the Contessa was and the potential profit she would generate for Hawke Industries, age had taken its toll on the structure. The hotel would continue to deteriorate unless it underwent the necessary maintenance and upgrades it so sorely needed. He intended to see that the hotel was returned to its former glory and became profitable—with or without Laura Spencer's cooperation.

She stood. "As you heard, I'm late for a meeting, Mr. Hawke. So this discussion is over."

It wasn't often that he found himself so clearly dismissed and certainly not by someone who was in no position to call the shots. A part of him was annoyed. While another part of him couldn't help but admire her spirit. Standing, Jack adjusted his gray suit coat. "I suggest you call your attorneys, Ms. Spencer, and have them review the documents I gave you."

"I intend to."

"Once you've confirmed that Hawke Industries is now the majority stockholder of the Contessa Hotel, I want to meet with you to discuss the hotel's operations. Preferably, tomorrow morning."

"I won't be available tomorrow morning," she informed him.

"Then the afternoon. Two o'clock okay with you?"

"I'll be tied up then, too."

Jack stared at her. Once again, he was surprised by her defiance. His name alone had struck fear in the hearts of many a hardened CEO. Apparently, that wasn't the case with Laura Spencer. He liked the fact that she wasn't afraid of him. And he wasn't averse to the rest of the package, either, he admitted. Under different circumstances he might have entertained the idea of something more personal with her. While he didn't consider himself to have a specific type, he enjoyed the company of intelligent, attractive women. He knew from her education and work history that Laura Spencer was smart. With her big eyes, soft skin and hair that was some shade between red and brown, she certainly was attractive. The perfect package really—except for her connection to the hotel deal. It was that connection that was the problem. Regardless of how attractive he found her on a personal level, he had no intention of letting it get in the way of business. Reminding himself of the business at hand, he said, "Tomorrow evening then. We can discuss my plans for the hotel over dinner."

"I already have plans," she told him.

The intercom buzzed. "Laura, they *really* need you for that meeting."

"I'm on my way," she said. "I have to go."

"I don't suppose there's any point in suggesting another day or time because you'll be tied up then, too," he stated, knowing full well what she was doing. If she agreed to a meeting with him, then she would, in effect, be admitting that everything he had told her was true. Her family no longer owned the Contessa Hotel.

"How perceptive of you, Mr. Hawke. As a matter of fact, my entire week is full and I won't have a moment to spare."

"Then I suggest you make time, Ms. Spencer. Because like it or not, you are going to have to deal with me." And without waiting for her to respond, Jack turned and exited the office.

As she left the hotel's kitchen, Laura pressed her fingers to her temple. The splitting headache that had started with the arrival of Jackson Hawke earlier was quickly working its way toward a migraine. Nodding to various hotel em-

ployees, she made her way across the lobby to the elevators. At least her temperamental chef's latest emergency—table salt being substituted for kosher salt—had
been fixed relatively easily. She'd simply borrowed some
kosher salt from a neighboring restaurant so Chef André
could finish his masterpiece. Then she had dispatched one
of the busboys to the supply house to swap the incorrectly
delivered salt. While the celebrity chef she had hired away
from a major restaurant caused her a few hassles, the
income he generated by keeping the hotel's dining room
filled far outweighed the headaches, she reminded herself.
Besides, at the moment dealing with a temperamental chef
was the least of her worries. Her real worry was Jackson
Hawke. Just the thought of him made the pounding in her
head increase.

Laura stepped into the elevator and pressed the button
for the executive floor. If only the *real* emergency that
Jackson Hawke had dropped in her lap could be solved as
easily. Of course, she could always hope that the man was
wrong—that her mother hadn't pledged her hotel stock and
that Hawke hadn't actually bought her note. Laura called
up an image of him in her mind's eye. She thought about
the way he'd trained those blue eyes on her, the confidence in his expression, the hard line of his jaw. She sighed.
Sure, she could hope he was wrong, Laura told herself. But
Jackson Hawke hadn't struck her as a man who was often
wrong about anything.

Stepping out of the elevator, she headed down the
corridor toward the block of offices. When she entered the
reception area and discovered her assistant on the phone,
she retrieved her messages and began to flip through them.

Penny placed her hand over the receiver and mouthed, "Everything okay?"

Laura nodded and motioned for Penny to join her when she was finished with the call. Once inside her own office, Laura snagged a bottle of water from the mini-fridge and walked over to her desk. She opened the side drawer and reached for the bottle of aspirin. After shaking out two tablets, she washed them down with water and then sat in her chair. But five minutes later, Laura could feel the aura starting around the edges of her eyes and she knew the aspirin wasn't going to cut it this time. She was going to need the pills her doctor had prescribed for the migraines. She hated taking the meds, she admitted. While they knocked out her migraine, they also zapped her energy and made her feel fuzzy for the rest of the day. And today of all days, she needed a clear head and all the energy she could muster.

Shifting her gaze to the credenza, Laura glanced at the framed photo of her with her various half siblings and step-siblings at her mother's most recent wedding. She looked at the smiling green-eyed blonde beside her—her half sister, Chloe. At twenty-two, Chloe was four years her junior and the product of her mother's fourth marriage to soap opera star Jeffrey Baxter. An actress living on the West Coast, her sister was into healthy eating and treating the body's ailments with alternatives other than drugs.

Deciding it was worth a shot to try one of Chloe's methods before resorting to the pills, Laura began the deep-breathing techniques that her sister had shown her. And because she couldn't bring herself to chant the mantra aloud without feeling like an idiot, she repeated the words silently.

I can feel my heartbeat slowing. I can feel the blood flowing down my arms, to my fingertips. My fingers are growing warmer. I can feel the tension leaving my body. I am relaxed. I am calm.

Continuing the silent chant, she closed her eyes. But the minute she did so, an image of Jackson Hawke filled her mind. She remembered in vivid detail the cut of the charcoal-gray suit he wore, how the blue in his tie was the exact shade of his eyes. Even seated, he had looked tall and forbidding as he'd told her that he now owned the Contessa. And just thinking of Hawke made her head pound even harder.

"So much for natural healing," she muttered and opened her eyes. Still reluctant to take anything stronger than aspirin, Laura lowered her gaze to the bottom drawer of her desk.

*Don't do it.*

Ignoring the voice in her head, Laura pulled open the drawer and stared at her stash of candy. She had banished the forbidden sweets from her sight two weeks ago in her effort to cut her sugar intake and take off the five pounds she'd been carrying on her hips since Halloween. Biting her lower lip, she recalled the promise she had made to herself only three days ago. No more junk food. That meant no cookies. No candy. No ice cream. No milk-chocolate bars with the gooey caramel inside.

*Don't do it, Laura.*

Torn, Laura stared at the tempting treats. Her mouth watered. Still she hesitated. She'd promised herself, no sweets unless it was an emergency. Didn't Jackson Hawke and a monster headache constitute an emergency? Of course they did, she reasoned. Snatching up the bite-sized chocolate-and-caramel bar, she ripped off the wrapper, bit into the decadent treat and moaned.

"Uh-oh."

Laura opened her eyes and spied Penny standing in the doorway. She popped the remainder of the forbidden chocolate into her mouth and swallowed. Calories or not, she felt better already, Laura decided.

After taking a seat in the chair across from her desk, Penny glanced at the candy wrapper and said, "Since Chef André didn't walk out like he keeps threatening to do, I'm guessing that guy Hawke is the reason you deep-sixed the new diet. Who is he, Laura? And what did he want?"

Laura gave her assistant a quick rundown of the situation and the stunned look on the other woman's face mirrored her own feelings when Jackson Hawke had dropped the bombshell on her an hour earlier. But now that some of the shock had started to wear off, she knew she had to figure out a plan to stop Hawke. "I know this is a shock, Penny. It was to me, too. But I need you to keep quiet about this—at least until I can find out exactly what our position is. If word were to get out, it could cause a panic among the staff and I can't afford that. It's been difficult enough getting workers since Hurricane Katrina," she said, referring to the storm that had nearly destroyed New Orleans in 2005. Not only had the city lost more than half of its population, but the destruction had claimed entire neighborhoods and depleted the workforce. "And any buzz in the marketplace about management changes could set off a run of cancellations, not to mention that we'd probably lose out on any contracts."

"I won't breathe a word," Penny assured her. She paused, worry clouding her brown eyes. "But what if what this guy Hawke says is true? What if he really does own the hotel? Do I need to start looking for another job?"

"Hawke didn't strike me as a stupid man. Regardless of what happens, he'll need someone who knows about the day-to-day operations of the hotel, where and who to go to for the emergencies that pop up. And that person is you. I don't think you need to worry about your job, Penny."

But her assistant's concern made her realize that if Hawke did take over the hotel, Laura would need to do everything she could to ensure the job security of her employees. It was what her grandfather would have done, what he would have wanted her to do. If only her grandfather were here now, she thought.

"What about you? If Hawke is telling the truth, what will you do?"

"I don't know," Laura told her honestly. She thought about her childhood, of moving to new places each time her mother married and started a new life. But come summer, she had always returned to New Orleans, to her grandfather, to the Contessa. Even when she'd gone away to college and then had gone to work for other hotels out of state, she had known that the Contessa was still there, waiting for the day when she would return home for good. Only now when she had finally come back, her grandfather was gone. And Jackson Hawke was here, trying to take the Contessa from her. She wouldn't let him.

She couldn't. She looked at her assistant. "But I can tell you what I'm not going to do and that's roll over and play dead. Try Benton's office again, then get my attorney, my mother and my sister on the phone for me."

If Jackson Hawke wanted her hotel, then he was darn well going to have to fight her for it.

# Two

So far, she'd struck out. Sighing, Laura put down her pen and stretched her arms above her head. She still hadn't spoken with her attorney or her sister. And her conversation with Benton had not gone well at all. She still couldn't believe her mother had actually used the Contessa as collateral on a loan and not told her. Benton hadn't given her much in the way of details. Instead he'd referred her to her mother. Unfortunately, the time difference and distance between New Orleans and France had made reaching her mother difficult. Glancing at the clock, she calculated the time overseas and concluded it was now after two o'clock in the morning in France. Aware of her mother's love of the night life, Laura tried the number again.

"*Oui,*" her mother answered on the fourth ring, her voice breathless.

"Mother, it's Laura."

"Laurie, darling," she replied, genuine pleasure in her voice. "Philippe, it's Laurie calling from America."

She could hear Philippe shout out a greeting from the background and Laura made the obligatory hello to her mother to give to him. "Mother? Mother?" Laura pressed when her mother began to converse with Philippe in French.

"I'm sorry, darling. Philippe wanted me to tell you how well things are going here with the new club and to see when you can come for a visit. He's eager to show it off to you and Chloe." Without waiting for her to answer, her mother went on, "Do you think you girls could come? Why, it's been nearly a year since I've seen you, Laurie. And it would be so lovely to have my babies here for a visit. We could…"

Laura closed her eyes a moment as her mother rambled. She didn't bother trying to explain to her that at twenty-six and twenty-two, she and Chloe could hardly be considered babies. Finally, she said, "Mother, please. This is important. I need to know if you used your stock in the Contessa as collateral for a bank loan."

For a long moment, her mother was silent. Then she said, "It was just as a formality. A guarantee, until I paid back the loan."

Telling herself not to panic, that not even her mother could have spent all that money so quickly, she asked, "How much of the money do you have left?"

At her mother's silence, the knot that had formed in her stomach when Jackson Hawke had walked into her office tightened. Just when she thought her mother wasn't going to respond, she said, "I don't have any of it left."

Laura felt as though the wind had been knocked out of

her. There was nothing left? All of the money was gone? Suddenly a roaring started in her ears. Her stomach pitched. Feeling as though she were going to be sick, Laura leaned forward and put her head between her knees.

"Laurie? Laurie, are you still there?"

When the initial wave of nausea had passed, Laura straightened and leaned back in the chair. Lifting the phone receiver she still held in her hand to her ear, she managed to say, "I'm here."

"Darling, you sound…strange. Are you okay?"

No, she wasn't okay, Laura wanted to scream. Her foolish, reckless mother had placed the Contessa at risk. And because she had, Jackson Hawke might very well be able to take the hotel away from them, away from her. "You're sure it's all gone? There's nothing left?"

"I'm sure."

"What did you do with all that money?" Laura demanded.

Her mother explained how she had invested six million dollars into the nightclub that Philippe had been so keen to open in France. "I used some of it to pay for repairs to the hotel that the insurance didn't cover after the hurricane and the rest of it went to pay the back taxes on the hotel."

Laura knew the hotel had been underinsured at the time of the hurricane and, as a result, not all of the repairs had been fully covered. But the taxes? "The taxes couldn't possibly have been that much," Laura argued. "Since the hurricane, the assessment values have decreased, not increased."

"The taxes were from before the hurricane…from when your grandfather was still alive and running the hotel."

Laura frowned. That didn't make any sense, she thought and told her mother so. "Granddad always paid the Contessa's bills—even if it meant using his own money to do it. He would have made sure the taxes were paid."

"Apparently, he didn't. Or he couldn't. Evidently, the hotel wasn't doing well for quite some time before your grandfather became ill and he got behind on some of the bills. The tax assessor came to see me not long after the funeral and told me the taxes were three years in arrears, plus there were penalties. He was going to put a lien on the hotel. So I went to the bank and borrowed the money to pay them off."

Once again, Laura felt as though she'd had the wind kicked out of her. She'd known the hotel had gone through a rough patch and that her grandfather had hired a marketing firm to help him. But she hadn't realized things had been that bad. "Why didn't Granddad tell me? I would have come home and helped him with the hotel."

"That's probably why he didn't tell you, because he knew you would have come rushing home. And that wouldn't have been good for your career."

But Laura suspected her grandfather hadn't told her because he hadn't believed she was capable of running the Contessa. A sharp sting went through her as she recalled her grandfather dismissing the idea of her working at the Contessa after she'd graduated from college. He'd insisted she was too green to run a property like the Contessa and had told her to take the job she'd been offered by Stratton Hotels. Lost in thought, Laura didn't realize her mother had spoken until she heard her name said sharply. "I'm sorry. What did you say?"

"I said, how did you find out I pledged my stock to the bank for the loan?"

"Because the bank sold your note, Mother."

"Yes, I know. To some company with a bird's name."

"Hawke Industries," Laura supplied and she certainly didn't consider the man for whom the company was named to be some tame, feathered creature. Rather he was a predator—just like his name implied.

"That's right. I remember getting a notice from them, telling me they owned the note for my loan now."

"They own more than the note, Mother. You defaulted on the loan and now Jackson Hawke owns eighty percent of the stock in the Contessa."

Jackson Hawke sat in the penthouse suite of the Contessa Hotel late that evening and waited for the e-mail on Laura Spencer to arrive on his computer. Following his meeting with her, he had had the investigative firm he used compile a complete background check on her. He'd asked for everything—from her favorite flavor of ice cream right down to her shoe size. He frowned as he recalled his assistant's remark that it sounded personal. It wasn't, Jack told himself. It was business. Strictly business. And he intended to keep it that way.

As he waited for the file, Jack took a sip of his wine and considered, once again, his earlier encounter with Laura Spencer. While he had anticipated her objections and could even understand her denial at losing the hotel, he hadn't expected to find her outright defiance so stimulating. If he were honest, Jack admitted, the woman intrigued him. And it had been a very long time since anything or anyone had truly intrigued him.

A beep indicated the new e-mail and Jack clicked onto

the file document and began reading the investigator's preliminary report. Much of the information he was familiar with already, having attained the data during his initial investigation of the Contessa and its principals. But he skimmed through the basics on Laura Spencer again anyway—noting the names of her parents, the schools she had attended, the places she had lived, her employment history. As he perused the information in the file, he paused at the newspaper and magazine clippings Fitzpatrick Investigations had included with the report.

He studied a color photo that had appeared in a soap-opera magazine more than twenty years ago of a young Laura on the steps of a church following her mother's wedding to an actor. Another photo showed a six-year-old Laura standing with her grandfather in front of the Contessa Hotel as the older man shook hands with the city's mayor. Even then, there was no mistaking the stubborn tilt of Laura's chin, the pride in her eyes, the promise of quiet beauty in her features. More clippings followed. Laura graduating as valedictorian from a high school in Boston. Laura in her freshman year at college in New Orleans. Laura making her society debut as a maid in one carnival ball and reigning as queen in another. Laura named as an assistant manager at the Stratton West Hotel in California. He paused at a more recent clipping of an elegantly dressed and smiling Laura on the arm of a man wearing a tuxedo. Jack clenched his jaw as he recognized her escort—Matt Peterson. Just the sight of his stepbrother's face sent anger coursing through him. And along with the anger came the painful memories, the old hurt. Jack read the caption beneath the picture.

*Ms. Laura Spencer and Mr. Matthew Peterson at the Literacy Gala hosted by Mr. and Mrs. Edward Peterson.*

How had he missed this? And just how serious was Laura's relationship with Peterson? he wondered. After dashing off an e-mail to Fitzpatrick Investigations, demanding answers, he considered how Peterson's involvement with Laura might impact his deal. While his stepbrother didn't have the money to bail Laura out, Peterson's old man and stepmother did. And there was nothing the pair wouldn't do for their golden-boy son.

Bitterness rose like bile in his throat as Jack thought of Peterson's stepmother—his own mother—who had left her family for her husband's business partner and best friend. Whether Laura was seriously involved with Matthew Peterson didn't matter, Jack told himself. All that mattered was the deal. If his stepbrother tried to play knight in shining armor for Laura, it would only make the deal that much sweeter when Jack foreclosed on the hotel and crushed Matthew in the process.

Irritated, but not sure why, Jack shut off his computer. Deciding he needed to stretch his legs and clear his head, he pocketed his room key and exited the hotel suite.

Twenty-five minutes later, he returned to the hotel, carrying a paper bag filled with a large cup of coffee and a chocolate éclair that he'd picked up at a hole-in-the-wall coffee shop located a few blocks from the hotel. While the crisp November air had refreshed him and tempered his restlessness, it had also awakened his appetite. One foot inside the tiny shop and he'd opted for the sugar-laden pastry.

"Evening, Mr. Hawke. I see you found the place I told you about," the doorman remarked as he approached the hotel.

"I sure did, Alphonse. Bernice said for you to come by and have a slice of apple pie and a cup of coffee after your shift," Jack said, relaying the message the waitress had asked him to pass on to her sweetheart.

Alphonse grinned, showing a mouthful of even white teeth. "That little girl makes the finest apple pie in all of New Orleans," he boasted. "You be sure to try some before you head home."

"I'll do that," Jack promised as he entered the hotel, his gaze sweeping over the lobby. He noted the magnificent chandelier, the marble floors, the artwork and massive urn of fresh flowers that spoke volumes about the hotel's quality. As nice and lucrative as the newer chain hotels were, they couldn't duplicate the old-world elegance and sense of history found in a place like the Contessa.

Despite the toll time and the lack of funds had taken on the hotel, the Contessa still exuded an air of luxury and privilege to those who walked through her doors. It was on the promise of that luxury and privilege appealing to the discriminating traveler, as well as the movie community that had adopted the city, that he had banked fifteen million dollars. It was a good investment, one based on numbers, not sentiment, Jack told himself as he pressed the button for the elevator.

After pushing the button again, he waited for one of the hotel's two elevators to arrive. Two minutes turned into three, then four. When he hit the button a third time, he took another look at the large dial above the elevator banks that indicated the cars' positions. He noted that one of the elevators remained on the eighth floor while the other was making a very slow descent from the twelfth floor. When it, too, stopped at the eighth floor, he frowned. Walking over to the front desk, he read the clerk's name tag and said, "Charlene, I think there's a problem with the elevators. They seem to be stuck on the eighth floor."

"I'm sorry for the inconvenience, sir. We've been having a little trouble with the elevators lately. I'll notify maintenance right away and have them check it out. I'm sure they will be operational in a moment," she advised him and picked up the phone to report the problem.

Making a mental note to add servicing and refurbishing the elevators to his list of immediate hotel improvements needed, Jack headed for the stairs. When he reached the sixth floor where the executive offices were, he paused before opening the door. He told himself he was simply going to check the status of the elevators and find out if they were moving again. But when he reached the elevator bank, he angled his gaze down the hall toward the management offices, where the lights were still burning.

A check of his watch told him it was after ten o'clock— long past quitting time, even for the hotel's general manager. But as he approached the suite of offices, he didn't have to wonder who'd be working so late.

Jack looked to his left toward Laura's office. The door was slightly ajar and he could hear music—a hauntingly beautiful piece that was one of his own favorites. Obviously, he and Laura shared similar tastes in music.

Pausing in the doorway, he saw that Laura was seated behind the mahogany desk, her head tipped back against the massive black leather chair and her eyes closed. He used the moment to study her. The hair that he had classified as a color somewhere between red and brown that morning was a deep, rich red in the lamplight. Her skin was fair and had a smooth, creamy glow. Jack could just make out the faint dusting of freckles across Laura's nose. His gaze dipped to her mouth. Her lips were bare—no splash of bright color, no slick of gloss—which made her far more attractive in his book. She'd shed the red suit jacket she'd worn earlier to reveal a long, smooth neck and more creamy skin. The white silk blouse gently skimmed her shoulders and draped breasts that were neither large nor small, but just the right size to fill a man's hands.

As though sensing his presence, she opened her eyes. For the space of a heartbeat, she didn't move. She simply stared at him. Then suddenly she straightened and reached for the stereo remote. The music died midnote.

"You didn't have to turn it off. That CD is a favorite of mine," he told her and stepped into the room.

Ignoring his comment, Laura's voice was cool as she said, "If you're looking for your room, Mr. Hawke, it's on the top floor."

"Thank you for pointing that out, Ms. Spencer," he said. So she had discovered he was a guest in her hotel. He'd known that she would. A good general manager made a point of reviewing the hotel's guest list. She had apparently reviewed hers and found his name on it, which, judging from her expression, had not pleased her. He walked over to her desk and set down the bag with his coffee and éclair.

"The business office is closed."

"And yet you're still here," he pointed out. "I didn't realize being the hotel GM meant working day *and* night. I'm surprised your boyfriend doesn't object to the long hours."

"Was there something you wanted, Mr. Hawke?"

He paused a moment, considered the loaded question and the woman. Evidently from the way she narrowed her eyes, Laura realized what he was considering had nothing to do with business. Deciding it was best not to go there, he finally said, "Actually, I was taking the stairs up to my room when—"

"Why were you using the stairs?"

"Because the elevators aren't working."

When she grabbed for the phone, he reached across the desk and caught her wrist. Gently removing the telephone receiver from her hand, he replaced it on the cradle. "The front desk has already alerted maintenance."

Laura pulled her wrist free. "I'm sorry you were inconvenienced," she told him. "I'm sure maintenance will have the problem fixed shortly. In the meantime, if you need to get to your room, you can use the service elevator. I'll show you where it is."

"That's okay. I'm in no hurry. I'll just wait for the elevator," Jack told her. Deciding to take advantage of the fact that he had her one-on-one, he sat down in the chair in front of her desk. "But since I'm here and you don't appear to have any pressing meetings scheduled at the moment, maybe now would be a good time for us to talk about the hotel. I'm assuming you've spoken with the bank and confirmed my ownership position of the hotel."

"Actually, I haven't confirmed anything other than the fact that you purchased my mother's note. And until I speak with my attorney and find out what your legal claim is on the property, I see no reason for us to have any discussion about the hotel."

"All right. We won't discuss the hotel. But I would like

to drink my coffee before it gets cold. That is, if you don't mind," he added even as he removed the large foam cup from the paper bag. He took out the chocolate éclair that was wrapped in a thin white pastry sheet. Looking over at her, he noted that her eyes were trained on the treat. "Maybe you'd like to join me? I bought the large-size coffee."

"No, thank you," she said.

"Some of the éclair, then?"

"No, thanks," she told him, but Jack didn't miss the way she looked at the pastry.

Ignoring her protest, he divided the éclair in two and placed half of the chocolate pudding-filled confection on one of the napkins, then set it in front of her. When she simply stared at it, he said, "Go ahead."

"I'm not hungry," she told him.

"What's hunger have to do with it?" he asked and bit into his half. He didn't bother to hide his enjoyment. The rich pudding inside the chocolate-iced pastry shell was delicious. "Alphonse was right. Bernice does make the best éclairs."

"This came from Bernice's Kitchen?"

He nodded, took another bite, swallowed. "I was looking for a cup of coffee and wasn't exactly dressed for the dining room," he said, indicating the casual slacks, sweater and bomber jacket he wore. "Alphonse recommend Bernice's."

"Bernice is a genius when it comes to baking." The wariness in her expression faded, giving way to a look of anticipation as she dragged her fingertip through the choco-late pudding spilling from the torn pastry. "I tried to hire her as a pastry chef for the Contessa, but she turned me down flat. Said she didn't think it was a good idea for her and Alphonse to be working at the same place, that it might take some of the mystery out of their relationship."

Jack arched his brow. "I got the impression they were in a…um…long-term relationship."

"They've been dating for fifteen years, engaged for the last four. They don't want to rush things," she told him, the hint of a smile curving her lips.

"After fifteen years, I'd say there's little chance of that happening."

"It seems to work for them," she said and brought her finger to her mouth.

There was something inherently sensual about the sight of Laura licking her finger, Jack thought. He found himself wondering what she would look like while making love. Would those green eyes darken with need and heat? Would her lips part, her breathing quicken? Would that smooth, cool skin feel as soft as it looked?

The direction of his thoughts annoyed him, but it didn't surprise him, he admitted. He was a healthy male who enjoyed the opposite sex and the pleasures to be found in a woman's body. But when it came to women and sex, he had no delusions. Plain and simple, he believed in lust, not love. And right now he was experiencing a serious case of lust for Laura Spencer.

She scooped another finger full of pudding and as though sensing his gaze, Laura looked up. Her body went still. Her eyes locked with his as awareness sizzled like electrical currents between them.

Jack watched as Laura's lips parted and when he heard the slight hitch in her breath, he felt another stab of lust. The pudding on her fingertip fell with a splat onto the napkin on her desk. But her eyes remained locked with his. Not bothering to think about what he was doing or how it might impact his business, Jack pushed back his chair and started toward her. He had just reached the side of her desk when he heard the tap at the door.

A disapproving male voice came from the doorway asking, "Am I interrupting something?"

# Three

For a moment, Laura couldn't breathe. The air seemed to have backed up in her lungs as Jackson Hawke stood at the side of her desk looking at her as though he wanted to swallow her whole. And heaven help her, for a moment, she had almost wanted him to.

"Laura?"

Shaking off the moment of insanity that had gripped her, Laura yanked her attention to the doorway where her attorney, Daniel Duquette, stood looking both concerned and curious. "Daniel," she said, her voice sounding more breathless than she would have liked. She cleared her throat. "What are you doing here?"

Daniel strode from the doorway into the office, slanted a glance at Hawke before shifting his focus back to her. "I've been tied up in depositions in Baton Rouge all day and just got back. When I picked up my messages, there was one saying that you needed to see me, that it was urgent. The front desk said you were still here, so I decided to stop by on my way home. Is everything okay?"

Everything was far from okay, Laura thought. But now was not the time to go into all that was wrong—not with Jackson Hawke standing there, measuring Daniel with his eyes and on the heels of whatever madness had stricken her. Because it certainly had been sheer madness that had caused her to react to Hawke as she had. The man was her enemy, she reminded herself. "Not exactly. And I do need to talk with you," she said, hoping Hawke would take the hint.

"I think that's supposed to be my cue to leave," Hawke said drily before he shifted his gaze from her to Daniel. "I don't believe we've met. I'm Jackson Hawke," he said and extended his hand.

Daniel shook his hand. "Daniel Duquette," he replied, his brow creasing. "You wouldn't happen to be the same Jackson Hawke with Hawke Industries who engineered the takeover of the Wilhelm family's company last year, would you?"

"Guilty as charged."

As she witnessed the exchange, Laura had a vague recollection of the small chain of family-owned inns that had been bought out by a corporation. She'd heard that the sale hadn't been a friendly one, that the two brothers who'd owned the properties that had been in their family for years had been split on whether or not to sell. There had been a great rift in the family because of it and because of the sale. The man behind that had been Jackson Hawke?

"So what brings you to New Orleans, Mr. Hawke?"

"Business."

"Thanks for sharing the éclair," Laura said, eager to get rid of Hawke and talk to Daniel about the mess her mother had gotten them into.

Hawke held her gaze for several moments. "You're quite welcome."

"Good night, Mr. Hawke."

He dipped his head in acknowledgment, but Laura didn't miss the gleam in his blue eyes that told her he hadn't forgotten what had almost happened between them. "I'll call your assistant in the morning about scheduling that meeting. Duquette," he said with a passing glance, and without waiting for a reply he strode out of the room.

The door had barely closed when Daniel asked, "What was that all about? And what's Jackson Hawke doing here?"

Laura sat down in her chair and released a breath she hadn't even realized she'd been holding. "He's the reason I called you. My mother pledged her stock in the Contessa as collateral for a bank loan and defaulted on the loan. Hawke bought her note and now he's trying to take over the Contessa."

Daniel let out a whistle. "Damn."

"My sentiments exactly," she said. "I spoke with the bank chairman briefly by phone and he wasn't much help. I'm going to meet with him after the Thanksgiving holidays. I know it's late, but could you take a look at these documents and tell me if there's anything I can do to stop Hawke from taking over the hotel?"

"Sure. Let's see what you've got." Daniel removed a pair of glasses from his coat pocket, slipped them on and began to read through the sheaf of papers she'd handed him. "I assume your mother received notices from both the bank and Hawke telling her she was in default of the loan," he said as he flipped through the pages.

"She remembers receiving something about the payments being late. She meant to contact them and explain she needed an extension, but because of the time difference and the new club opening, she never got around to making the call." Laura cringed inwardly as she heard herself repeating her mother's excuse. It was typical Deirdre behavior, she thought. When confronted with a problem, more often than not, her mother would go into her Scarlett O'Hara mode and plan on dealing with the matter another day. Only she never did deal with the problem. It either took care of itself or it got worse. But this time her mother's irresponsibility had proven disastrous.

Finally, he removed his glasses and looked up. "It looks legit. Unless your mother can come up with fifteen million dollars in the next thirty days to repay the loan, Hawke Industries can claim the stock she pledged as collateral and take over the hotel. I'm sorry, Laura."

So was she. But she refused to give up and play dead. Already, a plan was forming in her mind. "In other words, if I can come up with the fifteen million dollars and pay off the loan before the thirty days are up, then Hawke can't take the hotel. Right?"

"Right. But where are you going to get fifteen million dollars?"

"I don't know," she told him honestly. "But I'm not going to just hand over the Contessa to Jackson Hawke without at least trying to save her."

* * *

He had given her enough time, Jack decided. It hadn't been easy, but he had made himself wait three days—until after Thanksgiving had passed. Since his mother had walked out on him and his father all those years ago, holidays had been just like any other day as far as he'd been concerned. On those few occasions when his father had attempted to make Thanksgiving or Christmas some warm, fuzzy family event, it had invariably ended with Samuel Hawke pining for the woman who'd run out on them both, then drowning his heartache in a bottle of whiskey. Once his father had died, Jack had been able to stop pretending that holidays were some special family affair.

But something told him that that was just what they were for Laura Spencer—special, warm and fuzzy family affairs. He couldn't help wondering how she had spent her Thanksgiving. He knew her mother was in France and that her father lived on the East Coast. He also knew she had a slew of step and half siblings scattered across the country. Evidently, she hadn't traveled to see any of them since she was already at the hotel on the Friday morning following the big turkey day.

Or had she canceled her plans because of him? It was a strong possibility that she had, he conceded. Pushing aside a twinge of guilt that he might have caused her to spend Thanksgiving alone, Jack assured himself that Laura would make up for it at Christmas. She'd probably fly to France and spend it with her mother, he reasoned. Unless, of course, she was planning to spend Christmas with his step-brother, Matt.

Jack considered that a moment, recalled one of the few

times he had visited his mother, her new husband and stepson. The visit had been at Christmas and the entire scene had been something out of a Norman Rockwell painting—only it was a picture in which Jack hadn't belonged. Laura would belong though. He frowned at the image of Laura with Matt and his family gathered around a Christmas tree, opening gifts, drinking eggnog. According to Fitzpatrick Investigations, she and his stepbrother had been seeing each other for more than a year and it was rumored they'd been seriously involved when she had moved back to New Orleans.

Jack frowned. He knew Matt Peterson. The man thought far too highly of himself to restrict himself to any one female. A leopard didn't change its spots and neither would his stepbrother. Laura might think that she was the only woman in Peterson's life, but Jack would bet his vintage Corvette that there were several someone elses. But if Peterson had devoted a year to Laura as the report indicated, his stepbrother had done so for a reason. More than likely that reason had something to do with the senatorial race Peterson was rumored to be considering. Jack considered that angle for a moment. Laura was pretty, smart, well educated and poised. While her parents might be maritally challenged, her family tree was a good one and Laura herself was scandal-free. She would definitely be an asset on a senatorial candidate's arm and help him to get votes. Her return to New Orleans would have put a kink in Peterson's plans, but Jack doubted the man had abandoned his goal. He might have shelved it for a while, but Peterson didn't like losing any more than Jack did. It had been one of the few things they'd had in common. According to

Fitzpatrick's report, the pair had supposedly remained "close" friends despite her move. Just how close were they? he wondered. How many times had Matt tasted her mouth, touched that soft-looking skin, felt her body beneath his?

Envy sliced through him like a scalpel, swift and sharp. Annoyed by the stab of jealousy, Jack reminded himself that his stepbrother had nothing that he wanted. All Jack wanted was to get down to business. Determined to do just that, he entered the executive offices of the hotel. "Is she in?" he asked the receptionist, his voice sharper than he'd intended.

"Yes, but—"

Ignoring her attempts to waylay him, he marched into Laura's office. "Good morning," he said as he approached her desk.

"It was."

Dismissing the barb, Jack met her gaze. Her eyes were the same clear green as the waters in St. Thomas, he decided, and damned but he couldn't help wondering what it would take to make those eyes turn dark and smoky for him. Irritated with himself and her, Jack decided there was no point in dancing around his reason for being there. His voice was cold, brusque, as he said, "I assume you've had an opportunity to speak with your attorney by now."

"I have."

He put down his briefcase and withdrew the management contract he had prepared for Laura, along with the purchase agreement for her stock. He also pulled out the letter of resignation he'd had drawn up in the event it was needed. While the transition would be simpler for him if she stayed on at the hotel, he was prepared for her to quit and to buy out her stock. "Then you know that my purchase of your mother's note is legal."

"Legal, maybe. But certainly not ethical."

Refusing to debate her, he continued, "Then you also know that by defaulting on the loan, she forfeited the stock that she pledged as collateral on the loan. Which means Hawke Industries now owns the controlling interest in the Contessa."

He paused, waited for her to respond. But Laura remained silent. Her demeanor remained unchanged.

Keeping his voice level, he said, "My plan is to turn the Contessa into a five-star property again and recapture the market share it's lost. As I've already told you, I would prefer that you stay on at the hotel as the general manager. But if you choose not to stay, then I'm prepared to accept your resignation and purchase your stock." He slid both agreements and the resignation letter across the desk so that they rested in front of her. "It's your call, Ms. Spencer. Are you going to stay? Or are you leaving?"

Laura didn't even look at the documents he had placed before her. Instead, she met his gaze. There was something hard and determined in her eyes as she said, "I'm not going anywhere, Mr. Hawke."

The news surprised him. After their previous conversations, he had been sure she would turn him down flat. The fact that she hadn't both pleased and concerned him. He was pleased because it would be good for business to have her stay on. It concerned him because he had the hots for her, he admitted. And she was more than likely sleeping with his stepbrother, he reminded himself. The thought of Laura with the golden boy his mother had chosen as her son over him chafed at Jack, made him feel raw. He couldn't help wondering how Peterson would feel to come out on the losing end for once. Irritated with himself for allowing his thoughts to stray from the business at hand, he tapped the documents on the desk. "In that case, I'll need you to sign a new management contract with Hawke Industries. It's pretty straightforward, with all the standard clauses and the increase in salary I mentioned earlier."

"I'm sure the contract is fine."

He nodded. "Still, you may want to have your attorney look it over anyway."

"That won't be necessary."

"It's your call," he told her.

"Yes, it is."

Jack wasn't sure why, but her agreeable demeanor seemed off. "There's also a purchase agreement for your stock, if you should change your mind about selling it. My previous offer of—"

"I won't change my mind."

Something was off, Jack told himself again. Instinct, some unexplained ability that told him if a venture would be a hit or a flop, kicked in now. The woman was up to something. He felt it in his gut, felt it in his bones. "Why do I get the feeling that you're just itching to throw those contracts in my face?"

She picked up the contracts, fingered them. Looking directly at him, she smiled and said, "Because I am."

There was a confidence in her smile, a spark in her green eyes that he found intriguing. Intriguing and sexy as hell. "I admire your honesty. But you might want to think twice before you do that."

"Why? Because it would be an unwise career move on my part?" she asked.

"Something like that."

"You'd probably be right—if you were my boss and had the authority to fire me," she began. Obviously too edgy to sit, she stood and paced behind her desk. She paused, turned and looked at him. "But you don't."

"The last time I checked, owning eighty percent of the stock in a company constitutes the controlling interest, which does make me your boss and gives me the authority to pretty much do whatever I damn well please."

"That would be true—if you owned the stock. But you don't own it. At least not yet," she informed him triumphantly.

"Is that so?"

"Yes, that's so. You see, that note that you so cleverly got the bank to sell you gives me thirty days to cure the default on my mother's loan. Once I do that, my mother keeps her stock in the Contessa and your deal, Mr. Hawke, is null and void."

So that was her plan. Jack would have laughed were it not for the fact that this stunt of hers would cost him both time and money with delays. He didn't intend to allow her to cost him either—not without a price. "You think you can go out and find fifteen million dollars like that?" he asked with a snap of his fingers.

"I didn't say it would be easy."

"Try next to impossible."

"Nothing's impossible," she fired back at him.

"Trying to block my purchase of this hotel is," he assured her. Standing, he walked around to her side of the desk, a deliberate move on his part to intimidate her.

Instead he found himself far too aware of her, of the way the office light caught the copper in her hair, the way her black silk blouse curved over her breasts, the way the scent she wore reminded him of exotic islands and sex. Desire hit him like a one-two punch. He wanted her. Maybe part of him wanted her because she belonged to his stepbrother. But another part of him wanted her because he sensed a fire in her and he wanted to be the one to ignite it.

"Why? Because you're so rich and powerful?"

"Yes." Leaning closer, he lowered his voice and said, "And because I never lose."

"There's a first time for everything."

Jack didn't bother to hide his amusement. "And you think that you'll be the one to beat me?"

"I don't think I can beat you, Hawke. I *know* I can."

"You sound pretty sure of yourself."

"I am," she insisted.

Before he could quell the impulse, he countered, "Sure enough to wager on the outcome?"

"You mean a bet?"

"That's right. You say you can stop me from taking over the hotel. I say you can't. Are you willing to put your money where your mouth is?"

"I am, if you are," she told him.

"Oh, I am. I most definitely am."

She was insane to have dared the man the way she had, Laura admitted. But blast him, he had been so smug, so sure of himself. The fact that he had been standing so close to her hadn't helped, either. She had hoped those moments of heightened awareness between them in her office a few nights ago had been a fluke, that stress and thoughts of spending the Thanksgiving holiday without any of her family had caused her sexual chemistry radar to go askew. But if it had, then her radar still wasn't working because she'd felt those same ripples of awareness when he'd entered the room, that same quickening of her pulse each time he drew closer.

"So what are the stakes?"

"The stakes?" she repeated, doing her best to shake off his effect on her nervous system.

"Yes. You know, the prize that you're going to fork over to me when you lose our bet and I foreclose on the Contessa."

Laura sobered at his cocky remark. Taking a step back, she said, "You mean the prize that *you're* going to fork over to me when I beat you at your own game."

His lips twitched. "So what are the stakes?"

"Dinner," she suggested. "The loser pays for a seven-course meal at the restaurant of the winner's choice."

"Dinner?" he scoffed. "That's your idea of a bet?"

"What do you expect me to offer? My car? My condo?" she tossed back at him, and suddenly felt queasy at the thought of losing either.

"I don't have any use for a three-year-old BMW and you don't have enough equity in your condo to make it worth my trouble."

Anger bulldozed right over any misgivings she'd had about challenging the man as she realized he had had her investigated. Temper driving her, she put her hands on her hips and looked him square in the eyes. "And just what are you going to give up when you lose and *I* win?"

"I have a Jaguar that you'd look good in," he said with

a smile that lit up his eyes and made his face go from handsome to dangerously sexy.

"Far be it from me to take away your little toy and force you to be driven around in a limo."

"And I'd hate to have to see you hoof it to work in those high heels or be forced to sleep on the couch in your office," he countered.

He didn't think she could do it, Laura realized. He honestly didn't believe she could outmaneuver him and save the hotel. She could see it in those blue eyes, sense it in the way his muscles had tightened when she'd challenged him. She could feel it in the way he was watching her now—like a hawk with a helpless mouse in his sights. The realization that he thought she'd already lost only fed her temper. And it was her temper that had the words falling off her tongue as she declared, "Believe me, I won't be the one hoofing it to work or sleeping on a couch, Hawke."

"You won't have to. After all, it really wouldn't be fair of me to foreclose on your hotel, then take your car and home, too."

Suspecting that he was trying to bait her, Laura kept a rein on her temper, determined not to let it get her into any more hot water. With a nonchalance she was far from feeling, she said, "Well, since you ruled out dinner, I guess the bet's off."

"Not necessarily," he said.

"We can't agree on the stakes," she pointed out.

He stared at her for a long moment, long enough for Laura to see his enjoyment in sparring with her turn to something else, something hot, something sexual. "I have another idea on what the stakes could be," he said finally. "But I've got a feeling you're not going to like it."

Laura knew at once what those stakes were. She'd seen it in his eyes the very first time he had looked at her, felt it the other night when he had almost kissed her. He wanted to have sex with her. That he would even suggest such a thing infuriated her. It also made her stomach tighten, her skin heat. "You're right. I don't like it. And despite what you might think, going to bed with you just isn't my idea of a prize."

He laughed. "That's a pretty big assumption you've made."

Laura could feel the color rush to her cheeks and cursed her fair skin. Refusing to back down, she said, "All right. So what *did* you have in mind?"

"Never mind my idea," he said, his amusement fading. He inched a step closer. That dark and hungry look was back in his eyes, in his voice, as he said, "While it's not what I had in mind initially, I like your idea better. A lot better."

"The bet was a stupid idea in the first place. Let's just forget the whole thing," she told him, hating the fact that just having him move closer made her heart start racing again.

"Why? Don't think you can pull it off after all?"

Pride had her spine stiffening and the words firing from her lips. "I know I can pull it off."

"Then the bet stands. When I win, you spend the night in my bed."

Laura's pulse scattered. "And what do I get when I win?" she demanded, wishing she had never started this thing, wishing she could figure a way to get out of it without losing face…or something more.

"Your mother's promissory note—free and clear—and you get to keep or return the money you borrowed."

Laura blinked. "You can't be serious. That would mean you'd lose the fifteen million dollars you paid for the note."

"I won't lose," he assured her.

His words set her competitive juices stirring once again. She so wanted to wipe that smug look off his face. "Like I said, there's a first time for everything."

He grinned. "If you're right, then you have nothing to worry about. But if you're wrong and you can't come up with the money in time, then I foreclose on the hotel and I get you—in my bed for an entire night."

It was crazy. No, it was beyond crazy, she thought. It was insane. *He* was insane. Because only a madman would make such a bet. "Not that I'm complaining, mind you. But don't you think the stakes are a bit lopsided? At least for you. I mean, it hardly seems fair that I stand to have a fifteen-million-dollar loan wiped out whereas all you stand to gain is a night of sex."

He ran his eyes down the length of her in a way that made her skin feel as though he had touched her. "I'm satisfied with the stakes."

"I should think a man with your ego could satisfy his sexual needs for a lot less money," she tossed back, annoyed by her reaction to him.

"Oh, but I'd much prefer to have those needs satisfied by *you*, Ms. Spencer," he said, his voice dropping to a seductive whisper that sent a shiver along her nerve endings. "So, do we have a deal?"

For a moment, Laura said nothing. She was every bit as crazy as he was to even consider such an outrageous thing, she reasoned. The man was a corporate shark. Every article and interview she had been able to dig up on him all proclaimed his genius as a businessman. He hadn't lied. He seldom lost. When it came to doing business—or in the

Contessa's case, engineering a hostile takeover—Jackson Hawke would be a lethal opponent. And regardless of how good she was at her job, she'd be lying to herself if she thought that finding the money she needed to cure the defaulted loan would be easy. At best it was a long shot. But if she could pull it off, somehow raise enough money in time, she would win the bet, get the Contessa and be able to pay back the loans. "You're really serious? You'd risk fifteen million dollars against a night…a night of sex?"

"A night of sex with *you*," he amended. "And, yes, I'd risk it."

Still, she hesitated. She'd be a fool not to accept the deal he was offering her. And if she lost?

"Of course, if you're ready to concede that you can't come up with the money and dispense with the thirty days so I can foreclose, we can call off the bet."

Laura yanked up her chin. "I'll do no such thing. You've got yourself a bet. And if I were you, Hawke, I'd get ready to lose fifteen million dollars."

He smiled, a knowing smile that made the air in her lungs grow shallow. "And if I were you, Spencer, I'd get ready to spend a night in my bed—without the benefit of sleep."

# Four

Jack stood on the corner outside the restaurant where he'd gone for dinner and waited for the light to change. Still restless despite the long walk, he hit the speed dial for Fitzpatrick Investigations. When it went to voice mail, he grimaced. "It's Hawke. I need you to get me whatever you can find on Matthew Peterson, both personal and business. And I need it ASAP. Send whatever you find to my e-mail address."

Hitting the off button, he considered calling his assistant at home, then opted against it. Unless it was an emergency, Dotty would not be at all happy to have him calling her at home on a Sunday night. As she'd told him often enough, weekends were for family.

Instead, he holstered his cell phone and when the light changed, he headed back down Saint Charles Avenue in the direction of the hotel. The air was cool, but not cold like

New York. Not that you could tell by the way the people were dressed with their gloves and heavy coats, he thought. And given the number of red-and-green scarves he'd seen, people were already into the Christmas frenzy. December was still a few days away, but the storefronts and restaurants were already trimmed in lights. Christmas trees filled several windows and wreaths hung from doors. Even the lobby of the Contessa sported pots of red and white poinsettias and a huge tree.

Jack frowned as he thought of how all the Christmas craziness was going to impact him getting business done. He hated the distraction the holidays caused almost as much as he hated weekends. And he really hated weekends, Jack admitted. Nobody wanted to work on weekends and unless you were in the retail or service end of business, nobody did. That meant there were no stock deals to be done, no bank transactions to be made, no business brokering to negotiate and no attorneys or board of directors available to draw up contracts and vote on his deals. He hated that. He hated wasting time and he hated waiting for the hours to tick by until Monday morning rolled around and he could get back to work.

Sidestepping a couple with a baby stroller, Jack continued toward the hotel. Despite what his assistant claimed, he was not a workaholic who needed a wife. He had all the female company he wanted. As for work, it was mastering the game that drove him. That and the need to win. And having Laura in his bed was a bet he was looking forward to winning. He was thinking about all the delectable ways he intended to enjoy Laura when he neared the hotel and spied her standing under the porte cochere with her back to him and a cell phone at her ear. As he drew closer, he caught the tail end of her conversation.

"No. It's just that I was hoping we could go tonight to see the Celebration in the Oaks together."

He knew from the doorman that the Celebration in the Oaks was some big Christmas thing at the park. Was she talking to Peterson? he wondered. Was he in town? Was Peterson the reason he hadn't seen Laura at the hotel all weekend? Jack clenched his jaw as he thought about Laura spending the past two days with his stepbrother. He had never liked Matt Peterson. Even when their fathers had been partners and friends, the two of them had never gotten along. Two years older than him, Peterson had been a manipulative bully who had gotten his kicks by getting Jack into trouble. Later, when his mother had run off with Peterson's father, Matt had delighted in taunting him, calling him and his father losers.

"Yes. Of course I understand. Business should come first."

For a moment, Jack heard his mother's voice in his head, admonishing him for eavesdropping when he'd overheard her making plans to meet his father's partner. He didn't care if it was wrong or rude, he decided, and dismissed the memory. He remained where he was, several feet away from Laura, but close enough to listen to what she was saying. Although he made a show of studying the firs that had been draped with white lights near the hotel's entrance, his focus remained on Laura and her conversation.

"I know. It's just that it's been a while since I've seen you and I was looking forward to us spending some time together."

The disappointment in her voice had envy curling in his

gut. The fact that he was fairly sure it was his stepbrother she was pining over made the uncharacteristic jealousy he was experiencing all the more difficult to swallow. It also made him angry—with her and with himself—and all the more determined to wipe every memory of Peterson from her mind when he claimed her as his prize. The admission sent a stab of guilt through him. Just as quickly, he dismissed it. He was not using Laura to exact revenge on Peterson, he told himself. The chemistry had been there between them even before he'd known she was involved with his stepbrother. The fact that he would be taking her from Peterson when he bedded her would simply be an unexpected bonus.

"No. Don't worry about picking me up. I'm just going to take a taxi home and call it an early night." She paused. "You, too."

After she flipped the phone closed, she turned around and stopped cold when she saw him. "Hawke, what are you doing out here?"

"I was on my way into the hotel when I thought I recognized you standing over here. I wasn't sure it was actually you at first since this is the first time I've seen you in jeans—which, by the way, look great on you," he added. It was the truth. Those long legs of hers were made for skirts, but they looked every bit as sexy in the snug-fitting jeans.

"Thanks."

"You're welcome." Judging by her body language, Jack could see that he was making her nervous and he wasn't sure if that pleased him or not. He wanted her nervous with anticipation about being in his bed, not nervous because she was afraid of him. "I haven't seen you around the hotel the past couple of days and was beginning to think you were avoiding me."

"I decided to take the weekend off and catch up on some personal stuff."

Personal stuff like hooking up with his stepbrother? he wondered and felt that envy burning his gut again. "Have you told your boyfriend about our little bet yet?"

"I haven't told *anyone* about our bet," she informed him.

"Why not? Afraid he won't like the idea of you sleeping with me?"

"*I* don't like the idea that there's even the remote possibility that I might have to sleep with you. So I'd just as soon no one else know that I agreed to something so stupid."

Irritated by her response and his need to prove her a liar, Jack inched a step closer. He wanted to haul her up against him, kiss her senseless until she was begging him to make love to her. And because his own need was so great and he feared he wouldn't stop with a kiss, he did neither. Instead, he reached out and drew the back of his fingers gently down her cheek. His gaze never left her face and he watched her eyes widen, darken at his touch. Then slowly, very slowly, he rubbed his thumb along her bottom lip. Her lips parted. He heard her gasp, felt the warmth of her breath against his fingertips. He was reconsidering kissing her after all when Laura stepped back.

"I need to go," she said and started to leave.

"Laura, wait," he called as he followed her toward the hotel's entrance.

He wasn't sure if it was because he'd called her by her name or if she heard the regret in his voice, but she stopped, turned. Before he could apologize for coming on like a Neanderthal, she held up her hand and said, "No, you wait. I don't know if you're trying to intimidate me or seduce me, but it isn't going to work because I'm not going to sleep with you. At least, not unless I have to."

"Fair enough."

"I—" Evidently surprised by his answer, she fell silent, leaving the rest of what she'd planned to say unfinished. "Then I guess there's nothing more to say except good-night. So if you'll excuse me, I think I'll go grab a taxi and head for home."

"What about the Celebration in the Oaks?" Jack asked as he fell into step beside her. When she slanted a glance his way, he explained, "I couldn't help overhearing. Sounded like your boyfriend canceled on you."

He waited for her to confirm or deny his statement. She did neither. Not until they stopped at the end of the line for the taxi stand did she say, "Something came up. I'll just go another time."

The disappointment in her voice was also in her expression. And, once again, Jack found himself irritated by the notion of her with Peterson. A burning need to wipe his stepbrother's memory from her mind and replace it with his spread through him. "Alphonse said this Celebration in the Oaks is some kind of Christmas-lights display in the park. He said that it's worth seeing."

"It is," she assured him as a gust of wind blew down the street. Pulling up the collar of her denim jacket, she brushed the hair away from her eyes. "The gates open at dark every night from now until the end of the year. You should go see it while you're here."

"You still here, Ms. Spencer?" Alphonse said as she reached the front of the taxi line. "Evening, Mr. Hawke."

"Alphonse," Jack said.

"I thought you were over at City Park looking at the pretty Christmas lights with your—"

"Something came up and we had to cancel," she told him. "But I'm going to need a taxi to get home."

"No problem," he said and whistled for the next cab to come forward. "Sorry you didn't get to go see the Oaks, ma'am. I know how much you loved going to see them with your grandfather."

"Thanks, Alphonse. But I'll just go see them another time."

The taxi arrived and Alphonse opened the door. But before Laura got in, Jack caught her arm and said, "Why wait? Why not go now? With me."

Laura still wasn't sure what had possessed her to agree to accompany Jack to view the Celebration in the Oaks. Granted, her moods had been all over the place for nearly a week now—ever since Jackson Hawke had walked into her office and pulled the rug from beneath her high heels. Her emotions had run the gamut—from anger to despair and fear, from hatred to outrage and lust—and every one of those emotions had been ignited by Hawke. But of all of them, it was her attraction to the man that worried her the most. When she'd found herself wanting him to kiss her, she'd realized just how dangerously close she'd come to making a monumental mistake.

The man was her enemy, she reminded herself. He was a thief out to steal her legacy. And whether she won or lost the foolhardy bet they'd made, she'd be an idiot to risk losing her heart to the man. Yet, when he'd asked her to come with him to the Celebration in the Oaks, there had been something in his eyes, a loneliness, that had touched something deep inside her. She'd remembered the staff telling her that he'd ordered room service and spent Thanksgiving Day alone in his room. It made her realize how fortunate she'd been because she'd never spent any holiday alone. It was one of the advantages, she supposed, of her parents' multiple marriages. There was always family somewhere and she was always welcome. Last year had been one of the few times she hadn't celebrated Thanksgiving with her own family, opting instead to join Matt and his family.

She thought of Matt, realized she hadn't called him back as she had promised. And while she had used her sister, Chloe's, visit as an excuse for cutting the conversation short, the truth was she hadn't wanted to go another round with Matt. While she cared deeply for him, she didn't love him—at least it wasn't the kind of love that her grandparents had shared, the kind of love that she wanted. And despite his claim, she didn't believe that Matt really loved her that way, either. If he did, he would have understood why the Contessa meant so much to her. He didn't. Nor did he understand why she'd left California and returned home to try to salvage the hotel. He certainly wouldn't understand her desperation now to save it from falling into the hands of Jackson Hawke.

Shifting her glance, she took advantage of the dimly lit backseat and studied Hawke. In the jeans and bomber jacket, he seemed far less forbidding, she thought. With his black hair mussed from the wind and the beginnings of a five-o'clock shadow darkening his jaw, he was, surprisingly, even more handsome. But even dressed casually, there was an air of alertness, a fearlessness and determination that exuded power. There was also something inherently sensual about him that told her this was a man of passion, a man of strong appetites. The fact that he'd made it clear he wanted to indulge those appetites with her should have appalled her. And it did. But it also ignited a longing inside her that had desire curling in her belly whenever she was near him.

Embarrassed by the admission, Laura stared out of the taxi window and warned herself what a mistake it would be if she were ever to let Hawke know just how tempting she found him. Her silent warning was still ringing in her head when the taxi swerved to avoid a pothole and sent her body careening sideways, nearly into Hawke's lap. Pressing her hands against his chest to right herself, Laura looked up and made the mistake of glancing into his eyes. The heat simmering in them set off a tingling sensation inside her. Suddenly aware that his arms were cradling her, she straightened and scooted back to her side of the seat. "Sorry," she murmured.

"No problem," he told her, the husky timbre in his voice only adding to the charged atmosphere.

"Sorry about the rough ride, folks," the driver said, his eyes meeting theirs in the rearview mirror. "These here streets took a real beating in Katrina, and being under water for all those weeks didn't help."

"We understand," Hawke told him, but his gaze remained fixed on her.

"The streets weren't in the best of shape even before the

storm and now they're a whole lot worse," she commented, trying to diffuse the moment. As though to prove her point, the car hit another rut that had her body bumping against his again. He made no comment as she returned to her side of the taxi and this time, she held on to the hand grip above the door.

"She's right," the taxi driver commented, apparently oblivious to the tension. "A lot of the streets are still a mess. But the people are starting to come back. And mark my words, New Orleans is gonna be just fine. It's just gonna take more time than most folks thought."

While the driver answered a call from his dispatcher, Jack said, "He's right about it taking longer for the city to recover. I imagine leaving a hotel like the Stratton West to take over operation of the Contessa wasn't an easy decision."

"It was for me," she said, grateful that he was focused on business and not on her.

"Really? Most people in your position wouldn't have given up a big paycheck with a growing operation so easily."

"I'm not most people," she informed him.

"No, you're not. Maybe that's why you intrigue me, Laura Spencer."

Unsure how to respond, Laura chose to remain silent and spent the final minutes of the drive looking out the window, trying to ignore the man seated beside her. Eager to escape the intimacy of the darkened car, she was already unbuckling her seat belt as the taxi pulled up to the entrance of the park.

"This is as far as I can take you, folks," the driver informed them as he parked the car. "No driving tours allowed anymore, not since Katrina."

After paying the taxi driver, Jack joined her in line.

"Since you paid for the taxi, I'll take care of the entry fees."

But before she could even open her wallet, he handed the admission clerk a crisp fifty-dollar bill. "I've got it," he said. "You can buy us coffee later."

Too eager to see the display to argue with him, Laura said nothing. Once they had their hands stamped, they walked into the park and she entered a virtual wonderland of lights. She tried to take in everything at once—the towering oak trees dripping with white lights that looked like stars, the Christmas trees and storybook characters fashioned from lights, the delight on the faces of the children as they spied Santa Claus.

"Is it like you remembered it?"

Laura glanced to her side and realized Jack was watching her. "Yes. And no. A lot of it's the same, but it's different, too. There used to be more trees, more lights," she explained as the two of them began to walk through the park. "There was a road over there where cars could drive through and see all the lights. On the really cold or rainy nights, that's what a lot of people did. There were also horse-drawn carriages you could take the tour in. When Chloe and I were younger, we used to sing 'Jingle Bells' and pretend we were riding in a one-horse open sleigh."

"A sleigh, huh?"

She didn't have to look at him. She could hear the smile in his voice. Laughing, she shrugged. "What can I say? We're snow-deprived Southerners."

He laughed.

The sound surprised her. It was the first time she'd

actually heard him laugh. Unable to resist, she sneaked a peek up at him. He was smiling, and not just that slight twitch at the corners of his mouth, but an honest-to-goodness smile that revealed perfect teeth and radiated in his eyes. For the first time since she'd met him, Jackson Hawke actually looked happy, she thought. And she wasn't sure why, but knowing that she was responsible made her feel warm inside.

"Is that a train I hear?" he asked.

"Yes," Laura told him, suddenly enjoying herself. "There's a miniature train ride that goes through the park and there's this huge elevated train exhibit that has these tiny replicas of the streetcars and historic buildings and landmarks around New Orleans. It's like a mini-version of the city. Come on, I'll show it to you."

Laura showed him the train exhibit. She showed him Storyland. She showed him the vintage rides in the Carousel Gardens, sadly pointing out that several were no longer working because of the damage they'd sustained in the storm. She showed him the gallery of Christmas trees decorated with handmade ornaments made by local schoolchildren that lined the walkways of the Carousel Gardens. Finally, she showed him her favorite part of the exhibit—the antique wooden carousel. "It's more than a hundred years old," she told him and explained how the severity of the storm and the exposure to water had left the carousel inoperable. "I know it doesn't look all that great now because the paint is faded and chipped and so much of the gilding still needs to be redone, but you should have seen it before the storm. It was beautiful."

"I'm sure it was. It's amazing it even survived the storm."

"It's a miracle. I just hope they'll be able to get the funds they need to restore it. Since the park doesn't get any state or federal funding, the only money for repairs has to come from donations and admissions. With the population half of what it was pre-Katrina, there's less money." She sighed. "It would be such a shame if other little girls and boys never got to ride on it like I did."

"Boys, don't run," a harried-looking and very pregnant woman called out to the twin boys wearing green jackets and matching hats who were streaking toward them. "Please, would you catch them for me?"

"Whoa," Jack said, reaching out and corralling them. "Hey, buddies, what do you say we wait for your mom?"

"You're big," one of the boys said. "Are you a Saints football player?" he asked, referring to the city's beloved team.

"Afraid not. But you guys are so fast, I bet you could play for them when you get big."

"I'm so sorry," the woman said as she reached them. She smoothed a hand over her stomach. "Their little sister makes keeping up with them harder than it used to be."

"Not a problem," Jack told her. "We were just chatting about football. I think you've got yourself two running backs in the making here."

The woman laughed and ruffled their heads. "Their daddy would love that. In fact, he's home watching Sunday-night football right now. I must have been out of my mind to not make him come with me."

"We're going to see *The Cajun Night Before Christmas* exhibit," one of the boys said.

"Are you now?" Jack replied.

Both boys nodded. "It's supposed to be just like the book. If you want to see it, you just need to follow this road."

"Over there?" he asked, pointing in the direction they'd indicated.

"Yeah."

Still hunkered down beside the boys, Jack lowered his voice and said, "You know, I could have sworn I saw one of Santa's elves hiding up in one of those trees over there."

Both boys' eyes grew wide as they looked toward the trees. "Really?"

Jack nodded. "I figure they must be here, checking out the boys and girls and reporting to Santa which ones are extra good. You boys might want to walk with your mom so they can tell Santa how good you two are."

"Come on, Mom. You'd better hold our hands and take it slow."

"Yeah, you shouldn't run. You might trip or something," the other twin added.

"Thanks," the woman mouthed as she and her sons headed in the direction of the trees with the elves.

"That was really sweet of you. I'm sure their mother was very grateful," Laura told him, touched by his actions.

"Hey, I was telling the truth. I think I did see an elf in those trees," he said, smiling once again.

"Which tree?"

"That one right over there," he said and, grabbing her by the hand, he brought her several yards back from the road and pointed up to a huge oak. "That one. I saw a pair of little green eyes peeking out of those branches."

Laura peered up at the branches in question. "I don't see anything," she told him and when she turned to look at him, the smile dissolved on her lips. He was still holding her hand and he was watching her with an intensity, with a longing, that stole her breath.

She didn't know how it happened. She didn't know if he took another step toward her or if she moved toward him. Then his mouth was on hers. The kiss was gentle, slow, just a simple brushing of lips against lips. Then she felt the tip of his tongue. Sighing, she opened her mouth to him. Heat exploded inside her and just when her senses hit overload, he was easing back, ending the kiss. Still dazed and wondering why he had stopped, she heard the voices. A family was approaching on the path near them.

"I didn't think you would want an audience," he said simply.

He was right. She wouldn't and it embarrassed her that she had been so engrossed in the kiss that she hadn't heard them. "Thanks."

"Don't thank me. For a moment there, I considered not stopping," he told her as he brushed his thumb along her jaw.

Confused and shaken by his effect on her, Laura stepped back and in doing so pulled her hand free. She walked back over to the carousel to take another look at it before leaving.

Jack followed and stopped beside her. "So tell me about the carousel."

"What do you want to know?"

"About the history of it. How long it's been here. How old you were the first time you came to see it."

Laura filled him in on the history, or as much of it as she knew. She told him how it had been her grandfather who had first brought her to see it. "I was four at the time," she told him. "My mom was married to Jeffrey Baxter, the soap star, then, and we were living in California. She had just had Chloe and was finding a four-year-old and a newborn a lot to handle. So she sent me down here to visit my grandfather. I was feeling a little homesick, so he took me to see the Christmas lights in the oaks to distract me. And the minute I saw the carousel, I fell in love with it."

"Which one was your horse?" he asked.

Laura looked over at him, surprised at his perceptiveness. "The palomino over there, with the red saddle," she said, pointing out the horse she had always ridden. "I named him Pegasus."

"The flying horse, huh?" he remarked because it was one of the horses crafted with its legs in flight.

"Yes," she said and laughed at herself. "I really did think he could fly. In fact, I had myself convinced that the carousel was enchanted and that when everyone left for the night all the horses and animals would come to life."

"Ever test your theory?"

"Yes," she admitted proudly and smiled at the memory. "When I was six, I snuck away from my grandfather just before closing time and went and hid in the carousel house."

"What happened?"

"None of the carousel animals came to life, but everyone else did. My grandfather and the security guards and staff were looking for me. My grandfather thought I'd been kidnapped and everyone was upset. I got in a lot of trouble with my granddad and wasn't allowed to have any desserts or treats for an entire week after that."

He let out a whistle. "No desserts for a week? That must have been really tough," he said, but from the grin on his face, it was clear he didn't think it had been tough at all.

"Trust me, it was torture," she assured him with a laugh. "I'd have sooner given up my favorite doll than give up dessert for a week."

"Have a sweet tooth, do you?" he teased.

"I was six," she pointed out. Then recalling how his appearance had caused her to hit her candy stash, she amended her answer by saying, "I've gotten better." But the memory of *why* she'd hit the candy stash in the first place brought reality crashing back. The man she had been sharing such tender moments with was Jackson Hawke. Her enemy. The man who was trying to foreclose on her hotel. The man with whom she'd made the crazy bet and agreed to sleep with if she lost. "It's getting late. I'd better see about getting a taxi and heading home."

"What about the rest of the exhibit?" he asked.

"I think we've seen everything."

"What about that new one—that Cajun story one."

"*The Cajun Night Before Christmas.* It's an animated children's story by a local author and artist. I wouldn't have thought you'd be interested," she said honestly. In fact, she wouldn't have thought he'd be interested in any of the exhibits, but he'd seemed to genuinely enjoy himself. And if she were honest, she had enjoyed sharing them with him.

"I wouldn't have thought I'd be interested, either, but I am."

The man confused her. He was a mass of contradictions. Just when she had him pegged as a rich and arrogant man who would wager a fifteen-million-dollar note against a night with her in his bed, he spendt an evening looking at Christmas lights with her and listening to stories about her childhood. On the one hand, she despised the businessman who threatened to take away a part of her heritage. On the other hand, she liked the kind man who had been so gentle with the little boys and considerate of their mother. She liked the man who had laughed with her, the man who had made her first visit to the carousel since her grandfather's death a happy one.

"Laura?"

The sound of him calling her by her first name snapped her out of her reverie. "Yes?"

"You zoned out there for a minute. Either that or I shocked you into silence. Which is it?"

"Both," she admitted.

"So what do you say? Do you want to see that other exhibit with me?"

Laura hesitated. Spending more time with this man wasn't a good idea, she told herself. She was beginning to like him, feel drawn to him. The last thing she could afford was to lose her focus when the Contessa was at stake. "I think I'll pass. But you go on ahead."

"Maybe another time, then," he said. "I'll head back to the hotel."

But when the taxi arrived, Jack insisted on sharing it with her. He also insisted the driver take her home first. Once they reached her place and she'd tucked her share of the cab fare into his hand, she said, "Good night."

He touched her arm. "Laura?"

She paused, turned to face him. "Yes?"

"Thanks for tonight. I'll see you in the morning."

And in the morning, he would be her enemy again, she reminded herself as she quickly exited the taxi and raced up the steps to her house.

# Five

Seated in the dining room of the Contessa Hotel, Jack kept his eyes trained on the doorway and awaited the arrival of Chloe Baxter. Fitzpatrick had managed to locate Laura's half sister—in New Orleans, where she had been since Thanksgiving weekend. Funny how Laura had failed to mention the fact that her sister was visiting. But then, she had studiously avoided him since that night they'd gone to see the Christmas lights in the park. On those occasions when their paths had crossed, she had been all business. It was as though the woman he had laughed with and kissed in the park had never even existed.

Only he hadn't been able to stop thinking about that woman. It was difficult for him to look at her and not remember how sweet she had tasted, how good she had felt in his arms. Even more difficult was wondering if his stepbrother was the personal business she'd left town for two days ago. Jack closed his fist around the glass of Scotch as he considered that possibility. According to the detective, there had been no record of Peterson booking a flight in or out of New Orleans last weekend. But knowing Peterson's tastes and ability to manipulate, he could just as easily have gotten someone to fly him in on a private plane. Maybe one of his rich college buddies or someone in the moneyed crowd his father was so tight with. Or maybe even one of the corporate idiots that Peterson had conned into backing his political run.

Or maybe he'd been wrong and Peterson had never been in town after all. Had Laura gone to see him? It certainly would explain her sudden leave on personal business. According to Fitzpatrick Investigations, she had booked a flight to San Francisco with a stop in L.A., and there were no hotel reservations anywhere in her name. But then, why would she need a hotel room if she was sleeping with his stepbrother?

A white-hot anger seethed inside him at the image of Laura with Peterson. He tossed back a swallow of Scotch, but it did nothing to soothe the gnawing in his gut. If she was with his stepbrother, it wouldn't be for much longer, he assured himself. He knew through his sources in the financial arena that her attempt to secure a personal loan from the bank by pledging her own stock as collateral had been turned down. With only twenty days left on the thirty-day proviso, she was running out of options quickly. Once the designated time to cure the default was up, the hotel—or at least eighty percent of its stock and the controlling interest in it—would belong to him.

And so would Laura.

He would win their bet. And once he had her in his bed, he would wipe any trace of his stepbrother from her body, from her mind, from her soul.

Jack frowned. He was competitive. No one did what he did for a living without possessing a strong competitive streak. The truth was he enjoyed a challenge, thrived on taking risks. The higher the stakes, the more exciting he found the game. And he'd be lying to himself if the thought of taking Laura from Peterson didn't appeal to him on a very personal level. It did.

But it was more than that, Jack admitted. Even before he'd known about her connection to his stepbrother, she had set his competitive juices flowing and his hormones into a state of lust. Just remembering how she'd looked that night in the Carousel Gardens with her cheeks flushed, her eyes filled with desire and her body taut sent adrenaline pumping through his system. She'd been like some wild creature and every male hormone in his body demanded that he capture and possess her.

Disturbed by the admission, Jack shoved the images from his mind. Laura had been right. Making that bet with her had been crazy. *He* had been crazy. To offer the note he'd paid fifteen million dollars for against a night with her in his bed had been insane. It didn't matter that she stood little chance of winning the bet. The fact that he had even agreed to the terms had been flat-out reckless. Worse, it had been the act of a man making a decision guided by his hormones instead of by sound business sense.

*So why did you do it, Hawke?*

Because he wanted her. And he fully intended to have her.

"Would you like another Scotch, Mr. Hawke?"

Jack glanced down at his empty glass, then up at the waitress who stood at his table. Dressed in a crisp black-and-white uniform and wearing a name tag with Tina written on it, she gave him a friendly smile. Reasoning that he had no farther to travel than the elevator to his room, he said, "Sure."

"I'll be right back," she told him and wove her way through the busy restaurant toward the kitchen.

Shaking off his disturbing thoughts about Laura, Jack glanced around the restaurant. There was a nice crowd, he noted. Laura's decision to open the dining room on week-nights to draw from the local business clientele leaving work had been a smart move. So had extending the dinner hours on the weekends. Both were moves he would have implemented himself. Some well-placed advertisements and a few local TV and radio spots to capitalize on the popular chef's affiliation with the Contessa would fill the remaining tables. He made a mental note to discuss a series of print and TV ads with Laura. Of course, that was assuming she agreed to stay on as general manager when she lost the bet.

The bet.

Had Laura been thinking about those stakes as much as he had? he wondered. That kiss they had shared had given him a glimpse of what it would be like between them. Even now he wondered how the night might have ended had he not played the gentleman and ended it when he had.

"Here you go," the waitress said as she placed the Scotch in front of him.

"Thanks." Jack started to take a sip, then decided against it. Instead, he picked up the knife on the place setting before him. Made of quality stainless steel, he noted as he traced the blade with his fingertip. It was also sharp enough to cut his finger if he wasn't careful. A lot like Laura, he thought—attractive, of excellent quality and dangerous if a man wasn't careful.

He was always careful, Jack reminded himself. Putting aside the knife, he checked his watch. Thirty minutes late. Evidently, punctuality wasn't one of Chloe Baxter's virtues, he decided. He was just beginning to wonder if the woman would be a no-show when he spied the striking blonde in the doorway. At first, he wouldn't have pegged her for Laura's sister. On second glance though, he noted the shape of her eyes and the long legs were very much like Laura's. She was a real head-turner, Jack thought as the hostess led her toward his table. Judging by the number of appreciative male looks cast her way, he wasn't the only one who thought so. He stood as she approached. "Ms. Baxter," he said and extended his hand. "I'm Jackson Hawke."

She shook his hand firmly. "Mr. Hawke," she said in a voice that had a smoky tone to it.

Once she was seated, he asked, "Would you care for something to drink?"

She looked up at the waitress, smiled. "I'd love a glass of merlot."

Jack ordered a bottle from a select vintage and once the waitress was gone, he said, "I appreciate your agreeing to meet with me."

Amusement lit her hazel eyes. "We both know that I came here in exchange for your promise that you'd schedule a meeting with Meredith Grant to discuss her company, Connections."

"Yes. And I have to say, your request surprised me. As an actress, I would have thought you would have traded for an introduction for yourself to a producer or casting director. After all, I do know several. But instead, you asked for something for a former stepsister. Why is that?"

"Meredith's my sister. Just because our parents divorced doesn't mean she and I stop being sisters. And contrary to what most people think, not all actresses are self-centered divas. Meredith has been trying for months to get an appointment with you and your office keeps turning her down." She sat back in her seat, crossed her legs and met his gaze. "When you called and asked me to meet with you, I saw an opportunity to get her that appointment and took it."

Jack nodded. "I appreciate your candor, Ms. Baxter."

"Then I hope you'll appreciate that I intend to have you book that meeting with Meredith before I leave here today."

"I'll book the meeting—just as long as both you and Ms. Grant understand that I'm not interested in a matchmaking service."

"Connections does more than matchmaking," she told him. "It connects people for business reasons, too. That's what Meredith wants to meet with you about."

"Very well, Ms. Baxter. I'll keep my promise and book the meeting with Ms. Grant," he assured her. "In exchange, you promised to listen to my offer and hear about my plans for the hotel with an open mind. Agreed?"

"Agreed," she replied. "And the name's Chloe."

"Very well, Chloe. And my name's Jack."

"All right, Jack. I'm listening."

She listened while he told her about his reasons for wanting to buy the hotel. She listened as he explained the difficulties of competing in the hotel market in the post-Katrina city. She listened as he told her about his plans to restore the Contessa and make it a viable, revenue-producing property.

"If you're able to do what you say, it seems the smart thing for me to do would be to hold on to my stock because it'll be worth a lot more down the road."

"That's true. But that's at least a year or two away," he said as he leaned back in his chair. "Accepting my two million dollars now would mean you wouldn't have to take another waitress job and you could study full-time at the L.A. Theater Institute."

She lifted her eyebrow. "I suppose I shouldn't be surprised you did your homework on me. Laura said you were smart."

"Did she now? What else did your sister say about me?"

She smiled. "I think she mentioned something about your being an arrogant Neanderthal who—"

Laughing, he held up his hand. "I think I get the picture."

"I thought you would," she said with a twinkle in her eye. "Although I'm not sure the Neanderthal fits. I expected you to be bigger...and ugly."

He laughed.

So did she.

And they were both laughing when an unsmiling Laura walked into the dining room. Damn, but she looked good, Jack thought. No suit today, he noted. She was dressed in an ivory sweater with a red ribbon bow shooting across the shoulder and a skinny-fitting skirt of lipstick-red that gave him an enticing view of those killer legs. Her mouth was painted that same shade of red and Jack found himself itching to taste it.

"See something you like, Jack?"

Jack shot a look over at Chloe and, given the amused expression on her face and tone in her voice, his appraisal of her sister hadn't gone unnoticed. As Laura approached their table, Jack stood. "How was your…vacation? It was a vacation, wasn't it? Your assistant said you were off on personal business."

"My trip was fine," Laura said drily, her attention focused on her younger sister. "Hello, Chloe."

"Hi, sis. You're back early. I thought your flight wasn't due in until after nine tonight," Chloe said.

"I was able to get an earlier flight. I thought you had a date tonight," Laura said, accusation in her voice.

"I do—but not until later. So I decided to take Jack up on his dinner offer."

He knew very little about siblings, particularly siblings who loved one another. His only experience had been the hurtful experiences and bitterness that permeated his relationship with Matt Peterson. Whatever was going on between Laura and Chloe was different—and whatever it was, it was generating a lot of tension. In an effort to diffuse some of that tension, he said, "We were just about to order coffee and dessert. Would you like to join us?"

"No, thanks. I've got some paperwork to catch up on. Besides, I wouldn't want to interrupt you while you're trying to charm my sister into selling you her stock."

Chloe waved her hand in dismissal. "Lighten up, Laura. As charming as he is, Jack already knows that I have no intention of selling him my stock. Don't you, Jack?"

He did know it. But judging by the look of relief on Laura's face, she hadn't been quite so sure. "Yes, I know you're not going to sell," he said. "But it doesn't mean I haven't enjoyed our time together or that I'll stop trying to convince you." He looked over at Laura. "Either of you."

"And as I've already told you, you're wasting your time," Laura said.

Annoyed by her dismissal and wondering whether or not a rendezvous with his stepbrother, Matt, was the reason, Jack said, "Speaking of wasting time, before you take off on another trip, you might want to remember that there are only twenty days left before one of us has to pay up on that bet. I'm counting on that someone being you."

Back in her office, Laura tried to focus on the letters awaiting her signature and block out all thoughts of Jackson Hawke. The man was infuriating. She'd wanted to wipe that cocky smile off his face. And at the same time, she'd wanted to jump his bones. Just remembering the way he had looked at her—as if he'd wanted to swallow her whole—made her pulse stutter, her body hot.

"All right," Chloe said, marching into Laura's office and slamming the door behind her. "What's going on between you and Jack? And what's this about a bet?"

Laura didn't bother to look up from her paperwork. "I thought you had a date."

"Forget about my date. I want some answers."

Laura sighed. "Nothing's going on and the bet doesn't concern you."

"It sure didn't look like nothing to me. You two were generating enough heat between you to keep this hotel warm for the entire winter. And when Jack mentioned that bet, you turned as red as that skirt you're wearing before you stormed out of the dining room."

"You're wrong."

Chloe planted her hands on the desk, got in her face. "Laura, this is me you're talking to. I may not know anything about running a hotel, but I do know about sexual chemistry. And believe me, there was definitely some serious sexual chemistry cooking between you two."

Her sister was right, Laura admitted to herself. There was sexual chemistry between them. And for her there was something more, something she hadn't wanted. She had hoped that kiss in the park had just been a fluke, that these feelings she was starting to have for Jack weren't real and would disappear with the light of day and with some distance. But they hadn't disappeared. If anything, they were getting stronger. In fact, he was the reason she had come home early from California. She had actually missed him, had even wondered if she had misjudged him. She had gone so far as to hope that maybe she wasn't the only one who had felt there was something more than desire happening between them. Only when she'd seen him with Chloe, believing he was trying to buy her sister's stock, she'd realized she had been kidding herself. Sure, Jackson Hawke might want to have sex with her, but what he really wanted was the Contessa. His reminder that in twenty days he intended to take the Contessa from her only served to bring home that fact.

"Since I turned down two million dollars for my stock because this place means so much to you, I think I deserve some answers," Chloe pointed out. "Tell me what's going on and why you're so upset."

Laura told her sister everything. She told her about the bet she had made with Jack in the heat of the moment. She told her about the evening they had spent together at the park viewing the Christmas lights. She told her about the kiss and the feelings it had stirred inside her.

"It sounds to me like you might be falling for the guy," Chloe responded. "There's nothing wrong with that. You said you and Matt weren't exclusive anymore. And you can bet the wannabe-congressman isn't spending his nights alone. Or did he manage to convince you to change your mind about that when you were out in California?"

"Matt didn't convince me to change my mind about anything because I didn't see him. I went to see Papa Vincenzo and his family because I canceled on them at Thanksgiving," she said, referring to one of their former stepfathers.

"Then I don't see where you hooking up with Jack should be a problem."

"It's a problem because I'm not into one-night stands or casual sex. And that's what it would be with a man like Hawke."

"You don't know that," Chloe argued.

No, she didn't know it for a fact. But she had a pretty good idea that Hawke was not a man who was into long-term relationships or commitments. She was. "But I do know that the man's a shark. He's a corporate raider. Half the companies he buys, he dismantles and sells them off in pieces for a profit. And now he's intent on doing that to our hotel."

"Not according to him," her sister told her. "Besides, if you ask me, Mr. Jackson Hawke seemed a lot more interested in winning that bet and you than he is in foreclosing on the hotel."

"Yes, he is. Isn't he?" He did seem intent on the bet, Laura realized, and found herself wondering why. While she didn't doubt for a second that he wanted her, there had been moments when she'd caught him looking at her, with something more than desire in his eyes. There had been anger and determination and something else all mixed in with his wanting her. What she didn't understand was why. "Don't you find that odd? That he's more focused on the bet than the hotel?"

"What I think, dear sister, is you think too much." Walking around to the other side of Laura's desk, Chloe opened the drawer and stole a bag of chocolate-covered nuts from her stash. When Laura attempted to take them back, Chloe quickly moved out of her reach. "You know what else I think?" she asked as she ripped open the bag and popped several of the candies into her mouth.

"No. But I imagine you're going to tell me."

"I think Jackson Hawke's got a case of the hots for you. And I think you've got the hots for him. So I say quit analyzing it to death and enjoy it."

"And I say you're going to be late for your date," Laura said, wanting to end the discussion.

"All right, I'm going. But seriously, Laura, there are a lot worse things that could happen than to find yourself waking up in Hawke's bed."

There were a lot worse things that could happen than her ending up in Jackson Hawke's bed, Laura conceded. One worse thing that came to her mind was losing the

Contessa Hotel. Not wanting to think about that possibility or about Jack, she fortified herself with a chocolate peanut-butter cup, then tackled the mountain of reports and correspondence that had accumulated in her absence.

After she'd finished going through the budget reports and projections, she reached for the folder of incoming mail. A quick glance revealed several solicitations, bills and subscriptions. Then she spied an unopened envelope from the Jardine Law Firm. Her stomach pitched. It was the same firm that had handled the foreclosure paperwork for Hawke. Ripping open the envelope, she pulled out the document.

Quickly, she skimmed the legal jargon and zeroed in on the name *Hawke Industries*.

In accordance with Hawke Industries' purchase of the above-referenced note, Hawke Industries and/or its appointed representative are hereby granted access to said hotel property in order to perform the due diligence afforded Hawke Industries as purchaser of said note. Hawke Industries and/or its appointed representative will not be afforded the right to take any actions or implement any changes in the hotel, its management, personnel or operations until such time that the thirty-day grace period on the loan has expired and the shares of stock in the hotel are transferred to Hawke Industries. Also in accordance with the purchase of the above-referenced note, Hawke Industries and/or its appointed representative will be provided suitable office work space to perform said due-diligence process connected with the sale.

Laura didn't bother reading any further. He couldn't do this. He couldn't just waltz in and take over before the thirty days were up. And if he'd been planning to do this, why hadn't he told her? With temper blazing and the attorney's letter crumpled in her fist, she headed for the penthouse suite. The ride up the slow-moving elevator only added to her mood. By the time she exited the car, she was nearly trembling with anger and frustration. Marching over to the ornate door of the penthouse, she punched the doorbell to the suite. She counted to ten and when Jack didn't answer, she pounded on the door with her fist.

No answer.

She beat on the door again. "Hawke, open this door now." When he still failed to respond, Laura didn't hesitate. Reaching into her skirt pocket, she pulled out the master key card she always carried that allowed management access to all rooms in the hotel for emergency purposes. She zipped it into the lock. The green light kicked on, unlocking the door.

"Hawke, get out here," she demanded from the entrance.

Nothing.

"Hawke," she yelled as she tried to find him in the living and dining room areas. Ignoring the laptop computer and mounds of files, she began searching the rest of the suite. The first two bedrooms were empty. Growing angrier by the second, she pushed open the door to the master suite. Still no Hawke. She spied the door to the bathroom ajar, heard the buzz of an electric razor. Intent on confronting him, Laura made a beeline for the bathroom. She shoved the door open and sent it banging sharply against the wall. And there Jack stood in front of the sink, naked from the waist up, with a towel anchored around his hips and a razor buzzing in his hand.

Surprise flickered across his features for a moment as he shut off the razor. "Hello, Laura. Was there something you wanted?" he asked, an edge in his voice.

At the sharp tone, Laura jerked her gaze from his bare chest to his face and remembered that she was the one with reason to be angry—not him. But before she could tell him so, he was moving toward her.

"Let me guess. Your trip didn't turn out quite the way you'd planned and your friend didn't come through with the money like you thought he would."

"What are you talking about?" she replied, confused.

But he didn't seem to hear her. "Isn't that why you're here, Laura? Because you know you can't beat me, so you've come to pay off on our bet?"

"In your dreams."

"Actually, I've had quite a few dreams about having you in my bed, Laura. Especially after that night in the park. What about you? You have any dreams about what it'll be like between us?"

"*Nightmares* is more like it," she lied, vowing he'd never know that she had wondered what it would be like to make love with him. Even now she wasn't immune to him and was having a devil of a time ignoring the way the sprinkling of dark hair made a vee down his chest to his sexy abs before it disappeared beneath the towel hitched around his hips. Suddenly realizing what she was doing, Laura yanked her gaze back to his face. His mouth looked hard. His expression closed. But his eyes, his eyes were dark and hungry as they watched her watch him.

"If you're not here for sex, then why did you break into my room?"

"I didn't break in. I used the pass key," she informed him, holding up the card that she still held in her hand.

"Which is a violation of a guest's privacy and illegal."

"It's not illegal if you enter with cause," she defended, knowing that was a stretch.

He moved toward her, causing the towel to shift precariously. "And just what would that cause be, Laura?" he asked, his voice dangerously soft.

"This," she said, shoving the attorney's letter at him.

He barely gave the letter a glance. "How does notification that I'll be starting the due diligence on the hotel qualify as cause for illegal entry to my room?"

"Because I came to tell you that there isn't going to be any due diligence because there isn't going to be a foreclosure."

"Why? Did the friend you spent the past couple of days with lend you the money to stop me?"

"No. At least not yet." The truth was Papa Vincenzo hadn't given her an answer yet on lending her a portion of the money because he and his wife needed to meet with their accountants first. But even if they did give her a loan, it would only be for a fraction of the money she needed.

From the scowl on his face, her answer hadn't pleased him. "Pardon me," he said and she stepped to the side while he stretched out his left arm to the towel rack behind her. But instead of taking the towel and moving away, he continued to hold on to it, effectively caging her between him and the counter.

There was that look in his eyes again, that mingling of anger and desire, she noted. Laura's heart pounded as he leaned closer. Suddenly she was aware of how tall he was, just how wide those shoulders were. He smelled like soap and outdoors, she thought. Lifting her gaze, she stared at his face and noticed for the first time that his eyes were a blue so deep they were almost black. His hair was still damp and mussed from his shower, and she had this crazy urge to brush it away from his forehead. She noted the stubble along his chin that he hadn't had a chance to shave. She looked at his mouth, recalled how those lips had felt on hers that night in the park and all she could think was she wanted to kiss him again.

As though he could read her thoughts, Jack lowered his head until his mouth was only inches from hers. He waited a fraction of a second, no more. Yet it seemed like an eternity during which she could feel her pulse race, could feel her heart beat frantically like the wings of a hummingbird. And just when she thought surely she would explode, his mouth was on hers—hot, hungry, demanding. Somewhere Laura heard a moan. But she wasn't sure if it came from her or from Jack.

Then she couldn't think at all as Jack continued to kiss her. When she touched her tongue to his, Jack gentled the kiss. He kissed her slowly, deeply, thoroughly. Her head spun. Her stomach quivered. Every nerve in her body seemed to have come alive at the touch of his lips.

And she wanted more.

The papers she held in her hand fell to the floor, freeing her fingers to explore his face. She could feel the whiskers where she had interrupted his shave. She could smell the mixture of soap and a woodsy scent. She sieved her fingers through his damp hair and kissed him back.

One kiss strung into another and then another, each feeding that ache inside her, each one demanding more. Of their own volition, her hands slid down to his shoulders, to his chest, along the dusting of dark hair. When her fingers moved lower and unknotted the towel at his waist, Jack sucked in his breath. This time when she heard a groan, Laura knew it was Jack's. He devoured her with his mouth.

So caught up in the feel of him and the heat of his mouth, it took her a moment before she realized that Jack had stopped kissing her. When she opened her eyes and saw the hunger in his blue eyes, her heart began to race all over again.

"One of us is wearing too many clothes," he whispered in a voice that sent another wave of desire pumping through her. He drew the backs of his fingers slowly, gently, along the line of her breast.

Her nipples puckered. Her breath lodged in her throat and she closed her eyes, overwhelmed by the sensations. Even through her sweater and bra, she could feel the heat of his touch and another wave of desire pulsed through her. Opening her eyes, she looked at him, witnessed the strength of his arousal. The sight of him had heat pooling in her belly, between her thighs.

She took a step back and heard the papers crunch beneath her heel. Laura looked down, saw the letter from the attorney that had driven her to his suite in anger.

Suddenly sanity came crashing back. What was she doing? What had she been thinking? Hadn't she just told Chloe earlier that the man was a shark, that he was out to steal their hotel and score a one-night stand? She couldn't let him do either. Not and look at herself in the mirror in the morning. "This was a mistake. I never should have come here."

And without waiting for him to respond, Laura turned and ran from the bathroom and out of the suite.

# Six

"I agreed to allow you to start the due diligence, didn't I?" Laura argued as she stood across the desk from Jack the next morning.

"Yes, you did. And I appreciate your cooperation," he told her, not bothering to point out that she really hadn't had much choice. She'd been on the defensive since his arrival that morning.

As he listened to her excuses for not providing him with the office he'd requested, he noted that she had taken great care to keep the subject on business. She'd made no mention of her visit to his suite the previous night or what had happened between them. He thought about that initial kiss, the anger that had driven him to possess her, the need to wipe Peterson from her mind and body until all she wanted was him. Only when she had kissed him back, she had tasted sweet and hot, just as she had that night in the park. Then all he could think about was quenching the thirst inside him with her. He had thought she'd felt the same way—until she had bolted from his suite.

Why had she bolted? It was a question he'd asked himself long after she had gone. And the answer he kept coming back to was Peterson. If she had been with his step-brother as he suspected, Peterson wouldn't have told her about their connection since he'd never claimed Jack as part of his family. Instead he would have warned her to stay away from him, that he was ruthless, the son of a loser and not to be trusted. The last thing Laura would want would be for her lover to find out that she had slept with his sworn enemy. And Peterson would find out he'd bedded Laura, Jack vowed. He would make sure of it. Then he would see how his stepbrother felt to be the one who came out the loser. As for Laura, he wouldn't hurt her, he promised himself. He'd simply let the sexual chemistry run its course and when it was over, they would both move on with their lives. No, the only one who would be hurt would be Peterson—and the blow would be more to his ego than anything else.

"…and all things considered, I don't think it's in the best interest of the hotel," Laura continued, laying out her reasons for not wanting him there and omitting the primary one; that they had been within minutes of tumbling into bed.

Despite her all-business attitude, the sexual tension was still there—like the proverbial pink elephant in the middle of a room that no one admitted to seeing. He could see it though. It was there in the way she avoided eye contact with him, in the way she seemed unable to remain still, in the way she tensed each time he came within a few feet of her. And from the shadows under her eyes, he suspected he wasn't the only one who'd had trouble sleeping last night. Not even a cold shower had been able to stop him from thinking about her, from wanting her. He still wanted her. Fortunately, he knew how to control that wanting and not allow it to control him and interfere with his business.

Unlike his father.

An image flashed through Jack's mind of his father sitting alone in the dark with a drink in his hand. His father had made the mistake of letting sentiment override his business sense and look what it had cost him. Samuel Hawke had lost not only his wife and company when Nicole had taken off with his business partner, but he'd also lost his will to live. He had learned from his father's mistakes, Jack reminded himself. He had no intention of letting that happen to him—regardless of how tempting he found Laura Spencer. Bedding Laura and shoving it in his stepbrother's face would be a fringe benefit, one that he would enjoy. But he wouldn't put it or her before business. No, business would always come first. That was why he'd decided to get the due diligence on a fast track, so that when the thirty-day proviso was up, he'd be ready to close the deal and set his plans for the hotel in motion. Whether those plans included Laura or not would be up to her.

"...so if you'll just give me a list of what reports and information you need to perform the due diligence, I'll see that they're sent to your suite."

Tuning back in to what Laura was saying, Jack caught only the tail end of her remark. But it was enough for him to know that she was still balking at giving him a work space in the corporate offices. "Maybe you didn't hear me the first time," Jack said, his voice firm. "I have no intention of working from my suite. I need an office, preferably one on this floor where the data is more accessible. It's all spelled out there in the letter from my attorney," he said, referring to the document he had returned to her. He walked around the desk and picked up the letter. Holding it up, he pointed to the appropriate clause. "According to those terms, the Contessa Hotel and its representative, that's you, will provide Hawke Industries and/or its representative, which is me, adequate office space to perform the due-diligence portion of the contract."

Laura snatched the letter from him, crumpled it in her fist. "I know what it says. I can read. But I can't give you what I don't have. There is no office available," she argued. "So you're just going to have to suck it up and work out of your suite like you've been doing."

"Wrong. I have no intention of spending my time coming down here to access data or having you send the information upstairs to me," he told her. "Even you have to agree that would be a waste of valuable time for both of us."

"I do agree. But I don't see where you have any choice. There is no office available."

"Then I suggest you make one available," Jack insisted.

"And just how am I supposed to do that?" she snapped.

"You're a smart woman. Figure something out. After all, you're the one who insisted we play by the rules, remember?" he pointed out, referring to the thirty-day grace period in the contract that she'd insisted on exercising. "The rules say I get an office."

"Anyone ever tell you what a jerk you are?"

"Repeatedly," he said.

She sat down in her chair, shoved the hair back from her face. After letting out a breath, she looked up at him again and said, "All right. Since I want as few people as possible to know why you're here, you can have my office."

"Where are you going to work?"

"What difference does it make? You're getting your office."

"It makes a difference because you're the hotel's general manager, at least for the time being, and I need you to run this place. After the foreclosure if you don't want to stay on, I'll bring someone else in to take over. But until then, your contract says that you're the GM. So I repeat, where are you going to work?"

She looked mad enough to chew nails, Jack thought. "I'll just work out of one of the suites—the way I wanted you to do."

He didn't want to displace the woman, he admitted. She also had a point about not wanting to ignite the rumor mill about the hotel's new ownership—at least not until he had finished his assessments and was ready to take the appropriate action. In the post-Katrina climate, staffing remained a problem citywide and he didn't want to lose valuable employees needlessly. "That won't work. You need to be here."

"Well, I don't see where I have a lot of choices. As you pointed out, I have to provide you with an office. Since there's none available, someone has to give up theirs and it's not going to be one of my staff. Your being here to supposedly conduct an evaluation of the hotel's operations for marketing purposes is going to raise enough questions. So the only option is for you to take my office."

"Then we'll share the office."

She blinked, evidently stunned by the suggestion. "You've got to be kidding."

"I seldom kid," he told her. Shoving aside a pile of folders, Jack sat on the edge of her desk. He didn't miss the sudden tension in her body at his close proximity. Nor did he miss the awareness that crept into her eyes. He'd seen it last night when she'd realized he was wearing nothing more than a towel. He'd watched desire cloud her anger. And watching her had fed his own hunger for her. The memory set off a sharp jab of need as he recalled how she'd tasted, how her hands had felt on his skin.

"The idea is ridiculous," she told him and averted her gaze.

Annoyed with himself and with her, Jack shut off the memories and stood. Determined to focus on business, he picked up the amethyst paperweight from her desk, tested its weight in his palm. "What's ridiculous is for either one of us to work out of a suite when this office is more than big enough for the two of us. And since a lot of the information I'll need will have to come from you, it makes sense for us to both work out of here."

"That may sound good in theory, but—"

"Would you rather have me in an office where someone might overhear me on the phone and learn something they shouldn't? If I'm working from here, neither one of us has still to worry about that happening." He paused, gave her a moment to digest the idea.

"I guess it could work," she conceded, reluctance in her voice. "But…"

"But what, Laura?" he countered, irritated by her refusal to look at him. "What's the real reason you don't want me here?"

Finally, she looked at him and the coolness was back in her green eyes. "Besides the fact that you're trying to steal my family's hotel, I don't want you here because I don't trust you."

Her words hit him like fists. Angry, he walked over to her and said, "Is it really me you don't trust, Laura? Or is it yourself? Could it be you're worried that if we're alone together we'll finish what we started last night?"

"That monster-size ego of yours is showing again, Hawke."

"My ego has nothing to do with it. You and I both know that you wanted me every bit as much as I wanted you last night. And the only reason you didn't wake up in my bed this morning is because you got cold feet."

She pushed away from the desk and stood, taking a step back and putting distance between them. "I didn't get cold feet. I came to my senses. Last night I was tired after my trip and I was upset and wasn't thinking clearly. What happened was a mistake."

Her mention of her trip to California, coupled with her denial, angered him even more. "Is that what it was?" he asked as he moved closer, crowding her personal space. "When you had your hot little hands all over my body and my tongue was in your mouth, that was a mistake?"

"Yes," she insisted. "And it's one I have no intention of repeating."

"Then tell me, sweet Laura. Just how do you intend to pay off on our bet when you lose? Because you are going to lose. And when you do, I intend to collect."

* * *

"I can't tell you how much I appreciate this and I promise I'll pay you back just as soon as I can arrange refinancing of the hotel," Laura told her former stepfather, who had just called to inform her he'd wired five hundred thousand dollars to her account.

"You just pay me back when you can and come for another visit soon," Vincent Vincenzo told her. "Be sure to say hello to your mother for me. *Ciao.*"

"*Ciao.*" Laura hung up the phone and leaned back in her chair. A range of emotions rushed through her. Relief. Gratitude. Love. Regardless of all the chaos her parents brought into her life with their merry-go-round of marriages, she had definitely been the lucky one because she had ended up with a wonderful extended family.

Grateful to have the office to herself for a change, Laura retrieved the plan she'd devised to come up with the money to pay off her mother's note. She added the loan from her stepfather to the list and studied the totals. Thanks to Chloe signing over her stock to her, she'd used it and her own stock as collateral on a four-million-dollar loan from another bank. Of course, the interest rate was outrageous. But she'd been desperate and had agreed to the terms. She'd netted another two hundred fifty thousand by cashing in her stocks, IRAs and savings account. Her accountant had warned her that the tax penalties would be a killer, but a big tax bill was the least of her worries at the moment. With the one hundred fifty grand she'd gotten from her own father and the one hundred grand from Chloe's dad, she had managed to come up with five million dollars. Now all she needed was for her mother to be successful in refinancing the nightclub for at least ten million dollars and she would have the fifteen million she needed to cure the defaulted loan.

Then the hotel and its stock would be returned to her family and Jackson Hawke would be out of her office, out of her hotel and out of her life. So why did the prospect of never seeing Jack again leave her feeling more unsettled than pleased? Not sure she wanted to examine the reasons too closely, Laura returned her finance plan to her drawer and dove into the weekly reports. She was still going through the reports when Jack entered the office.

In the nearly two weeks that they had shared an office, he had done nothing to be overly intrusive. His phone conversations were brief. His questions minimal. His interruptions few. He had made no further references to their bet. Nor had he attempted to kiss her again. Yet she had been keenly aware of his presence. The tension between them had been like a live wire dangling in a storm, leaving her on edge, waiting for the sparks to ignite. And each time she looked across the room and found his eyes on her, the desire she saw in them made her blood heat.

It simply made no sense. While she was no prude, sex wasn't something she took lightly. She'd only slept with two men in her life—her first love and Matt Peterson. In each case, she'd known the man for nearly a year and had strong feelings for him before she'd shared his bed. She'd known Jack for less than a month and the feelings he aroused in her were certainly not feelings of love. Yet, there was no denying her physical attraction to him. The admission worried her as much as it annoyed her.

"Isn't there someone else who can generate a copy of the report?"

Laura looked up at the sound of Jack's voice and glanced over to the table where he had been working. He'd shed the dark suit coat and silk tie he'd worn that morning, she noted. The crisp white shirt was open at the collar. The gold cuff links at his wrists caught the light as he put down his pen. Sitting back in his chair, he shoved a hand through his hair, and Laura couldn't help remembering sliding her own fingers through his damp hair that night in his hotel suite.

"All right, then. Just leave a message for him to call me when he gets in," Jack said and hung up the phone.

"Is there a problem?" she asked.

"I'm missing the copy of the marketing projections for the first quarter of next year and the guy who handles it took off this afternoon to go to see his daughter in a school Christmas pageant."

She smiled. "Jerry's daughter is in kindergarten and she's an angel in the pageant. I told him he could have the afternoon off," she told him. "But I should have a copy of the report you can use."

A few minutes later, after she'd located the report and handed it to him, he said, "Thanks."

"No problem." Curious, she asked, "So how is the due diligence coming? Have you been able to get everything you needed?"

"It's going pretty well. And yes, so far I've been able to get or access all the data I've asked for."

"How much longer do you think it'll take before you finish?"

His lips twitched. "What's the matter? Tired of sharing your office or just anxious to get rid of me?"

"Both."

He chuckled. "At least you're honest."

"You asked."

This time he actually laughed aloud. And Laura realized it was the first time she had heard him laugh since that night in the park. She couldn't help thinking that despite his fortune and power, Jack didn't seem to have a lot of laughter in his life. Or people, she realized. While he had lots of employees, she could never recall him mentioning any family or close friends.

"You're right. I did ask. And in answer to your question, it should only take me another week, maybe less to finish." He sat back, stretched his arms behind his head and looked up at her. "How about you? Any problems with the employees buying the story about me doing a marketing analysis?"

"Not really. Some people are curious and there have been a few questions," she advised him. Most of those questions had come from the accounting department, which she had expected since the info that Jack had requested was much more expansive than the data needed for marketing purposes. "But they seemed satisfied with the explanation I had Penny give them. And it hasn't been a secret that I'm trying to increase the hotel's revenues. They think that you're part of that plan."

"I guess I am, in a manner of speaking, if things go down as I plan."

"But not if they go as I've planned."

"True," he said with a smile. "Other than for the obvious reason that your family owned this hotel, why a career in hotel management?"

The question surprised her. It was the first time in nearly two weeks that he'd spoken to her about anything that didn't relate to the hotel's operation. "The truth is, I knew from the time I was a little girl that I wanted to be a hotelier. More specifically, I wanted to run this hotel." For the next fifteen minutes she told him about how enamored she had been by her grandfather's stories about the people who had stayed in the hotel, how he had taught her that each person was like a guest in their home. She told him how for nearly a hundred years the lives and loves of countless people had played out within the walls of the Contessa, that the hotel stood as a witness to history. "Did you know that an Austrian duke once stayed here?"

"A duke, huh?"

"Yes. It was in the early 1930s when my great-grandfather was running the hotel. Anyway, the duke and his consort were here for the Mardi Gras festivities. In particular, they were special guests attending the meeting of the courts of Rex and Comus on Mardi Gras night," she explained, telling him about the momentous occasion that had, for nearly a century, signaled the final events of the holiday. "They supposedly chose to stay at the Contessa because of it's old-world charm."

"That must have been quite a coup for your great-grandfather."

"It was. In fact, there's a photograph of him and my grandfather with the duke and duchess hanging over there." She stood and walked over to the wall in question where the photo from the bygone era was displayed.

"I assume the serious little boy is your grandfather," he said from behind her.

"Yes, and the man wearing the costume and mask is my great-grandfather, Robert Spencer," she said, and was surprised to turn and find Jack standing so close to her. Disarmed by his nearness, Laura returned her attention to the photograph and adjusted it.

"Is that your grandfather, too?" he asked, indicating another shot of a young man in a doorman's uniform, smiling and holding the door for guests. After assuring him the young man was indeed her grandfather, he said, "He certainly looks like he's enjoying his job."

"He did. My grandfather loved this place. Instead of having bedtime stories read to me as a child, I got stories about movie stars and royals and even bank robbers who had stayed here. I knew that I wanted to have my own stories to tell my children and grandchildren someday," she said wistfully and traced her fingers over the photo before turning. "What about you? What did you want to be when you grew up?"

"Rich."

Surprised, she thought he was kidding and said, "What happened to wanting to be a fireman or a cowboy?"

"They don't make enough money."

Again surprised by his response, she asked, "And just how old were you when you reached that conclusion?"

"Six."

He said it so matter-of-factly, she realized he was serious. She couldn't help wondering what had happened to him at six that would have had him set such a serious goal. So she asked, "What was so important about being rich?"

"Because when you're rich, people like you better. They want to be around you. They're nice to you because they know you have money and can buy them things, can take them places," he said.

"Having people hang out with you just for your money doesn't sound all that great to me. It certainly isn't the kind of friends that I would want."

"Maybe not," he said, a sardonic note in his voice. "But it sure beats people treating you like a loser because you don't have money or ditching you for somebody else who does."

Judging by the hard look in his eyes, Laura was sure Jack was speaking from personal experience. And the realization made her feel sad for him. "What they say is true, Jack. Money isn't everything."

"Sure it is. Money is power. And power is all that really matters."

"So is that why you do what you do? Buy companies like the Contessa for the power?"

"That's a big part of it," he conceded. "But there's also the challenge of turning a company around and making it profitable."

"So that you can make more money," she added drily.

"Yes."

"But where's the joy in that? Where's the passion?"

"The joy is in being able to make it happen. As for the passion, I find all the passion I need with the woman who's in my bed. You're the woman I would have found that passion with if you hadn't run out on me." He edged a step closer, cupped the back of her head with his hand.

"Jack," she said, her voice suddenly dry. Despite her attempts to resist him, Laura could feel her pulse start to stutter.

"You can still be that woman, Laura," he told her as he brushed his mouth against hers. "I want you."

She pressed her hands against his chest, unsure if she

intended to push him away or draw him closer. He slid his hand down her back, drew her to him, and the feel of his arousal sent waves of heat through her.

"All you have to do is say yes and we can go to my suite now. Then I'll show you what real passion is."

She was tempted. Oh, she was tempted, Laura admitted as he kissed her jaw, moved to her neck. The nip of his teeth to her sensitive flesh sent a shiver of need through her body.

"Laura." Penny buzzed through on the intercom. "I have Matt Peterson on line one for you."

It took Laura a moment before she registered the sudden stiffening of Jack's body or the way the hand that had been caressing her was now curled into a fist in her jacket. But that momentary cease in the assault to her senses was enough for Laura to catch her breath and realize where she was, what she was doing and who she was doing it with. The realization that Penny or anyone could have walked in on them was like a sobering blast of cold air. She eased back from him and his hands fell away. "I really need to take this call," she said.

"Right," he told her, his voice cool, his expression shuttered. And before she could say another word, his back was to her. After shoving his laptop into its case, he snapped it shut, then grabbed his jacket and started for the door. "When you make up your mind, you know where to find me."

# Seven

"Hello, Matt," Laura said as she stared at the door through which Jack had exited so abruptly.

"Hi, beautiful. How are you?"

"Fine," she said absently, her thoughts still on Jack and his swift change of mood. "How about you?"

"Much better now that I've finally reached you."

At his sweet declaration, Laura shoved thoughts of Hawke from her mind and thought about Matt. An image of his face filled her mind's eye. Tall, blond and brown-eyed, Matt Peterson had Brad Pitt good looks and a double dose of charisma. A partner in a major law firm in L.A., he was smart, civic-minded and a man of action. He was sexy, exciting and fun to be with. In short, he was everything she thought she wanted in a man. And even though she cared deeply for him, she didn't love him—not with the deep-rooted passion she'd seen her parents find with their partners, but mostly not with the unshakable love that her grandparents had shared for one another.

"You're a hard woman to reach, babe. Have you been getting my messages?"

"Yes, I got them. And I'm sorry for not calling you back. It's just that I've been swamped and haven't had a moment to spare." It wasn't entirely true, she admitted silently. While the problems at the hotel and Hawke had eaten up most of her time, she hadn't called Matt back because she simply hadn't wanted to go another round with him about her returning to California.

"Sounds to me like you need a vacation. Why don't you take a break and come out here this weekend for a visit? It's been too long since I've seen you, Laura. I miss you."

"I can't, Matt. I've got too much going on here right now."

"Is there a problem?" he asked. "You sound…on edge."

His remark reminded Laura how perceptive Matt could be. For a moment, she considered telling him about the problem with Hawke, her mother's note and the impending foreclosure on the hotel. He was an attorney and businessman from an affluent family and could probably help her secure the funding she needed. But something told her the price he'd expect in return for his help would be too high. Matt wanted a socialite wife like his mother, a woman to adorn his arm, host his parties and be devoted to him and his interests. While some women would be happy in that role, she knew that she wouldn't. Even if that weren't the case, she would still be reluctant to tell him about Hawke. The thing with Hawke had turned personal and she didn't trust that Matt wouldn't sense the truth. It didn't matter that

Matt had dated others since her departure and done so with her blessing. Matt was far too competitive to view her interest in Hawke as anything other than a threat to him. If he knew how close she had come to sleeping with Hawke, he'd see it as a challenge to his manhood. And the last thing she wanted was to deal with Matt's ego.

"Laura, is everything all right?"

"Yes. I'm just tired," she told him, which was the truth—if only part of it.

"I told you going down there and trying to salvage that old place was a mistake. You're wearing yourself out. You should have stayed here in California."

"I didn't want to stay in California," she reminded him. "And I really don't want to argue with you about this again."

"I'm sorry, babe. I just hate the thought of you pushing yourself so hard. I worry about you."

"I know," she said with a sigh because she knew that he did care about her. And for the first time, she wondered if maybe she should have just ended things as she'd wanted to do six months ago instead of allowing Matt to convince her that they could still remain a part of each other's lives. If her move had done nothing else, it had confirmed her re-alization that she didn't want a future with Matt as anything more than a friend. Of course, this crazy attraction to Hawke certainly proved that she could never love Matt.

"Listen, I know you're too busy to come back now. But Christmas is only a couple of weeks away. What do you say you come spend Christmas here in L.A., then we'll drive up to see my parents at their place in Big Bear and do some skiing. I know they'd love to see you."

"It all sounds wonderful, Matt. But I can't," she told

him, realizing it wouldn't be fair for her to end things with him over the phone. "Chloe's staying with me for a few weeks and I don't want to leave her alone at Christmas."

"All right," he said, an edge in his voice. "Then I guess I'll just have to settle for seeing you after Christmas. In fact, see if you can get into L.A. by the twenty-eighth. One of my backers for the senatorial race is throwing a big party then to introduce me to some of his friends. And my parents are hosting their big New Year's Eve party, so there'll be lots of press coverage."

"I'm afraid I won't be able to make it then, either," she told him. "I promised Papa Vincenzo that I'd come see him and Maria and the boys before the New Year."

"Dammit, Laura. I get your feeling you need to be with Chloe for Christmas. Even if she is just your half sister, there's blood there," he said. "But what I don't get is you blowing off spending New Year's with me for those...those people?"

Angry now, Laura said, "Those people happen to be my family."

"Give me a break. Just because the guy was married to your mother for a little while doesn't make them your family. For crying out loud, the man's your ex-stepfather and his kids are your ex-stepbrothers. There's no blood tie there. Those people are nothing to you."

"That's where you're wrong, Matt. Those people are everything to me." And without waiting for him to reply, she hung up the phone.

Stepping inside of his suite at the hotel, Jack dumped his laptop case and coat on the chair near the door, then tossed his key card onto the table. He wanted to punch something. No, he amended, he wanted to punch *someone*.

Matt Peterson.

Anger ripped through him as he recalled Laura all hot and sweet and soft in his arms only to turn away from him to take his stepbrother's call. It wasn't about her rejecting him, Jack told himself. He could handle rejection. If a woman wasn't into him, that was fine. He certainly didn't lack for female company and finding a woman willing to share his bed had never been a problem. Hell, Laura had been more than willing to share his bed. She had been as hot and eager for him as he had been for her.

Until Peterson had called.

When given the choice, she had walked away from him for Peterson. The son of a rich man, the golden boy that people flocked to, the one his own mother had adopted as her son all those years ago and had preferred over him. The fact that Laura had chosen Peterson over him fed his anger. But beneath that anger there was something else—an ache that felt dangerously close to hurt.

Enraged with himself that he had allowed Laura to affect him so deeply, that he had somehow given her the power to cause him this hurt, Jack stormed through the suite. He pushed open the door to the bathroom, went to the sink and doused his face with cold water. It hit him like a slap and helped clear his head somewhat.

Grabbing a towel, he dried his face and shoved the hair from his eyes. He braced his hands on the sink, drew in a breath. Satisfied he had his emotions under control, he hung the towel on the rack beside the counter. As he did so, memories of Laura flashed through his head. Laura staring at his naked chest, unknotting the towel at his waist. Laura looking at him, her eyes dark with desire, her mouth hot and hungry as she kissed him. Then suddenly it wasn't him Laura was looking at. It wasn't him she was kissing. It was Peterson she was clinging to, Peterson whose name she was gasping.

All the anger came rushing back. Furious with her and with himself, Jack turned away and stalked back into the living area. He headed straight to the bar where he snatched a glass and poured himself two fingers of whiskey. Wrapping his fist around the glass, he brought it to his lips and was about to toss it back when he realized what he was doing. He slammed the glass down on the bar untouched, sending liquor sloshing over the rim. He would not use liquor to numb the anger and pain the way his father had done.

Instead, he did what he always did. He took refuge in his work. Jack wasn't sure how long he worked. Long enough for him to plow through a mountain of e-mails and reports from his various holdings. Long enough for his shoulders to become stiff. Long enough for his stomach to remind him that the minibar snacks he'd fed it during his infrequent breaks weren't doing the job. But the thought of venturing out to dinner held no appeal. Besides, he was on a roll, Jack told himself.

Retrieving his cell phone, he punched in his assistant, Dotty's, home number. The second she answered, he barked out, "I want you to call Jardine's office and tell them to make sure they have everything ready to close on this deal," he said, referring to the attorney handling the sale. "And the minute the thirty days in that default clause are up, I want the deal closed." When she didn't respond, he asked, "Dotty, did you hear me?"

"I heard you," she said. "But if it's okay with you, I'll wait until morning and call Ms. Jardine at the office because I'm guessing she and her family might be getting ready for bed about now."

The sarcasm in her voice wasn't wasted on him. "It's not that late," he told her. But a glance at the clock on the bedside table proved him wrong. It was after ten o'clock, which meant it was even later in New York. The silence that followed was telling. "All right, it is late," he conceded. "And I'm sorry if I disturbed you. But I want you to call first thing in the morning and tell her—"

"I know. You want the deal closed ASAP. I'll call Ms. Jardine's office in the morning and make sure everything's on track."

"Good. I also want you to make some calls and find out exactly where Laura Spencer stands on raising that money. I know her mother and stepfather are trying to refinance the nightclub in Paris. Find out where they are on that." He filled her in on what he already knew. Namely that Chloe had signed over her stock to her sister and Laura had pledged it and her own stock for a loan. He also knew that she had cashed out her stocks and savings. What he didn't know was if Peterson had loaned her the money. "Give Sean Fitzpatrick at Fitzpatrick Investigations a call, too. Have him see if Matt Peterson or his family have made any large cash transactions."

"Jack, you never said anything about your stepbrother being involved in this deal," Dotty told him and he didn't miss the worry in her voice.

"I don't know that he is. But he and the Spencer woman are close friends and I don't want any surprises."

"All right," Dotty told him. "And since I've got you on the phone, what do you want me to tell the people at City Park about that donation you made to restore the carousel? They're most appreciative and want to have a commemorative plaque installed, acknowledging the donation. They also want to hold a press conference to announce Hawke Industries' generosity."

Jack hesitated a minute, then recalled the night Laura had shown him the Carousel Gardens and told him about her grandfather taking her there for the first time. "Tell them the plaque should read In Memory of Oliver Jordan, Hotelier."

"And the press conference?"

"Tell them I want to wait until after the first of the year and have the Contessa Hotel listed as the donor. List Laura Spencer as their contact person."

"Got it," Dotty told him. "Anything else?"

"That's it. Just make sure our people are ready to come in here and get things rolling once this goes down so I can get started on the Henderson's Plastics deal," he said, referring to a company he'd been eyeing in California.

"So you won't be sticking around New Orleans?"

"No. There's no reason for me to stay here once things are under way. Besides, my home is in New York."

"You live in a hotel suite," she reminded him.

"Which has a laundry, a housekeeper and twenty-four-hour room service."

"That's not a home, Jack."

"It's the only home I need. Good night, Dotty." He hit the off button on the phone. Annoyed by his assistant's remark,

Jack went over to the minibar, grabbed a can of nuts and a bottle of water. He popped the top on the can of nuts, ate a handful and then washed it down with water. As he munched on the snack, he looked around the luxurious room.

There wasn't a thing wrong with living in a hotel, he told himself. Living in a hotel suited him just fine. There was no fuss, no maintenance, no lawn to cut and a hot meal was only a phone call away. If it felt a little empty or pristine at times, so what? Besides, he wasn't there all that much anyway.

Polishing off the rest of the nuts, Jack walked over to the window and drew open the drapes to look out at the city. The threat of rain that had lingered all day had finally arrived and fell steadily on the streets below. The sky was starless thanks to the dark clouds. Even the moon struggled to be seen through the rainfall and clouds. The streets below were nearly empty, save for an occasional car. Jack suspected that the lack of traffic had more to do with people's lingering fears of flooding in the aftermath of Hurricane Katrina than it had to do with the actual threat of a rainstorm. He couldn't help feeling empathy for the people who had lived through the nightmare and had bravely returned.

Since the stormy weather suited his mood, Jack left the drapes open. After trading his dress slacks and shirt for a pair of jeans, a shirt and sweater, he returned to the table and his laptop where he went back to work. He was knee-deep in the projected operating budget for the hotel when he looked for the report that detailed the operating expenses for the prior five years and realized he didn't have it. Evidently, he had left it in Laura's office when he'd stormed out that afternoon. Still too restless to call it a night, Jack took the elevator downstairs to the executive office to retrieve the report.

Exiting the elevator, he started down the hall toward the office. He had the key to the door in his hand when he reached the suite of offices and found it unlocked. When he entered the reception area, he spied the light shining from Laura's office. The door was ajar and he could hear her speaking to someone.

"Yes, I know," she said. "I know that, too."

She was on the phone, he realized, and felt that punch in his gut again as he remembered who she had been speaking to when he'd left her this afternoon. Refusing to allow himself to go down that road again, Jack reminded himself he was there to get a file. He pushed the door open and walked over to the table.

Laura turned as he entered and there was no mistaking the surprise on her face. Lightning flashed outside the window behind her, illuminating her face. Her skin was pale, her eyes huge. She'd repaired the damage to her hair and lipstick that he'd done earlier, but it did little to disguise her fatigue.

"I'd better go, Mother. It looks like this storm is turning nasty. I should probably head home before it gets worse," Laura said.

It was her mother, Jack realized. Annoyed with himself because he was pleased that it hadn't been Peterson she was talking to, he began searching through the files for the report he needed.

"Yes, I understand. Just let me know as soon as you hear."

So her mother still hadn't been able to get the refinancing on the nightclub, he surmised. Did that mean Peterson hadn't come through for her yet? Even if his stepbrother didn't have that kind of money himself to lend her, his parents certainly did. It would take moving some stocks or pledging other assets, but Edward and Nicole Peterson were very wealthy people and they had never denied his son anything. Too bad the same couldn't be said for her son. But then, Jack had stopped being Nicole's son a long time ago, he reminded himself. All he was to her was a reminder that she had once been married to a loser.

"I will, Mother. Yes. I love you, too," Laura said and hung up the phone. After a moment, she said, "Jack, I'm sorry about…about earlier."

"Don't sweat it. I didn't," he told her and continued rummaging through the files.

"No, I guess you wouldn't," she tossed back.

There was something in her voice, a weariness beneath the sharp retort that caused him to look over at her. She looked sad and confused and vulnerable. But it was the sadness that touched something inside him, something he didn't want her to touch. And because she had the ability to make him feel, he resented her for it. Unable to locate the report he wanted, Jack dumped all the files into the briefcase he had left on the table. He'd take them all back to his suite and look for the one he needed there, he decided. Another bolt of lightning streaked through the sky. Thunder boomed. The lights flickered and he jerked his gaze up. "How good is the backup generator?"

"Good enough."

"When was the last time it was serviced?"

"I don't know the exact date. But it was sometime last year, shortly before I took over management," she told him as she began shutting down her own computer system. "We haven't had a major storm since Hurricane Katrina."

But he knew that the backup generator was old. In fact, according to the records, it had been retired and designated as the backup more than ten years ago when a new generator had been purchased. Given the difficulties experienced in restoring power to the ravaged city, he wasn't sure that either generator could sustain a minor storm, let alone a major one. And this one sounded like a big one if that last blast of thunder meant anything. "You may want to rethink trying to get home in that mess and take a room here for tonight."

"I'll be fine," she assured him as she switched off her desk lamp and gathered her briefcase and purse. When she reached the door, Jack allowed her to precede him and then he followed her out. After locking up the offices, they walked in silence down the corridor to the elevator banks. Jack punched the up button. She pressed the one for down. And they waited.

And waited.

She punched the button again. So did he. But according to the floor indicator, both elevators continued to move at a snail's pace. "I'll just take the stairs," he told her.

"Jack, wait," she said when he started for the stairwell door. "That's a lot of stairs. I'm going to take the freight elevator. If you don't mind riding down to the first floor with me first, you can use it to go up to the penthouse."

"Sounds good to me," he told her and followed her down to the far end of the hallway where the elevator the staff used for servicing the guest floors was tucked in a corner. Within moments of pressing the button, the elevator doors opened and they stepped inside.

Laura hit the down button for the first floor and the elevator started to descend.

Jack watched as the car lumbered down, passing the fifth floor, then the fourth floor. And then the elevator slammed to a halt, nearly knocking Laura off her high heels. Jack caught her arm to keep her from falling forward.

"Thanks," she murmured as she straightened herself. Then she hit the button for the first floor again.

Nothing happened.

When she tried three more times and the car failed to move, she said, "What in the devil's wrong with this thing?"

Jack frowned. "What's wrong is it's stuck. And so are we."

# Eight

Stuck?

They couldn't be stuck, Laura told herself. The elevator was just having a little hiccup. That was all. No way was she stuck in this elevator with Jack. "It'll start again in a minute," she said more to herself than to him. She set her briefcase and purse down on the floor and punched the floor buttons—all of them.

Nothing happened.

"I told you, it's stuck. Try pushing the emergency lever."

She tried. But still nothing happened. She pulled open the door to the red emergency box that contained the phone only to find that someone had cut the phone cord. Laura could feel her heart begin to race. Telling herself there was no reason to panic, she snatched her purse from the floor. "I'll just call the front desk on my cell phone," she said and began digging through the handbag. When she located it, she flipped it open. "No signal," she told him. "Either the storm took out the satellite or the walls of the elevator are interfering with the reception. You'll need to call the hotel on your phone."

Jack reached for the clip on his belt, but it was empty. "I left it in my suite."

Her stomach sank at the news. She was in trouble. She was alone with Jack in a space the size of a small closet. And no one even knew she was there. Not Chloe. Not her assistant, Penny. Not any of the hotel staff. The realization sent a wave of panic rushing through her. She had to get out of here. She had to, Laura told herself and she began slapping at the buttons again.

"Hey, take it easy," Jack told her as he caught her hands, holding them in his fists. When she started to struggle, he narrowed his eyes. "What's wrong? Are you claustrophobic?"

"No," she responded. But as she looked around, noting just how small the elevator was, she felt even more trapped. The air suddenly seemed thin, as though she were on a high mountaintop. "At least I wasn't until you mentioned it," she told him, both annoyed and scared. Pulling her hands free, she tried her phone again.

"It's okay," he told her.

Laura ignored him. Struggling to breathe, she tried to fight off the growing panic while she continued to hit at the buttons on the panel. She had to get out. She had to get out. She repeated the words silently like a litany.

"Laura," he said.

When she failed to respond, he stepped in front of her. But with the tide of panic sweeping through her and her breathing growing more difficult by the minute, she struck at him. Her blows seemed to bounce off his chest, but still she continued to fight him to get to the control panel. She needed to get the door open. She needed to get out of the elevator.

Jack caught her fists, sandwiched them between his palms and held them. "Laura. Laura," he repeated her name softly. "Breathe. Try to breathe."

It was the gentle way he had said her name that eased some of her panic. No longer struggling, she drew a deep breath, released it. As her heart rate slowed, so did her breathing. She looked up at Jack, stared into blue eyes that were warm, caring, concerned.

"It's okay," he told her gently.

But it wasn't okay. It might never be okay again, she thought. She was running out of time to get the money and her mother's attempts to refinance the nightclub had been turned down by two banks already. Her hopes of retaining the Contessa were on the verge of sinking and had a great deal to do with her stressed-out state. The ugly conversation with Matt and the realization that their relationship was nearly over had only added to what had turned into a lousy day. But it was the knowledge that she was swimming in dangerous waters on a personal level where Jack was concerned that worried her the most. She didn't want to be attracted to him. She didn't want to want him. And she didn't want to like him, to care about him. Even if the Contessa was not an issue between them, the emotional risks were far too great. Jackson Hawke was not a man who believed in love and commitment. He'd made that abundantly clear. And she... She was a woman who believed in and wanted both. To be trapped in an elevator with him was only asking for trouble that she didn't need, that she wasn't sure she could handle. That night in his hotel suite had proven that. So had this afternoon in her office. Had it not been for Matt's call, she wasn't at all sure she would have called a halt to things.

"Better?" he asked.

She nodded, drew another steadying breath. "You can let me go now."

He hesitated a moment, then released her. "I don't think it was a power outage. The light in here is still working. It's probably just the elevator."

Thinking more clearly, she noted that the light was indeed still working and told herself that was one thing for which she could be grateful. Otherwise, they would be trapped together in the dark. She waited, expecting him to remind her what poor condition the entire elevator system was in, but he didn't. Probably because he knew that she was well aware of it already. "It still doesn't change the fact that the car is stuck."

"No. But it means the rest of the hotel has power. The next time someone goes to use the service elevator, they'll discover it isn't working and report it to the maintenance department. Once maintenance is aware there's a problem, they'll correct it and get the car running again. Then we'll be able to get out."

"That would be fine except for the fact that no one's likely to discover the elevator isn't working until morning. It's after eleven o'clock. Room service stopped fifteen minutes ago and most of the housekeeping staff are gone for the day," she explained. "The chance that anyone will even try to use this elevator before morning is very slim."

"Maybe. Maybe not," he conceded. "The front-desk staff know you're still in the hotel. They might be used to you keeping long hours, but when you don't leave, someone's bound to come looking for you."

Laura shook her head. "There was a shift change two hours ago. I doubt anyone knows I'm still here. If they do, they'll think I just decided to spend the night on the couch in my office. I've done that before."

"What about Chloe? She's staying with you, isn't she? She'll come looking for you when you don't come home," he reasoned.

Laura would have laughed if she hadn't felt so dismayed. "Her stepsister, Meredith Grant, was arriving this evening for that meeting Chloe conned you into taking to discuss Meredith's company. Tonight Chloe was introducing Meredith to the city's nightlife. Knowing my sister, her chance of getting in before dawn is about as good as my chance of winning the lottery."

"What about your friend Peterson, the one you had to take the call from this afternoon?" he asked, an edge in his voice. "Won't he get worried when he calls you tonight and can't reach you?"

"Matt won't be calling me," she said firmly. Knowing Matt as she did, he would see nothing wrong in what he'd said and would expect her to make the next move by apologizing to him. "So unless someone is expecting you, no one knows we're missing."

"No one's expecting me," he told her, and Laura could have sworn the hardness that she'd detected a moment ago was gone.

"Then that means we're stuck here for at least…" she

glanced at her watch and continued "...the next five hours, maybe six, depending on when someone needs to use the service elevator."

"In that case, I suggest we make ourselves comfortable."

"What do you think you're doing?" she asked as he sat down on the floor and leaned against the wall.

"I told you. I'm getting comfortable. So should you."

"Aren't you going to at least try to get us out of here?" she asked, wondering if the man had lost his mind. Didn't he realize they were trapped in an elevator and no one knew they were there?

He glanced up at her. "And just what is it you expect me to do? The alarm on this thing is shot. I don't have my cell phone and yours won't work. And you said yourself that we're going to have to wait until one of the staff comes along and discovers the elevator is broken."

"But that won't be until morning," she pointed out.

"Precisely. That's why the smart thing for both of us to do is to try to get comfortable while we wait," he said and stretched out one leg while he bent the other. Leaning his head against the wall, he closed his eyes.

Irritated with him and frustrated by the situation, Laura looked around, then up at the tiled ceiling of the car. She knew that there were pulleys on the elevator car that were checked whenever the system was serviced. Through the ceiling, they could also get access to the next floor.

Opening his eyes, he followed the direction of her gaze. "You've got to be kidding," he said, sitting up.

"Why? If you get up on top of the car, you can crawl up to the next floor and get out through one of the vents in the elevator shaft." At his look of skepticism, she added, "It's done all the time."

"In the movies, maybe. But not in real life. Forget it. No way am I going to climb around in that elevator shaft and risk falling and breaking my neck. I can wait until morning for someone to find us."

"Well, I can't wait," she told him. But there was no way she could make it up to the ceiling without help. "All right. I'll do it. You just need to give me a boost up so I can reach the ceiling."

He looked at her as if she'd lost her mind. "In that outfit? You've got to be joking. That skirt isn't exactly made for climbing."

He was right. The skirt's straight cut was designed to showcase her legs, not for climbing around in an elevator shaft. "Then you go."

"No." He said the word firmly.

"Why not?"

"Because I don't like heights, okay?"

The admission stunned her. Jack had struck her as a man who feared nothing. Learning he had a fear of heights made him more real somehow and reminded her of the tender man she'd spent time with in the park. "I'm sorry. I didn't realize. I'll do it then. All you have to do is help me get up there."

He muttered something about stubborn women and pushed himself up to his feet. "You know, I should let you do it and just sit back and enjoy the view. But I'd hate like hell seeing you break your pretty neck and cheat me out of that night of sex you're going to owe me."

Ignoring the reference to their bet, she said, "Jack, I said I'll do it."

He pulled off his sweater, handed it to her. "Hold this."

Feeling unfair to have pressured him if he actually was afraid of heights, she said, "Really, Jack. Maybe you should let me go up."

"I said I'd do it," he told her. He stared up at the ceiling tiles for several months, then down at her briefcase. "How sturdy is that briefcase?"

"Very," she said.

"I'm going to need you to hold it as steady as you can while I stand on it so I can reach the ceiling. You wouldn't happen to have a flashlight in there, would you?"

"No, but I've got a penlight," she said, which she retrieved from the key ring in her purse and handed to him.

"Thanks," he said and slid it into his pocket. He tested his weight on the briefcase. Once. Twice. Then he turned to her. "Ready?"

"Ready."

Jack stood on top of the briefcase again and, stretching upward, he pushed on the cover tile in the ceiling that led to the elevator shaft. Once he had managed to nudge the tile aside, he looked down at her for a moment. "All right. Here goes."

"Jack." When he looked back down at her, she said, "Be careful."

"Don't worry, Laura. I intend to collect on that bet." Then he jumped and the tips of his fingers caught the edge of the opening in the ceiling. He clung to it for several long seconds.

Laura let go of the briefcase and moved beneath him so that she could hold either side of his legs. He glanced down at her. "It's okay," she said at his questioning look. "Use my shoulders to brace your feet."

Jack said nothing. And instead of using the leverage she had offered, he tightened his grip and pulled his body up until his shoulders were inside of the opening. Bracing himself on his elbows, he climbed through the rest of the way. For several moments he just seemed to stay where he was, hovering near the opening.

"Are you okay?"

"Yes," he told her and then he moved.

Laura tried to see inside the opening, but it was too dark. She did see a sliver of light occasionally and assumed it was her penlight. Trying to be patient, but finding the wait interminable, she asked, "Jack? Can you see the air vent yet?"

"Yeah," he yelled. He came back to the opening, knelt on one knee and looked down at her. His expression was grim and there was an odd look in his eyes that quickly turned to one of determination. "It's dark as sin inside this thing. But it looks like we're caught between floors. The nearest vent that I can see is a few yards above us. I'm going to see if I can get to it."

"Be careful," she repeated her earlier warning, but she wasn't sure Jack heard her because he had already disappeared back into the dark shaft.

It seemed as though an eternity passed, during which she heard Jack swear twice. Her heart stopped a moment when she heard something fall down the shaft before she realized that it must be the penlight. Finally, he returned to the opening and lowered himself down into the elevator.

"I'm sorry. I tried, but I couldn't get the thing opened. It's sealed tight," he told her as he brushed off his clothes. He sank to the floor, pressed against the wall. His jeans were dusty. His shirt was torn, his hair mussed. "And I owe you for the penlight. I dropped it."

"Forget about the penlight," she said, too worried by the sight of the gash on his forehead to recognize that he was being facetious. She didn't care about the penlight. She didn't even care about them being stuck in the elevator. What she did care about was the fact that Jack was hurt. "You're bleeding," she told him then grabbed her purse and dug through it for the packet of tissues she always carried.

He touched his forehead, looking surprised when he saw the blood. "Must have hit my head harder than I thought. I couldn't see much after I dropped the penlight."

Laura pushed his hand away and dabbed at the cut with a tissue. She was relieved to see that it wasn't as bad as she had first thought. She held the tissue for several moments to stem the bleeding. When she lifted it again, the flow of blood had lessened. "I've got a couple of Band-Aids in my briefcase. Hold this," she said and took his hand to place it on the wad of tissues. "Try to keep pressure on it while I get them."

"If you happen to have a couple of aspirin in there, I could use them. I've got a killer headache."

She did have aspirin, which she gave to him, along with the bottle of water she had tucked in her purse. Once she had cleaned the cut as best she could with the water and tissues, she placed a bandage over it. Sitting back on her heels, she said, "You've got a knot on your forehead and you're probably going to have an ugly bruise, but I don't think you need stitches."

"So I don't need to worry about looking like Franken-stein, huh?"

She knew the comment was meant to be funny. But she didn't feel the least bit amused. What she felt was guilty because he could have been seriously hurt. "I'm sorry. I should never have insisted you climb into that shaft."

"Hey, you didn't hold a gun to my head," he reminded her.

"I might as well have. The only reason you went in there was because of me." And it was knowing that, realizing it was her fault he was hurt, that he could very easily have fallen or worse, that made her feel even more guilty.

Jack tipped up her chin with his fingertip. "It's just a little scratch, Laura."

"But—"

He pressed his fingers against her lips, silencing her. "I'm fine."

"Are you sure?" she asked him.

"I'm sure," Jack lied. The truth was his head felt as if someone had hit him with a sledgehammer. But Laura looked so worried and guilty, he knew telling her so would make her feel even worse. In an effort to distract her, he said, "Any chance you've got some candy stashed in your purse? My dinner consisted of a raid of the minibar in my room, so I'm starving."

She didn't have any candy in her purse, but she did have some in her briefcase. It was her emergency stash, she explained to him as she divided the cache of chocolate-nut bars, peanut-butter cups and chocolate-covered wafers between them.

"I don't have any cups. I don't mind sharing, if you don't," she told him and offered him the bottle of water. He took it. For the next several minutes they ate in silence and as the silence grew he could see the nerves and guilt settling in again. To distract her he asked, "What's it like having such a big family?"

"Crazy. And wonderful," she told him.

As he hoped, she began to relax as she told him about her large, extended family and spending her summers in New Orleans with her grandfather at the Contessa. "It sounds pretty chaotic, all the moving around, people in and out of your life."

"It was, but in a fun way. Chloe used to say we were gypsies and had relatives in every state. But I didn't mind. I always wanted to be part of a big family and every time one of my parents remarried, I inherited another set of relatives."

"What about when they divorced?" he asked. "Didn't it hurt to lose all those new relatives?"

She grinned. "But I didn't lose them. Chloe and I decided that just because our parents got divorced didn't mean we had to. So we just kept the relatives. At last count I had fifteen grandparents and eleven brothers and sisters."

"That's a big family, all right."

"What about you?"

"My father died about ten years ago," he told her. But, in truth, Samuel Hawke had died long before then. He'd died the day his wife had left him for Edward Peterson.

"What about your mother?"

"She walked out on us when I was six. She's remarried now and has another son. I haven't seen much of her since the divorce."

"What about your brother? Are you and he close?"

"Hardly," Jack said, a wry smile twisting his lips as he thought of Matt Peterson. "He's my stepbrother. And there's never been anything that even remotely resembles family love between us. In fact, it's just the opposite. He detests me as much as I detest him."

"But why?"

Jack sighed. "I guess a lot of it had to do with my parents' divorce. It was a pretty ugly scene and watching people you love hurt each other, make selfish decisions you don't understand, isn't easy," he said, recalling his devastation back then.

"If you'd rather not talk about it, I understand," Laura told him.

Normally he wouldn't have told her about it. He seldom talked to anyone about that time in his life when his entire world seemed to have fallen apart. But looking at Laura now, recalling how she had shared the Carousel House with him that night, told him about her dreams, it felt somehow right to tell her. "My father had a construction business. Nothing big or fancy, but it supported our family. Then he landed a big contract to build a couple of office parks and hotels. It was great and there was the potential to make a lot of money on the deal. It would have made us rich. But he needed money to get the insurance and bonding. So he turned to an old friend who had hit it big in the real-estate business. He agreed to put up the money my Dad needed in exchange for half of the company."

"So your dad agreed," she added.

"Yes. Everything seemed to be going well for about six months or so. But my dad was gone a lot, busy with the business. And my mother wasn't the type of woman who liked being alone. Anyway, my dad's partner was around a lot and after a while I guess he wasn't content with just half of the business. He wanted my dad's wife, too. And my mother apparently didn't need much persuading. She was more than willing to swap what she considered a life of loneliness and pinching pennies for a life of fun and luxury."

"But what about you?" Laura asked. "She just left you?"

"I didn't want to leave my dad. He needed me," Jack explained as he recalled how difficult those first few years had been. "Besides, her rich new husband was a widower with a young son just a little older than me. Even when she was still married to my dad, she paid a lot of attention to him because he didn't have a mother," he told her, using the explanation his mother had always given him for her doting on Matt. "Anyway, once they were married, she adopted his son. So I guess you could say she traded me for him."

"But you were still her son," Laura said, her outrage clear.

"My stepbrother didn't think so. Whenever I'd go to visit, it was clear he didn't want me around. And the truth is, I didn't like being around them anyway. I didn't fit in. I just didn't belong." A fact that Matt had made sure he knew, Jack recalled. "After my dad sold his share of the business to them, he and I moved to New York. The visits grew fewer and fewer and eventually they stopped altogether. We haven't seen or spoken to each other in years."

"I'm so sorry, Jack," she said and reached out to touch his hand. "Your mother leaving you and your father like that for someone wealthy, she's the reason you said you wanted to be rich."

"Yes," he admitted. "I thought if I could find a way to make a lot of money and become rich then my mother would come back to us. Pretty stupid thinking, huh?"

"No. It was pretty smart thinking for a six-year-old," she

told him. "And I guess it's served you well. Because you are rich now."

Yes, he was rich, Jack thought to himself. Yet, lately, he had felt just as lonely and poor as he had been at six. He looked at Laura, thought about her crazy family, how her mother's selfishness and irresponsibility threatened to take away the hotel Laura loved, how she was willing to risk everything she owned to save something created by her family. Despite all the turmoil and financial strain, it was clear that she felt rich and was confident in her family's love. When she stifled a yawn, he suggested, "We probably ought to try to get some sleep. It's nearly one in the morning."

"Do you think that's a good idea? I mean, you have a head injury. You're not supposed to let someone with a head injury go to sleep."

He half smiled. "I don't think a little bump on the head qualifies as a head injury."

She frowned. "You were bleeding and you've got a knot on your head. As far as I'm concerned, that qualifies as a head injury."

When she stifled another yawn, he said, "All right. I do. But I read somewhere that when someone has a head injury, they can go to sleep. You just need to wake them up every hour to make sure they're okay. So why don't I set the alarm on my watch to go off in an hour. If I don't hear it when it goes off, you will and you can wake me up. How's that sound?"

She seemed to consider that. "I guess that would be okay."

So he set the alarm. Already stretched out on the floor, he leaned his head back against the wall and shut his eyes. She, on the other hand, couldn't seem to get comfortable.

He opened one eye, watched her stretch out her legs and put her head back against the wall the way he had. She tried tucking her feet beneath her and crossing her arms over her chest. She tried lying flat on her back and then curling into a ball on her side.

"Come over here," he told her.

Laura flushed. "I'm sorry. I didn't mean to wake you. I don't seem to be able to get comfortable and it feels like it's getting colder."

"Here, put this on," he said and tossed her his sweater.

"What about you? Aren't you cold?"

"Just a little. But I imagine it's going to get colder before the night's over. We might as well use our body heat to keep us both warm. So come on over here." When she hesitated, he said, "You don't have to worry, Laura. Being stuck in a cold elevator with a monster-size headache has pretty much put any thoughts of me having sex with you on the back burner for now."

Evidently taking him at his word, she scooted over to his side of the elevator. And when he opened his arms, she settled her head against his chest. Within moments, she was asleep.

But for him, sleep was a long time in coming. There was no need to reset the alarm on his watch when two o'clock rolled around because he was still awake. He was also still awake at three o'clock and four. And his inability to sleep had little to do with his using the floor as a bed and more to do with the woman whose shapely bottom was pressed against his arousal.

Laura stirred against him, adding to his torment and pleasure. He ached to slide his hand beneath her blouse, to feel the heat of her bare flesh against his palm. But to do so now when she was so vulnerable wouldn't be right, he told himself. He'd promised her she was safe. Besides, how would she feel if he slept with her and then foreclosed on the hotel? She already saw him as her enemy. Would she view her actions as a betrayal to herself and her family? Something told him that she would.

There was also the problem of Matt Peterson. How would she feel if she slept with Jack and then discovered that he was Matt's stepbrother, that he had considered bedding her for revenge? It would devastate her. Ashamed that he had ever thought of using her that way, he promised himself she would never know.

Still restless, she turned so that she was facing him, which drove all thoughts of Matt Peterson from his mind. Jack watched her. He noted the sweep of dark lashes that shielded her eyes, the gentle curve of her cheek, the way her lips parted ever so slightly in sleep. He remembered how soft and warm those lips had felt when he'd kissed her, the way she had tasted of both innocence and sin. The memory sent a sharp stab of desire through him, making him painfully aware of why he had been unable to sleep despite his own exhaustion.

She shifted again, adding to his discomfort. This time when she settled, she placed her hand trustingly against his chest. And then she opened her eyes.

# Nine

Laura wasn't sure what had awakened her. One moment she'd been dreaming about riding on the carousel and the next moment she'd been under the oak trees in the park with Jack. Then his arms had been around her, pulling her close, engulfing her in the most delicious warmth. And when she had tipped her face up to him, desire had pooled in her belly as he'd watched her out of deep blue eyes that were hot, hungry.

Opening her eyes now, she stared into those same hungry blue eyes. His arms were wrapped around her with one of his hands cupping her rear and one of his legs resting between her thighs. A hard warmth pressed against her belly and heat spread through her like lava as she realized it was Jack's arousal. Suddenly the events of the previous night came rushing back. Being trapped in the elevator. Her panic. Jack soothing her and sharing with her painful memories about his past. Something told her that Jackson Hawke was not a man who shared much of himself with anyone. That he had shared it with her touched something deep inside her.

"Good morning," he said.

"Is it morning yet?" she asked and was surprised how rusty her voice sounded.

Without removing his arm from around her, Jack slanted a glance at the watch on his wrist. "Technically, it is. It's just after six. But the sun probably won't be up for at least another hour. You sleep okay?" he asked.

"Yes," she admitted, surprised by just how soundly she'd slept. Then she remembered the alarm. "I didn't hear the alarm."

"I did," he assured her. "I dutifully reset it for an early hour."

"Did you sleep at all?"

"A little."

But she suspected that wasn't true. There were shadows under his eyes and a tension in his body that told her he'd probably not slept at all. Whiskers darkened his jawline and an ugly bruise spread from beneath the bandage. "How's the head?"

"The jackhammer that was beating in it stopped a couple of hours ago."

She reached up, tested the area around the bandage with her fingertips. "It doesn't look as swollen. But you definitely have a bruise and probably a concussion," she told him. "You should have a doctor look at it once we get out of here."

"I will," he promised.

A wave of tenderness washed through her. She hadn't wanted to desire this man. She certainly hadn't wanted to care for him. He was her enemy, the man who threatened the hotel she loved so dearly. And yet she did want him with an intensity that shocked her. Worse, she was beginning to care for him—more than she should. More than was safe.

But then she had never been one to play it safe, Laura reminded herself. She didn't want to play it safe now. She smoothed her fingers down his face, felt the prickle of his whiskers against her skin, heard him draw in a breath. When he caught her fingers, a thrill went through her as she realized that her very touch had excited him.

"We've probably got at least another hour before someone discovers the elevator is out of commission and finds us. Why don't you try to go back to sleep?"

"I don't want to sleep," she told him. "Do you?"

Heat flashed in those blue eyes. "No."

"Then what do you want to do?"

"This," he said and kissed her mouth.

Excitement swept through her at the feel of his mouth on hers. Her skin burned everywhere his lips touched. He tasted of heat. He tasted of danger. He tasted of need.

When Jack's hands sloped her body, cupped her breasts, Laura thought she would explode. And the more he kissed her, the more he touched her, the more she wanted him. She couldn't get enough of him. Judging by his groan when she stroked his manhood, he couldn't get enough of her, either.

He flipped her onto her back, kissed her again. Harder. Deeper. Her tongue matched his, stroke for stroke. Needing to get closer to him still, she pulled at the buttons on his shirt and when his chest was bare, she pressed her mouth to his chest. When she flicked her tongue over his male nipple, she felt his body quiver.

Then his hands were on her again. "I want you naked," he told her and made short work of the buttons on her blouse. He unhooked the front of her bra, bared her breasts. And the look in his eyes sent a shiver through her. "I've dreamed of seeing you like this, of doing this," he said as he lowered his head and took her nipple into his mouth.

Laura gasped. She speared her fingers through his hair. Desperate to have him inside her, she reached for her belt. "Not yet," he whispered as he laved the nipple with his tongue then moved to the other breast and started the process all over again. The sensations were exquisite and maddening. But still he refused to hurry.

While his mouth enjoyed her breasts, he smoothed his hand down her waist, over her hips and beneath her skirt. By the time he slipped his hand inside her panties and cupped her, Laura was quivering with need. When he eased one finger inside her, she could hardly breathe.

He took his time. He stroked the nub of pleasure at her center slowly at first and with each stroke, Laura could feel the need build. She could hear her breathing quickening. He increased the pressure, quickened the pace. And she could feel his own need mounting, hear it with each ragged breath he drew.

"Jack," she cried out as she felt the orgasm building. She pulled his mouth to hers. She kissed him hungrily, greedily, wanting to send him over the edge as he had sent her. Then suddenly the orgasm hit her.

Pulling her mouth free, Laura clutched at his shoulders. She dug her nails through his shirt and into his skin.

Closing her eyes, she tipped her head back and shuddered as she reached the crest and went over. Just when she started to settle, Jack took her up again and again.

But it wasn't enough. Keeping her eyes on his, she reached for him. She heard his breath catch, felt a thrill of power go through her at his reaction to her touch. The feel of the large bulge in his pants sent another wave of desire through her. She fumbled with his belt, got the button of his jeans open. She had just started to ease down his zipper when the elevator jerked to life and they began moving.

Jack didn't know whether to be grateful or seriously ticked off when he realized the elevator was moving and that they were about to be rescued. He'd been moments away from making love with Laura on the floor of the elevator and a part of him was tempted to hit the stop button on the car and finish what they had started.

But then he thought of Laura. Her hair was tumbled and wild-looking. Her eyes were dark and smoky with desire. Her lips were swollen from his kisses and whisker burns were visible on her pale skin. Her skirt was a rumpled mess and she was struggling to button her blouse. She would be mortified for anyone to find them like this, to see her disheveled appearance. And for the first time in a long time, someone else's needs mattered more than his.

"Here," he said, handing her her jacket.

"Thanks," she murmured and slipped it on.

Quickly, Jack buttoned his shirt. When he realized some of the buttons had been broken in her haste to rid him of his shirt, he grabbed his sweater from the floor and pulled it over his head.

Laura had just managed to smooth her hair when the elevator doors opened. And madness ensued.

"Ms. Spencer, are you all right?" the building's maintenance engineer asked.

"What happened?" the housekeeping supervisor asked, concern in her voice.

"I'm fine," Laura said. "The elevator shorted out in the storm."

"Laura, for heaven's sake," Chloe exclaimed as she muscled her way to the front of the elevator and blocked the door. "I was worried sick about you when you didn't come home last night."

"I'm surprised you got home that early," Laura said.

Chloe scowled at her. "Funny."

"What are you doing here at this time of morning, anyway?"

"Looking for you. When you didn't come home and didn't answer your cell or office phones, I was worried. I thought something bad might have happened to you."

"Something bad did happen," Laura replied. "I got stuck in an elevator."

"Is that Mr. Hawke with you?"

"Yes," Jack replied in answer to the hotel bellman's question.

"The front desk has been trying to reach you since last night," he explained. "I think they had an important message for you."

"Thanks. I'll check with them," Jack said.

"What happened to your head?" Chloe asked him.

Jack pressed his fingers against the bandage, but before he could respond, Laura said, "Mr. Hawke tried to get us out of the elevator by climbing up into the elevator shaft, hoping he could reach the next floor through a vent and get help. Unfortunately, the vents were sealed shut. But in the process, he injured himself."

"Pretty brave of you, Jack," Chloe remarked.

"It *was* brave of him," Laura fired back. "But it was also very foolish." She looked at him then, remorse and concern filling her eyes. "We're lucky he didn't fall and seriously injure himself or worse."

"It's just a scratch," Jack replied, more for Laura's benefit than anyone else's.

"You still should see a doctor," she told him.

"I will," he promised. Aware of the curious eyes watching the exchange, Jack wanted to spare Laura any more awkwardness with her staff or her sister, so he cleared a path by saying, "Now, if you'll excuse us. I think you'll all understand that after spending the night on the floor of a hard, cold elevator, Ms. Spencer and I could both use a hot shower, something to eat and some sleep."

Taking the hint, the people began to disperse—everyone except Chloe, who followed them both to the main lobby. "So you two were stuck in that little old elevator together all night, huh?"

"Yes," Laura said, but Jack noted that she didn't look at her sister. Nor did she look at him. Instead she kept her gaze focused on the floor numbers above the main elevator.

Chloe looked at him and then at her sister. "What did you two do all night?"

"Waited," Laura replied.

Chloe moved a step closer to Laura. "What's that on your face?"

Laura touched her cheek where his whiskers had left their mark. "Nothing. Probably from lying on the floor."

"Doesn't look like a mark from the floor tile to me." She got even closer. "Looks more like whisker burns. Wonder how they got there?"

Laura flushed and Jack expected her to deny it. Instead, she surprised him by turning to her sister and saying, "Probably the same way you got that hickey on your neck the night you went out with Bobby Connors and his car broke down during your senior year in high school."

"His car did break down," Chloe assured her, color creeping into her cheeks.

"And the elevator did get stuck," Laura countered.

Jack wasn't sure if the argument had continued or not because just as the elevator arrived, the front-desk clerk spotted him. "Mr. Hawke," she called out. "I have your assistant on the line again, sir. She says it's important."

"Tell her I'll be with her in a moment," he told her. Then he turned to Laura, touched her arm. "We need to talk later."

She nodded. "Be sure to have someone take a look at that cut."

"I will," he promised again.

"And when you two finish your 'talk,' don't forget you're supposed to meet with Meredith this afternoon," Chloe reminded him.

Jack didn't miss the knowing look in Laura's sister's eyes. But he didn't shy away from it, either. "I won't forget," he assured her. Once Laura and her sister disappeared into the elevator, Jack headed to the house phone to take Dotty's call, wondering what was so all-fired important.

What was so all-fired important, he soon discovered,

was that his stepbrother's father had just initiated a series of stock sales and transfers that, when complete, would net him a cool fifteen million dollars. The exact amount needed to pay off Laura's mother's note, cure the default and stop Jack from foreclosing on the Contessa. Jack had never believed in coincidences. He didn't believe in them now.

Laura didn't believe in omens. She'd never believed that spilling salt, walking beneath a ladder or having a black cat cross your path were signs that something bad was about to happen. But she was beginning to seriously reconsider her decision. After that night she and Jack had spent in the elevator, the main heater in the hotel had died, the sous-chef had quit and a group scheduled to take thirty of the hotel's hundred rooms for a week had canceled due to crippling snowstorms in the north that had shut down the airports. But it was the fact that she had neither seen nor heard from Jack for nearly two days that worried her the most.

When he'd said they needed to talk, she had agreed. While she would have liked nothing better than to go with him up to his suite right then and there, it hadn't been possible. She'd had Chloe itching to hear details, a staff with a million decisions that needed to be made, and she'd been in serious need of food and a bath. But from the way Jack had looked at her, the tender way he had touched her arm, she had been positive he had wanted them to finish what they had started as much as she had.

She still didn't know what the important business was that had caused him to leave abruptly that morning. Nor did she know why he hadn't told her he was leaving. Had it not been for Chloe mentioning that he'd had to cancel the meeting with Meredith for that afternoon, she wouldn't have known he'd left town. But he was back now. She knew from Alphonse, the doorman, that he had returned late that afternoon. So why hadn't he attempted to see her? They had almost been lovers, for pity's sake.

Lovers.

Just the word sent a thrill through her. She wasn't an innocent young girl. She was a grown woman who had made love before and had enjoyed it. But never, not ever, had she experienced anything close to the pleasure that she had experienced in Jack's arms.

At the mere memory, a ripple of heat swirled through her body. Lifting her hand to her throat, Laura recalled with vivid clarity the feel of his mouth, hot and eager, on her breasts, the feel of his hands, so strong and yet gentle, on her skin. She had no doubt that had it not been for the untimely rescue, they would have made love completely that morning. It was what they both had wanted, what they had been heading toward for weeks now, she admitted.

So why, two full days later, had they still not made love?

Was it possible that she had been mistaken about how much he wanted her? Had those hours they'd spent together really meant nothing to him?

It was imperative she discover the truth. Because somewhere between fighting to stop his takeover of the hotel and lying half-naked in his arms, she had fallen for Jackson Hawke. She'd known him less than a month, had resented the threat he represented to her beloved hotel and she was starting to fall in love with him.

Laura was still digesting the fact that she had feelings for a man who, for all intents and purposes, was her enemy when her cell phone began to ring. Grabbing her purse, she dug into the leather bag and hoped it was Jack. But when she located the phone, she saw her mother's number instead. "Hello, Mother."

"Laura, darling. You'd better sit down."

He was in a foul mood, Jack admitted as he walked over to the window and looked out over the city. Night had fallen. On the streets below he could see people scampering, their arms most probably laden with shopping bags and wrapped packages. Everywhere he'd turned over the past two days, people were in a cheerful, holiday mood.

Not him.

He was angry, Jack acknowledged. He was angry with Matt Peterson. He was angry with Laura for lying to him. But most of all, he was angry with himself. He'd allowed himself to become distracted. He'd allowed his emotions to interfere with business. He'd allowed his attraction to Laura to distract him. And because he had, he was on the verge of blowing a fifteen-million-dollar deal.

Peterson was going to bail her out. Unless Jack found a way to foreclose before Peterson could get his funds in place, his deal was dead and Laura would keep the hotel. And Peterson would keep Laura. He didn't like losing. But he'd lost deals before and probably would again in the future. He wouldn't have even minded losing to Laura and seeing her win their bet. What he did mind was losing to his stepbrother. Losing *Laura* to him.

He didn't want her to matter. He didn't want to care about her. But it was because he did care for her that he hated like hell to see her with someone like Peterson. She deserved better than his stepbrother. Hell, she deserved someone better than *him*.

Caught up in his musing, it took Jack a moment to register that the pounding he heard was coming from the door. Turning away from the window, he strode through the suite and opened the door to Laura.

He knew instantly that something was wrong. Her eyes had a wild look to them. Her dark red hair, a tangled mass around her face and shoulders, looked as though she'd been running in the wind. Her eyes were dry, but there were tear streaks down her cheeks. "What's wrong?" he demanded.

"I guess that depends on who you ask," she told him and pushed past him into the suite.

Jack closed the door and followed her. "Since you're the one who came barging into my suite, I'm asking you. What are you doing here?"

"I'm here to pay off on our bet," she told him and stepped out of her heels.

Jack narrowed his eyes. Keeping his voice even, he said, "You're a little early. You've still got another five days."

"Five days or five months. It won't matter," she informed him. "My mother came up two million short in the refinancing. You've won, Hawke," she said, her voice cracking. "The Contessa is yours and I'm here to deliver on my end of the deal."

What was she talking about? Didn't she know Peterson was going to give her the money? But if she knew, she wouldn't be there. She would be with Peterson. "As much as I'd like to collect on our bet," he began with a casualness he didn't feel, "you might want to hold off. The rest of the money could still turn up."

"It won't. And I want to pay off now."

"Laura, you don't have to do this," he told her. "You don't want to do this."

"Sure I do." She pulled her sweater over her head. "We had a bet and I lost. I'm here to pay off the debt."

Jack's mouth went dry at the sight of her in the black lace bra. He was rock hard in an instant. Fighting the desire clawing at his gut, he told himself he shouldn't do this. He would not do this. He would not take advantage of her when it was obvious that she was upset and apparently didn't realize that Peterson was going to come through for her. When they'd started this thing, there had been a part of him that had wanted to bed her, had deliberately planned to do just that, to get back at his stepbrother. But that had changed and he knew he could never use her that way. He refused to do so now. Snatching up her sweater from the floor, he threw it at her and walked over to open the door of the suite. "Go home, Laura," he said through a voice that had gone hoarse with need.

He didn't expect the flash of anger in her eyes. She threw his sweater back on the floor and followed him across the room where she slammed the door shut. Then she turned to look at him. Taking his face in both of her hands, she kissed his mouth. When he didn't respond, she ran her tongue across his lips. Lifting her head, she looked up at him and said, "I'm not going anywhere, Hawke. Not until I've paid off my debt."

His body trembled with need. He wanted to haul her into the bedroom and make love to her until neither of them could remember their names. He wanted to feel her body shudder and clench around him when he filled her. He wanted to hear her call his name and cling to him as he took them both over the edge.

But he didn't.

He couldn't.

Not now. Not when she was so vulnerable, when she was still reeling because she thought she'd lost her hotel. Not when he knew that his stepbrother was going to bail her out even if she did not. He couldn't make love to her with the lie between them. If he did, she would hate him. And the idea that Laura would look at him with disgust and hatred hurt far worse than he ever imagined it would.

With a strength he hadn't known he possessed, Jack caught her hands and ended the kiss. "I was never serious about the bet. It was just a joke," he lied. "Go home, Laura. Before you embarrass us both."

He braced himself, sure he would see shock and hurt in her eyes. Instead he looked into the green eyes of a siren. "So you're saying you don't want me?"

"That's right."

The smile that curved her lips was pure sin. She stepped into his space, stroked his arousal through his slacks. "Liar."

Jack groaned. Unable to resist her, he pulled her into his arms and kissed her with all the hunger, all the need that had been building inside him from the first time he'd laid eyes on her. Tonight, he told himself, tonight she was his. Lifting her in his arms, he carried her into the bedroom.

# Ten

Laura could feel the coolness of the silk sheets on her heated skin as Jack placed her on the bed. The contrast served to sober her for a moment. She'd come to him in a frenzy of despair and hurt following her mother's phone call. Those feelings had soon given way to anger. Anger at herself, her mother, her grandfather for not trusting her with his hotel. And anger at Jack for taking the hotel. At Jack for making her love him and then turning away. So she'd come to him. One look into those cool blue eyes and she'd known he was shutting her out. She didn't know why he had turned away from her. She didn't understand why he would deny what was between them. She only knew that she needed him to feel as she was feeling.

He stood beside the bed looking down at her. He wanted her. She could see it in his eyes, etched in the rigid way he held his body. But she could also see he was struggling with the decision to make love with her as he wanted, as they both wanted.

Determined not to let him deny them both, she took his hand and brought it to her breast, held it there. Desire flared in his blue eyes as he squeezed her sensitive flesh through her bra. "Make love with me, Jack," she whispered.

"Laura, you don't need to do this."

"Yes, I do. I want you, Jack. And I know you want me."

This time he didn't deny it. And when she reached for him, he came to her. The feel of his body against hers drove all thoughts away save for the feel of him, the taste of him, the ache at her center that grew stronger with each stroke of his tongue. In a frenzy to be one with him, Laura reached for his zipper.

He tore his mouth free and captured her fingers. "No," he told her. "I'm not going to let you rush this. I'm going to make love to you slowly and enjoy every inch of you. And when I finish, I'm going to start all over again. I want you to remember tonight, Laura. I want you to remember me."

She started to tell him that she doubted she would be able to forget him if she tried, but then he was kissing her again and she forgot what she wanted to say. All she knew was that her body was taut with need and awash with sensation as Jack moved his mouth from her lips to her jaw. From there he worked his way down her neck to her shoulder. He veered left and without removing her bra, he closed his mouth over the tip of her breast. When his teeth closed around her nipple, Laura nearly came off the bed at the exquisite sensations that rolled through her.

He unhooked her bra, bared her breasts and took them

in his hands. Laura moaned as he kneaded and kissed and plucked at her nipples. Then his clever mouth kissed a path down her rib cage to her belly. Her stomach quivered as his tongue circled her navel. By the time he pulled off her skirt and panties, tossing them aside, Laura was frantic to feel him inside her. She reached for him, fought with the buckle of his belt. "You're wearing too many clothes," she complained.

Between them, they made short work of his shirt and slacks. His groan as she freed him from his briefs sent a thrill of excitement through her. But excitement turned to white-hot need as he moved down her body and parted her thighs. "Jack, no."

"Yes." Opening her, he kissed her.

The first stroke of his tongue sent an explosion of sensation through her. When he repeated the process, she gasped. He continued to kiss her, to taste her, to nip her with his teeth. And with each flick of his tongue she could feel the pressure building. Just when she thought she couldn't stand the pleasure another second he increased the pressure and Laura felt the world explode.

"Jack," she cried out, reaching for him.

Then he was inside her. One smooth, slow stroke after the other, moving in and out. In and out. Nearly withdrawing, then filling her again. Then he started to move faster and faster still as he pushed her, pushed them closer and closer to that precipice.

"Look at me, Laura," he commanded.

She looked at him, stared into eyes that had gone dark with need. And desperation. She wondered at the desperation, wanted to ask him what was wrong. Then he entered her again, and the room around her shifted, shattered. And then she was tumbling into space.

Wave after wave shuddered through her, stealing her breath, stealing her ability to think. All she could do was feel. When the orgasm ripped through Jack, it sent her free-falling again. Driving into her one last time, he cried out her name. As his body convulsed, she held on to him, felt each spasm as it hit him before it rolled into her. Finally, when the shudders stopped, they continued to cling to one another.

For a long time, she said nothing. Neither did he. She contented herself with the feel of his body next to hers, the strength of his arms wrapped around her. She didn't allow herself to think beyond the moment. She didn't know where they went from here, if they went anywhere at all. Jack had made no promises. Neither had she. But she knew in her heart that it was promises she wanted.

"We need to talk, Laura. There's something I need to tell you about the foreclosure. You—"

"I don't want to talk about business," she told him. Turning over, she faced him. "What happened between us just now wasn't business."

"But—"

"It was personal, Jack. And I didn't come here tonight to try to convince you not to foreclose on the hotel. I came here tonight because I wanted to be with you. I wanted you. I needed you."

"But there's something I need to tell you. Something you need to know about me," he began.

Laura pressed her finger to his lips. "I know everything I need to know about you. I know that you're smart and arrogant and a tough businessman. I know you can be ruthless, but that you're brave and more caring than you want anyone to know. I know you're a wonderful and generous lover," she said softly as she stroked his jaw.

"I was inspired," he told her, then captured her hand and placed a kiss in her palm.

As impossible as it seemed, she could feel desire curling in her belly again. With a boldness she would never have imagined she possessed, she said, "Maybe I can inspire you again."

Heat flared in his eyes, but his expression grew somber. "You inspire me just by breathing. But you may feel differently when you know the truth about me, about who I am."

"I know who you are, Jackson Hawke. You're the man I'm in love with." When he went still, Laura quickly added, "I didn't tell you how I feel because I expect a declaration from you. I don't. But I wanted you to know the way I feel. I love you."

"Laura, if you knew the truth—"

"The only truth that matters to me right now is that you want me. Do you want me, Jack?"

"Yes," he said, his voice gruff. "I want you…more than I've ever wanted anything or anyone in my life."

"Then show me," she told him.

Jack showed her over and over again throughout the night. With his mouth. With his hands. With his body. And when she awoke in the morning, feeling tender and achy from their lovemaking, he lifted her in his arms and carried her into the bathroom. In the shower, he soaped her body, bathed every inch of her, discovered new pleasure points she hadn't known existed.

"You're so beautiful," he murmured. "So soft," he told her as he worked his way up from her feet to her thighs and the sensitive spot between them. With a slowness that she found maddening, he finally reached her breasts. Then his mouth was on hers, pressing her against the wall while the shower poured over them.

He lifted her onto him and she wrapped her legs around his waist and then he began to move. With each thrust, Laura could feel herself moving closer and closer to the edge of the cliff. And with the water streaming down around their joined bodies, she felt herself begin to fall,

"Jack," she called out, clutching his shoulders as the sensations took her over that cliff.

Moments later, she heard him shout her name as he followed her over the edge.

By the time she exited the bedroom forty-five minutes later, Jack was already dressed in a suit and tie, sitting at the table talking on his cell phone. She noted his briefcase and laptop sat near the door.

"I know it's last-minute, Dotty. But try to set the meeting up with as many of them as you can. If they can't make it, get them to agree to be available for a teleconference." He paused. "Just tell them it's a one-time chance for them to make a thirty percent return on their investment, but I need an answer by tomorrow."

For the first time since she'd shown up at his hotel room door the previous night, Laura felt awkward. They were lovers and she loved him, but she didn't know how he felt. Had last night been a one-time fling for him? Would he want to continue to see her? Or would he foreclose on the hotel and return to New York and never see her again? A sinking feeling settled in her stomach as she realized she didn't have the answers and that those answers may very well not be what she wanted. It also reminded her that Jack had wanted to tell her something last night. Only she had been fearful that whatever he wanted to tell her would ruin what was happening between them, so she had refused. Now in the clear light of day, she realized that might not have been the smartest thing to do.

As though sensing her presence, Jack looked up. "I've got to go, Dotty. I'll see you in a couple of hours." Ending the call, he went to Laura and kissed her. When he lifted his head, he smiled and said, "Good morning, again."

"Good morning."

"I ordered some coffee, croissants, eggs and bacon from room service," he told her and Laura noted for the first time the serving cart piled with silver trays. "I wasn't sure what you liked to eat in the morning."

"Just coffee for now," she said and sat down while he retrieved the silver pot. "Are you going somewhere?"

"I have to go to New York this morning," he told her as he poured her a cup of coffee.

"I see," she said, but she clearly didn't. "Will you be coming back?"

He stopped in the middle of pouring his own coffee at the question. "Of course I'll be back. Why would you think I wouldn't?"

Both relieved and somewhat embarrassed, she said, "I just wasn't sure. I mean, I was the one who showed up here last night and refused to take no for an answer."

He caught her hands, pulled her to her feet. "And I'm glad you did. I meant what I said last night. I've never wanted anything or anyone as much as I wanted you. As much as I *still* want you," he added.

Laura went into his arms, laid her head against his chest. As she breathed in his scent, reveled in the feel of him, she asked, "Do you really have to go to New York now?"

Taking her by the shoulders, he gently set her from him. "I'd like nothing better than to take you into that bedroom and make love to you again. But there's something I have to do first, something I have to fix. Once I've made things right, I'll be back."

"How long will you be gone?"

"A day, maybe two tops. And when I get back, we'll talk."

"About the foreclosure," she said, realizing he would be back right before the scheduled foreclosure on the hotel.

"Yes, we'll talk about that. And about us."

It took a lot longer to fix his situation than he'd anticipated, Jack admitted as he sat across the table the next afternoon with the signed documents in hand. It had also cost him an additional million dollars to sweeten an already very sweet deal. But he'd done it. The foreclosure on the Contessa Hotel by Hawke Industries was now officially canceled. In turn, the investors he'd originally sold the idea to were enjoying a hefty return for their initial investment. And he was now the sole owner of the promissory note and the foreclosure was called off. The entire process had been tricky at best and he'd had to tiptoe around the legality of his actions because of the potential conflict of interest. Fortunately, the attorneys had hammered it out.

Standing at the door, Jack shook hands with each investor and bade them goodbye. "Thanks again, Carlton," Jack said.

"Anytime, Hawke," the other man said and shook his hand. "You call me again the next time you're willing to offer these kind of terms on a deal."

"Me, too," one of Carlton's cronies said with a laugh.

Everyone left but his final investor and his father's old friend, Tom Ryan. "Thanks for coming, Tom."

He nodded. "You know, son, I've known you since you were knee high. I watched you go through your parents' nasty divorce and your father's bout with the bottle. I watched you grow into a fine young man, but a hard one, a man who never allowed himself to feel anything deeply or look at anything beyond the bottom line. For you, everything has always come down to money. I suspect a lot of that had to do with what happened with your parents. And I understood it, but I worried about you."

"Is there a point here somewhere, Tom?" Jack asked, not particularly happy with the portrait he'd heard painted of himself.

"The point is that today you made a business decision that I suspect had nothing to do with the bottom line. Unless I miss my guess, you just blew several million dollars for personal reasons."

Which was true, Jack admitted silently. Feeling somewhat defensive, he said, "What if I did? You and the others certainly profited from it."

Tom smiled, his brown eyes twinkling. "Yes, we did. And I wasn't being critical, son. Hell, I'm pleased about it because I was worried you were going to end up a rich but lonely man."

And he just might have, Jack realized. Had it not been for Laura. Laura had changed all that. Laura had changed him. "Glad I could make you happy," Jack said. "But if you don't mind, I've got a plane to catch."

"Just one more thing, Jack. Tell me. Was she worth it?"

Jack smiled for the first time since he'd left New Orleans two days ago. "Yeah, she was."

And as he dashed from his office to the waiting limo for the airport, all Jack could think about was that Laura had been worth not only the millions it had cost him on this deal, but she had been worth everything he had and more. Now all he had to do was hope that she would forgive him for not telling her right from the start that Matt Peterson was his stepbrother and convince her that a future with him was worth the risk.

"Thank you. Yes, I'll get back to you about the date for the press conference," Laura said then hung up the phone with the business office at City Park.

Jack. Jack had done this for her.

Picking up the letter from the park's Celebration in the Oaks Improvement Committee, she reread the words of thanks for the donation to restore the Carousel House. She skimmed the remainder of the letter, asking her to confirm the wording on the commemorative plaque that would grace the Carousel House in her grandfather's name. Her heart swelled. Jack had made the donation before their night together. Surely for him to do such a thing had to mean he felt something more for her than lust, she told herself.

She thought of his phone call earlier, telling her he was on his way back and would meet her at her house. He'd said he had something to tell her. Was this what he'd wanted to tell her earlier? Then she'd let him surprise her and after he did, she would show him just how much she appreciated what he'd done.

"That's an awfully dreamy expression for a woman who's supposedly working. Don't you agree, Meredith?"

Laura opened her eyes and looked over at the doorway where her sister stood with Meredith Grant. The daughter of a Boston blue blood and an opera diva, Meredith had been Chloe's stepsister during the brief marriage of Chloe's father and Meredith's mother. As in Laura's own case, divorce had not severed the family bonds. Laura smiled at the two of them.

"I think she looks like a woman who's working at dreaming up some wonderful new marketing plan for her hotel," Meredith offered diplomatically, a hint of her Boston roots in her voice.

"Thank you, Meredith," she said and couldn't help but notice the contrast in the two women. While her sister, Chloe, was striking, in-your-face sexy and fun, Meredith was a quiet beauty with an abundance of grace and poise. And where her sister's style was up-to-the-minute chic and bold, Meredith's was elegant.

"You're quite welcome," Meredith told her politely.

"So what are you two doing here? I thought Chloe was dragging you off to some party tonight."

"Not some party," Chloe corrected. "It's a party being hosted by the director of the new action/adventure movie they're planning to shoot here. Oops," Chloe said as her cell phone started to ring. She glanced at the number. "I need to take this," she told them and exited the office.

"Your sister seems to think there could be a few poten-tial clients for me among the Hollywood South set,"

Meredith explained, referring to the name many were now calling New Orleans's fast-growing movie industry. "Laura, I hope you don't mind, but Chloe told me about your situation with the hotel. I have some money in a trust fund I could borrow against and lend you if it would help."

Moved by the gesture, Laura reached out and squeezed the other woman's hand. "I can't tell you how much I appreciate the offer, Meredith. But I can't accept. I've pretty much resigned myself to the fact that come Monday, Hawke Industries will be the majority owner of the Contessa."

"I'm sorry," Meredith told her.

"So am I." She sighed. "But I guess the one good thing that's come out of all this is that I met Jack."

"Oh. I didn't realize the two of you were…involved."

Laura frowned, not sure what to make of Meredith's reaction. "Is there any reason I shouldn't be involved with Jack?" When the other woman remained silent, Laura pressed, "Please, Meredith, if there's something you think I should know, tell me."

The clear blue eyes that looked at her were filled with concern and empathy. "It's just that…in my business I try to keep up with the society columns and based on what I'd read and things Chloe said a while back, I was under the impression that you were involved with Matthew Peterson. In fact, I thought it was rather serious."

"Matt and I did date for a while," she confessed. "And for a short time, I thought it might become more serious. But when I moved back to New Orleans, we agreed to take a bit of a break. We have sort of had a long-distance relationship since then. But it isn't serious. At least not anymore," she told her, which was something she realized she still needed to make clear to Matt. Now with Jack in her life, she could see even more clearly that what she shared with Matt was not real love and to allow him to believe otherwise would not be fair.

"Does Jackson Hawke know that? I mean, does he know that you and Matthew Peterson are no longer a couple?"

"I'm not sure. But then I'm not sure he ever knew Matt and I were involved in the first place. Why? What difference does it make?"

Meredith clasped her hands in that way well-bred women do when they need to compose themselves. When she looked up at Laura, her gaze was steady and her voice gentle as she said, "It might make a difference because Matthew Peterson and Jackson Hawke are stepbrothers."

The news hit Laura like a blow.

"You didn't know." It was a statement, not a question.

"No, I didn't."

"I guess it's not surprising that he didn't tell you," Meredith said. "From what I'm told there's a lot of bad blood between the two of them. It goes back to when Hawke's mother left him and his father for Matt Peterson's dad. I understand Matt Peterson doesn't even acknowledge there's any family connection between the two of them, even though it was Hawke's mother who adopted Peterson. And before you think I'm some terrible gossip, the only reason I know all this is because my mother is friends with Nicole Peterson. She performed at some charity event Mrs. Peterson was chairing."

"I don't think you're a gossip at all," Laura assured her. "Is there… Is there anything else I should know?"

Again, Meredith hesitated. "Just that the rivalry between

Jackson Hawke and his stepbrother has only gotten worse
as they've gotten older. In fact, when I was having such a
difficult time getting an appointment with Hawke to
discuss my business proposal, my assistant went so far as
to suggest I approach Matt Peterson with the proposal
because the chance to snatch a deal from his stepbrother
would be a sure way to draw Hawke's interest. I'm
ashamed to say I actually considered it."

"No one would have blamed you, if you had," Laura
said absently.

"I would have blamed me. That's not how I do business," Meredith explained. Then her expression softened
again. "I'm so sorry, Laura."

"Me, too. I just still can't believe that Jack didn't tell me
he and Matt are stepbrothers."

"Maybe he didn't know about you and Matt Peterson,"
Meredith offered. "I mean, I read the gossip and society
sections because of my business. It's possible Hawke
doesn't pay any attention to them and never realized you
had been involved with his stepbrother."

Had Jack known about her involvement with Matt? Of
course he would have known. He'd had her investigated. Her
personal relationships, particularly a long one with a wealthy
and well-connected businessman would have been noted.
Suddenly memories came flooding back—of the night in her
office when Matt had called and Jack had left abruptly in a
surly mood. She also remembered his odd remark about what
would Peterson say when he called for her and she wasn't
home. Yes, Jack had known about her relationship with Matt.
What she didn't know was if Jack had really wanted her, or
had he only wanted what he thought belonged to Matt?

As though sensing her turmoil, Meredith said, "Laura, if he did know about you and his stepbrother and didn't say anything, he might have had a good reason."

"Can you think of a good reason?" she asked.

"No, but if I were you, I would talk to him and find out what his reasons were."

"I intend to," Laura told her. And she prayed that when she did talk to Jack, the answers he gave her wouldn't break her heart.

"Good luck, then."

"Thanks," she said. "And thanks for being honest with me. I know I put you on the spot."

"I just hope that when you talk to Hawke that you get the answers you want."

"So do I," Laura said.

# Eleven

Jack spied the flashing police car lights behind him and breathed a relieved sigh when the officer whizzed past him. He had no doubt he'd broken several speeding laws in his race from the airport to Laura's house. Reminding himself to send a donation to the policemen's fund as atonement and thanks, he exited Interstate 10. As he waited for the light to change, he turned on the radio and found himself listening to the Christmas carol about being home for Christmas. Jack smiled, realizing that in a manner of speaking he was coming home—to the first home he'd had in a very long time. And for the first time in even longer, he was actually looking forward to Christmas.

Because of Laura.

His heart seemed to swell in his chest as he thought of her, remembered the feel of her, the scent of her, the sound of her telling him she loved him. He wanted to see her face, hold her close and hear her say those words to him again. And she would, he told himself. Once he told her that the foreclosure on the Contessa had been canceled, it would no longer stand between them. She would no longer need to worry about losing her beloved hotel and he would no longer have to worry about Peterson injecting himself into Laura's life.

Later, he would tell her about Peterson, explain their connection and hope she would forgive him for not telling her about it earlier. But no matter what happened, she would never know that he had even considered seducing her to get back at his stepbrother. That he had thought of doing so still shamed him. He could live with his shame, but he couldn't live with the hurt that it would cause Laura. Whatever it took, he would keep that truth from her.

Deep in thought and eager to see Laura, Jack didn't even see the man standing on the stairs in front of her house until after he had parked and exited the car. Even though his back was to him, Jack recognized the tall figure in the black overcoat sporting his two-hundred-dollar haircut. Jack also recognized the voice talking on the cell phone.

"Laura, it's Matt again. I've got a surprise for you, babe. Give me a call."

Jealousy and anger gripped Jack by the throat and refused to let go. He balled his hands into fists. And when Peterson turned around, he didn't look at all surprised to see Jack there.

"Hello, Hawke."

"What are you doing here?" Jack demanded.

"I could ask you the same thing. This is Laura's apartment, after all. And she is *my* girlfriend. Not yours."

"She might have been your girlfriend at one time, but she's not anymore," Jack told him.

"Are you sure about that?" Peterson asked. He leaned back against the door, a smug look on his face. "Laura and I have been seeing each other for more than a year. In fact, Mom and Dad adore her and they're eager to welcome her into our family."

The mention of his mother and the insinuation that Laura would be marrying Matt infuriated Jack. But he forced himself not to give in to Peterson's baiting. It had been a mistake he'd made far too often in their youth. As a result, he'd ended up being the one getting the bad rap and Peterson had come out smelling like a rose. "Give it up, Peterson. Laura's done with you."

"I don't think so."

Jack couldn't help noticing that his stepbrother had made the statement with the same confidence he'd possessed as an eight-year-old when he'd told Jack that his mother wouldn't be coming back for him. Peterson had been right. His mother hadn't come back for him. She had started a new life with a new son. But Peterson wasn't right this time, Jack told himself.

When he didn't respond to the provoking, Peterson continued, "As a matter of fact, I'm so sure about Laura that I'm planning to announce our engagement at Christmas. She'll make the perfect candidate's wife, don't you think?" He paused. "After all, she is the whole package. Smart, beautiful and of course, there's that sexy little body of hers."

"Shut up," Jack warned.

Peterson smiled, his lips twisting malevolently. He was clearly enjoying himself. "What do you think she's going to say when I give her the check to pay off her mother's loan and stop you from foreclosing on that hotel that she loves so much? I've got it right here," he said, patting his pocket. "I imagine she's going to be very grateful and I certainly am looking forward to letting her show me her appreciation."

Jack wanted to plant his fist in Matt's face. Instead, he took a step forward. "I said to shut up!"

"Why? Don't like the idea of Laura showing me her gratitude with that sweet little body of hers?"

"Don't hold your breath, Peterson. She isn't going to show you anything but the door because the foreclosure was canceled. I bought out the other investors. So you see, Laura doesn't need your money or you. Now why don't you go hop on the plane and go back home to mommy and daddy."

Peterson laughed and the sound did nothing to ease Jack's temper. "Come on, Hawke. Do you honestly believe that given a choice Laura would choose you over me? Face it, you're a loser. Just like your old man was."

Jack wasn't sure if it was hearing Peterson tag him as a loser again or if was the seed of uncertainty that Laura might indeed choose his stepbrother over him, but something inside of him snapped. Grabbing Peterson by the lapels of his coat, Jack hauled him up to get right in his face and said, "Since it's my bed Laura's been sleeping in and my name she screams when I'm buried inside her, I'd say you're the loser this time. Not me."

At the sound of a gasp behind him, Jack spun around and saw Laura standing there on the sidewalk. In the streetlight, her face was the color of chalk and her green eyes were the size of quarters. But it was the look in those eyes, the shock, the hurt, that ripped at him now. Releasing Peterson, he started down the steps toward her. "Laura—"

"Don't," she said, holding up her hand.

"I can explain," he told her, desperate to wipe that shattered expression off her face. "It's not what it looks like."

"Isn't it?" she asked, her voice flat, cold.

"No," he told her firmly. "It's not."

"Don't listen to him, Laura," Matt said as he straightened his coat. "It's exactly what it looks like. Hawke has hated me from the day his mother left his old man and him to be with me and my father. He's always been jealous that his mother chose us over him and what he hated most was that I was the son she really loved, not him. He'd do anything to get back at me for that."

"Including using me," Laura remarked, but her eyes remained fixed on Jack.

"No," he told her.

"That's exactly what he did. It's all a game to him," Matt assured her. "He found out about us, knew that I was in love with you and he devised this elaborate scheme to try to hurt me by taking you from me. Why do you think he bought your mother's note? He knew the threat of foreclosing on the hotel would make you vulnerable to him. He even went to the trouble of getting the foreclosure canceled just so he could play hero and make you indebted to him."

"And what about you, Matt? Why are you here? To play white knight for me, so that I'll be grateful to you?"

"Babe, I'm here because I love you. I knew something was wrong the last time we talked. As soon as I found out what was going on here I knew that Hawke had to be involved. And I'll admit, I did get the money you needed but that's because I know how much that old hotel means to you."

"Or maybe you got the money so that I would be indebted to you instead," she countered and there was no mistaking the cynicism in her voice.

"I did it so that you would see how much you mean to me. I want a lifetime with you, Laura, not a few nights of cheap sex. Because that's all it was to him," Peterson told her. "You heard him yourself. He bragged to me that he'd slept with you just to get even with me."

"That's a lie," Jack insisted.

"Is it, Jack?" Laura asked. "Did you know about me and Matt?"

"Yes, but—"

"Don't listen to any more of his lies, Laura," Peterson told her. He came down off the steps, stood before her and reached for her hands. And the sight of Peterson touching her was like a knife in Jack's heart.

"I love you," Jack told her, saying the words he'd never said to anyone since he was a six-year-old boy, pleading with his mother not to leave him. "And that's not a lie. It's the truth. I may not have been honest about anything else, but that much is the truth. I love you."

"I'm afraid that's not enough," she told him and pulled her hands free from Peterson. "Now if you'll both get out of my way, I'd like to go inside my house."

"Laura, please let me explain," Jack said as she brushed past him and climbed the stairs.

"It's a little late for explanations," she told him. "You'll have my letter of resignation in the morning."

"What about your staff?" he asked, hoping her loyalty

and concern for her employees would persuade her to re-consider and give him time to somehow convince her that he hadn't meant to hurt her, that he loved her.

"I'll draft a statement and speak with them individually. But under the circumstances, I won't be giving the customary two weeks' notice because I'll be leaving town." She unlocked the door, paused and turned. "Oh, and if you still want to buy my stock, Jack, it's yours."

"You've made the right decision, Laura," Peterson told her, triumph in his eyes as he started to follow her. "We'll go back to California and put this whole ugly thing behind us."

Laura blocked him at the door. "You'll go back to California, Matt. You and I are done."

"You can't mean that," he countered.

"Oh, but I do mean it. I'm not in love with you, Matt. I don't think I ever was. So I guess you were right, Jack. Matt is the loser this time. But so are you. Because I loved you, but I'll never forgive you for what you've done."

"Come on, Laura. It's Meredith's last night here. You have to come with us," Chloe all but whined as she followed her out of the house to her car.

Laura loaded the empty cardboard boxes into her trunk and closed it. "I told you, I have too much to do. I've got to clear out my desk, make a list of personal items at the hotel that belong to the family, draft a statement for the employees and update my résumé. I don't have time to go to the Celebration in the Oaks. You and Meredith will just have to go without me."

Besides, Laura thought as she walked around to the front of the car and unlocked the driver's-side door, she didn't know if she could face seeing the lights in the oaks with the memory of her evening there with Jack still so fresh in her mind. She'd spent the remainder of Friday evening and the better part of Saturday alternately crying and cursing Jackson Hawke. But nothing she had done had assuaged the ache in her heart over what he'd done.

"But it's Christmas," Chloe continued, refusing to give up. "This will be my first time going to see the lights since Granddad died. And who knows, it might be my last time to see it. And it might be yours, too, if you insist on selling your shares of the Contessa to Jack and leaving New Orleans."

Her sister was right. She didn't know if she would come back again. With her grandfather gone and the Contessa belonging to Jack now, there seemed little reason for her to return to New Orleans. The realization sent another swirl of sorrow through her. New Orleans had always been the one place to which she'd returned. It was her anchor. It was her home.

"Oh, do come," Meredith urged in that perfect diction that Laura found so lovely. "I've heard so much about this Celebration in the Oaks and the antique carousel. I can't wait to see it and Chloe tells me you're a fountain of information about it."

Feeling as though she were being double-teamed, she said, "I'd hardly call the few facts and figures I know a fountain. And as much as I'd like to go, I really am too busy."

"Don't you want to see the Carousel House one last time? Say goodbye to Pegasus?" Chloe asked.

"Pegasus?" Meredith repeated.

"Her favorite horse on the carousel," Chloe explained.

But mention of the horse brought tears to Laura's eyes.

She thought of her visits to the Carousel Gardens with her grandfather, the young dreams and fantasies she'd spun while riding on that horse. She thought of telling Jack about those dreams and fantasies, of the tender way he had looked at her while he'd listened, of that first time he'd kissed her under the trees in view of the carousel. Then she thought of the donation he'd made in her grandfather's name to restore the antique ride. An act of love, she had thought at the time. Only she had been wrong. Instead of an act of love, it had merely been part of his great plan to seduce her as a means of revenge against his stepbrother.

Evidently taking her silence as refusal, her sister decided to change her tactics and said, "It's because of Jack, isn't it? He's the real reason you won't come with us."

"He's part of it," Laura admitted. A big part, she added silently.

Chloe planted her hands on her hips, flattened her lips in a disapproving line. "I get that you love him and he hurt you. I even get that you're willing to let him take the Contessa from you and leave town because of what he did. What I don't get is why you would let him steal all the good memories you have of that carousel and the Christmas lights in the oaks."

"I'm not."

"Aren't you? I know how special that old carousel is to you, how much you looked forward to going to see it and the lights each Christmas. It's all you talked about from the moment you saw October on the calendar. You couldn't wait to come home to see the lights and ride your horse on the carousel. But you won't even go now to take a look at it and share it with me or Meredith and it's because you went there with Jack." She paused. "He stole your heart and broke it, Laura. Don't let him steal all your precious memories, too. Say you'll come with me and Meredith tonight."

"All right. I'll come with you," Laura said.

Chloe all but beamed and Laura didn't miss the satisfied smile she sent Meredith's way. "Great."

"You won't be sorry, Laura," Meredith told her. "Tonight you'll make a new memory, a happy memory."

Although she thought the remark odd, Laura shrugged it off. "I'm not going to be making any memories at all if you two don't let me get out of here so I can get to the office and pack."

Both stepped back from the car while Laura got in behind the wheel. "The gates open at dark, which will be around five, but I'll probably be lucky to be finished before six. Why don't I just meet you guys there for around seven," she suggested.

Chloe's smile faded. "But I thought we'd all go together and get there when it opens."

Laura considered all she had to do and the already late hour. She didn't want to let clearing out her office drag on to the next day. Her plan was to go into the office in the morning, speak with Penny and a few of the other longtime employees before making her announcement and leaving.

"Won't it be especially crowded if we wait that late?" Meredith asked.

Meredith was right. On the weekend before Christmas, attendance was highest. "The best I can do is six-thirty," Laura said.

"Six," Chloe insisted. "Six-thirty is when all the people who went to early dinner will be stopping to tour the lights."

"All right. Six o'clock," Laura relented.

"And we'll pick you up at the hotel," Meredith informed her. At Laura's querying look, the other woman simply explained, "I understand parking is a problem. Best to not have to worry about two cars."

"All right. I'll see you at six."

By the time six o'clock rolled around, Laura was emotionally and physically exhausted. After loading the boxes into her car, she returned to the office for one final look. She had known that packing up her office would be difficult. She had also known that packing away family mementos like the photos of her grandfather and great-grandfather would be bittersweet. She had even known that losing the Contessa would hurt. She had had so many dreams about running the hotel, continuing her grandfather's legacy. What she hadn't known was that losing her dream of a future with Jack would hurt even more.

It wasn't meant to be, she told herself and sighed. She looked around the office, ran her fingertips across the old mahogany desk one final time, then she shut the door and went downstairs to meet her sister and Meredith.

When Laura exited the hotel, she wasn't surprised to see a limo parked out front. Limos were as common as taxis it seemed. What did surprise her was Alphonse, the doorman, informing her that the limo was for her. Wary, Laura approached the sleek black vehicle and when the driver opened the back door, she was equally surprised to see her sister and Meredith. Chloe was dressed in an eye-catching red leather skirt and boots and Meredith in chic mocha-colored suede slacks with matching jacket. But it was the red Santa hats, champagne glasses and the ear-to-ear grins that caused her to do a double take. "What's going on?" she asked.

"Hurry and get in," Chloe insisted. "You're letting all the cold air inside."

Laura climbed into the backseat. "All right, what's with the limo? Did you to hit the jackpot at Harrah's?" she asked, referring to the city's only land-based casino.

"Actually, we're celebrating," Chloe said and poured her a glass of champagne.

Laura took the glass, but didn't drink. "Just what is it we're celebrating?"

"I landed a contract with Hawke Industries yesterday to act as a matchmaker between businesses," Meredith told her.

"That's wonderful, Meredith. Why didn't you say something earlier?" Laura asked. "We should have celebrated last night."

"Given the situation with you and Jack…Mr. Hawke," she amended, "I didn't feel it was appropriate. But Chloe insisted I tell you. She said you would be happy for me and want to celebrate my success."

"She was right. I am happy for you," Laura told her honestly. "Just because things didn't work out for me and Jack personally is no reason for you to pass up a good business opportunity. I wish you every success," she added, clinking her glass with theirs in a toast.

"He was quite remarkable, you know," Meredith told her. "He had some wonderful ideas, ones I had never even thought of."

"I'm not surprised. He's a brilliant businessman," Laura remarked.

While Meredith and Chloe chatted, Laura fell silent. She stared out the window of the limo, but her thoughts remained filled with Jack. She had half expected to see him at the hotel when she'd gone to pack. If she were honest, a part of her had even hoped she might see him. The truth was now that the initial shock and hurt had subsided some, she wanted to believe that he hadn't meant those things he'd said to Matt, that he hadn't used her. She wanted to believe that what they had shared hadn't all been a lie.

She'd refused to speak with him when he'd tried to talk to her that night. She had ignored each of his calls and not even Chloe's urging her to speak with him had made her relent. But she'd known he'd been outside her apartment most of the night. Between bouts of crying and anger, she'd looked out the window and seen him standing there next to his car. With his arms folded, seemingly oblivious to the bone-chilling cold that was part of New Orleans's winter, he had stood there watching her house window. And each time he'd seen her at the window, he'd straightened and started toward her. So she'd pulled the drapes closed and walked away. She'd almost expected to find him there in the morning. But when she'd awakened, he'd been gone. And there had been no more calls, no more attempts on his part to see her. The memory brought on another wave of hurt and longing.

"We're here, ladies," the driver announced.

"Oh my, look," Chloe exclaimed.

Shaking off her sad thoughts, Laura set her untouched champagne glass down and exited the limo. And she stepped into a winter fantasy. There on the ground at the entrance to the park were mounds and mounds of white snow. "I don't understand," she said as she walked over to join her sister and Meredith.

Kids were squealing all around her, frolicking in the mountains of white. Even the adults were laughing and carrying on like children who were seeing snow for the very first time.

Stooping down, Laura picked up a fistful of white, let it fall from her fingers. "It's snow. It's really snow," she said and when she looked up, she saw Jack. He looked so tall and handsome and wonderful standing there. But it was the look of longing and fear in his eyes that made her heart skip a beat.

"Technically, it's called artificial snow," Meredith told her. "It's made with machines called snow canons by spraying water and using air pressure—"

"I'll take it from here, Meredith," Jack said as he approached her.

She shot a glance at Meredith and her sister. "You knew about this?"

Chloe made a show of being fascinated with the snow. Meredith smiled and said, "I actually made two deals yesterday. One with Hawke Industries for business and one with Jackson Hawke personally."

"You may have to give a refund on that last one," Laura told her, still not sure she was willing to trust him with her heart again.

"All I guaranteed him was that I'd get you here so you could listen to what he has to say. I told him getting you to believe him was up to him," Meredith said. "But personally, Laura, I'd listen. I've made enough matches to know when two people have found something special. It would be such a shame to walk away from that without being absolutely sure."

"All I'm asking for is ten minutes, Laura," Jack said. "Listen to what I have to say and if you still can't forgive me and want me out of your life, I'll sign over the Contessa to you and never bother you again."

A part of her was afraid to listen. She was afraid because she wanted to believe that what they'd shared had been real and that she would fall for more lies now.

"Please, Laura. Ten minutes. It's all I ask."

"All right," she said.

"This way," he told her and led her through the gates of the park to a waiting horse and carriage.

"I don't understand," she said as he helped her into the carriage where he settled them both under a bright red throw and nodded for the driver to leave. "How did you manage this? The park is closed to all vehicles. It's walking tours only since Hurricane Katrina."

"Meredith arranged it. And the snow," he told her.

The horse's hooves made a clip-clopping sound as the carriage drove along the winding path through the huge oaks glittering with white lights. Everywhere she looked, there were mounds and mounds of white snow lining the paths, turning the park into a winter wonderland. "But why?"

"Because that night you took me to see the lights, you told me about your snow-deprived childhood here."

That he had remembered softened something inside her, made Laura hope. And because she felt herself weakening, she made a point of looking at her watch. "Seven minutes."

"I also remembered you telling me about thinking the carousel was enchanted. Unfortunately, Meredith couldn't come up with a way to arrange that so quickly."

Laura remained silent; she was moved that he had remembered what she'd told him. As the horse continued on its way amid more snow, she said, "All of this… It must have cost a fortune."

"I considered it a small price to pay to get you here."

When they reached the Carousel Gardens, the horse stopped and Jack said, "I thought we'd walk from here."

They exited the carriage and when Jack helped her down, he held on to her for several seconds. When she stepped back, he released her. For the next few minutes, he said nothing and when they reached the Carousel House, they stopped.

"I got the letter telling me about the donation you made to restore the carousel in memory of my grandfather." She turned to him then and asked the question that had plagued her. "Why did you do that, Jack?"

"I made the donation after you took me here. I could see how much that carousel meant to you. And you taking me here, sharing it with me, meant a lot to me. I think it's when I fell in love with you."

Laura looked away, wanting to believe him, afraid, too. "If you loved me, how could you use me the way you did?"

"I didn't."

"I heard what you told Matt. I heard the way you told him, about us making love, about how he was the loser now because you'd taken me from him." Even now, the memory of his words made her feel raw inside.

"I never meant to hurt you, Laura. It was anger and years of bitterness that caused me to say those things."

"If you're saying you didn't know about me and Matt, I don't believe you."

He frowned and she thought she could detect a trace of

temper as he insisted, "I *didn't* know about the two of you. At least not at first. And I'll admit that when I found out and we made that bet, I did think about seducing you to get back at him. But that plan lasted about a minute because as hard as I tried to convince myself that I was pursuing you because of Matt, it didn't work. Matt was the last thing on my mind when we were together." He caught her by the shoulders, turned her to face him. "He was the last thing on my mind when I kissed you, when I held you, when I made love to you. Because I fell in love with you, Laura."

"Then why didn't you tell me about Matt being your stepbrother after we became lovers? Why let me think you didn't even know him?"

"I wanted to tell you. I started to tell you that night in my hotel suite. But then you were upset about losing the hotel and were insisting you pay off on our bet. I wanted you so badly that night and then once we made love, I was afraid to tell you because you would think that I'd used you. I also was afraid that Matt would come through with the money to pay off the note and I would lose you to him."

"You should have trusted me, Jack."

"Yes, I should have. But at the time, I was in a panic. All I could think of was that I didn't want to lose you to him the way my father had lost my mother to Peterson's father."

"I'm not your mother, Jack. And you're not your father."

"Don't you think I realize that now?" he demanded. "I'm sorry I hurt you. I'd sooner cut my heart out than hurt you. Don't you think if I could take it all back, take all those horrible things I said back that I would?"

"I don't know, would you?" she asked, but she already knew the answer, Laura admitted as she felt her heart lighten.

"Yes, I would, dammit. But I can't. All I can do is tell you that I love you. And hope that you still love me enough to give me another chance. Will you give me another chance?"

Laura heard the plea in his voice, saw the care shining in his eyes. She slid her arms around his neck, and, smiling up at him, she said, "Yes, I'll give you another chance, Jackson Hawke, because I love you, too."

# Epilogue

*December, one year later.*

When the car turned onto the exit for City Park, Laura looked over at her husband and said, "Jack, I thought we were going to dinner."

"We are. But there's a little stop we need to make first," he told her as the car pulled to a stop at the entrance to City Park.

After Jack helped her ease her very pregnant body from the vehicle, Laura couldn't help but notice there were no lines stretched around the block to view the lights in the oaks as there normally would be just days before Christmas. "Please tell me you didn't rent the park just for us."

"Only for an hour," he assured her as he led her to the gate.

"But it's Christmas, Jack. The children—"

"Will see the lights for free tonight. Everyone will. It's part of the deal I worked out with the park. But there's something I want to show you first."

"Another surprise?"

"Yes," he told her and, cupping her chin, he brushed his lips against hers.

In the ten months since she'd married Jack, her life had been filled with one surprise after another. After funding the initial improvements for the Contessa, Jack had turned over the hotel to her completely. He hadn't interfered or offered advice unless she'd requested it. She'd implemented her marketing plans and the Contessa was doing remarkably well. Her marriage to Jack had proved equally surprising. They had merged their lives, as well as their hearts. He sought her opinions, shared his thoughts and feelings with her as she never dreamed he would. While his relationship with his mother and stepfamily remained strained, the bitterness seemed to have waned and he'd grown more comfortable being part of her family.

To her surprise the passion between them remained just as powerful now as it had a year ago—despite her watermelon-size belly. But it had been the life growing in her belly that had come as the biggest surprise. She wasn't sure who was more thrilled about the baby—her or Jack. What she was sure of was that she had never felt more loved or cherished or happy in her life.

"Good evening, Mr. Hawke. Mrs. Hawke," the clerk at the gate said.

"Evening," Jack said. "Everything ready?"

"Yes, sir. Everything's ready."

"This way, Mrs. Hawke," Jack told her.

Rather than surprised, Laura was deeply touched by the sight of the horse and carriage. After Jack assisted her into the carriage and covered her with a throw, she rested in the comfort of his arms as the driver took them through the park. The horse and carriage made its way along the winding path through the oaks glittering with white lights. Laura couldn't help remembering a similar ride with Jack in the park last December and her shock to discover he'd had snow pumped along the roads to give her the white Christmas she'd dreamed of as a child. A gust of wind whipped through the trees and set the lights to shivering. Laura shivered, too, and burrowed under the blanket closer to Jack.

"If you're too cold, we can go back," Jack offered.

"No, I'm fine. It's just the humidity," she explained to him. "It makes it seem colder than it is."

When they reached the Carousel Gardens, the carriage stopped and Jack helped her from the carriage. He frowned and looked up at the sky. "I swear it's dropped ten degrees since we got here. And if I didn't know any better, I'd swear those were snow clouds."

"I wish," she said and she did. Snow in New Orleans was a rare thing indeed.

"You sure you're not too cold?"

"Quit fussing, Hawke, and show me the surprise."

Taking her hand, Jack led her down the path toward the Carousel House. As they made their way to her favorite part of the park, Laura felt another wave of love for the man she'd married. Thanks to Jack's donation, the antique carousel that she adored was on its way to being fully restored. Unfortunately, the expertise needed and painstaking detail could not be rushed. As a result, the carousel was still inoperable for this holiday season.

When they turned the corner, Laura heard the music and smiled at the familiar sound. "The calliope is working."

"Yes," he told her and guided her along the next curve of the path.

And then she saw it. Her beloved carousel aglow with lights, music playing, horses weaving up and down as it turned in a circle. "But I thought it wasn't finished. The restorer said it would be another month," she exclaimed.

"They managed to finish ahead of schedule," Jack told her.

Laura looked at her husband. "How? By working around the clock?"

Jack's cheeks darkened slightly. "Trust me, they were well compensated. Wait here a second," he told her and hopped onto the carousel. After disappearing inside the maze of mirrors for a moment, the carousel slowed to a stop. Returning to her, he offered his hand and said, "Come on."

He helped her up onto the carousel and once she was on, she went straight to Pegasus and lovingly stroked the horse. "It must have cost you a fortune to do all this."

"It was a small price to pay to see that look on your face. Do you like it?" he asked.

"I love it. And I love you, Jackson Hawke," she said, wrapping her arms around his neck.

"Not half as much as I love you, Mrs. Hawke," he responded and covered her mouth with his. When he slid his hands down her body, cupped her bottom and pulled her to him, Laura thrilled at the feel of his arousal. Knowing that he wanted her so much even now fed her own hunger for him.

Another blast of wind sent her scarf and coat whirling

around her and Jack ended the kiss. He tugged the scarf around her neck and there was no mistaking the love and desire in his eyes as he looked at her. "I think I'd better get you out of this cold, Mrs. Hawke," he said.

But Laura barely heard him as she spied the white flakes beginning to fall. Surprised and delighted, she said, "Jack, look. It's snowing."

"I'll be damned," he said, laughter in his voice. Scooping her up into his arms, he stepped off the carousel and began walking back to the carriage. "Looks like you're going to finally get your Christmas fairytale," he told her.

Oh, but she'd gotten so much more than her Christmas fairytale, Laura thought as she reached up and brushed snow from his brow. She'd gotten the whole fairytale when she'd gotten Jack's love.

* * * * *

# SPENCER'S FORBIDDEN PASSION

### by
### Brenda Jackson

Dear Reader,

It's hard to believe that *Spencer's Forbidden Passion* is my eleventh book in the Westmoreland series. Time sure flies when you're having fun, and I've really had a ball bringing you stories about these gorgeous Westmoreland men.

Spencer Westmoreland would be a challenge for any woman. Besides being too handsome for his own good, he's also smooth, suave and seductive. He believes in getting whatever he wants, no matter what it takes…and he really wants Chardonnay Russell! Will he succeed in charming the elusive Chardonnay? His quest to win her results in a red-hot, sizzling pursuit that I hope you will enjoy.

All the best,

*Brenda Jackson*

## BRENDA JACKSON

is a die "heart" romantic who married her child-hood sweetheart and still proudly wears the going steady ring he gave her when she was fifteen. Because she's always believed in the power of love, Brenda's stories always have happy endings. In her real-life love story, Brenda and her husband live in Jacksonville, Florida, and have two sons.

A *USA TODAY* bestselling author, Brenda divides her time between family, writing and working in management at a major insurance company. You may write to Brenda at PO Box 28267, Jacksonville, FL 32226, USA by email at WriterBJackson@aol.com or visit her website at www.brendajackson.net.

## Acknowledgements

To Gerald Jackson, Sr Happy Anniversary!
Thanks for 35 years of love, happiness
and romance.

To all my readers who joined me on the
Madaris/Westmoreland Cruise. Thanks for
making it special, and this book is
especially for you!

To my Heavenly Father. How Great Thou Are.

Let us go early to the vineyards
to see if the vines have budded, if their blossoms
have opened, and if the pomegranates are in
bloom – there I will give you my love.

—*Song of Solomon 7:12*

# Prologue

"We've encountered a problem, Spence."

Spencer Westmoreland briefly closed his eyes to blot out two things—the look on his mother's face across the room and the frustrating sound of his attorney's voice on his cell phone.

He opened his eyes to find his mother was still looking at him with that, *I-wonder-who's-next* expression. He was in Bozeman, Montana, attending the wedding of his cousin, Casey, and his childhood friend, McKinnon Quinn. The couple was still inside the ranch house taking pictures. Everyone else who hadn't been a member of the wedding party was in the huge barn that had been miraculously transformed into a spacious ballroom for the reception.

He glanced around. Everyone seemed to be having a good time, smiling and happy. Everyone except him now that he'd been interrupted by a phone call from his attorney. Stuart Fulmer was one of the most competent men he knew, known for his precise and expeditious handling of all business matters, which meant if he felt there was a crisis then there definitely was one. "Okay, Stuart, what's the problem?" he asked.

"The Russell Vineyard."

Spencer lifted a dark brow and decided to step back into a corner of the room for privacy, as well as distance from his mother's intense gaze.

A few months ago he had gotten wind that the vineyard, located on over three hundred acres in the Napa Valley, was up for sale. He took the drive to the valley, saw it and fell in love with the area immediately. His research revealed that the owners, the Russells, were having financial difficulties and were struggling to hold onto the land. Spencer had sent his attorney to make the Russells an offer that had been more than generous. His plan for the property, once he became the owner, was to close down the winery and convert the place into a vacation paradise by adding a plush resort hotel and trails for hiking, biking and backpacking. It'd be the perfect tourist getaway.

The last he'd heard the negotiations were going smoothly and it would merely be a matter of days before the property became his. So what went wrong at this late date?

"What kind of problem are we talking about?" he asked abruptly.

"A young woman by the name of Chardonnay Russell."

He lifted a brow. "Chardonnay Russell? Isn't that the old man's twenty-seven-year-old granddaughter?"

"Yes, that's her. Somehow she has gotten the old man to change his mind."

Spencer frowned not liking the sound of that. "That's not acceptable. And I thought we pretty much had this deal wrapped up."

"We did."

"I also thought the Russells had a slew of money problems."

"They do."

"Then how can they afford *not* to sell?" he asked. When he noticed a couple of people who were standing around had turned to stare, he became aware that he'd raised his voice.

"They can't. But it's my understanding that she's making one last ditch effort to get the financing they need to hold onto the place. After all, it's been in the Russell family for over fifty years. I guess she's not ready for the family to throw in the towel just yet."

"That's admirable but too friggin' bad and too damn late. I want that property, Stuart. Do whatever you have to do to get it."

"It's going to be difficult, Spence. Chardonnay Russell isn't making things easy on my end."

Frustrated, Spencer rubbed a hand down his face. This was the first time in the fifteen years he'd known Stuart that he'd heard such aggravation in the man's voice. And all because of one female? Hell, how difficult could a single woman be? He then decided to find out for himself.

"Look, Stuart, let me handle things from here. I'll fly to Napa in the morning and meet with the Russells. Please let them know I'm coming."

He actually heard a sigh of relief in Stuart's voice. "I'm giving you fair warning to prepare yourself, Spence. The granddaughter may have been named after a wine, but there's nothing sparkling at all about her. Believe me when I tell you that she has the distinct sting of a scorpion."

Spencer couldn't help but grin at the words coming from the mouth of one of the most polite and mild-mannered men he knew. Chardonnay Russell must really be a handful. "Thanks for the warning. I'll keep that in mind."

# One

"That man has arrived, Donnay."

Chardonnay Russell lifted her head and gazed into her mother's worried eyes. She tossed aside the pencil and notebook as she stood up. She hated to see her family agonize over money problems now. The winery had always brought in a substantial profit, but her grandfather's hospital bill earlier that year, and the subsequent cost of his medications had eroded their extra funds. Now they were barely hanging on.

So far every bank they had applied to for a loan had turned them down. Their last hope was the bank she had visited a few days ago in San Francisco. Mr. Gordon, the bank manager, had seemed positive and she had left in a better frame of mind.

"Donnay?"

The nervous tone of her mother's voice cut into her

thoughts. A smile played across Chardonnay's face as she crossed the room, not for the first time realizing her mother was a very beautiful woman. Donnay never knew her father. In fact, the only thing she'd been told about him was that her mother had met and fallen in love with him at eighteen. Chad Timberlain was a soldier on extended leave who had worked at the vineyards one summer and then returned to duty before finding out his short stay had produced a child.

"It's okay for him to wait, Mom. I'm sure it won't be the first time."

*Or maybe it would be*, she silently concluded. Earlier that day she had scanned the Internet to read up on Spencer Westmoreland. The thirty-six-year-old had made his first million before his thirtieth birthday. According to what she'd read, the wealthy tycoon had retired last year with more money than he could ever spend. Evidently he had gotten bored and wanted a new toy—her family's winery.

"Where's Gramps and Grammy?" she asked softly. She knew her grandparents were even more worried about their meeting with Mr. Westmoreland than her mother.

"They're in the kitchen. Janice has escorted our visitor to the study and he's there waiting."

Donnay nodded. "All right then. It's time for us to meet Mr. Westmoreland, and remember the three of you agreed to let me handle him my way."

Spencer paced the room and glanced at the various framed awards on the wall with a wry smile. Timing, he mused, was the reason he was being kept waiting. He hadn't become a successful businessman without knowing how the game was played. He was fully aware that the best way to keep a business opponent on edge was to make them wait. Stall them. Test their patience and their ability to endure.

He shook his head as an even broader smile touched his lips. The tactic was a waste of time with him, but Chardonnay Russell wouldn't know that. She had every reason to believe she was the one calling the shots and no doubt would be surprised to discover she wasn't.

"Sorry that you were kept waiting, Mr. Westmoreland."

*Yeah, I bet*, he thought, slowly turning toward the sound of the soft, feminine voice. Any further thoughts on his mind died a sudden death the moment his gaze connected to the most gorgeous pair of eyes he'd ever seen. They were silver-gray and he wondered if she was wearing colored contacts lenses, but quickly concluded she wasn't when he noticed the other three persons standing beside her had the same eye coloring. Evidently a family trait.

He quickly gathered his composure and said, "It was no problem."

The truth to the matter was that there was a problem and it came in the form of Chardonnay Russell. The woman was absolutely stunning. In his lifetime he had met and dated numerous beautiful women, but standing before him was definitely a rare beauty.

She was tall, at least five-nine. Slim and curvy in the short-sleeve white blouse and printed gypsy skirt she was wearing. And her facial features were exquisite. Dark, luxurious brown hair flowed around her shoulders. She had long lashes, mocha colored skin that looked incredibly soft, a perfect nose and kissable lips.

The hoop earrings dangling from her ears made her look even sexier. Made him feel hotter.

Never had Spencer's gut clenched so tight or every muscle in his body felt so taut because of a woman. But there was something flagrantly erotic about her, and while looking into her gray eyes all he could think about were satin sheets and entangled bodies.

"I think introductions are in order," she said curtly, slicing into his personal perusal of her and his lusty thoughts. He watched her kissable lips move; however, he wasn't listening. His thoughts were too centered on the alluring package she presented and how he would like opening it up, enjoying it.

"We have you at a disadvantage," she continued saying. "We know who you are, but you don't know us since we dealt with your attorney, Mr. Fulmer, in the past."

His gaze picked up her every movement when she crossed the room, giving him a chance to check out those long legs underneath her skirt as well as her small waistline. And to make matters worse, all it took was one sniff and he picked up her scent. The arousing fragrance only added to his inner frustrations. He had a natural ability when it came to business, but handling such an intense degree of lust was another matter.

"I'm Chardonnay Russell," she said, offering him her hand. "And this is my mother, Ruth Russell, and my grandparents, Daniel and Catherine Russell."

Spencer took Chardonnay's hand in his, and the moment their hands touched, an electrical current raced through him. The sensation annoyed the hell out of him and he tightened his jaw. This was not the time to be reminded that since he'd been extremely busy lately, he hadn't had a woman in over seven months. Unfortunately his increased heart rate was reminding him of that very fact and he was fighting hard to keep his features impassive, his mind sharp.

"Ms. Russell," he said, quickly releasing her hand. He then moved to shake the hands of her mother and grandparents. He noted her grandfather didn't look well and recalled reading in one of the reports that the winery's financial woes were due to the man's escalating medical bills.

"Now that introductions have made, please, let's sit down."

Chardonnay's voice cut into his thoughts, reminding him of why he was there. "Yes, I suggest that we do," he agreed.

"Like I've told Mr. Fulmer, the vineyard is no longer for sale. And I might as well warn you, Mr. Westmoreland, that if you assume you'll be able to change our minds about that then you are vastly mistaken," she said the moment she took her seat.

Spencer liked her spunk. She was definitely no pushover. "On the contrary, Ms. Russell. In business, one never operates on assumptions—at least not if one intends to be successful in getting what he wants."

He saw the quick frown that appeared around her eyes. Those same eyes he thought looked sexy as hell. "And you think you're going to get what you want, Mr. Westmoreland, even after I've said we no longer want to sell?" she asked, narrowing her gaze at him.

"Yes, I think so," he said rather arrogantly. "Mainly because you haven't seen my new proposal."

He couldn't help cutting her a very cocky grin, one he

was certain irritated the hell out of her. But at the moment he didn't give a damn. He was feeling adrenaline of another kind flow through his bloodstream. The one he always felt when pitted against a worthy opponent.

"Now," he said calmly, "I suggest you let me present a new proposal to you."

Donnay's head snapped up from the report she was reading. "What you plan to do with our land is unacceptable."

She saw the look in his eyes was tempered steel, and he didn't blink when he said, "It really shouldn't concern you what I plan to do with the property once I acquire it. All you need to be concerned with is that the price I'm offering is more than fair."

Donnay frowned. He was sitting across from her on the sofa, casually sipping the wine her grandfather had offered him before they got started with business. Some of Russell Vineyards' finest.

"Well, it does concern us, which is why we've decided not to sell. And now after reading this proposal I'm sure my family and I have made the right decision."

"If you think that, then you're wrong. Look at the proposal closely, Ms. Russell," he said in an annoyed tone, sitting up and leaning forward. "I'm willing to pay you a half million more than what I'd authorized my attorney to offer. I think that's more than generous and it's all the increase I'm willing to make. Can you and your family truly turn down the deal I've placed on the table?"

Donnay nervously bit her lip. Truly they couldn't. She didn't want to think about what could happen if the bank didn't approve their request for a loan. She glanced over at her mother and grandparents. They were depending on her to make the right decision for the family, especially her grandfather with his heart problems and diabetes. Still, she refused to let someone like Spencer Westmoreland waltz in and take advantage of their situation.

But then she should have known she was in trouble when she'd entered the room and he stood there, impeccably dressed in an Armani suit and looking like he was ready to buy or sell whatever suited his fancy. Then there were his looks that were sharp, sexy and suave. He had to be over six-three, with coffee-colored skin, short, dark hair, a generous mouth and the darkest pair of eyes she'd ever seen on a man. In fact, they were so intense that each and every time they connected to hers she felt a tingle slowly make its way up her spine.

"I asked you a question, Ms. Russell."

She glared at him, not liking his tone. She drew in an agitated breath as she glanced back over at her family. Her grandfather nodded and a slight smile touched his lips, giving her the encouragement she needed to give Spencer Westmoreland her answer. She had to believe that a miracle would come in the form of that friendly banker in San Francisco, who actually seemed sympathetic to their financial problems.

Taking such a chance might be foolish but, sighing deeply, she met Spencer Westmoreland's gaze and said, "Yes, we can turn it down and we will turn it down."

She then stood. "We've taken up too much of your time already, Mr. Westmoreland, and we have work to do around here. My family appreciates your interest in the Russell Vineyard but like I said earlier, it's no longer for sale."

Spencer stood and snapped his briefcase closed. He was silent for a long moment then he said, "If you think you've seen the last of me, you are sadly mistaken."

Donnay saw the smile that touched the corners of his lips when he added, "I'm finding you a worthy opponent, Ms. Russell."

She stiffened her spine. "Don't count on being a nuisance, Mr. Westmoreland. Just go find another vineyard to buy. And if you try making trouble for us, you'll be sorry."

His smile widened and the look he gave her sent shivers up her spine. "I promise I won't be the one making any trouble for you, but I can guarantee you that in refusing my offer, you've just made a lot of trouble for yourself. Good day."

Once Spencer had gotten at least a mile from the Russell Vineyard, he pulled the rental car to the shoulder of the road and placed a call on his mobile phone. He couldn't get out of his mind just how beautiful Chardonnay was and the degree of his attraction to her. Never before had he been so aroused by a woman.

He was intuitive enough to know that even with others in the room she had been acutely aware of him, just as he had been aware of her. And she'd been fully conscious of the sexual attraction between them, although in the midst of a business battle they had attempted to stay focused and downplay it.

"Stuart? This is Spence. I want you to find out which bank is leaning toward loaning the Russells the money and let me know immediately."

He clicked the phone shut and sat there for a long

moment, focusing on his surroundings. It was a gorgeous day for early December, and the land around him was beautiful. He wanted that land. A thought then flickered across his mind. In addition to the land there was something else he now wanted.

Chardonnay Russell.

His brows knitted together in deep thought. The single Westmorelands were dropping like flies, and from the look on his mother's face at McKinnon and Casey's wedding, she expected the next victim to be another one of her sons. So why should he disappoint her?

After Lynette Marie's betrayal, the thought of ever marrying for love was as foreign to him as a snowstorm in the tropics. He had mourned the loss of his fiancée, who had died in a jet-ski accident over four years ago in Bermuda, only to discover from the coroner's report that she had been six-weeks pregnant. That meant she had gotten pregnant sometime during the two months she had been there on business. That had also meant he had not been the father of her child.

His hand tightened on the steering wheel. A marriage for love was out of the question but he would definitely entertain a marriage for lust. Besides, at thirty-six he had accumulated a lot of wealth, wealth he had worked hard to acquire. It was time to think about his future and make some important changes.

Although he wasn't looking for a love match like three of his brothers, Jared, Durango and Ian, had been blessed with, it was time for him to settle down, marry and secure his future with a child who would one day inherit all of his wealth.

He couldn't help but smile when he thought of all the

babies born in the Westmoreland family just this year. His cousin Delaney and her husband, Sheikh Jamal Ari Yasir, had given birth to their second child, a girl, whom they had named Arielle. His cousin Dare and his wife Shelley also had a daughter born in August. Durango and his wife Savannah had been blessed with a daughter in September; and his cousins Thorn and Stone and their wives were expecting new additions to the family as well. Thorn and Tara's baby was to be born at the end of the month, and Stone and Madison were expecting their firstborn in February.

Spencer restarted the car's engine. As he continued the journey to the Chablis, the resort where he was staying, he knew the next time he and Chardonnay's paths crossed, he would be making her an offer. And this would not be one that she would refuse. He would make damn sure of it. He was now a man on a mission. He was also a man who was known to go after whatever he wanted and didn't let up until he succeeded in getting it.

And what he wanted with Chardonnay was a merger of the most intimate kind.

# Two

"You have a phone call, Donnay."

Busy in the winery doing inventory, Donnay quickly turned and glanced at her mother, "The bank?"

Ruth shook her head, an anxious look on her face, "No, it's not the bank. I believe it's Mr. Westmoreland," she said handing her daughter the phone.

Donnay sighed deeply. Why hadn't her mother told the man she wasn't available? She was well aware that Spencer Westmoreland had gotten on her daughter's last nerve yesterday. "Thanks a lot, Mom," she said sarcastically, taking the phone. "Why didn't you tell him I wasn't here?" she whispered, placing a hand over the mouthpiece.

"But, his call might be important."

She rolled her eyes and gave a little huff under her breath. "I doubt it. The man just wants to harass me some more." She placed the phone to her ear when her mother left the room.

The last thing Donnay wanted to do was talk to the man whose image was still blatantly clear in her mind. Although she hadn't wanted to, she had thought about him after he had left yesterday, and even worse, she had thought about him last night. She had made the mistake of noticing how much of a man he was instead of concentrating on what a forceful, imposing individual he represented. That was one mistake she wouldn't make twice.

"This is Ms. Russell," she said rather gruffly.

"Ms. Russell, this is Spencer Westmoreland. I'm calling to ask if you would have dinner with me tonight."

Arousing sensations automatically flowed through Donnay's body at the seductive tone in his voice. She fought the feelings, not quite sure what to make of the man. She pursed her lips, trying to decide whether to hang up or continue the conversation.

She inwardly sighed before saying, "Mr. Westmoreland, why would I want to have dinner with you?"

"To save your family's winery."

Donnay's arched brow rose a fraction. "I hate to shatter your illusions but Russell Vineyards doesn't need saving."

"Are you absolutely sure about that?"

Donnay leaned back against a wine rack. No, she wasn't absolutely sure; especially since she hadn't heard back from the bank. Mr. Gordon had indicated he would let her know something by noon today. Although she felt fairly confident they would get the loan, she also felt it would be in her best interest to see what Spencer Westmoreland might have up his sleeve.

"I'm willing to listen to what you have to say. However, it doesn't have to be over dinner."

"For me it does. That's the way I conduct most of my business meetings."

Her words were edged with anger when she asked, "And what if I prefer not having dinner with you?"

"Then you don't get to hear what I have to offer."

Donnay tipped her head back. The man had offered a lot of money for the vineyard yesterday, more money than she or her family could have ever expected. "Do you not recall me telling you yesterday that we aren't interested in any offer you make?" she asked bluntly.

She could hear his soft chuckle and liked the sound of it. "I do, but I'm hoping that I can change your mind," he said.

"That's not possible, Mr. Westmoreland. Like I told you, the vineyard is no longer for sale."

"And you're willing to turn your back on my offer on the chance that some banker is going to come through for you?"

An intense degree of uneasiness prickled Donnay's skin. "What do you know about my dealings with any banker?" Her stomach churned as suspicion raised its ugly head.

"I merely assumed as much since a few weeks ago your family was desperate to sell the winery and now you're not. Besides, I make it my business to know the financial position of any potential business partners."

She didn't like the sound of that. "We aren't partners, potential or otherwise."

"If you want to believe that, go ahead. Now back to

dinner. We'll go to Sedricks. I'll be there to pick you up around six. Is that acceptable?"

She wished she could tell him that it was not acceptable, but as she stared out the window at the lush vineyard in the distance, she knew doing so might not be a smart move. She had no intentions of ever parting with the vineyard she was looking at, no matter how confident Spencer Westmoreland seemed to be. She had a feeling he was up to something and there was only one way to find out what. "Yes, six will be fine."

"Wonderful. I'll see you then."

As soon as he clicked off the line Donnay wasted no time contacting Wayne Gordon at the bank. Her stomach settled when he told her he had good news for her. The loan her family had applied for had been approved. Donnay felt happiness all the way to her toes. Spencer Westmoreland hadn't bested them after all. That remark he'd made earlier about her business with the bank had been meant to throw her off, emitting smoke when there really wasn't any fire. Their money worries were now over. She would pull out a bottle of their finest wine and her family would celebrate.

A smile touched her lips. She would take great joy in letting Mr. Westmoreland know she expected him to get out of their lives forever. And she couldn't think of a better opportunity to tell him than that night over dinner.

Spencer smiled as he settled comfortably in the back seat of the limousine he had hired for the night.

The call he had received earlier from Stuart had him in high spirits. Things were definitely going as he had planned. Thinking about the offer he would make to

Chardonnay later tonight sent heat all through him. The thought that he would be the one who made love to her with the full purpose of giving her his child practically had his loins on fire. Of course, not for one minute did he assume she would go along with his proposal.

His lips curved into another smile. There was no doubt in his mind that she would turn him down flat, fight him with every breath she took, which was why he intended to give her no choice in the matter. Not if she really wanted to retain possession of her family's winery.

He glanced out the tinted window, seeing the beauty of the countryside of the Napa Valley. He had fallen in love with California the first time he had visited over twenty years ago after accepting a scholarship to attend Southern California University. As much as he loved Atlanta, California had eventually become his permanent home. After obtaining a bachelor's degree in finance and then a M.B.A., he began a career in banking at one of the most prestigious financial institutions in San Francisco.

He loved going back home to Atlanta for family gatherings, but always looked forward to returning to Sausalito, the charming waterfront community that was located just across the Golden Gate Bridge. The town was often compared to the French Riviera because of its Mediterranean flair and breathtaking views.

His house, a distinguished looking two-story structure, sat on four acres of land with beautiful San Francisco and Bay views. But he had to admit there was something peaceful and charming about Napa Valley. Away from the hustle and bustle of traffic, it was an idyllic setting. The perfect place to settle down and raise a family.

His mind was set, his agenda clear. It was not in his nature to tolerate resistance when it came to meeting any of his goals. And this time would not be an exception.

Chardonnay stared at her reflection in the huge mirror, wondering why she was putting so much effort in looking good tonight, granted Sedricks was a very elegant and sophisticated restaurant.

She turned slightly and smiled. The strapless, backless black dress made of a sheer material clung to her hips, showing curves she had a tendency to forget she had until she dressed up in a manner such as this. She couldn't remember the last time she had gone out on a real date with a man. After that fiasco with Robert Joseph, her former college professor whom she had fancied herself in love with a few years back, she had a tendency to watch herself around men, especially those who thought they had it all together and expected women to fall in place and cater to their every whim.

She had been twenty-four and in her last year at UCLA, earning a degree in horticulture, when she had met Robert, a divorcé fifteen years her senior. The older man had dazzled her, swept her off her feet and into an affair that had lasted almost a year. A month before she was to graduate, he broke the news to her that he and his ex-wife had worked things out and were getting back together. She had realized then that she had been nothing more to him than a fun pasttime. The pain had taught her a valuable yet hard lesson when it came to men.

She tossed her head, sending her shoulder-length hair forward, framing her face. She grinned at the seductive effect and laughed. The rich sound vibrated in the room and made her realize it had been weeks since she'd had a reason to laugh. Almost losing the only home she'd ever known had taken its toll, but now she had a reason to rejoice.

"You look pretty."

She turned at the sound of her mother's voice and smiled. "Thanks, Mom, and I feel pretty tonight. I can't wait to tell Spencer Westmoreland that we have no reason to sell the vineyard, no matter how much he offers for it."

A worried look touched her mother's features. "Be careful, Donnay. It's my impression that Mr. Westmoreland isn't a man who likes losing."

She chuckled. "That's my impression of him as well, but I can't worry about that. How he handles bad news is no concern of mine."

"I know, but still, Donnay, he's—"

"Mom," she said, reaching out and grabbing her mother's hand. "Don't worry, I can handle Mr. Westmoreland." A smile curved her lips as she glanced at herself in the mirror again, thinking of the sheer arrogance of the man. "The big question of the night is can he handle me?"

Spencer slid out of the back seat of the limo when the chauffeur opened the door. He nodded, thanking the driver before walking briskly toward the huge house. When a cool breeze slid through his leather coat, he slipped his hands into the pockets in defiance of the crisp December air.

Although the sun had set and there was very little light, he could recall vividly the Russells's sprawling country home that seemed to loom out of the hills and sat on over a hundred acres of vintage land. Yesterday he had trekked this same path to the front door. The stone walkway, which seemed a mile long, was bordered with numerous flowering plants that seemed to welcome him.

Anticipation ran through his body with every step he took, and his heart began pounding furiously in his chest when he finally reached the door and pressed the bell. He tried ignoring the rush of excitement, thinking no woman had ever affected him this way, but then he conceded there was a first time for everything. And as long as he didn't let it dull his common sense, he could handle a little bit of craziness on a nippy December night.

The door opened and Chardonnay stood there, a vision of loveliness that practically took his breath away. His mouth pressed in a thin, hard line when he felt his common sense deserting him, and immediately he fought back the feeling. He liked being in control, but at that moment he feared that he was losing it.

She stepped back to let him enter. "It will take me only a minute to grab my wrap," she said, walking off.

His gaze sharpened when he saw her bare back. Her dress seemed perfect for her body and emphasized the svelte lines of her curves and the gracefulness of her long, gorgeous legs. The effect was stunning and he felt it all the way to his groin. He shifted, deciding it best to stay in place by the door, grateful for the full-length leather coat he was wearing.

He watched her grab her wrap off the table, place it around her shoulders and turn. Their gazes locked and at that precise moment, something passed between them. He felt it and was convinced she had felt it as well. Like him, she stood perfectly still, their gazes leveled, connected.

Then suddenly the sound of a door closing somewhere upstairs in this monstrosity of a house broke the spell, and she tilted her head and frowned at him. A deliberate smile curved his lips.

"Are you ready to leave?" he asked, deciding the sooner he got her out of this house, off this land and into the cozy confines of the limo, the better.

She nodded and he had a feeling that the smile she proceeded to plaster on her lips was just as deliberate as his had been. She crossed the room and, as graceful as a swan, came to a stop in front of him. "Yes, I'm ready."

As Donnay settled into the soft leather cushions of the limo, she inhaled the familiar scent of ripened grapes that drenched the night air. This was wine country. The hills, valleys, fields and meadows bowed to that very proclamation and had done so for years. She had been born here and they had buried a host of other Russells here on this land. This was her legacy. But even more importantly, this was her home.

Through the tinted windows and in the darkness her gaze still scanned the land the car passed. She was grateful she and her family no longer had to worry about losing what was theirs to someone who wouldn't appreciate the valley for what it was. Someone who wanted to destroy the land instead of wanting to cultivate it. Someone intent on turning what would always be a vineyard into a playground for the rich and famous. A vacation spot.

That very someone was sitting a decent distance from

her on the seat and hadn't spoken since the limo had left her family's home. She had to admit to surprise once she had walked outside and had seen the limo parked in the driveway. She should not have been. Spencer Westmoreland was a man who evidently enjoyed basking in his wealth.

In the dark interior of the car she allowed her gaze to scan his silhouette, bathed in the moonlight. He wasn't looking at her. In fact his gaze seemed fixed on the objects they passed; although she doubted he was actually seeing anything. That meant he was deep in thought, or just plain ignoring her.

The thought of him doing the latter should not have bothered her but it did. After all, he was the one who had invited her to dinner. She wondered if he'd already detected that this was one deal he'd thought he had wrapped up that he could now kiss goodbye. Not bloody likely. He was probably sitting there thinking of a new strategy to get what he wanted.

Hopefully after tonight she would make it clear as glass that her family would not entertain notions of selling the vineyard. She smiled thinking her mother and grandparents would certainly rest a lot better tonight. But when it came to how well she would sleep, she wasn't as certain. Not with the man sitting beside her on the seat causing all sorts of turbulent emotions to rise within her.

While he was looking elsewhere, she scanned his face. His features were sharp, as sharp as his arrogant tongue, a tongue he was holding tonight, thank goodness. But everything else about him was out there, in the open. He was handsome. That fact was a given.

Every single detail about his features—the rounded chin, the short dark hair, the full lips—contributed to a face that would make any woman take a second look. Then there was the way he fit his clothes. Yesterday she hadn't failed to notice he was a sharp dresser. No doubt beneath his leather coat was a designer suit.

"Have you been to Sedricks before?"

She blinked, realizing he had spoken. He had shifted positions in the seat and was staring at her. When had he done that? While she had been admiring his clothes? If that was the case, he hadn't missed her studying him.

Deciding she needed to answer his question, she said, "Yes, several times. Have you?"

"Once. I was impressed with both the service and the food."

"The food is wonderful," she said, suddenly wondering if they needed more space between them. For some reason it seemed the distance separating them had decreased.

"And that will give us a chance to talk."

She lifted a brow. "About what?" she asked, wanting him to get specific.

"A number of things." With a move that was so premeditated that it caught her unawares, he eased closer to her on the seat. Her heart rate escalating at an alarming rate, she glanced up at his face and fought back the panic she felt rising in her throat. She had made light of her mother's warning, however, when it came to experience, she was no match for Spencer. He had a sensuality about him that made the pulse in her throat twitch. Robert had been an older, handsome man who had impressed her with his intellect. But when it came to style, sophistication and fashion, he'd been slightly unkempt. He was a professor, and in his social circles and profession, one wasn't supposed to look like he belonged on the cover of GQ.

But it was a whole different story for Spencer Westmoreland. He was a businessman, suave, debonair, handsome…arrogant. Even now his presence was dominating the interior of the car. There was no doubt in her mind that in his world, his word ruled supreme. She doubted very few opposed him. And those who did probably paid the price. One didn't make it to where he was in life, and at such a young age, without being ruthless to some degree. Donnay shuddered at the thought. He wanted Russell Vineyards. She wondered how he would handle knowing it was no longer within his grasp?

She drew in a deep breath when he stretched his arms across the back of the seat. "I really wasn't sure you would go out with me tonight," he said in a throaty tone.

Her senses became focused fully on him when she said, "I'm a woman full of surprises, Mr. Westmoreland, and there's one I intend to share with you later."

"Is there?"

"Yes."

She saw his gaze study hers intently before he said, "You have beautiful eyes."

She could respond by echoing the compliment, but instead she decided to play it safe. "Thank you."

"You're welcome. You're also a gorgeous woman."

She slanted him a cool glance. It was on the tip of her tongue to tell him she was too levelheaded to fall for sweet talk. She wondered why he was wasting his time and couldn't imagine what he hoped to gain by using such flattery. It might work on other women but not on her.

"I must thank you for a second time, Mr. Westmoreland."

"Let's dispense with the formality. Call me Spencer."

She nodded. "All right, and I'm Donnay."

He smiled. "I like Chardonnay better."

She mentally shook aside the sexiness in his voice when he said her name. The scent of grapes, she noticed, had been replaced with the scent of man. Whatever cologne he was wearing was manly, robust and sexy. She knew for some woman he would probably be the perfect lover since there was no doubt he would be good at anything he attempted.

"Chardonnay."

She glanced up and saw his gaze was focused exclusively on her. She wondered what he was staring at so intently. Then she realized her lips had captured his attention and were holding it. She drew in a quick breath and felt a stirring begin in her stomach and slowly spread to all parts of her. And then there had been the way he'd said her name. Placing emphasis on certain syllables in a way no other man ever had, giving it an undeniably sensuous sound.

She parted her lips to draw in a much needed breath, and in a daring move he leaned closer and darted out his tongue to moisten her lips, before capturing her mouth with his. The contact had been so unexpected, so sudden, that instead of pulling away she felt every cell in her body vibrate under the onslaught of a combustible combination of overzealous hormones and much-deprived lust.

It was too late to revamp her senses. Too late to think about resisting. The moment his tongue touched hers she was a goner and she had a feeling that with his arrogant, utterly confident self, he very well knew it. What other reason could there be for him deepening the kiss and pulling her closer to him in such a way that had her moaning sounds she'd never heard before.

No man had ever kissed her this way. So completely, so totally, so downright absolutely. The kiss aroused her, stimulated her like none before. She responded to his actions on instinct and not experience. Her tongue had never participated in a kiss the way it was doing now, emanating a need within her that she didn't understand. But evidently he did, because the more she greedily demanded from him, the more he gave.

Suddenly he pulled back, and disappointment poured through her like cold water on overly heated skin. She noted she was draped over him, practically in his lap. And he was staring at her with an intensity that held both longing and possession. She knew at that moment, as she tried pulling herself back together and away from him, that she was out of her league. And to think she'd actually thought she could handle him.

"Your taste is one I'll never forget, Chardonnay."

She focused her full attention on him when he added, "And one I intend to indulge in time and time again."

His words were filled with confidence, as if barring any opposition or debate. By the same token, her reaction to them was immediate and instinctual. "I disagree."

He shook his head and smiled at her. It was a smile that touched his lips, corner to corner. "That's your prerogative. But the way I see things, your loyalty will be your downfall, but then at the same time it's what sets you apart from all others. It's what I admire most about you."

She frowned, not understanding what he was saying or what he meant. Before she could ask, he glanced out the car window and said, "We've arrived at our destination and I prefer resuming this discussion over dinner."

# Three

Spencer knew he had selected the right restaurant the moment he led Chardonnay through the doors. The ambiance alone deserved the establishment's five-star rating.

Situated on a grassy slope in the heart of the Napa Valley, the huge European-style structure boasted elaborate stone and brickwork. The interior glistened with holiday decorations. Even on a Tuesday night the place was packed, and he couldn't help but note that more than a few males looked his way with envy in their eyes. More on instinct than anything else, he entwined his arm with Chardonnay's. When she gave him a questioning look, he smiled and said, "I made reservations so we shouldn't have long to wait."

No sooner had he said the words then the maître d' appeared to escort them through the throng of well-dressed patrons to a private room in the back of the restaurant. Brick walls with dark wooden beams and cast-iron chandeliers that hung overhead created a romantic setting.

After being seated at the only table in the room they were given a wine list and their menus. They were informed that a waiter would arrive shortly to take their wine selection and dinner order.

Moments later he was alone with Chardonnay. Spencer glanced up at her face, trying to read her expression as well as guess her thoughts. He knew he had surprised her when he had touched her arm with such possessiveness. Hell, he had surprised himself. Never had he been jealous of another male's attention to any woman he was with. It wasn't in his makeup to do such a thing.

Giving himself a few moments to clear his rattled mind, he followed her gaze around the room. It was quaint and cozy, almost completely surrounded in tinted glass, and it provided a beautiful illuminated view of an outdoor gazebo that was surrounded by thick shrubs, blossoming flowers and running vines.

"The room is lovely."

Chardonnay's comment caught his attention and he met her gaze. It was on the tip of his tongue to say that the room had nothing on her. "Yes, it is," he said instead. The taste of her was still on his lips and he doubted even the strongest drink would be able to remove it. He had enjoyed kissing her, sliding his arms around her and holding her close to him while he mated with her mouth at will. And when her arms had wrapped around him, and he'd heard the soft moans from her throat, he had done what had come naturally. Deepen the kiss even more.

Not that he was complaining, but the intimate

exchange had lasted longer than he had intended. All sense of time and place had flown from his mind in the awakening lust that had consumed his body. And when she had stretched up against him, he had effortlessly pulled her into his lap without disengaging their mouths.

His thoughts came to an abrupt end when the waiter brought in glasses of water and then took the time to take their wine and dinner order. They both agreed on a veal dish and a bottle of Russell Chianti.

"Have you ever tasted our wine before?" Chardonnay asked after the waiter had left, leaving them alone again.

He shook his head. "No, but I understand it's delicious."

She frowned. "It's more than delicious. It's superb. The best in the land."

He chuckled. "You would say that but I'll see for myself in a minute." He then leaned back in his chair. "What exactly do you do at the winery?"

She shrugged. "A little bit of everything, depending on the season. I handle PR during the winter months—spring and summer I work the vineyard, pruning, planting and I even know how to operate the equipment to crush and ferment the grapes. In the fall I take on the role of wine taster. So I guess you can say I enjoy wearing several different hats."

After taking a sip of her water, she asked, "Why are you interested in what I do?"

He smiled, wondering if she was always so suspicious of people or just him. Then again, she had good reason to be. "Um, just curious."

She placed her glass down and met his gaze. "And I'm just as curious, Spencer," she said, leaning forward and saying his given name for the first time. "What is tonight all about? Why did you invite me to dinner?"

He leaned forward as well and countered by asking in a low, husky voice, "Why did you accept?"

She slowly drew back and lifted her chin. "Because there was something I wanted to tell you."

"What?"

She inclined her head toward the closed door. "I prefer we wait for our food, especially the wine, since what I have to say is a cause to celebrate."

He lifted a brow. "Is it?"

"Yes, I think so."

"All right then. In the meantime tell me about yourself."

He immediately saw defiance light her gray eyes before she said. "I already have. It's your turn."

Spencer started to say she was wrong. She hadn't told him everything about herself. Since she would eventually become his wife, he had an urge to know a whole lot more. However, he said, "I'm a Westmoreland."

The smile that touched her lips stirred something deep in the pit of his stomach. "And that's supposed to mean something?" she asked, seemingly amused.

He shared her smile and felt rather comfortable in doing so. "In Atlanta it does. Just like your family has deep roots here, mine has deep roots in Atlanta. My cousin Dare is sheriff of College Park, a suburb of Atlanta. And my cousin Thorn Westmoreland is—"

"The man who builds motorcycles and races them as well," she finished for him, smiling brightly. "I didn't make the name connection until now. I used to have a poster of him on my bedroom wall when I was sixteen. Boy was he hot."

Spencer chuckled. "I understand there are some women who think he still is. He's happily married, and he and his wife, Tara, are expecting their first baby later this month. It's going to be a boy."

"That's wonderful. And what about siblings? Do you have any?"

"Yes, I have an older brother, Jared, and four younger brothers—Durango, Ian, Quade and Reggie."

"They all live in Atlanta?"

"Jared and Reggie do. Ian lives in Lake Tahoe and Quade works for the government in D.C."

"Really, what sort of work does he do?"

"Quade works in security at the White House. Because of the high level of security entailed, we're not really sure what he does and he's never divulged any details." And so she wouldn't ask any more questions about Quade's job, he asked a question of his own. "What about you? Is it just you, your mother and grandparents?" he asked.

"Yes, and the four of us are very close."

"And your father?"

She shrugged. "I never knew him and he never knew me. End of story."

Spencer knew it was the end of the story only because she deemed it to be. At that moment the waiter returned with their wine. After he filled their glasses and left the room, a smiling Chardonnay held hers up for a toast. "To Russell Vineyards, may we last forever, and with the loan we got approved today from the bank, we are well on our way of doing just that."

She glanced at him over the rim of the glass as she then took a sip, smiling. Spencer knew she was feeling really good right now, thinking she had just burst his bubble.

She lifted a brow as she put her glass down, evidently disappointed that she had failed to get a rise out of him. "Well?"

He lifted his own brow. "Well, what?"

"Don't you have anything to say?"

He smiled and then replied, "Yes, I have quite a lot to say, but I prefer to do so after we enjoy our meal. I wouldn't want any words we might exchange to ruin our dinner."

Apparently thinking she *had* succeeded in getting him riled after all, she leaned back in her chair and said smugly, "You'll get over it."

"And if I don't?"

He watched as she drew her breath, saw how her lips curved in a frown. She leaned forward again. "It will be a waste of your time since there is nothing you can do about it."

The waiter entered with their food. Spencer smiled at her and said, "Our dinner has arrived, Chardonnay. Please hold your thoughts until after our meal. Then I will tell you why you're wrong."


Donnay declined dessert, thinking she was tired of this cat-and-mouse game she and Spencer were playing. During the drive over, she had felt elated, confident, thrilled at the prospect that he would be experiencing a letdown like he hadn't felt in a while, given what she had read about him. He should be totally disappointed, frustrated and probably more than a little upset to learn Russell Vineyards was completely out of his reach. Instead it didn't appear that the news had affected him at all, which made her wonder if perhaps he knew something that she didn't.

And then there was the kiss she couldn't get out of her mind. The one that still had her insides sizzling. His lips had connected to hers in a way that immediately set off a rush of heat within her. And the chemistry that had been stirred between them was as potent as anything she'd ever felt before. His taste had literally zapped her of her senses and it was taking everything she had to get her entire body back on track.

Not able to handle the tension or curiosity any longer, she tilted her head up and looked into his face. "Tell me why you think I'm wrong, Spencer."

She watched him set aside his wineglass. He then eased his wallet out of his jacket pocket and withdrew a business card. He offered it to her.

Donnay took it, studied the information that was printed on it before looking back at him with a questioning look. "What am I supposed to be looking at?"

"My profession."

She glanced at the card again before raising her head to meet his gaze. "Financial management investor?"

"Yes. Like you, I enjoy wearing several different hats," he said, putting his wallet back in his pocket.

Donnay sat straighter in the chair. Their gazes held for a long time when she finally asked, "Meaning what?"

Spencer continued to hold Chardonnay's gaze. There was no doubt in his mind that she wouldn't like what he was about to say. She would probably like even less the proposal he intended to offer her. For a fleeting instant he thought of undoing all he'd done; let her and her family keep the land and just walk away. He knew that although he could walk away from the land, he could not walk away from her. Spending time with her tonight had only solidified his interest, attraction and desire. He wanted her with a passion unlike anything he'd ever known.

He met her eyes as intently and said, "Earlier you said your family had managed to secure a loan."

"Yes, it's been approved."

"I know it has."

"And how would you know that?"

When he didn't answer her right away, she repeated the question. "How would you know that, Spencer?"

He leaned back in his chair. "Banks offer loans to individuals that sometimes have to be underwritten by a third party because of their risky nature."

He gave it a few moments and then he saw the light that came on in her eyes, letting him know she was finally getting the picture. That same light suddenly flared with fury when she asked. "Are you saying you're the one who underwrote the loan?"

He answered her, deciding to speak slowly and deliberately, making sure she understood completely. "Yes. The bank couldn't find any other investor to do it. So basically, once you sign the loan papers I'll be the one holding the mortgage to the vineyard."

His words had the effect he knew they would. Her eyes hardened and began shooting fire at him. "You want our land that much?" she asked in a tone he knew she was trying to control.

He decided to be completely honest. "Yes, but there's something else I want, Chardonnay, and it has become even more important to me than Russell Vineyards."

"And what is that?"

He only paused a second before saying, "You."

* * *

It took Chardonnay a few moments to gather her composure. And she couldn't help inhaling a deep breath several times before asking what may have been a relatively stupid question. "For what purpose?"

He took his time in answering her. "I want to marry you and give you my child. In fact, several of them."

She gasped first in surprise, then in outrage. "Do you honestly think I will go along with a notion as crazy as that?"

"Yes. You will if you want to keep your family winery," he said, looking her straight in the eye. "Evidently you don't fully understand your family's predicament, Chardonnay. Without the backing of a third party, no bank will agree to loan you the amount of money your family needs. You've depleted a lot of the business assets, not to mention you continue to be a mom and pop operation that has been operating in the red most of this year. However," he continued, "I'm willing to guarantee the loan for whatever amount you need. And to show what a generous person I am, I'm giving you two options. You can take out the loan but it will have to be paid back in full within six months."

"Six months!"

"Yes. If you default on the loan, everything will be mine. Or you can consider the second option. Agree to marry me and have my child and I will let you continue to run and operate the winery as you see fit. In fact I will put a lot of my money behind you to expand the winery to an international one."

Anger swept through her. Neither were acceptable options. She leaned over and glared at him. "Forget both options."

He gave a small nonchalant shrug. "If that's what you really want. But either way, Chardonnay, I will own your land one day and will do whatever it takes to do so. I suggest you take the second option. It's less risky. And if you do, I will even forgo my dream to build the vacation resort on the land. Instead I will devote my time and attention, when I'm not trying to get you pregnant, to building up Russell Vineyards' reputation and standings."

"I will not be your brood mare!" Donnay stood, amazed at just how much anger she could feel toward one single individual. "You have to be the vilest man I know to suggest something so despicable. The last thing I'd want is to marry you. And as far as having your baby, I can't imagine the two of us ever sharing a bed to do such a thing."

"Are you saying that you're willing to walk away from everything I'm offering knowing the outcome?" he asked in a calm voice.

"Walk away and not look back. Take note, Spencer Westmoreland, because that's just what I'm doing. And don't worry about taking me back home. I'll call a cab."

And then she did just what she'd said she would do. With her head held high she turned and left the room. And she did so without looking back.

When Spencer caught up with Donnay outside the restaurant, she was thanking one of the valet's for calling her a cab. "I'm taking you home, Chardonnay," he said, coming up behind her.

She swiveled and the look she gave him would have turned lesser men to stone. "No, you're not. I refuse to have anything to do with you, and if you try forcing me to do anything against my will, I will let out a scream the likes of which you've never heard before."

He believed her. "Very well, then," he said quietly, taking a step back. "But there is one thing I'd like to ask."

"What?" she all but snapped.

"Forget about the vineyard for a moment and all the things my proposal entails. I want to know what is there about me that rubs you the wrong way."

Donnay shook her head. The man really didn't have a clue. Did he not know how degrading his offer was to her? He wanted to marry her and use her to have his child. What could possibly be romantic about that? The sad thing about it was that she wanted the very things he was proposing—marriage, babies, a way to take the winery to an international scale. But not this way and definitely not on his terms. What he was proposing only showed just how ruthless he could be and how far he would go to get anything he wanted.

She tilted her head up and looked him dead in the eye when she said, "The reason I can't conceive of the two of us ever coming together romantically, Spencer, is that personally, you are *not* my type."

"Miss, your cab has arrived."

The attendant's words claimed Donnay's attention. She hurried over to the parked cab, leaving Spencer standing there alone.

"How was dinner with Mr. Westmoreland?"

Donnay glanced up at the stairs at the sound of her mother's soft voice. She could not tell her mother or grandparents the true nature of her evening with

Spencer. The last thing she wanted was for them to worry about anything.

"Dinner was okay," she said as she watched her mother descend the stairs.

When her mother reached the bottom stair, Ruth smiled at her and said, "It was just okay? I've never known a time that I went to Sedricks that the evening ended up being just okay."

Donnay smiled back at her mother. "Well, considering the company, it was just okay."

"And?" Ruth probed.

Donnay lifted a brow. "And what?"

"And how did he handle the news that we had secured a loan?"

"Better than I wished he had, giving me the feeling that he won't give up," Donnay said, admitting that much.

"Well, considering everything, how much ruckus can he stir? Getting the loan puts him totally out of the picture now since we won't need his money."

"Let's hope so," she said guiltily in response to her mother's words. She wished she could be completely honest and tell her mother that Spencer and the loan were tied together as one. The first thing she would do tomorrow would be to visit with Glenn Forbes, their attorney. She was certain Spencer had done something unethical in the handling of the loan. If fighting him legally was the only way then she would do so.

Needing to change the subject, she glanced at what her mother was wearing. It didn't take much to tell that her mother, who rarely went out, had gone somewhere tonight. "And where have you been?" Donnay asked, curious. Years ago, she had stopped encouraging her mother to get out more, meet a nice man, have fun and date, since her mother claimed there would never be another man in her life she could possibly love more than she had Donnay's father.

"McClintock Café," her mother answered. "After you left I got a call from a friend I hadn't seen in ages who was passing through. We got together for coffee and to catch up on old times."

Donnay nodded. It was good seeing her mother taking interest in something other than the winery. "Well, I'm glad. You look nice."

Yawning, her mother said. "Thanks. And I believe we're both up later than usual and need to go up to bed. The next few weeks will be busy ones for everybody."

The winter months were usually less hectic. Except for winter pruning, there wasn't much to do but take precautions to assure that the sometimes harsh weather didn't cripple or destroy the crop. It was also a time for staff members to discuss how to increase productivity and retain quality.

But a couple of weekends from now, downtown Napa would be hosting the annual Taste Napa Downtown event, which for wine lovers was the most popular wine tasting event in the world. Russell Vineyards would be represented again this year.

"Yes, and I can't wait. The excitement is spreading already," Donnay said, giving her mom a hug. "Good night, Mom."

"Good night, Donnay."

Donnay was halfway up the stair when her mother called out to her "Donnay?"

She turned. "Yes?"

Her mother stared at her for a moment then shook her head and smiled. "Nothing, sweetheart. At least it's not anything that we can't talk about later."

"You're sure?" she asked, studying her mother's features to detect if something was wrong. When she couldn't identify anything, she relaxed her brow.

"Yes, I'm sure. Go on to bed and get a good night's rest."

Donnay smiled. "I will and you do the same."

# Four

*You are not my type...*

Irritation lined Spencer's brow as he took a sip of coffee. He couldn't imagine any woman saying such a thing to a Westmoreland. And if Chardonnay thought for one minute her words would stop him for acquiring the single most important thing he wanted—namely her— then she needed to think again. But still, what she'd said had irritated him, although he didn't have to speculate on the reason she'd said it.

He took another sip of coffee. He didn't care what she claimed, especially when her lips had said differently. He might not be her type but she had enjoyed the kiss they had shared. There was no way she could convince him otherwise. And he couldn't help wondering if memories of being in his arms had kept her awake last night as they had him. In addition to her beauty, there was something so beguiling about her that he hadn't been able to take his mind off her, even when he'd slept.

And that wasn't good.

With a frustrated sigh he pushed away from the table and stood. How could he have become so mesmerized by one woman? And so quickly. Even now the scent of her still lingered with him. It was such an arousing fragrance, one he couldn't let go of. He had left his cousin's wedding with the intent of coming to California to turn a deal around. Instead he was the one getting turned around. The woman was having just that kind of effect on him. He wanted to marry her. He wanted her to have his children. He wanted it all, and as far as he was concerned, no one else would do. On the other hand, he didn't expect this to be any sort of love match. Everything was strictly a business affair.

However, she had made it pretty clear, business or otherwise, she wasn't interested. He would turn up the heat a little, because in the end, he very much intended to have every single thing that he wanted, especially her. And he wasn't someone who wasted time once he'd made up his mind. He glanced at his watch. It was almost noon and time for him and Chardonnay to have another talk.

Less than an hour later he was strolling up the walkway toward the Russells' front door. He refused to entertain the notion that considering how they'd parted the night before, Chardonnay would refuse to see him. Whatever it took, he would get her alone so they could talk.

He was halfway to the door when suddenly it was flung wide open and Chardonnay's mother appeared, frantic, almost hysterical with tears streaming down her face. "Mr. Westmoreland, please come quickly! Help us. It's my father. He's collapsed and is unconscious."

"Are you saying there's nothing that we can do, Glenn?"

Glenn Forbes had been the attorney for Russell Vineyards for years and Donnay was trying hard not to let the man see her frustration.

"Unfortunately that's exactly what I'm saying," the sixty-something year-old man answered. "It will be Westmoreland's money that he's loaning out so he can set up any terms and restrictions that he wants. And chances are, he will be giving you stiff ones since the bottom line is that he wants your land."

"How stiff?"

"He will probably call in the loan during a time he knows you can't possibly pay it back, or hike your interest rates up so high that you'll have difficulty making the loan payments, which will ultimately push you into defaulting. On the other hand, if you don't take the loan and he's the only one interested in buying the property or if he keeps the same offer on the table that he made a few days ago, then you and your family will make a lot of money."

"But we'll lose our home." She sighed deeply, knowing Spencer had backed them into a catch-22 situation. Either way he stood to gain and they could lose everything that truly mattered to them. "Thanks for the information, Glenn."

"No problem. How's your grandfather's health?"

Donnay smiled. "It's been good. His medication is expensive but we've been able to handle it so far. He's a little disappointed that we've had to put aside our plans for expansion for a while. Right now our main focus is surviving."

For years her grandfather, who was the master wine-maker in the family, had worked hard to improve the quality of the wines they made. Although Russell wines had a great reputation in the United States, the next stage in their plan had been to start doing business in the overseas market. That meant hiring more employees, some with specialized winemaking skills. That was one of the reasons Spencer's offer to transform the winery from a mom-and-pop operation to an international one had merit. It was the same plan her grandfather had been dreaming of for years. But the price Spencer demanded was too high.

She stood. "Well, I need to be going, Glenn. I've taken up too much of your time already."

"Nonsense," the older man said, also standing. "Just be careful with those city slickers like Westmoreland. He'll take advantage of any mistake you make. If he wants that land bad enough he'll do just about anything to get it."

Donnay didn't need to be warned. She already knew how far he'd go. She gave Glenn a small smile and was about to make a comment when her cell phone went off. Pulling it from her purse she checked caller ID. "Excuse me, Glenn, it's Mom calling." She flipped open the phone. "Yes, Mom?"

Seconds later she grabbed the edge of Glenn's desk for support when a lump of panic swelled within her throat. "What! How is he?"

She nodded anxiously. "I'm on my way."

"Is anything wrong, Donnay?"

She glanced up and met Glenn's concerned expression right before she quickly headed for the door. "Yes, it's my grandfather," she said to him over her shoulder. "He collapsed and had to be rushed to the hospital."

Donnay rushed through the E.R. doors and looked around frantically for her mother and grandmother. Relief washed over her when she saw them, but tension and anger quickly consumed her when she saw who was with them.

What was Spencer Westmoreland doing here? Was he responsible for whatever was happening to her grandfather? Had he said something to upset him? Her grandfather had been perfectly fine when she had eaten breakfast with him that morning, long before her mother and grandmother had awakened. And now he was here in the hospital.

Inhaling deeply and trying to consume the anger she felt, she crossed to where the three individuals sat. Spencer was the first to see her and stood after whispering something to her mother and grandmother. They glanced up and rushed over to her.

"How's Gramps?" she quickly asked.

"We don't know," her mother responded softly. "The doctor hasn't come to talk to us yet. Everything happened so fast. We were all in the kitchen. He was fine one minute and the next thing we knew he was clutching his chest and then he collapsed."

"There's a possibility he had a heart attack," Spencer said when he joined them.

Donnay's eyes locked with his. Rage consumed her. "And what do you know about any of this?"

Her mother answered. "He was there to—"

"He was there!" Donnay broke in as her anger escalated even more. "What did you say to my grandfather? You had no right to upset him. If anything happens to him I will never forgive you."

"Donnay, you're wrong. Mr. Westmoreland—"

"Sorry your opinion of me is so low, Chardonnay," Spencer cut into her mother's words. "And since my being here has upset you, I'll leave." He turned and quietly headed toward the exit.

Ruth grabbed her daughter's arm, highly disturbed. "What is wrong with you, Donnay? Why would you talk to Mr. Westmoreland that way?"

"I can't stand the man. You know that, Mom."

"Yes, but it was a blessing that he showed up when he did today or your grandfather might not be alive."

Donnay was too stunned to speak. After a moment she asked in an unsteady voice. "What do you mean?"

"After your grandfather collapsed, I was rushing out of the house to get one of the workers when I saw Mr. Westmoreland coming up the walkway. He ran in and administered CPR to your grandfather until the paramedics arrived. He was not responsible for what happened to your grandfather. Instead of sending that man away, you should have thanked him. What you just did was incredibly inconsiderate."

Donnay knew she looked as totally embarrassed as she felt. The floor could open up and swallow her whole and she would deserve it. "Mom, I didn't know. I truly thought he was responsible."

"I don't know why you would think such a thing. You owe him an apology."

Before she could respond, they turned when the doctor walked into the waiting room. Donnay rushed over to him. "How is he, Dr. Miller?"

The older man, who had been her grandfather's doctor ever since it was discovered that he had a heart condition earlier that year, gave them a small smile. "He's resting and, yes, he did have a heart attack. One that could have taken him out of here had it not been for the quick thinking to use CPR. As soon as he's stable we want to run more tests. That surgical procedure we discussed a few months ago would help tremendously although most insurance companies won't pay for it since it's still considered experimental in nature."

"Can we see him?" her grandmother asked softly.

"Yes, but one at a time and for no more than five minutes. It's important that he continues to rest."

It was only after her grandmother's and mother's visits with her grandfather that Donnay entered his room. She had seen him like this before, hooked up to various machines and monitors, but seeing him now profoundly affected her. In her eyes he had always been strong, robust and bigger than life. Now he appeared tired and weak.

She walked quietly across the room to stand beside his bed. She gazed down at him, remembering years when he represented the only father-figure in her life. She couldn't think of losing him, like she had refused to let him consider losing the one thing that meant everything to him, other than her grandmother—the vineyard.

When the family hadn't been able to see through their

financial situation, he had been willing to part with the one thing that had been in the Russell family for generations, although she'd known doing so was killing him inside. She'd known then that it would be up to her to make sure he'd never have to do that. That burden was still on her shoulders.

"Donnay."

She blinked back tears when he opened his eyes, met her gaze and said her name, barely murmured under his breath. "Yes, Gramps, I'm here."

"Pretty."

She smiled. He'd always told her she was pretty. She watched as he tried moving his gaze around the room and knew why. "Grammy and Mom were here earlier. They will only let us see you one at a time."

He nodded, letting her know he understood. "I'm nothing but trouble."

She frowned upon hearing his words. "No, you're not, so don't even think that. Everything is going to be all right."

He looked up into her face. "The winery?"

She felt a thick lump in her throat as she nodded and brushed moisture off his forehead. "The winery is going to stay with us. We got approved for the loan, remember?"

He nodded again and a slight smile formed on his lips. "We're going to keep it."

She blinked back more tears. "Yes, we're going to keep it."

"For your kids."

A smile touched her lips. Even in his condition, he was again dropping hints about her personal life. "Yes, one day for my kids."

"My great-grands."

"Yes, Gramps, your great-grands." She watched as his eyes closed. He was dozing off again, apparently being tired out from talking to her.

"Miss, I hate to interrupt but your five minutes are up," a nurse stuck her head in the door and said, smiling apologetically.

"Thanks, I'm leaving." Leaning over she placed a kiss on her grandfather's cheek, then clutched the shoulder strap of her purse as she left the room.

Spencer stared down into the dark red depth of his wine before swirling it around in the glass. Russell Vineyards' finest. Last night Chardonnay had referred to it as superb and he had to admit she was right. He'd never had a reason to taste the wine before last night but now he was mildly surprised. He hadn't expected such a fruity, yet tartly smooth taste. He found it incredibly pleasing to his palate.

Instead of sipping he put the glass to his lips and thought, what the hell. He had ordered it. Room service had delivered it. And at the moment, he needed it. He took a rather large gulp and then licked his lips while the warmth of the liquid flowed straight through his body to settle in a part of him right below the belt.

Seemingly sensual. Definitely erotic.

It was then, and only then, that he took the time to fully recall every vivid moment of the scene that had played out at the hospital with Chardonnay. A hard muscle twitched in his cheek. She had wrongly accused him, but instead of defending himself, he had walked away. He had discovered last night that once Chardonnay became upset about something, the woman was downright hard to deal with … even when her facts were wrong.

But unlike his attorney, Stuart, he had no intentions of letting her test the level of his endurance or get on his last nerve. After all he still intended, whether she liked it or not, to marry her. She just wasn't making things easy for him, which meant he would continue to make things hard for her.

He crossed the room to gaze out the window in an attempt to calm his frustrated mind. The abundance of land his eyes touched was incredible, amazing, simply beautiful. The sun was sending golden highlights across the valley in a way that was astounding and peaceful.

As if to break that peace, his mind went back to Chardonnay. He loathed the very idea that she thought he would intentionally bring her grandfather harm. If she knew how much he had cherished and loved his own grandfather, she would know how totally wrong she was. Scott Westmoreland had made an impact on all of his grandchildren's lives, making them believe that they could fulfill their dreams, no matter what they were. Like Chardonnay's grandfather, he had been a master, not at wine but at food. His reputation as a cook and restaurant owner was legendary. And Spencer had loved him as deeply as Chardonnay loved her grandfather.

He turned away from the window when his cell phone rang. Thinking it was Stuart or one of his brothers, he answered. "Yes?"

"I owe you an apology."

Spencer felt a deep tingling in the pit of his stomach the moment he heard Chardonnay's voice. There was just something incredibly sexy about it. However, the effect it had on him was too intense for his frame of mind, and resentment set in. For a moment he didn't know what to say since he never expected her to call to apologize. "Do you?" he finally replied in a clipped tone.

"Yes."

"I'm sure it's something you don't do often. Do you really know how it's done?"

There was a slight hesitation on her part and then she said in an irritated tone, "Look, I don't need this."

He'd gotten her mad. Good. "And neither do I, Chardonnay. I don't like being falsely accused of anything."

"I told you I was sorry. What else do you want?"

"Have you decided to indulge me in the things I want?" he retorted coolly, waiting for her response, knowing it would probably be just as biting and sharp as his had been.

"You have got to be the most—"

"Be careful what you say, Chardonnay, or you might very well be apologizing for a second time." He was taunting her and he knew it. She had pushed a number of buttons that no other woman had pushed before and he didn't like it.

"I think we need to end this conversation," she said brusquely.

"I don't. The reason I was at your home earlier today was that I felt we needed to talk. I still feel that way," he said.

"Maybe some other time."

"No. Tonight."

For a moment she didn't say anything and then asked, "And if I refuse?"

"Then either way, you can kiss the winery goodbye." He had said the words calmly, but Spencer was fully aware she knew he meant them.

"One day you'll regret what you're doing."

She was probably right but as long as that day wasn't today he was fine. "We'll do dinner at seven, here at the resort. I'm staying at the Chablis." He also knew his words probably sounded like an order.

An incredulous smile touched his lips when he heard the sound of the phone clicking in his ear. That wasn't a dropped call. She had deliberately hung up on him.

Hours later, Donnay murmured not so nice things about Spencer under her breath when she headed down the stairs. Spending time with him again was not something she wanted to do. The less she saw of the infuriating man the better. However, she had to admit that they did need to talk. She just didn't want to do it tonight.

"There you are," her grandmother said smiling. "I was just about to come up and get you. The car has arrived."

Donnay lifted a brow. "What car?"

"The one Mr. Westmoreland sent for you. It's parked outside."

As soon as her feet stepped off the bottom stair Donnay walked over to the window and looked out. That same limo from the night before was parked outside. Why had he sent a car for her? Spencer said they would be dining at the Chablis, the luxury resort on two hundred acres of land that overlooked the Mayacamas Mountains and provided a stunning view of Napa Valley.

She turned to her grandmother wondering if she knew what was going on.

"Is Spencer outside waiting in the parked car, Grammy?"

"No, he sent his driver for you. The man came to the door to let us know he was here, and said he'd been instructed to take you to Mr. Westmoreland at the Chablis."

Donnay looked outside again at the limo and shook her head. The man really did have a lot of nerve. She turned back to her grandmother. "I'm using my own car."

She walked across the room and gave her grandmother a peck on the cheek. "I'll have my cell phone on if you need me."

They had already checked with the hospital and her grandfather was still resting peacefully. Her grandmother had wanted to spend the night with him but they had talked her out of it.

Donnay glanced around. "Where's Mom?"

"She went out."

Again? Donnay lifted a brow. Evidently that friend her mother had met for coffee last night was still in town. "Will you be okay here alone, Grammy?" she asked with concern.

Her grandmother waved off her worries. "Of course. Go on and enjoy the evening with your young man."

Donnay frowned, doubting that she would. "Well, if you're sure you'll be okay, I'll go and let the limo driver know I'm taking my own car."

"All right, dear."

Grabbing her purse off the table Donnay quickly walked out the door. She strolled down the long walkway to the chauffeur and smiled up at him. "Hello, I'm Chardonnay Russell, and I won't need your services since I'm driving my own car."

The man's face remained expressionless when he said, "Mr. Westmoreland instructed me that if you were to refuse my services, madam, to give you this," he said, presenting a sealed envelope to her.

Frowning, she took it from the man, quickly opened it up and pulled out the note.

> I prefer that you do things my way, Chardonnay. For your safety, comfort and convenience, I have sent the car for you and I expect you to use it. Failure to do so means all talks are off, including my backing that loan. Spencer.

A part of her wanted to say good riddance, but she knew she couldn't do that, especially after she had assured her grandfather today that all was well with the vineyard.

Keeping her irritation in check, she glanced at the driver and gave him a small smile. "It seems I'll be using your services tonight, after all."

# Five

His dinner guest had arrived.

A semblance of a smile danced across Spencer's lips as he reached for his jacket on the back of the sofa and put it on. He'd figured that Chardonnay would refuse to ride in the limo so he had taken the necessary steps to deny her a choice. It might have appeared underhanded on his part but he could not entertain thoughts of her driving back home alone late at night.

The moment the limo came to a stop, he walked out the front door of the two-story cottage he was occupying. Standing in the doorway he watched the driver walk around the front of the impressive shining black automobile to open the rear door. The windows were tinted so Spencer couldn't see Chardonnay, which he figured was just as well since chances were she wasn't too happy with him about now. She was a woman who didn't like being told what to do, especially when he was the one doing the telling.

He continued to watch as the chauffeur presented her his hand and she stepped out of the car. Tonight she was wearing her hair up and several strands had escaped confinement and were curling around her face. To his disappointment she was wearing a pair of slacks, which meant he wouldn't be ogling her legs tonight. Too bad, they were such a stunning pair, too gorgeous to be hidden.

His senses remained locked on her every movement and when she glanced his way, a frown settled on her features. He was tempted to cover the distance separating them and kiss that frown right off her face. Instead he continued to stand there, portraying an expression of nonchalance when he felt anything but.

Seeing her again was having one hell of an effect on him, an effect he was struggling to control. Lust in itself was a killer, a yearning of the worst kind. But when you mixed it with obsession, especially one that kept you from thinking straight, you were in deep trouble. The bottom line was that he wanted her. At almost any price. However, she would be the last person to know since that kind of information in her hands would be tantamount to lethal.

"Glad to see you arrive in the car I sent, Chardonnay," he said when she began walking toward him. He tried deciphering her mood and quickly reached the conclusion that she was definitely not a happy camper.

"Did I have a choice?" she asked curtly when she stopped in front of him, tilting her head back to look directly into his eyes.

"No," he said simply, truthfully, before moving aside

to let her enter. It was either that or be done in by the turbulent depths of the stormy gray gaze that narrowed at him. His restraint not to reach out and pull her into his arms to smooth her ruffled feathers was weak.

"I thought we were having dinner."

She was standing in the middle of the living room, glancing around. Evidently she had expected to see a table set for two and had noted there wasn't one. He moved toward her, deliberately slow, fighting back the urge to let his gaze slide over her from head to toe. She looked good in her black slacks and a turquoise top. The shade, he thought, complemented her coloring. Since the evenings and nights in the valley could get rather chilly, she had brought a tweed jacket, which was slung over her arms.

"We *are* having dinner," he said. "But I didn't want the food to get cold before you arrived. It won't take long for room service to set things up, and I hope you enjoy the entrée I ordered for us."

She glared at him. "And if I don't?"

She was itching for a fight and he sure as hell had no intentions of obliging her. He was getting used to her moods. Besides, he would be calming whatever storm was brewing inside of her soon enough. Therefore, he responded to her question with a dispassionate shrug and said, "Then I suggest you don't eat it."

He saw the way her lips tightened into an even deeper frown. "Do you always manage to have things your way?" she asked coolly.

"On the contrary," he replied, thinking if that was true she would be in his bed this very moment.

"There are some things I find myself doing without,"

he added, sliding his hands into his pockets so he wouldn't be tempted to reach out and pull her into his arms, capture her mouth beneath his, and touch her all over. The thought of doing any of those things had his heartbeat accelerating.

To counteract the effect, he nodded toward the huge window and said. "So, what do you think of the view?"

She followed his gaze and an unexpected smile touched her lips, making his guts clench. "It's beautiful," she said with something akin to spellbinding awe in her voice. "But then this is home for me and I've always thought the valley was the most exquisite place to live."

"I'm beginning to believe that, although I love my home in Sausalito."

She turned back around, and met his gaze with an arched brow. "You live in Sausalito?"

"Yes. You sound surprised."

"I am. I thought you would prefer the fast pace of San Francisco instead of the quietness of a small town."

He chuckled. "I grew up in a fast-paced town—Atlanta. I always wanted to live someplace peaceful and serene."

"I'm surprised such a thing doesn't bore you."

"I'm sure there's a lot about me that would surprise you, Chardonnay."

Her expression was one of indifference, and a part of him was determined to change that. "Make yourself comfortable while I call for dinner."

She didn't verbally acknowledge what he said. Instead she moved toward the sofa and sat down. He felt perspiration form on his brow while watching her graceful movement, appreciating the way her hips swayed, the slender curves of her body.

Deciding he needed to do something with his hands, he picked up the residence phone. "This is Spencer Westmoreland. You can deliver dinner now."

"When will we talk, Spencer?"

She asked the question the moment he'd hung up the phone. He met her gaze, saw the gray glint that was still ready for combat. His pure male persona was fighting an inner war not to put his plan of seduction in place before it was time. "We'll talk after dinner," he replied.

She reluctantly nodded and he knew that he would need as much strength as possible, because in dealing with Chardonnay Russell, only the strongest would survive.

Donnay drew a long, deep breath as she tried to keep her eyes off Spencer. It was hard. He had received a phone call and she'd been glad for the slight reprieve. Now she had time to study him without him being aware that she was doing so. He was rich, powerful and suave, and dressed in a pair of expensive trousers, a designer white shirt and a smooth-cut suede blazer, he definitely looked the part of a millionaire.

In addition to all that, he was magnificently built: tall, strong and masculine. The perfect male specimen. His very presence was causing emotions to flood her that were better left alone. The man was a predator. He was ruthless and lethal all rolled into one, but at that moment she thought he was the most desirable man she had ever come close to knowing. With a snap of his fingers he could destroy her and her family's livelihood. And she couldn't let that happen. What she wanted, what she needed to know was why he wanted to marry her. Why he wanted her to have his children. The man was as rich as he was good-looking, so finding a woman to fulfil his every need shouldn't be a problem. So why her?

"I just received good news from home," he said, hanging up his cell phone and reclaiming her thoughts.

She mentally shook off seeing the smile on his lips, the one that sent blood rushing through her veins. "And what is the good news?"

"Thorn and Tara's son came three weeks early."

"Is he okay?"

Spencer chuckled. "The baby and Tara are doing fine. However, I'm not sure about Thorn. I just finished talking to him and I think he's still in a daze. He was there with Tara during the delivery and said it was an awesome experience."

"I'm sure it was."

He didn't say anything for a moment, but his features held a pensive look. And then as if he'd made his mind up about something, he crossed the room and halted directly in front of where she sat on the sofa. "That's what I want, Chardonnay."

Donnay met his gaze. As far as she was concerned the man wanted a lot of things and it was hard to keep up. "And what is it that you want?"

He stared at her for a moment and then said. "I want to be there when my wife gives birth to our child."

To her surprise, his voice was gentle. Her senses registered his sincerity. And the look in his eyes was intense. Too intense. It was actually sizzling her insides. She hadn't expected that and lifted her head, narrowing her eyes. "Then I suggest you let the woman you intend to marry know that."

"That's precisely what I'm doing."

His gaze had her entire body feeling hot. "Don't fool yourself about that," she tried saying in a calm voice. "I am *not* the woman you're going to marry."

"Can you afford not to be?" he asked smoothly, cool and controlled.

She refused to let him back her against the wall any further. Her back stiffened. "You would use my family's land to force me into marriage with you?"

She watched his mouth hardened around the edges. "Yes, and I wouldn't hesitate doing so."

"And you would marry me, knowing I would despise you for it?"

He nodded. "Yes, because I'll put forth an extra effort each and every day to make sure you would eventually get over it."

She opened her mouth to give him the blasting retort she felt he rightly deserved when there was a knock at the door, indicating their dinner had arrived.

Chardonnay's fragrance was getting to Spencer. It was an arousing scent that made him think of everything other than the half-eaten steak on his plate. The food had been delicious. But then he figured, so was the woman sitting across from him. He wanted Chardonnay with a passion that, until now, had been foreign to him.

During his lifetime he'd never allowed himself to be swept away by passion, infatuation or obsession. He hadn't done that with Lynette Marie and he'd been quite taken with her. At least he'd thought so at the time. They had met and dated in college, and after graduating they had gone their separate ways, each wanting to devote time to their chosen careers.

Hers had been in broadcasting and she had immediately landed a job at CNN as a television journalist. They had renewed their relationship almost ten years later after bumping into each other while both had been in New York on business. Afterward, they began a long-distance romance, which had worked for the both of them, lasting a couple of years. When he'd felt the time was right, he had asked her to marry him and she had accepted.

A few months after announcing their engagement, she had gone to Bermuda on a three-month assignment. Unfortunately, with his busy work schedule, he never got a chance to visit with her while she was there. Then one morning while shaving, he'd gotten a phone call from her parents informing him of her accidental death.

The coroner's report had indicated that at the time of her death she was six weeks pregnant. Spencer had known the child wasn't his since they hadn't made love in over four months. Her betrayal left him determined to never share his emotions with a woman again. And he had sufficiently heeded that decision…until now.

Inwardly frowning, he lifted his gaze and looked over at Chardonnay from across the table. Other than inquiring about her grandfather's health and other mundane small talk, they hadn't said much during dinner; however, she seemed to be enjoying her meal.

Deciding they had put off the reason she was there long enough, he said, "Now we'll talk, Chardonnay. But keep in mind we need to stick to the important issues, and I want your decision in forty-eight hours."

She narrowed her gaze at him. "You can't expect me to make up my mind that soon."

"Yes, I can and I do. And I won't change my mind

about it. I refuse to give you time to drum up alternatives that I won't go along with. All you'll be doing is wasting both of our time. I presented the two options to you last night. Do you have anything you want to ask me about them?"

"Yes," she said, setting down her wineglass. "If we agree on the loan, what limits and restrictions will you be placing? And what happens if we miss a payment?"

He leaned back in his chair. "The interest rate will be higher than the present market and if you miss a payment, I'll begin foreclosure proceedings before you can bat an eye."

He had been brutally honest and from the look on her face she hadn't liked his answer. He was intentionally making the loan unattractive and blatantly risky.

He watched her hesitate a moment, fiddling with the food on her plate before lifting her head. Her stony-gray eyes met his dark ones when she asked in a curt tone, "This marriage of convenience you want. Just what would you expect of me?"

A smile touched his lips when vivid visions flooded his mind, some so blatantly sexual they made him ache. "I would expect of you what any man would expect of his wife. I want to sleep with you every night, make love to you, get you pregnant—several times—and provide a home for you and our family."

She hesitated again, and then asked, "And after I've ceased being of any value to you?"

He mused, surprised by the question. "Why would you think a time would come when you'd cease being of value to me?"

From the expression on her face he could tell his

question confused her, so he decided to ask another. "Just how long did you assume I wanted our marriage to last, Chardonnay?"

She shrugged her shoulders. "Until I had given you all the children you wanted."

He threw his head back and laughed. "Then what was I supposed to do with you after that?"

"Divorce me."

He arched an eyebrow upon realizing she was serious. "There hasn't been a divorce in the Westmoreland family since before I was born. In our eyes, marriage is sacred."

Donnay frowned. "Are you implying that you expect us to stay together *forever*?" she asked with disbelief in her voice.

"Yes, till death do us part. Why wouldn't that be the case?"

He could tell his question caught her off guard. "Because most marriages of convenience are for a set period of time, and usually a rather short one."

"Ours won't be. But I need to make sure you understand that love will not be a factor in our relationship mainly because it won't have a place in our marriage. I don't need it and personally I don't want it."

He paused, wanting to make sure she understood what he was saying. When he continued speaking, his voice was slow and his words were chosen carefully. "If you agree to marry me, you'll be agreeing to a loveless marriage, basically a business arrangement between us. I will treat you with respect and bestow upon you everything that comes with being my wife."

"Except love," she interjected.

He nodded. "Yes, except love."

She didn't say anything for a brief moment. "And if I go along with marrying you, what guarantee do I have that you will give up the idea of turning the winery into some vacation resort?"

"There aren't any guarantees other than my word. And I will give it to you now. If you agree to marry me, Chardonnay, you and your family's financial worries will be over. I will turn my attention toward three things. Getting married, getting you pregnant and doing whatever it takes to escalate the winery to an international scale. I agree that Russell wine is superb and I will put my money into making sure the entire world knows it as well. I will help build the vineyard into something that we can one day pass on to our children."

"Why?" she asked quietly. "Why is getting married and having children important to you all of a sudden?"

He lifted a brow. "What makes you think my wanting those things is a sudden urge?"

She met his gaze. "Because you would have them already, if you truly wanted them."

He wouldn't admit to her that he'd always wanted children. In fact, that was the main reason he had asked Lynette Marie to marry him. But after her death he had eradicated a family from his agenda… until the moment he had seen Chardonnay. Even now the thought of spending time with her in bed, getting her pregnant with his child, made him hard.

"I'll be thirty-seven in less than six months and over the years I've accumulated a lot of wealth. It's wealth I want to pass on to my offspring and I need a wife to do it," he said.

"No, you don't," she argued. "Men get women pregnant without marriage on their minds all the time." He couldn't help but wonder if she was thinking about her own father since he obviously wasn't in the picture.

"That's another Westmoreland rule," he said with strong conviction. "We take responsibility for our actions, no matter what they are. The only woman I ever intend to bear my child is the woman I'm married to."

His heart began beating like an insistent drum when he watched her push her plate away, signifying that dinner was officially over. He stood and walked over to the phone and called room service to come clear away their plates and to bring them another bottle of wine from Russell Vineyards. After that was done he leaned against the counter and said, "Now I have a question for you."

Her gray eyes flickered his way.

"I know about your involvement with that professor a few years back. Are you involved with anyone now?"

He watched as a dark color stained her cheeks and he could tell that once again she had been caught off-guard by one of his questions. She probably felt outrage in knowing he had dug into her past, knew her personal business. "Don't be bothered by the question, Chardon-nay. Like I told you before, I make it my business to know everything there is to know about any business partner, and that's exactly what you and I will be if we choose to marry. Partners. There won't be any secrets between us."

"Would it matter?" she all but snapped. "It appears I don't have any secrets you don't know about anyway."

"No, you probably don't," he agreed quietly, thinking he'd let one woman do him in with her secrets and blatantly refused to let such a thing happen again. "You never did answer my question as to whether you're involved with anyone now."

She glared at him. "You seem to know everything there is about me. What do you think?"

He slowly strode over to the table to stand in front of her. "It doesn't matter what I think, Chardonnay. It's what I want to know, what I want you to tell me, what I want to hear from your own lips. And if I ever find out you've deceived me, there will be hell to pay and the Westmorelands will have the first divorce in the family in over fifty years."

A sudden knock on the door announced the arrival of room service. Deciding to let her sit while his words sank in, he moved away toward the door. Minutes later, after the hotel staff had cleared the table and left, they were alone once more and he had no intention of letting her not answer the question he had asked earlier.

Seconds turned into minutes before she finally gave him an answer, after releasing what he considered a frustrated sigh.

"No, I'm not involved with anyone."

He took a step back, satisfied. A smile touched the corners of his lips. "That's good to know, especially considering what I'm about to do," he said, removing his jacket.

She frowned. "And just what are you about to do?"

He glanced at her. "Prove you wrong. I intend to show you that I am most definitely your type."

# Six

Donnay quickly got to her feet. "You will do no such thing!"

She stared at Spencer, wondering if he had lost his mind…and at the same time wondering if she had lost hers, when desire began heating her entire being. She gritted her teeth, refusing to give in to what she was feeling, what was trying to take control of her impeccable good sense.

"Why shouldn't I get the chance to prove I am your type?" he asked, taking off the cuff links to his shirt. "However, if you want to go ahead and concede that you're wrong—"

"I am not wrong!"

"Then prove it," he countered. "Or rather let me prove otherwise."

She held her ground, though she could feel herself

start to tremble. With fear…or desire? "I don't intend to let you prove anything, Spencer."

"That means you either don't know your own mind or you're afraid of what I'm capable of doing to that mind."

The latter was true and in acknowledging that fact, a sensuous shiver rippled down Donnay's spine. Their kiss last night had done things to her she hadn't expected. It had literally blasted her world into another hemisphere. Another kiss might be even more lethal than the last and she had no intentions of playing with fire. Seeing him now, standing there, staring at her with his intense dark eyes, was making her entire body flush with some sort of feminine heat she'd never encountered before. The room suddenly felt hot and she felt hot right along with it and wondered if she was running a temperature. The Spencer Westmoreland kind.

"Do you know what I think? What I truly believe?" he asked in a deep, husky voice that set her body throbbing.

She met his gaze. He was standing in the middle of the room, his legs braced apart in a sexy stance, with his hands in the pockets of his trousers, staring at her with an intensity that nearly made her weak.

"No, and I couldn't care less what you think or believe, but I'm sure you're going to tell me anyway," she said curtly, just as angry with herself as she was with him. Why was he the one man who could cause such conflicting emotions to rip through her?

"I think you're a very passionate woman."

Passionate? Her? He had to be kidding. If he was basing his opinion on what had happened the other night he was way off. Although Robert had never complained, to be quite honest, she never found sex to her liking. It was all right, but definitely nothing she couldn't do without. In her mind it was a process intended to make bodies sweat and give your muscles a fairly good workout. Nothing more, nothing less, and she was okay with that. But then, she couldn't explain what was happening to her now. She didn't think what she was experiencing had anything to do with passion. It was more akin to lust.

"I think you have me mixed up with someone else," she decided to say. "Either that or you've drunk too much wine and it's screwed up your brain."

He didn't respond and she eyed him as he bent over to remove his shoes and socks. "May I ask what you're doing?" she inquired. He straightened up and kicked his shoes aside.

Another smile touched his lips. "I told you what I'm doing. I intend to prove to you that I'm your type."

She placed her hands on her hips. "Evidently you didn't hear me when I said that you're not doing any such thing, and I don't take you as the type of man who would force himself on a woman."

He smiled. "I'm not, but if a woman begs, then—"

"Beg? The only thing I'll beg is your pardon. Do I look like a woman who would beg a man for anything?"

"Not yet."

He slowly began walking over to her, like a hunter cornering his prey. But she refused to back up. He intended to prove her wrong and she intended to show him she was right. He was cocky, ruthless, domineering…all the things she never liked in a man. Therefore, he wasn't her type. Men like him turned her off.

Usually.

So why not now? Why was the hard glint in his eyes daring her to look away, making certain parts of her body feel hot, wet, and amazingly charged? And why was she suddenly remembering the kiss they had shared last night? The one that had had her purring, had made her want to press closer to him, feel every inch of him against her. The one that compelled her to drape herself over him, find her way into his lap while he claimed her mouth in a way no man had done before.

He came to a stop in front of her and then stood there, almost body to body, face to face. "You're remembering last night, aren't you?" he asked, breathing the words against her mouth in a way that nearly moistened her lips.

"No, I'm not remembering last night," she denied.

"Then how about letting me jog your memory?" he said. At the same time he reached up and tenderly caressed her cheek with his fingers.

She forced the lump back down in her throat, the one that was almost responsible for the soft purr that threatened to come out. She was beginning to forget everything, especially just how much she didn't like Spencer. Instead she stood there and stared into his eyes in heated fascination while intense sensations flooded her stomach.

"Do you know I could actually taste you in my mouth all day?"

She licked her lips nervously, thinking Robert had never told her anything like that the day after they'd kissed. And when Spencer's fingers left her cheek to caress the underside of her right ear, she couldn't think at all. She swallowed and forced herself to speak, although the voice that came forth didn't really sound like her own. "Can we talk about something else?"

He chuckled, and she watched how the smile lines spread from one corner of his lips to the other. "Sweetheart, to be quite honest, we really don't have to talk at all. In fact I prefer that we didn't."

Donnay knew what was coming next and tried taking a deep breath to prepare for it, but nothing could have prepared any woman for the mouth that suddenly swept down on hers, taking it, capturing it while at the same time a sweet and delicious tongue danced inside.

Instead of resisting, she met him and let him lead. She thought he had the flavor of peppermint, but the tang of man. A part of her felt a deep need to savor both. Her mind wasn't prepared for this, although it seemed her body was. When she felt his arms wrap around her, pulling her body closer to the fit of his, she became aware of the way the hard, toned muscles of his abdomen complemented the lower part of her body, further stimulating its feminine heat.

In some part of her mind it registered that his hands had moved from her waist and had begun a journey, exploring every inch of her body within their reach. But she was too preoccupied to get caught up in what Spencer's hands were doing. She was too busy drowning in the warm scent of his cologne, and the way his tongue was melding to hers.

Suddenly, however, she did become aware of his hands again when they inched down the back zipper of her slacks and slowly went inside the waistband to touch bare flesh. Her skin sizzled beneath his caress; her entire insides began throbbing. His hands were made for a woman's pleasure. They were manly, yet soft to the touch.

A part of her couldn't believe this was happening or

that she was letting it happen. It was as if she'd given up any willpower she had, giving him the liberty to latch onto her mouth, to taste her senseless, to touch her in a way that had a rush of heat flooding her body. Never had she experienced a kiss so intimate, pleasurable, one that had her insides tingling all the way down to her toes. Beneath the onslaught of his mouth she felt breathless, weak in the knees, consumed with desire.

She suddenly realized Spencer had slid her slacks down to her knees and was gripping the bare flesh of her behind that the thong she was wearing didn't cover.

She felt herself slowly falling, then realized that wasn't the case, it was Spencer easing her down onto the sofa. And, as if it had a mind of its own, her body became supple, receptive and nonresistant in his arms. When she felt the soft cushions at her back she opened her eyes and looked up into his at the same time he pulled his mouth away to slip a hand beneath her head. His face hovered above hers as he shifted their bodies to a more comfortable position and lay half propped over her.

Her heart began beating at an alarming rate and the urgency she felt within her couldn't be held at bay. Their faces were close and their gazes were locked. She detected his change in breathing the same moment she detected her own.

Slowly he leaned forward, softly whispered her name before capturing her lips, playfully nibbling, licking and sensuously torturing them with his tongue and teeth. What he was doing elicited a fierce reaction from her and she closed her eyes against the sensations ripping through her, fearful of losing her sanity.

And then he was kissing her again, even more intensely than before, sweeping her away on a turbulent storm that made a guttural moan escape her lips. And just like before, she kissed him back, needing the taste of him, wanting to be physically close to him. She would probably regret all of this later, but for now, she accepted what she wanted and what she needed.

Drugged by desire, she returned his kiss with a passion and hunger she hadn't known till now. In his arms she turned brazen, wanton. Only Spencer had the ability to rob her of common sense and replace it with something so addictive she couldn't think straight.

The moment she felt cool air hit her skin, she realized he had lifted her blouse, and before she could give a moan of protest, he moved his lips from her mouth to undo the front clasp of her bra with his teeth. The moment her bra fell open and her breasts escaped confinement, he was there, greedily taking one into his mouth, his tongue lavishing pleasure of the most erotic kind.

Then she felt his hand ease inside her thong and possessively clutch her feminine mound just seconds before his fingers stroked her, making her wetter than she was before. She moaned out his name although she tried holding it back.

What he was doing to her down south, coupled with his mouth on her breasts up north was having one tremendous effect and she felt herself floating on a sensuous wave. Nothing she and Robert had done had ever escalated her to this degree of passion. This was foreplay at its finest and experiencing this kind of intimacy nearly shattered her brain cells. She closed her eyes, thinking she'd been dead wrong. He was her type in more ways than one. He was sharing with her the kind of passion she hadn't known she possessed. Forbidden passion. Hidden passion. He was exposing it and making her aware that not only did it exist but it was his for the taking.

And then he shifted his attention to her other breast while his fingers remained between her legs relentlessly stroking her. She opened her eyes, willing her strength back, but she felt as though she was drowning in delicious waves that were completely overwhelming her, possessing her, forcing her to acknowledge his power over her.

He finally let go of her breast and before she could say anything, he captured her mouth again. He interwove his tongue with hers, mated thoroughly, extensively, completely.

Suddenly he pulled back rested his forehead against hers, breathing in deeply. She had a feeling that like her, he was fighting hard to reclaim a normal heartbeat, which wasn't easy. Moments later he looked down at her, and she felt herself falling deeper into the intensity of his gaze.

"Tell me," he whispered hotly against her lips. "Tell me you were wrong and that I am your type, your perfect match in every way."

After the way he had made her feel, Donnay felt weak enough to say anything he wanted to hear, but another part of her knew if she did what he asked then he would always consider her putty in his hands. With the strength and willpower that had deserted her earlier, she refused to give in to what he wanted and stubbornly shook her head and said in as firm and absolute voice that she could. "What I just experienced meant nothing. I still say you aren't my type and we are far from being a perfect match."

"Meant nothing?" He gazed down at her, narrowed his eyes for a fraction of a second and then, to her surprise, seconds later smile lines replaced the frown. "Then I will have to work at changing your mind about that, Chardonnay. I hope you're prepared because I love a challenge."

She glared at him. "You can try."

A smile spread from one corner of his lips to the other, and he said, "Don't think for one minute that I won't."

After Spencer opened the rear door to the limousine for Donnay, she hung back. "You aren't riding in the limo to take me home, are you?" she asked with a serious frown on her face.

He met her gaze. "That's my plan."

She narrowed her eyes at him. "Then change it because it's really not necessary."

"I believe that it is. Your mother and grandmother have enough to worry about with your grandfather's illness. They shouldn't have to worry about you, too."

"They won't since they know I can take care of myself," she threw over her shoulder as she slid into the back seat of the car.

"Can you?" he asked, easing into the seat beside her. She scooted over, putting distance between them.

He laughed. "If I wanted to bite, Chardonnay, I would have done so earlier tonight when I had the chance."

His words reminded her of one of the places his teeth had been and the hardened tips of her nipples began throbbing in response to the memory. As much as she wanted to, she couldn't forget the skill of his fingers. She immediately glanced out the window so he wouldn't see her blush. The man had a tendency to say whatever it was that pleased him.

Sensing that his eyes were glued to her, she continued looking out the window as the driver pulled away from his cottage. A part of her was mortified at all the things she had allowed Spencer to do to her tonight, but then another part had been deliciously pleased, although she would never admit such to him.

"Don't forget you only have forty-eight hours to give me your decision, Chardonnay."

That statement made her turn toward him. Then she wished she hadn't. In the dimly lit backseat of the car they were separated from the driver's vision by a deep tinted glass plate. They could see the driver but he couldn't see them. Spencer was lounging casually against the seat in what she assumed he thought was a comfortable position. Personally she thought it was a thoroughly sexy position and to make matters even worse, his gaze was fixed on her.

Tension, as well as desire, began swelling up within and she dragged in a deep breath to force both back down. She knew at that moment that he was someone she should not get involved with, let alone contemplate marrying. Somehow, she would get out of this mess she had gotten both her and her family in. The last thing she wanted was to be under Spencer's control, because whether she admitted it to him or not, the man had proven tonight that he was more than just her type. He had shown just how easy it would be to lose control and give in to him during a weak moment—and she could see herself having plenty of those types of moments with him.

"I need more time than forty-eight hours."

"I'm truly sorry you think that but that's all the time you're getting. You'd have to agree that the plans I have to improve and expand the winery are pretty good ones."

"That isn't the only thing that concerns me," she said, breaking eye contact with him to glance back outside the car's window.

"It should be. Whether you want to admit it or not, I've already proven we're compatible."

She turned back and glared at him. "You've proven no such thing. It was simply a kiss and little fondling that got out of hand."

He started to speak again, stopped and then chuckled before saying, "Think whatever you want. I'm sure the decisions you have to make are rather hard for you, and it's obvious your family depends on you to make the right ones for them. But consider this one thing, Chardonnay. Will you be worse off with me ... or without me?"

Conversation between them had stopped several minutes ago and Spencer assumed she was huddled in her corner of the limo angrily sulking. But he should have known that a woman as tough and stubborn as Chardonnay didn't sulk. She had fallen asleep.

He could take that two ways. Either she had gotten bored with him or he had tired her out earlier. And she wanted him to believe she'd merely considered it as a kiss and a little fondling.

He leaned back against the seat as he continued to watch her, thinking she was definitely a sleeping beauty. His stomach knotted when he was assailed by a wave of memories of what had transpired between them earlier that night. Unfamiliar emotions filled him. He wanted more times like that with her, and he wanted the opportunity to take it further without any thoughts of stopping. He wanted her in his bed.

A shudder suddenly raced through him with that obsession. He'd never been so taken with a woman before. He had given her forty-eight hours but in his mind she was already his, and what she didn't know was that he would move heaven or hell to have her. When they had lain together on the sofa, her lithe body had seemed the perfect fit for his and they hadn't even connected intimately yet. Just the thought of being inside her sent previously checked emotions flooding all through him. Everything he was feeling was new to him. New as well as troubling.

He sighed deeply as he continued to watch her sleep, trying to remember the last time he'd done such a thing. With Lynette Marie perhaps? He truly didn't think so. And if he had, it hadn't been with such intensity and concentration like he was doing at this precise moment. Nor with such longing. She evoked a desire and need within him so strong that even now, he was tempted to pull her into his arms and wake her in one rather delicious way. And when the chauffeur turned down the mile-long, scenic lane that would carry them to her home, he thought, why the hell not?

He slid across the seat closer to her, gently caressed the side of her face with his fingertips. "Chardonnay, you're home."

He watched as her eyes slowly opened. She stared at him, seeing how close his face was to hers. "Let's kiss good-night before we get out of the car," he urged in a voice that sounded deep and throaty to his ears.

She continued to stare at him and for a minute he thought she would tell him where he could shove his kiss. Instead he noted the exact moment her breathing became labored. The exact moment her eyes became dilated with a need that mirrored his own.

And when she eased her lips closer to his, the warmth of her breath touched him. He decided at that moment that this kiss would be slow and easy but filled with a fervor he wasn't used to giving or sharing. Deciding he needed to hold her in his arms, hold the body he had possessed and claimed as his earlier, he shifted slightly and pulled her into his lap at the same time he reached out and ran his fingers through her hair before lowering his mouth hungrily to hers.

The moment their mouths touched, connected, locked hard, a hot tide of sensations surged through him. When he felt his insides start to burn, he pulled her closer, and the degree of desire and his ravenous need nearly undid him. She had a taste that was more fulfilling than any meal he could ever eat. Unique, rich and overpowering, it soothed a throbbing ache within him on one hand, and started an agonizing one on the other. He tried dragging his common sense to the forefront, forcing his body to get a grip. But the only grip he wanted was a tighter hold on her. The moment her tongue began dueling with his, pure exhilaration invaded his already fevered body.

He shifted his hips and her right along with them, determined to stroke her bottom. Even through her slacks, cupping her in such a personal way had heat blazing through his veins, groans sounding deep in his chest. The next time they were together this way, he wanted her to wear a dress. It would make it easier when he undressed her. And he intended to undress her and touch her all over. He wanted to make love to every part of her body. Just thinking about all he wanted to do had him wound up tight as a coil.

It was only times like this, when they were seeking mutual satisfaction, that they were on one accord and in tune with each other's wants and needs, willing to give in to their desires. Whether she wanted to accept it or not, she was giving herself to him, had given herself to him earlier that evening. Her actions spoke louder than any words could have, so she might as well make up her mind to become his wife. Besides, he wasn't going to listen to her refusal. He wanted to see that heat in her eyes again, hear her labored breath that signified she was as filled with desire as he was. He wanted to make her wet to his touch, sharing every kind of intimacy with her. He wanted to make her come while embedded deep within her.

Deeply engrossed in the kiss, he hadn't been aware the driver had brought the car to a complete stop until the man thumped on the top of the car. Spencer reluctantly broke off the kiss and pulled back and gazed down at her. There was nothing she could say. No denials, no accusations, no crying foul play. Not this time.

She had wanted the kiss, had enjoyed it as much as he had and they both knew it. Besides, over the next forty-eight hours they both had a lot to think about. He needed to understand why he was swamped by emotions he hadn't known he had. How this young, wisp of a woman could overwhelm him the way she had, so quickly and deeply.

"Forty-eight hours," he whispered softly against her moist lips.

Instead of the flaming retort he expected, she nodded and then pulled herself out of his arms, straightening her clothes. He watched her draw in a huge breath before glancing over at him. She exhaled slowly and said, "Are you sure you want me as a wife? I really don't think you know what you're asking for."

He thought about all the satisfaction he'd gotten from what they'd shared back at his place and the limo ride home, all the satisfaction and fulfillment a future with her would bring, and countered by saying, "Yes, I want you as my wife, and I know exactly what I'm asking for."

# Seven

Forty-eight hours.

She had only ten of those left and she'd yet to make a decision.

Donnay sighed as she stepped out of the shower and grabbed a towel to dry her body. She reassessed the predicament that she and her family were now facing, and although she didn't want to admit it, marriage to Spencer was the only solution, especially after talking to her grandfather's doctor yesterday. His condition was improving; however, sooner or later he would need the surgery, and the insurance company would deny paying for it since it was considered experimental treatment. That meant even if she opted for the loan, they would run the risk of not being able to keep up the mortgage payments.

She then thought, as she finished dressing for the day, about the pros and cons of marrying Spencer.

She would have to endure a loveless marriage, which was the main thing she couldn't get past just yet. She would have to willingly subject herself to spending the rest of her life with a man who didn't love her and would never love her. Given his attitude toward love, she wondered about the woman responsible for breaking his heart.

On the flip side, if she agreed to marry him, her family's financial worries would be over. And the added plus was that he had agreed to take the winery to the next level. Staying a regional mom-and-pop operation had served its usefulness. In order to compete in a broader market and bring in a higher profit, changes needed to be made, and they were changes that could only come about with Spencer's financial support.

She sighed deeply, feeling like the sacrificial lamb. If she were to tell her mother and grandparents about Spencer's outlandish proposal they would be outraged. On the other hand, if she were to waltz in and tell them she had fallen in love with him and planned to marry him, they would become suspicious anyway, since she had made it pretty clear that she detested the man.

The good thing was that she hadn't heard from Spencer since that night he had brought her home in the limo. She considered his absence a blessing. The last thing she needed was for him to further mess with her already muddled mind. With his hands she had been on the brink of her first real orgasm and just thinking about it had hot streaks of sensations rushing through all parts of her. One thing their marriage wouldn't lack was passion. He had more in his mouth and fingers than most men had in their entire body. He wanted kids and she didn't doubt he would have her pregnant within the first year. But then she had longed for kids, and a husband who would love her. Getting one out of two wasn't so bad, she told herself.

Her mind then went back to the passion. Spencer had touched her in ways she had never before been touched, making her feel things she'd never before felt. What happened to her whenever she was around him? Why was it so easy for him to entice her to indulge in things that she really didn't want to do? And why was the thought of being married to him turning her on instead of turning her off?

She knew one thing that was for certain, he was wiggling his way into her family's affections. According to her grandmother and mother, he had visited with her grandfather at the hospital yesterday, and of course everyone thought it had been extremely kind of him to do so.

She glanced around when she heard the knock at the door. "Yes?"

"I have a delivery for you, Ms. Russell."

Donnay felt relieved it was Janice, their housekeeper, and not her mother or grandmother. No doubt they would have questions about the loan. It had been three days since she'd told them they had been approved and she had yet to act on it and they had to be wondering why. As far as they were concerned the loan was the only hope for the winery's survival.

"Come on in, Janice."

Janice walked in carrying a huge vase of red roses that was almost larger than she was. In her late fifties, she was a tiny thing, barely five feet, weighing a little over a hundred pounds. She and her family had worked in one capacity or another at Russell Vineyards for years.

"What on earth," Donnay exclaimed, immediately crossing the room to relieve Janice of the megasize delivery.

The older woman smiled. "They just arrived for you. Aren't they gorgeous?"

Donnay smiled. Yes, they were, and it wasn't hard to figure out who had sent them. "Yes, they are nice," she said, pulling off the card and then making space for the vase on the table that faced the window.

"Well, I need to get back downstairs and prepare Ms. Ruth's and Ms. Catherine's breakfast."

As soon as the door closed behind Janice, Donnay pulled open the card that simply read: *Thinking of you. Spencer.*

Donnay rolled her eyes. In other words, he was sending her a reminder that her time was running out and he expected her decision in the time frame he had given. But when she glanced over at the roses, she had to admit he'd given her a very beautiful reminder.

She remembered the words Spencer had spoken two nights ago, and he was right. She had to decide, in ten hours or less, if she would be worse off with him in her life than she would be without him in it.

Spencer pulled his BlackBerry out of his jacket to check stock market results after noticing Daniel Russell had drifted off to sleep. He could vividly recall sitting at his own grandfather's hospital bedside years ago.

Scott Westmoreland's death from lung cancer had been hard on the Westmorelands since he had been the rock of the family. All of his grandsons, and at the time the one lone granddaughter, Delaney, had learned something from him that would carry them through life to face the many challenges and hardships.

As he placed the BlackBerry back in his jacket, he glanced back over at Chardonnay's grandfather. Yesterday, the two had talked and Daniel had asked if he would return today to shave him and he had. Also yesterday, the man had been a lot more talkative. He had shared with him all his hopes and dreams for the winery and had apologetically told Spencer that he regretted they wouldn't be selling the vineyard to him after all, but that they felt strongly that it should remain in the Russell family. His words had let Spencer know Chardonnay had yet to tell her family about his offer. He didn't know if that was a good sign or a bad one. But a part of him was confident she would end up doing the right thing—which would be to marry him.

Suddenly he became aware that someone was watching him. He glanced up and felt a tantalizing throb in his gut when he saw it was Chardonnay. At that very instant it seemed that he couldn't breathe. She was standing in the doorway to the hospital room staring at him. Her eyes weren't glaring or shooting daggers at him. They were just staring. He was certain she was wondering why he was there, and before she could ask, he stood and beckoned her to follow him into the hall so they could speak privately and not disturb her grandfather.

"I dropped by this morning to shave him," Spencer said as soon as they had stepped into the hall.

She nodded. "I know. Mom told me that he asked you to do it yesterday. Any one of us could have done it for him but I guess it's a man's thing." She then smiled sheepishly and said, "Or it could be that the last time we shaved him we left him with quite a few cuts and nicks."

"Ouch." His response made her laugh and Spencer found himself relaxing somewhat…as well as taking the time to notice her outfit. She was wearing a pair of jeans and a light-blue pullover sweater. Both looked good on her and the light-blue brought out the color of her eyes in a pretty way.

"Thanks for the flowers. They're beautiful," she said.

"You're welcome."

When a moment passed and they didn't say anything, she said, "We need to talk, Spencer. I've made my decision but I don't want to go into it here."

He met her gaze. "Okay. Let's have dinner tonight."

"All right, but not at your place again."

He started to argue, to tell her she was in no position to make decisions, but then thought better of it. Dinner tonight would be about decisions—hers—and he wanted to know which ones she had made no matter where they dined.

"And I prefer meeting you someplace. Don't waste your time sending a car for me because I won't get in it," she added curtly.

He nodded. "Okay, I won't be sending a car for you. I'm coming to pick you up myself and I do expect you to get in."

He saw her stiffen, her jaw set tight. "I'll be there to pick you up at five," he said.

She glanced down at the floor where she was tapping her foot. Probably counting to ten to hold back her anger, he thought. She had a tendency to dislike him giving her orders. "Are we on this evening for dinner at five, Char-donnay?" he asked, deciding to make sure they were on the same page.

She glanced back up at him. Her gaze was made of stone. "Do I have a choice?"

"No."

He said it quickly and unerringly.

"I have a request to make of you," she said, and from the look in her eyes he knew he wouldn't like it.

"What?"

"Promise me that you'll keep your hands and lips to yourself tonight."

He couldn't help but smile at that one. "Does that mean I can't kiss you…or touch you anywhere I want?" he asked as calmly as he could.

"Yes, that's exactly what it means."

He shrugged broad shoulders. "In that case I won't make such a promise because I plan to kiss you, Char-donnay. I like kissing you, and as long as you kiss me back, letting me know you're enjoying the kiss as much as I am, I see no reason to stop. And need I remind you that you initiated the last kiss we shared. I might have had my mouth in the right place at the right time, but it was you who made the first move."

He hated reminding her of that, but she needed to hear it. She needed to know that he was fully aware each and every time she participated in their kiss. "But as far as touching you like I did before, unless you give me a reason to think you want me to touch you there, I won't, since I've accomplished what I intended to do."

She frowned. "Which was?"

"Claim it as mine." Before she could open her mouth to deny his words, he said. "When your grandfather wakes, let him know I'll be stopping by again tomorrow."

"Why?" she asked when he was about to turn and leave.

He smiled. "Mainly because I like him. He reminds me a lot of my own grandfather and I was close to him. All his grandchildren were. He left a huge void in our lives when he died. He was a good man, and I believe your grandfather is a good man as well."

Deciding not to say anything else, he walked off toward the bank of elevators.


"Did your grandfather wake up and ask about me?"

Donnay turned from gazing out the car window to find Spencer looking over at her when he'd stopped at a traffic light. Just like he'd said, he had arrived exactly at five. She had been ready.

"Yes, and he seemed pleased that you would be returning tomorrow," she said, not liking it but being totally honest. She could tell her grandfather liked Spencer. So did her mother and grandmother. "You never said where we're going," she decided to say when the car began moving again.

"Into San Francisco. There's a nice restaurant I want to take you to. I think you're going to like it."

She was sure she would since it seemed that Spencer Westmoreland didn't do anything half-measure.

"Tell me about this surgery the doctor wants your grandfather to have."

She glanced over at him. "Who told you about it?" she asked, annoyed. It was family business and he wasn't family.

"Your mother and grandmother. They seemed worried that it wouldn't be covered by the insurance."

She wished her family hadn't taken Spencer into their confidence. But they didn't know how he could use such information to his benefit. However, since they had done so, she figured she might as well level with him. "There's a good chance it won't be since it's considered experimental."

"And if they don't, what's your next option?"

She sighed deeply. Did he look at all solutions by way of options? "If the insurance company denies payment then we'll pay for it out of our pockets. Either way, if Gramps needs that surgery then he's going to have it."

She knew Spencer was probably taking this all in and in doing so figured she had only one option open to her. The one he wanted her to take. He must be feeling pretty good knowing he had her family stuck between a rock and a hard place.

"You're right," he said, breaking into her thoughts. "Either way if your grandfather needs that surgery then he's going to get it. I'll take care of the cost, no matter what option you've decided to take."

Donnay snatched her head around, thinking she had definitely not heard him correctly. He'd come to another traffic light and was looking at her. "Why would you do that?" she asked, barely getting the words out and staring at him wide-eyed.

"Would you believe because I'm a nice guy?" he asked.

"No. I think that you can be a nice guy but that usually you aren't."

He chuckled. "My family would be the first to disagree with you. The personal side of me is nice all the time, but oftentimes, I have to take on another persona when I'm negotiating business. It comes with the territory. In that arena, nice guys finish last, and I like being first."

She believed him. "I don't want you to think the Russells are a charity case that need your handout, Spencer."

"I appreciate you telling me that, Chardonnay," he said, and she easily picked up the edge in his voice. "But the truth remains, charity case or not, your family needs my financial assistance and I'm willing to give it either way. Do you have a problem with that?"

Saying she did would, in essence, be the same as biting off her nose to spite her face, and she was too smart to do that. There was such a thing as family pride, but then there was also such a thing as knowing when to exercise good common sense. "No, I don't have a problem with it. Thank you for making the offer."

"You're welcome. And now it seems that we've arrived at our destination."

A frown darkened Spencer's brow as he watched Chardonnay finish the last of her dessert. What he'd told her in the car was true in most circumstances, but he was finding himself being a rather nice guy in his business dealings with her. Case in point, he hadn't immediately asked for her decision the moment the two of them had sat down to dinner. Nor had he inquired as to what it was over dinner. Instead he had engaged her in conversation about other things, things he normally didn't give a damn about, like who was messing around with whom in Hollywood or which rapper had offended Bill O'Reilly or vice versa.

Now he couldn't put off asking any longer, nor did he intend to. "So what have you decided, Chardonnay?"

He watched as she lifted her head and her gray eyes stared at him. She placed her fork down then took a napkin and wiped her lips. They were lips he had thought about kissing all evening. Suddenly the room seemed to get silent as he tuned everything out to concentrate on one thing. Her decision.

She continued to look at him directly and he knew whatever she'd decided that he hadn't made things easy for her. That had been deliberate on his part. But now, if her decision went the way he wanted, she wouldn't have to think of anything hard again. He would guarantee it… Almost. There was still that question regarding her degree of loyalty. That was important to him and it was something he had to be certain that he had from her, no matter what.

"I've decided to marry you, Spencer."

Her statement seared through him, made his heart squeeze tight and had blood pulsing rapidly through his veins. She bowed her head to resume eating and a frown gathered between his brows. Had she really meant it? His jaw tightened at the thought that she was playing with him.

"Chardonnay?"

"Yes?" She lifted her head again and for a long moment his eyes stared into hers. A deep desire to have her slowly replaced any irritating thought he'd had. She had been serious. She would marry him. For better or for worse. And she was accepting her fate of a loveless marriage. He gave a mental shrug, refusing to feel guilty. It was her decision.

"We need to make plans. I want the wedding to take place before Christmas."

Her eyes widened. "That's impossible. Christmas is less than three weeks from now."

"I know. We had a Christmas wedding in the family last year when my cousin Chase married. In fact it was on Christmas Day. Everyone had to make arrangements to be away from their homes during the holidays to attend. At this late date some people may have already made other plans this year. I prefer having a private ceremony before Christmas, here in the valley with just our families."

She narrowed her eyes at him. "What's the rush?"

"I'm surprised you would ask me that, Chardonnay." He knew she could read between the lines quite clearly and she proved it when her cheeks darkened.

"I guess you wouldn't entertain the thought of us waiting to get to know each other a lot better before engaging in something so intimate," she said softly.

"No, I wouldn't," he said quickly, deciding to once again make his position clear. "I want you, Chardonnay. I've never hidden that fact. And I want babies. Marrying you will give me all the things I want and you will benefit from the marriage as well."

A frown formed on her face. "And what will you tell your family about us? What am I supposed to tell mine?"

He picked up his wineglass to take a sip. "We'll tell them we met and fell in love immediately. It will be a lie of course, but considering …"

She raised a brow. "And they're supposed to believe it? Just like that?" she asked, snapping her fingers.

He leaned forward. "Yes, just like that," he said, snapping his own fingers. He chuckled. "My mother won't have a problem believing it since she's a true romantic."

He then straightened in his chair and said, "I'm flying out to L.A. for a few days to attend several prescheduled business meetings. When I get back I plan to move into your home, so make room."

"What?" She looked incredulous.

"Now that you've given me your decision—one I will trust you to keep—work will begin on the winery immediately after I get back and I need to be around for that. If there's not room for me at the main house, I'll settle with living in one of the guest cottages. I'll remain there until we marry."

From her expression he could tell he was moving too fast for her, but he had no intentions of slowing down.

Donnay stood outside her mother's bedroom door, trying to get a grip on her nerves. She had exchanged very few words with Spencer during the drive back home from the restaurant. Instead they preferred the silence since there had been very little left to be said.

Now she was to convince her family that she had miraculously fallen in love with him. Her grandparents might fall for that story but her mother would see through it. Taking in a deep breath, Donnay knocked on the door.

"Come in."

Donnay opened the door, stepped into the room and paused. Her mother was dressed to go out and she looked absolutely stunning. She couldn't recall the last time her mother wore something out other than slacks and a blouse. Tonight she was wearing a dress Donnay had never seen before. The soft tobacco-brown fabric slithered down her mother's curves.

"You're going out, Mom?" Donnay asked, although the answer was obvious.

Her mother gave her an easy smile. "Yes. How do I look?"

"Beautiful."

"That's good. That friend I told you about who's passing through, we're meeting for dinner tonight."

Donnay continued to look at her mom. "In that case I think you look too beautiful to be going out with an old girlfriend. You should be going on a date with a man."

Her mother chuckled. "Haven't we had this discussion before?"

"Yes, several times," Donnay agreed, leaning against the closed door.

"And what have I always told you?" her mother asked.

She'd always told her that she could never love another man the way she'd loved her father and that she was content and didn't need another man in her life, a man she could never love. Donnay wondered if that was the same for Spencer. Was there a woman out there whom he loved and that was the reason he could not love another?

"You're worried about something, Donnay," her mother said, breaking into her thoughts. "Come. Let's sit and talk." Her mother sat down on the bed.

With a deep sigh, Donnay crossed the room to take a seat beside her mother.

"Okay, tell me what's bothering you."

Donnay let out a breath, not sure how she was going to say it. Then she decided to just get it out. She turned toward her mother. "Mom, it's about Spencer Westmoreland."

Ruth raised a brow. "What about Mr. Westmore-

land? Did you know he came back to visit your grandfather today?"

"Yes, I know."

"I think your grandfather likes him."

"I can believe that."

Ruth studied her daughter. "So what's bothering you
about Mr. Westmoreland?"

Donnay felt her stomach tighten into knots. "He's
asked me to marry him, Mom, and he wants to have a
private ceremony here in the valley before Christmas."

Ruth looked stunned. "You're kidding aren't you,
sweetheart?"

Donnay shook her head. "No, Mom, I'm not kidding
and it's the only way."

Ruth frowned. "The only way for what?"

Donnay took the next twenty minutes to tell her
mother everything, including the details of the loan as
well as Spencer's proposal.

Her mother didn't say anything for a moment then
said in a relatively calm voice, "You must have mis-
understood Mr. Westmoreland."

Donnay rolled her eyes. Spencer had her mother and
grandparents convinced that he was Mr. Nice Guy.
"Trust me, Mom, I understood Spencer perfectly."

Ruth shook her head. "If what you say is true,
Donnay, then how can you even think your grandpar-
ents and I would let you go ahead with such a marriage?
You mean more to us than the winery."

Instinctively Donnay reached out and took her mother's
hand in hers. "I know, Mom, but it's something I must do."

Ruth studied her daughter. "And could it be something that you *want* to do as well?"

Donnay couldn't believe that her mother would ask such a thing. "Of course not. You of all people know how I feel about that man."

Ruth patted her daughter's hand a few times before asking, "Did I ever tell you that I disliked your father at first, too?"

Donnay looked back at her mother, surprised. "No, you never mentioned that. I assumed, considering how much you loved him, that it was love at first sight."

Ruth chuckled. "Far from it. I saw him as a threat."

Donnay lifted her brow. "A threat? To what?"

"To my relationship with Dad. Dad hired him on and the two of them quickly became close. I saw Chad as the son Dad never had, and I began thinking that Dad would regret I was born a girl and not a boy who would carry on the Russell name."

Donnay thought about what her mother had said for a moment then asked, "Did my father know how you felt?"

"Yes, I wasn't the easiest person to get along with and at times I deliberately made things hard for him. At least I tried to. But he saw through it all. And for some reason he understood."

Her mother got quiet and Donnay knew she was remembering those times, and recapturing those moments. It had to be hard for her mother. Donnay wished there was a way she could convince her to leave the valley for a while to find the man she loved and had allowed to walk out of her life. There had been times while in college when Donnay had been tempted to look up Chad Timberlain, get to meet the father she never knew and who didn't know she existed. But she never did.

For all she knew, and what her mother suspected, he

was now married with other children. Children who were her half siblings. She never got the courage to find him because she hadn't ever wanted to be the one to verify her mother's assumptions that the man she loved and had let get away had another life that included a wife and children.

"Mom, I appreciate you sharing that with me about you and Dad, but the situation with me and Spencer is totally different. I appreciate what he did for Gramps, but he's not the man you and Grammy think that he is."

Her mother touched her arm. "And considering everything, I have a feeling he's not the man you think that he is, either, Donnay."

# Eight

An aura of intense longing swept over Spencer the moment he rounded the corner of the building where he was told he would find Chardonnay doing a wine tasting. It had been almost a week since he'd seen her and he'd been stunned as to just how much he'd missed her, to the point that once his plane had landed in San Francisco, he had driven straight to the Russell Vineyard.

He followed the sound of voices and stepped into the crowded tasting room. Chardonnay was to taste the first wine to be bottled and packaged from this season's pruned crop. If the wine passed her inspection, it would continue to age.

Shivers of awareness passed through him when he saw her. She was standing on a platform facing the crowd—a Russell who was about to place verdict on a Russell wine. She stood before a table that held four glasses filled with wine. Sun shining through the huge windows slanted glints of gold on her head, adding highlights to her hair. Emotion gripped his gut at the sight of her. She was the most strikingly beautiful woman he knew, the woman who would become his wife and the mother of his children. She had been on his mind constantly since he'd left the valley, but no memory could compare with the woman in the flesh.

He watched as she rotated the glass a few times on the table. According to what he knew about wine tasting, she was swirling the wine around in the glass to mix it with air. The motion would cause the aromatic compound in the wine to vaporize and get that unique smell.

Moments later she picked up the glass and brought it to her face, sticking her nose into the airspace of the glass where the aromas were captured. Tempting visions, erotic in nature, filled his mind and fueled his imagination. While she was concentrating on the wine's scent, he was remembering hers, the one he considered sharply seductive, the one that could send sensations racing through him the moment it filled his nostrils.

Trying to get a grip, he watched as her eyes closed before she took a sip. He remembered another time he had watched her close her eyes like that. That night she had been at his place. The same night he had decided that no matter what it took, he had to make Chardonnay Russell his.

She opened her eyes and the smile that touched her lips was priceless. He knew the wine she had just tasted had successfully passed her inspection. Of course it would go through other tasters, but everyone knew her opinion counted most. Nodding her approval, she moved on to the next glass.

He leaned back against a solid wall. He had a clear view of her but doubted she had seen him yet, which was just fine. She would know his presence in all things, especially her life, soon enough.

His trip to Los Angles had been very productive. He had met with Steve Carr, the man whose construction company would be responsible for the expansions he wanted made to the winery. Work would begin rather quickly and he was getting excited about it and couldn't wait to tell Chardonnay so she could share his excitement.

When he heard everyone around him clapping, his concentration went back to Chardonnay. She had tasted all four glasses and evidently had approved all of them. Then, as her gaze spanned the crowd, she saw him. The moment their eyes connected, even if only for a brief second, he felt it as well as saw it. He saw the darkening of her eyes at the same moment he felt deep need pass through him.

She broke eye contact to speak with the people who had begun gathering around her. After she thanked them for upholding the Russell tradition in producing superb wine, she excused herself from the group and began walking his way. He hadn't moved an inch and his gaze flicked across her from head to toe as she made her way toward him.

He was mesmerized, utterly captivated. And not for the first time he was asking himself how one woman could snag a man's emotions so thoroughly and completely.

"You're back," she said in a tone of voice that didn't give away whether she was delighted or disappointed.

"Yes, I'm back. Have you set a date for the wedding?" he decided to ask, thinking there was no reason not to.

She gave a resigned shrug of her shoulders and her voice was very cool when she said, "Did I have a choice?"

If she expected a softening of his heart, she wasn't getting it today. "That depends on what you want and what's important to you," he replied in a voice that was painstakingly clear. "And I thought we'd gotten beyond all of that, Chardonnay. No need to whine about it now."

She narrowed her gaze. "Is that what you think I'm doing?"

"Sounds like it. What I was really hoping for was a nice welcome-home kiss."

"Sorry to disappoint you," she said sarcastically.

She had disappointed him but not surprised him. He smiled, thinking he would make doubly sure she made up for it later. However, he definitely wouldn't tell her that. Instead he decided to change the subject. "I spoke with your grandfather yesterday. He sounds good."

She smiled and he could tell it was genuine and sincere. "Yes, we're all pleased with his progress. If it continues he'll be able to come home at the end of the week. The doctor wants to give him time to build up his strength before planning the next phase of his treatment."

"The surgery?"

"Yes. They want to schedule it sometime after the holidays, providing his health continues to improve. I'm going to visit with him later. Would you like to come with me?"

He was surprised by the invitation and had no intentions of turning it down. "Yes, I'd like that, but first

I need to make arrangements to have my things moved here from the Chablis."

He watched her mouth tighten. "You're still planning on living here?"

"Yes, nothing has changed," he said in an even tone. "All my plans are still the same. The ones I have for the winery as well as the ones I have for us. And speaking of which, your mother said you would be the one to show me to the guest villa."

"Yes, I guess I am," she said, her voice trailing off as she turned around and noticed everyone had begun to leave.

"Yes, sweetheart, you definitely are," he said softly.

Donnay turned back to Spencer, trying not to let the throaty tone of his voice take over her senses and make her forget how he had succeeded in turning her entire life upside down. And then there was the term of endearment he'd just used. *Sweetheart*. It had a nice ring to it, but was actually meaningless in their situation.

The shutting of the door claimed her attention and she was grateful for the distraction until she saw that everyone had gone and she and Spencer were left alone. Definitely not a good thing. Especially when simply standing close to him was making all sorts of wanton thoughts flow through her head. Those boundaries she had set the last time they'd been together were fading away and she couldn't let that happen.

"If you're ready, I can walk you over to the guest villa. It's not far from here," she heard herself saying, as she took a step back, away from him.

In a surprised move, one she hadn't been prepared for,

he reached out, snagged her arm and pulled her back closer. "Not yet. There's something I need to do first."

His touch had every nerve in her body tingling and as usual she was immediately drawn to him. From the look in his eyes she knew he wanted to kiss her, was going to kiss her, and as much as she didn't want to, she was felt the anticipation of his kiss all the way down to the bone. She refused to play coy. She wanted this.

"Do you know how many nights I lay awake thinking about you?" he whispered, leaning closer to let his mouth brush her cheek. She could feel the warmth of his breath on the underside of her ear. Not waiting for her response, he answered his own question by saying in a husky voice, "Way too many nights."

And then unerringly, his mouth found hers, locked on to it, claimed it and successfully obliterated any and all coherent thoughts from her mind. Instead she concentrated on only one thing—his tongue and the way it was stroking hers, tangling with it in a deeply intimate way, sending sensuous chills up her spine, making goose bumps form on her arms and leaving no doubt in her mind that he had succeeded in touching something deep inside of her once again. He moved her in a way no other man could and she doubted ever would. A part of her knew she should reclaim her senses, put on the brakes. But she couldn't, nor did she want to. The way he was kissing her, so deep, sensual and intimate, he was making it plainly difficult, absolutely impossible, not to respond in kind. So she did.

She knew the exact moment her arms voluntarily reached around his neck to hold his mouth to hers, as well as when she felt his warm, hard fingers entwine in her hair. She also felt the heat of his body pressed intimately to hers, every hard plane and indentation, and she sank helplessly deeper into his strength, while he sank deeper into her mouth. His kiss was filling her with a physical yearning she only encountered with him.

When their lips finally parted, he pulled her closer into his arms, holding her, and they remained that way, silent for the moment.

Knowing she couldn't afford to give in to any sort of weakness or throw away good common sense, she pulled out of his arms. "I think we need to make some ground rules," she said in a shaky breath.

"I don't," was his response, as he brushed a stray curl back from her face. "Every time I kiss you that way, I want to proceed and strip you naked."

Like he'd come close to doing that other night, she thought. "I'd rather keep my clothes on around you. I think it's safer."

"Safer but not as satisfying. I think you should stop trying to fight me, Chardonnay, and give in to your wants and desires."

She shook her head. "I can't."

He held her gaze. "Yes, you can and eventually you will. We are perfect for each other."

She inhaled deeply as her mind absorbed his words. He might think the two of them were perfect but she did not. She refused to become too enthralled with any man again, let him take over her mind and thoughts. Besides that, Spencer was a man who could wiggle his way into a woman's heart if she wasn't careful. He would have her falling in love with him even though she knew he would never love her back.

"I would have to disagree with that," she said with conviction. "Now I suggest that I show you to the guest villa."

She hoped they were back to square one. No matter
how much she might respond to his kiss and intimate
caresses, she had to prove that nothing had changed. She
still considered him a threat to her happiness.

As they walked along the path, Donnay was surprised
at how relaxed she suddenly felt in Spencer's presence.
It was as if the torrid kiss they'd shared moments ago
had been what she needed to ease the tension.

"How many guest houses do you have?" Spencer
asked, breaking into the silence surrounding them. They
were strolling a path very familiar to her, one she had
always enjoyed as a child because the area surrounding
it was always manicured, while the land beyond was
overgrown with blackberry, raspberry and tomato vines.

"We have four guest villas, and a gardener's cottage
that's located at the edge of the vineyard," she said, remembering the day she had planted her very first grape-
vine nearby. Her grandfather had given her the space to
grow her own to keep her from picking and eating the
ones to be used for the wines.

"The guest villa you'll be staying in is actually where
I was going to live when I returned from college. I never
moved in since I preferred staying at the big house with
my mother and grandparents. I felt it would be lonely
living there and too far away from things."

"But you will be living there with me, once we're
married."

She glanced over at him. He hadn't asked a question
but had made a statement he expected her to obey. A

part of her wanted to rebel but she knew there was no use. In the end he would get what he wanted. "Yes, I'll be living there with you."

He smiled, seemingly satisfied with her acceptance of her fate. "Will you help me move in today?" he then asked.

Considering they seemed to be drawn together like magnets whenever they were alone, she didn't think that was a good idea. "There are some things I need to do before visiting Gramps at the hospital."

He nodded. "I understand and that's fine. But I'm counting on you to help me later since I'm sure I'll still have a few things that will need unpacking when we get back from the hospital."

She knew he was letting her know that he wouldn't allow her to put distance between them. Whether she liked it or not, they would be spending time together later tonight. "We had the phone service and electricity turned on a few days ago so you're all set," she said.

"Okay."

When they didn't say anything for several moments, he broke the silence by asking, "So you said you'd decided on a date?"

"Yes, I thought two weeks from this Saturday would do it. What do you think?"

He chuckled. "I think it's time to give my family a call and tell them about you. Of course they would want to attend the wedding ceremony. Wild horses won't be able to keep Mom away." He tilted his head and looked at her. "I see you've already told yours since your grandmother and mother congratulated me and welcomed me to the family when I arrived today."

She shrugged. "I saw no reason not to go ahead and

tell them. I basically told my mother the truth regarding our relationship. However, I led Grammy to believe we miraculously fell in love."

"And your grandfather?"

She stopped walking and gazed up at him. "I haven't told him anything yet, and Mom and Grammy promised they wouldn't, either. I thought it was best to wait until you returned so we could tell him together."

Spencer nodded. "And how do you think he'll take the news?"

Donnay couldn't help the wry smile that touched her lips. "Oh, he'll handle it quite nicely since your plans fall so neatly in with his. He's been after me for some time about finding a man, settling down and giving him great-grandkids. So in essence, you'll be giving him something he truly wants."

"And it's something I truly want as well," he said, smiling over at her. "And I'm more than happy to oblige."

They began walking again and she was glad moments later when they came to the private path that led to the guest villa where he would be staying. As soon as she got him there she planned to hightail it to the nearest shower to cool off. The man had a way of heating her body with a touch or a mere look. Resisting him was becoming a challenge.

"This path leads to the villa, the one you'll be using," she said, turning to walk a few steps ahead of him down the trail. "It's surrounded by a wrought-iron fence and is secluded enough to assure complete privacy. It's like your own little world inside a bigger universe."

He smiled. "It reminds me of a French château and I like it already," he said when he reached the gate and he saw the huge two-story structure. From his expression she could tell it was more than he had expected. "Who was this place built for?" he asked when she opened the gate for them to enter.

"No one in particular. The other villas are relatively small compared to this one and Gramps wanted to construct one that was larger and roomier. Like I said earlier, I think it was meant for me, although he would never admit he would do anything to persuade me to stay if I ever decided to leave. He felt pretty bad about what happened between my mother and father."

Spencer lifted a brow. "What happened between your parents?"

Donnay glanced over at him as they strolled up the walkway toward the front door. "They met when my father took a summer job here. He was in the army and was working at the winery while waiting to be deployed. He met and fell in love with my mother and she fell in love with him, too. He tried convincing her to marry him and travel the world with him since he planned on making the military a career. Although she loved him, she turned down his marriage proposal and sent him away because she didn't want to leave my grandparents alone. She felt her place was here with them at the vineyard. It was only after he left that she discovered she was pregnant with me."

Spencer paused, his hand on the doorknob. "So he never knew about you?"

"No. She tried writing him but the letter came back. Evidently he moved around a lot in the military."

"And you never tried finding him?"

She shook her head. "No. It's not that I never wanted to know Chad Timberlain—it's just that I knew developing a relationship with him would be a constant reminder to my mother of the love she gave away. That would be painful for her, especially if he had eventually married someone else over the years. My grandfather has always felt he and Grammy were unintentionally responsible for Mom turning her back on her true love, although they tried convincing her they would be fine here and that she should follow her heart."

When he opened the door she took a step back. "You don't really need me to give you a tour of the place so I'll leave you alone now."

He leaned in the open doorway, his stance nearly overpowering. "What time do you want to leave for the hospital?"

"Anytime after five will be okay. Grammy is spending the night with Gramps tonight. We prefer that she didn't because she'll be sleeping on a cot they bring into the hospital room, which won't be all that comfortable. However, no matter what Mom and I say she's determined to do so. After fifty years of marriage, I think she misses him."

He nodded. "I understand. Although my parents haven't been married quite that long, they have a strong marriage as well."

"Do they?"

"Yes. Like I told you, strong and long-lasting marriages run in the Westmoreland family."

Yes, he had told her that. "Well, I'll see you later," she said backing up to leave. If you'd like, you're welcome at lunch. Grammy usually has it on the table around one. If you want to get back to the main house just follow the path and you won't get lost."

"All right and thanks for the invitation. I might take you up on it."

"You're welcome," she said, forcing a cheerful smile before turning and quickly walking away.

"I appreciate you offering to help," Spencer said, ignoring Chardonnay's raised brow as he opened the door to the villa later that night. He knew she was thinking she hadn't offered. He really hadn't given her a choice in the matter.

She hesitated before stepping over the threshold and he strolled in behind her, closing and locking the door. He watched her glance around for a few minutes, and then she turned to him with a bemused expression. "I expected to see boxes all over the place."

He smiled in a perfectly calm way. "Did you?"

"Yes. You said you needed my help putting things away."

"I do. But everything didn't arrive today, so I have time."

The suspicion he saw in her eyes then became more pronounced. "In that case why am I here?" she asked, placing her hands on her hips "Why did you lead me to believe that you needed me tonight?"

*She would have to ask*, he thought as he leaned against the closed door and stared at her. And since she had, he would be completely honest when he gave her an answer. "Because I *do* need you tonight."

Donnay inhaled sharply. The tone of his voice, the intent of his words both were a soft caress across her skin. Their gazes held and she felt it, unquestionably.

His eyes were so dark she actually felt their intensity, could see the desire lining their depths. An instant passed, and then another and she felt herself getting breathless beneath the depth of their attraction for each other. Regardless of wanting to deny it, she couldn't.

She opened her lips to say whatever he needed tonight was his problem and not hers, but closed them when shivers raced up her spine. He was doing that to her and hadn't even touched her, hadn't even moved away from the door. His concentrated stare was making crazy things happen to her.

Sensations began gripping her and she felt the tips of her breasts grow hard as she remembered his mouth, tongue and teeth on them. She also remembered the place his fingers had been and felt a sudden ferocious ache right between her legs. She shook her head, trying to clear her mind of such memories and found it was no use. She then concluded that what she had deemed as *his* problem was now *her* problem as well.

She watched as he came toward her and she had the mind to take a step back and couldn't. Every fiber in her being was attuned to him, attracted to him, aroused by him. She couldn't resist him any longer. Nor did she want to.

"I want you and I need you, Chardonnay," he whispered huskily when he came to a stop in front of her.

She tilted her head back and looked at him, felt the heat coming from his gaze. And when he reached out and slipped his hands around her waist, bringing her body against the solid hardness of him, she inhaled when she felt his rock-hard erection press against the juncture of her thighs. Even the denim of her skirt couldn't downplay just how firm he was.

For moments he held her close against him, as if he needed the contact as much as she did. It then became crystal clear that her life and her future were going to be tied to him. He said he wanted a long-term marriage and a bunch of kids and she believed him; so why not accept how things were destined to be for her and move on? Why continue to fight what she couldn't change? Her grandfather was happy about their pending marriage, so was her grandmother. However, she could tell her mother was more worried than elated.

"Chardonnay?"

She tilted up her head to stare into his face. "Yes?" He was a strikingly handsome man. The thought of having a son or daughter who shared his features pulled on her heartstrings.

"I'ye told you what I want and need. Now it's your turn. Tell me what I can do for you tonight. If you say there's nothing you want or need from me then I will accept that and walk you back home. But if you have desires, I will not let you leave here unsatisfied."

Donnay swallowed because that's what she was afraid of. Spencer had unraveled her emotions in a way that Robert never had. What she should do was tell him good night and leave. Instead she found herself asking in a soft, curious voice, after remembering her intimate times with Robert, "What makes you think you can?"

He raised a dark brow. "Can what?"

"Satisfy me."

She watched as a slow, confident smile touched both corners of his lips. "Why would you think I can't?"

Since they would be getting married soon and he was determined that they would share a bed, she decided to be honest with him. She might be one of those women a man couldn't completely satisfy. "Robert didn't."

His brow arched higher. "The professor?"

"Yes, the one and only guy I've slept with."

"I can't imagine any man making love to you and not making you feel like an explosion hit and that every part of you has been shot to the stars and beyond."

Donnay's couldn't imagine anyone making her feel that way. "And how will you accomplish that?"

The look in his eyes indicated that he couldn't believe she really had to ask. But he answered anyway. "First, I'll undress you, kissing every part of you that I expose, lingering on some areas a lot longer than others. Next I'll take you into the bedroom and engage in foreplay of the most intense kind. So intense that I'll have you begging."

She shook her head. He'd made that claim before and she recalled how close she'd come to doing just that the night when he'd invited her to his place at the Chablis. "Is that what you think, that you'll make me beg?"

"No, sweetheart, that's what I know. In addition to long marriages, there's something else Westmorelands are known for."

She was almost afraid to ask but did so anyway. "And what's that?"

"Satisfying their mates. We are extremely physical beings who enjoy making love. Our sexual needs are sometimes inexhaustible."

Donnay felt a frantic tug between her thighs. "Thanks for the warning."

"It's the decent thing to do since I plan to keep you in bed with me quite a lot after we get married."

She wondered if he was joking, although the look in his eyes said otherwise. "Do I have a choice in the matter?"

His smile was amusing. "I guess you could always claim a headache, but I doubt that you would want to."

For some reason she doubted it as well, although she would never admit it to him. He was too sure of himself already.

"You know what?" he asked, breaking into her thoughts.

She heard the serious tone in his voice. "What?"

"I'm tired of talking."

A lump formed in Donnay's throat. She'd figured that sooner or later he would be.

"And if you plan on leaving, now is the time to do so because I told you what happens if you stay," he added.

She didn't move. She didn't say anything. She just stood there and stared at him. The more she stared, the more his gaze was touching her all over, making her feel hot and bothered, pushing her over the edge of her control.

And then he tipped the scales when he said in a voice too sexy for words, "Chardonnay Russell, soon to become Chardonnay Westmoreland, welcome to my world of forbidden passion."

He extended his hand out to her while locking his gaze on hers. She thought of everything he said he would do to her if she stayed and knew once she gave her hand to him, she would become his. For some reason that thought didn't bother her as it once had.

Inhaling deeply she placed her hand in his and watched his eyes darken even more before taking her hand and lifting it to his lips to kiss her fingers. And then he was slowly pulling her into his arms and taking her mouth with an intensity that would have brought her to her knees had his hands not wrapped around her waist.

His strength became the overt force that sustained her, the given power that was unconcealed and unrestrained. A shiver raced through her entire being when his tongue mated with hers in a way different from before. This was one of care, custody and control. He was placing ownership all over her mouth, claiming every breath she took and making the moans erupting forth from her throat totally his. The effect was enthralling, sensuously spellbinding and shockingly blazing.

Then she felt his hand working at the zipper at her waist, and moments later when he stepped back slightly without breaking the kiss, she felt her skirt slide down her hips to pool at her ankles. She was left in her blouse, a half-slip and a thong. And as she very well knew, this man had amazing fingers and definitely knew how to use them. He could strip a woman naked before she realized he was doing so. She then felt him slide his hand beneath the waistband of her slip to palm her almost bare bottom.

The moment he touched her, she moaned into his mouth and instinctively her body melded to his, felt his hardness, his erection, and the center of his arousal. He was taking more than she had been prepared to give, was priming her for what was yet to come and fanning a need within her to flashpoint. So she did the only thing she could. She let go.

Then suddenly he pulled back and swept her into his arms. Taking the stairs two at a time he entered the bedroom and placed her on the king-size bed. Her heart began beating faster, almost out of control, when he quickly worked at the buttons of his shirt.

Watching him, studying his eyes, she detected a hunger he was holding in check for now. Her mind began twirling with questions as to what could or would happen if he were to ever let go. She didn't want to think how he would overwhelm her if that were to happen.

He removed his shirt and tossed it on the other side of the room and her breath caught. His chest was so beautifully carved that she felt a moment of intense pride. This was the naked chest that would touch her own each time they made love, skin to skin; the chest she would rub her face in whenever she wanted to inhale the essence of his scent. And his shoulders, broad and firm, were the ones she would cling to when that explosion happened. And for a reason she didn't understand, she had believed him when he'd said it would.

A shiver racked Donnay's body when Spencer's hand went to the zipper of his pants. She held her breath as he eased it down, felt a lump form in her throat when he lowered his pants down his legs and stepped out of them. She finally released her breath and stared at him, her gaze more concentrated than before. It swept past his shoulders and chest to the area hidden by the black silk boxer shorts. The impression showed a very well-endowed man, a man who had everything to back up all the talk, and she believed he knew how to use everything he was packing.

She focused on that part of him that would soon connect their bodies, their minds, their entire beings. In the short time she knew him, she had come to realize that he didn't take too many things lightly. He was intense, demanding, a highly unmanageable person. But on the other hand, she believed he was fiercely dedicated. He would not deceive her like Robert had done.

"What are you thinking?"

His words broke the silence and she looked up to his face. She decided to be only half truthful. "I was wondering how I would handle you. Handle *it*."

He smiled at that. "You see both as a challenge?"

She blew out a breath. If only he knew. "Yes."

"Don't."

Evidently changing his mind about removing his briefs just yet, he moved back to the bed and pulled her up on her knees toward him and then bent down and captured her mouth in one smooth sweep. Something stirred the air surrounding them. She felt it as his tongue began mating with hers again. She felt it when his hands went to her blouse, when he broke the kiss just long enough to pull it over her head. And then he was easing her back into the bed, into the soft, thick cushions of the bedcovers, and straddling her body.

He pulled back and with a quick flick of his wrist and ready fingers, he removed her slip, thong and bra. Before she could inhale a deep breath, his lips were trailing a path down her body, continuing without pause until he reached the twin globes of her breasts. He began kissing them, devouring them, taunting them with his tongue, lips and teeth until she was moaning from deep within her throat. Desire set her ablaze when moments later his mouth began moving again, downward past her ribs and toward her navel. There he discovered her one moment of liberation during her first year in college. A belly ring.

He lifted his head, met her gaze and a broad smile touched his lips. She couldn't help but return his smile and at that moment something significant had passed between them. Acceptance of each other's likes, dislikes and values.

He lowered his head and her stomach tensed when he formed a ring on her belly with his tongue, a hot, wet one that seemed to brand her skin. And then he angled his head as his mouth began moving lower. She stiffened when he kissed the undersides of both her thighs while he reached down to let his fingertips trace a path along her calf.

She heard him murmur words that sounded foreign to her befuddled mind just seconds before he placed the other hand between her thighs to open her legs to him. And then she felt him there, his tongue touching her intimately in a way that lifted her hips off the bed. Her action only seemed to serve his purpose when he took the liberty to lift those same hips closer to his mouth and plunge his tongue inside her, even going so far to raise her legs over his shoulders for deeper penetration.

What he was doing was shooting sensation through her so intensely she felt every part of her shattering. With every flick of his tongue she felt a tug at her insides, as he deliberately pulled everything out of her, every single resistance, every rebellious thought. The feeling was excruciating, intense, unbelievably erotic. She reached out and gripped his shoulders, powerful and strong, and held on for dear life when he demanded anything and everything she was holding back from him.

And then she felt it. A wild, uninhibited dive into waters she had never been in before. But instead of drowning she was caught up on a wave so electrifying, she groaned deep within her throat before screaming out his name.

"Spencer!"

He refused to let up. His tongue went on in a frenzy,

as out of control as she was, and she arched her back as an explosion ripped through her. She felt every muscle in her body take a hit as she moved relentlessly against his mouth, unable to remain still.

She experienced a sense of loss when he pulled back and watched through glazed eyes when he shifted to pull off his boxers. And then he was there, straddling her, and in one swift, smooth move he entered her. Her body's reaction to his invasion was spontaneous. Flesh against flesh, he moved and she moved with him, every thrust as potent, deep and overpowering as the one before. Skin against skin, he slid against her, interlocking their limbs in a hold that was meant to go unbroken, uninterrupted, and unremitting. Any boundaries she'd established were shattered, totally demolished under the powers of his torrid lovemaking.

And then it happened again, another explosion tearing through her. She called out his name a second time, at the same moment he called out hers. And again she felt her body explode, shoot to the stars and beyond. Before she could gather her wits, Spencer's mouth covered hers in a long, slow and drugging kiss that erased all logical thought from her mind.

And she became caught up in Spencer's forbidden passion once again.

What woke Donnay was the feel of a masculine hand running along the side of her thigh, a slow and gentle caress. She slowly opened her eyes. And if she had any doubt just where she was, the hardness of the naked body pressed up against her own was a stark reminder.

She lay there knowing Spencer's hand was intent on

serving a very sensuous purpose; one she had come to expect since last night. He had warned her that when it came to making love he had inexhaustible energy, and over the past three hours he had proven that to be true. The man was so disturbingly virile she hadn't been sure she would be able to keep up. Surprisingly she had. There hadn't been a time when he had reached out for her that she hadn't willingly gone into his arms, knowing the pleasures that awaited her there. And at no time had she been disappointed. Each and every love-making session with him had left her totally and completely satisfied.

When she felt his hand ease between her legs and his efficient fingers went to work, she softly moaned his name.

"I see you're awake," he whispered, rising up on an elbow to gaze down at her.

She looked up at his naked chest, broad and muscular with a spray of dark hair. She remembered burying her face in that chest, taking her tongue and tracing a trail over it when he had been making love to her in one hell of a unique position. The man not only had an infinite amount of energy, he was also very creative. "Did you really expect me to sleep?" she asked, switching her gaze to his face and almost drowning in the depths of his dark eyes.

He smiled and that single smile, sexy to the bone, sent tingles through her body. "I didn't want you to get into any trouble."

She raised a brow. "Trouble?"

"Yes, it's rather late. And as much as I would love for you to stay here with me all night, I don't want to get on your grandmother's and mother's bad side by not returning you home at a decent hour."

She glanced over at the clock on the nightstand. It was already close to two in the morning. She couldn't help but chuckle. "Just what do you consider decent?"

His own voice was slightly amused when he said, "Anytime before daybreak."

Donnay inwardly shivered when his fingers began caressing her womanly core, making her hot and wet again. "Um, you don't have anything to worry about. Grammy is spending the night at the hospital and Mom is meeting a girlfriend in San Francisco and staying overnight. So I would have been home alone anyway."

His fingers went still, and he leaned in closer to her. "Are you saying that you can stay all night?"

She met his gaze and saw the intensity in it as well as the deep rooted desire. It did something to her to know that even after making love several times tonight he still hadn't gotten enough of her. Robert was always eager to send her away from his apartment afterward. Of course she later found out why. She nodded. "Yes, that's exactly what I'm saying."

His expression indicated her words had pleased him and he had no intention of letting her leave his bed now…which was fine with her.

When he lowered his head she was ready and parted her lips the moment he touched them, immediately becoming caught up in the throes of the passion he could generate so effortlessly.

From somewhere deep inside, she was suddenly struck with a terrifying realization. If she wasn't careful and protective of her heart, she could very easily fall in love with Spencer Westmoreland.

# Nine

The following morning, Donnay awakened to the loud sound of some sort of heavy machinery. She got out of bed, grabbed Spencer's shirt and slipped it on while quickly walking over to the window to peek out. The sun was just coming up over the horizon, and from a distance across the wide expanse of the vineyard she could see huge construction trucks making their way down the road toward the winery.

"I see Steve's men are on time as usual."

She swung around to see Spencer coming out of the bathroom. It was obvious that he had taken a shower. A towel was tied at his waist, and there were beads of water on his shoulders and chest. She narrowed her eyes and tried not to recall the role his shoulders and chest had played in their lovemaking during the night. There were more important matters to be concerned with right now. "What are those trucks doing here, Spencer?"

He walked over to the dresser, pulled a few items of clothing out of the drawer before dropping the towel. "I think it's obvious what they're doing here, Chardonnay."

She inhaled sharply the moment the towel hit the floor. He was standing before her stark naked and she was trying hard not to stare as he casually slipped into a pair of briefs. She had seen his nude body all last night and during the predawn hours, but seeing it in the bright sunlight was another thing altogether. The memory of all the things that body had done to her, shared with her, made sensations flood her insides. She shook her head and tried to clear her mind of such wanton thoughts and shift it back to what he'd said. "Well, it's not obvious, so tell me," she said.

He glanced over at her. "Those trucks belong to the company I hired to do the expansion to the vineyard."

She became livid. "How dare you!"

He raised a dark brow questioningly and leaned back against the dresser. "How dare I what?"

"How dare you take over. What gives you the right to make such a move without discussing it with any member of my family? We aren't married yet and already you're—"

"I discussed it with your grandfather."

Donnay locked her mouth shut but only for a second. "My grandfather?" she asked in a voice that had suddenly gone soft.

"Yes."

"Are you telling me that you told my grandfather everything about our arrangement?"

"Of course not. During our visits, he talked and I listened, which is a good thing because he shared his dreams with me for the winery. I took in all that he said. He was giving me the big picture—his hopes and dreams. I took it and consulted the best architect I know, and decided to try to make your grandfather's wants viable. Tonight, after telling him we would be getting married, I told him I would make his dream come true."

Donnay stared and then frowned. She didn't recall him saying anything like that to her grandfather. "When did you tell him this?"

"After you left the room to get him a blanket from the nurses' station."

She paused, tilted her head to one side as she considered his words and then asked softly. "And what did he say?"

"Thank you."

Every fiber in Donnay's body wanted to cry. She of all people knew just how long her grandfather had dreamed of expanding the winery, and how depressed he'd been the first time he had become ill and had seen those dreams slip through his fingers when the money for them was needed elsewhere. No one had to tell her that Spencer was giving her grandfather his life back, a reason to get better, a reason to want the surgery he'd been hesitant about having.

She met Spencer's gaze. "It seems I owe you an apology."

"Another one?"

He was standing in nothing but a pair of black briefs, in a sexy stance with his legs braced apart and his arms folded across his chest. From his expression it was obvious he was pretty annoyed with her for jumping to conclusions again. "Well, what was I supposed to think?" she asked in her own defense.

"I can tell you what you weren't supposed to think. The worst about me."

Okay, maybe she shouldn't have, but she had. What did he expect considering the reason he was in their lives? Their marriage would be nothing but a business deal.

As if reading her mind, he said, "I'm a man of my word, Chardonnay."

She slowly crossed the room to him. "And I'm a woman who doesn't have a problem admitting when she's wrong."

"And you're admitting it?" he asked when she came to a stop in front of him.

"Yes, on some things about you," she said, steadily holding his gaze.

He lifted a dark brow. "And the others?"

She shrugged her shoulders. "The jury's still out. But from now on you're innocent until proven guilty."

He caught her wrist and brought it to his lips and kissed it. "It's a good thing for you that I'm a very forgiving man."

"Are you?" she asked in a low tone, feeling heat travel all over her the moment his lips touched her flesh.

"Yes, on some things."

"And the others?"

"The jury is still out. But I don't have a problem with tampering with the jury if it will serve my purpose," he said, reaching out and slipping his shirt off her shoulders to fall in a heap at her feet. She stood before him naked but she had no intention of covering herself. From the look in his eyes, he evidently liked what he saw.

And he wanted what he saw. Again.

"You're very smooth," she said silkily, taking a step closer to wrap her arms around his neck and to bring her body close to his. "And you have one hell of an appetite."

"Don't say I didn't warn you," he said, sweeping her off her feet and into his arms to carry her over to the bed.

"I won't," she murmured into his strong, masculine chest.

Hours later after a long and lazy morning of love-making, Donnay and Spencer got dressed and he walked her home. Both her mother and grandmother were there but neither seemed inclined to ask where she had been.

Spencer then went to talk to Ray Stokes, the foreman for Carr Construction Company. Fred Akron, the architect he had paid, would be presenting his plans for the expansion of the winery by the end of the week. In the meantime, Ray and his crew's job was to clear land to extend the boundaries of the vineyard. Come spring they would be planting more grapevines for more wines to market.

It was way past noon when Spencer returned to the villa, and the moment he opened the door, memories of the night before assailed his mind when he picked up Chardonnay's lingering scent. It seemed to be all over the place. And he liked it. He had drunk chardonnay numerous times but never had he got the taste like he had last night. Good wine was supposed to have a lingering effect, get absorbed into your tongue, your mouth, your flavor palates. He licked his lips, still able to savor her taste on his tongue. Delicious.

He heard his cell phone ring and immediately pulled it out of his pocket. He glanced at the number. It was his brother Ian. Ian was the fraternal twin to his brother Quade and had gotten married that past June. Spencer fondly referred to his brother, who was six years his junior, as the gambler, since he had this unique ability to beat the odds, whether it was poker, a slot machine or blackjack. No one liked playing against Ian since he was known to walk away with everybody's money. He owned a casino and resort in Lake Tahoe, but if you were to ask Ian, his most prized possession was his wife, Brooke.

"And to what do I owe this honor?" Spencer asked teasingly. Since getting married Ian seldom called, saying his time was spent doing more important things. Spencer could just imagine what those other things were.

"Just checking to see if you're still living. Stuart was here at the resort last week and said something about how bad he felt about sending you to face a scorpion."

Spencer chuckled, wondered how Stuart would handle it when he found out that he would be marrying Chardonnay. "It's not that bad," he said and decided Ian would be the first family member he broke his news to. "In fact, it's pretty good. Her name is Chardonnay and I'm marrying her."

There was a pause and then, "You're joking, right?"

"No."

"You're marrying a woman name Chardonnay? Who would name their child after a wine?"

Spencer smiled. "Someone who owns a winery I would imagine."

"You're serious about getting married?"

"Yes. I'm giving the family a call later today. Your call was perfect timing and as a result, you're the first to know."

"When did you meet her?"

"A few weeks ago."

"Um, love at first sight?"

"No." The answer was simple, straightforward and true. "You know me better than that."

"Well, I'm one who knows that love can make you do foolish things."

"Possibly. But I'm not in love," Spencer said, being completely honest with his brother.

"Then why are you getting married? She can't be pregnant already."

Ian's words reminded Spencer that they hadn't used protection any of the times he and Chardonnay had made love last night. That thought didn't bother him since he wanted babies, plenty of them. "I'm getting married because I want to be married. Why let you, Jared and Durango have all the fun? Besides, Mom gets to put another smile on her face."

"But that won't stop her from going after Reggie and Quade," Ian advised.

"No," Spencer agreed. "But they're big boys. They'll have to handle Sarah Westmoreland as they see fit."

He glanced at his watch and saw it was almost two in the afternoon. He wanted to visit Chardonnay's grandfather and give him a report on today's activities. "Look, Ian, there's somewhere I need to be in about an hour. Keep your lips sealed about my upcoming marriage. I want to be the one to tell everyone."

"Okay, my lips are sealed…until such time as I use them to kiss my beautiful wife."

Spencer rolled his eyes heavenward. "Whatever." He then clicked off the phone.

* * *

"The two of you are marrying within two weeks? Why the rush?"

Donnay's looked at Spencer sitting beside her at the dinner table, wondering how he would respond to her mother's question. Not surprisingly, he met her mother's eyes and in a clear voice he said, "Because I don't want to wait."

She expected her grandmother or mother to ask, "Wait for what?" Instead both nodded their heads as if they understood his meaning.

She rolled her eyes. If they did she certainly didn't. It couldn't be that he couldn't wait for them to sleep together since they'd already done that. So the only thing she could figure was that he was anxious to get her pregnant since he was so gung-ho on starting a family.

"I think it's romantic."

Donnay's lips pressed together as she ignored her grandmother's words. Did she really think that or was she just in an extremely good mood because Donnay's grandfather would be coming home from the hospital at the end of the week? She felt Spencer's eyes on her and turned her head to meet his gaze. Fire immediately shot through her veins at the look he was giving her. She figured he was wondering why she had deliberately made herself scarce over the past couple of days. She'd had no choice because otherwise, she would fall deeper and deeper under his spell. And what was more pathetic than for a woman to fall for man who had no intention of ever falling for her?

"Daniel is going to be very pleased with all the work those men are doing on the vineyard," Donnay heard her grandmother say.

Spencer dropped his gaze from hers to look across the table at Catherine Russell. "I hope that he will be. I tried to follow his exact specifications."

Donnay would be the first to admit that he had. She knew that Spencer visited her grandfather daily and always kept him abreast of what was going on with the vineyard. One day she had walked into the hospital room to find her grandfather sitting up in bed with a bunch of architectural plans across his lap while he and Spencer had their heads together, making additional plans.

They'd been so absorbed in their discussion that they hadn't noticed her presence. For a moment she had felt the closeness of the two men and suddenly knew how her mother had felt all those years ago. It was as if Spencer had become the grandson Daniel never had. Not knowing how she felt about that, as well as the other emotions she'd begun feeling around Spencer, she'd decided the best thing to do was to stay clear of him while she screwed her head back on right.

After dinner while clearing the table, Spencer approached her when her mother and grandmother had left to take an evening walk. She'd been hoping that he'd accompanied them and soon discovered he hadn't.

"Okay, what's wrong, Chardonnay?" he asked, his voice low, strained and concerned.

For a moment she couldn't reply. What could she say? I'm falling in love with you and I refuse to do so and will do whatever it takes to make sure it doesn't happen? Instead she shrugged. "What makes you think something is wrong?"

"You've been avoiding me."

She decided to pretend she didn't know what he was talking about. "Avoiding you in what way?"

"You haven't been back to the villa."

Did the man expect her to seek him out and tumble in his bed every chance she got? Her stomach knotted upon remembering his ferocious sexual appetite and concluded that yes, he probably did.

"I've been busy," she responded, both angry and frustrated. They hadn't been alone but a few minutes and already she could feel heated tension sizzle in the very air they were breathing.

"Come to me at midnight," he whispered in a voice tinged with throaty sexuality. He moved closer and drew her to him.

She didn't think of pulling back and although she was trembling inside, she did manage to say, "No."

"Yes," he countered hotly. And then his mouth swooped down on hers before any further protest could come from her lips. The moment his tongue entered her mouth, she remembered, she relented and she surrendered. Every nerve in her body began quivering under Spencer's skillful tongue. The hand he had placed at her waist wasn't helping matters. It only pulled her closer, making her more aware of his powerful heat.

When he finally lifted his head, he had to tighten his hold to keep her from falling. "I won't go to sleep until you get there," he whispered hotly against her lips.

She gazed at him thinking that he wouldn't be going to sleep after she got there, either. There was no doubt in her mind that he intended to keep her awake and busy.

He leaned down and took her lips in his again and then she wasn't thinking at all.

* * *

Donnay couldn't sleep.

She had tossed and turned most of the night. Her body felt hot. It was sensitive. It was experiencing a need to get physical. She kicked back the bedcovers, got out of bed and began pacing the floor. Spencer Westmoreland had gotten under her skin and as much as she tried she couldn't get him out. As a result, she was torn between what she wanted to do and what she knew she should. She had underestimated Spencer.

The man was turning out to be the exact opposite of what she'd assumed he would be. Of course there was a brashness about him she wouldn't even try to discount. But there was also a sense of caring. Her grandfather was proof of that. It wasn't just the time he'd spent with him, but also the fact that he had shared plans of the expansion with her grandfather when he really didn't have to. And then he'd gone further by giving him peace of mind that the vineyard would remain in the Russell family. She had begun seeing another side of Spencer, and with it she felt a grudging respect for him and everything he was doing to be fair to her family.

And she felt something else, something she could no longer deny. Love. She loved him. She sighed. She would marry him, bear his children and make him a good wife. And she hoped and prayed that one day he would grow to reciprocate her love.

A glance at the clock on the nightstand told her that midnight was approaching. She wondered what Spencer was doing. Was he in his bed thinking about her? Waiting on her? Wanting her?

That thought triggered chills that traveled down her

spine. She took a few steps over to her closet and moments later she was slipping out of her nightgown and pulling a skirt and blouse over her head, not bothering with a bra and panties. The outfit was simple, easy to get out of and even a bit sexy. A few moments later after easing her feet into a pair of sandals, she opened her bedroom door and quietly slipped out.

Spencer refused to sleep.

He was feeling restless and positively filled with a need that only Chardonnay could quench. He glanced over at the clock on the wall. It was getting close to midnight. What if he'd pushed too hard and she didn't come? He breathed in deeply, refusing to consider that possibility.

He had spoken to his mother earlier and had given her his news. As expected, she had asked questions, but nothing had stopped her from being elated. Another one of her sons was getting married and she was tickled pink. He knew by tomorrow morning the entire Westmoreland clan would hear about it. He would get calls, probably more questions—especially from his brothers and cousins who knew how his mind operated—but that thought didn't bother him. Like he'd told his mother, Chardonnay was the woman he wanted and the woman he intended to marry here in the vineyard in two weeks.

A sense of accomplishment rolled over him as he thought of having the things that were most important to him. The most significant one at the moment was Chardonnay. He thought of her often, even times when he didn't want to. What he'd told her mother at dinner was the truth. The reason he wanted to rush into marriage was that he didn't want to wait … mainly to make her his.

Deciding if she were to come to him he preferred her not making the trip from the main house through the vineyard alone, he slid out of bed and slipped into the jeans and shirt he had on earlier. His skin felt hot to the touch and he wondered if the same heat consuming his body was consuming hers. When he'd kissed her earlier that night, he had felt her response, had tasted her desire, inhaled her heat.

He wanted it.

He needed it.

His mind was becoming mentally shaken, his body physically addicted. They had made love one night, numerous times over, and that was all it had taken to reduce him to a man who stayed royally aroused around her. A man who spent most of his day dealing with frustrated lust. As he left the bedroom and began walking down the stairs his mind was filled with one thing and one thing only. Making love to Chardonnay.

Moments later he was closing the front door behind him as he made his way down the path. It was dark and the only light was from the moon overhead. The night air was cool and he wished he had thought to grab a jacket. It had rained earlier, right after he had returned home. It hadn't rained a lot, but enough to dampen the earth, supplying a distinctive aroma of wet grass, blooming plants, thickening vines and the earthy fragrance of freshly turned soil.

Feeling his fingers go cold, he hooked them in the pockets of his jeans. He suddenly sharpened his gaze when he heard a rustling sound. Thinking it was Chardonnay, he was about to call out to her then stopped after seeing it was her mother instead. Then before he could blink, another figure—that of a tall, muscular man— stepped out of the shadows and into the moonlight in front of her.

Spencer's protective instincts kicked in and his senses immediately went on full alert. Then he watched as the man pulled Ruth Russell into his arms and kissed her, and it was quite obvious she was kissing him back.

Spencer lowered his head, not wanting to intrude on such a passionate moment between the couple who, like him, were meeting for a midnight rendezvous. Moments later he glanced up in time to see them disappear into the shadows heading in the direction of the empty gardener's cottage.

Not that it was any of his business, but he wondered if Chardonnay knew that her mother was involved in an affair. If she didn't, she definitely wouldn't hear about it from him. When it came to secrets, he was the king of discreet. Still he couldn't help but wonder about the man's identity. Was he one of the workers at the winery?

Fairly certain the couple was halfway to their chosen destination by now, he began walking again. The night was quiet so he easily picked up the sound of footsteps coming his way. He stopped and focused his gaze. And then he saw her.

She hadn't seen him yet so he leaned back against an oak tree to study her features in the moonlight. Beautiful. And then his body began thrumming at the realization that although he was fairly certain she hadn't wanted to come, desire had driven her to seek him out.

Something gave him away. Possibly the sudden intake of his breath when he saw her outfit. It was one of those fit-and-flare skirts and a jersey-knit top with billowy sleeves. The way they clung to her body sent a surge of adrenaline pumping through his veins. She stopped walking and stared at him and he pushed away from the tree and strolled toward her.

He had spent the last three hours wondering if she would show up, and now that she was here, his already hot blood was boiling even more at the thought of how they would spend the rest of their time together. He wasn't used to a woman taking control of his thoughts like she was doing.

"You came," were the only words he could fix his mouth to say at that moment, he was so filled with unleashed passion.

"Yes, I came," she whispered, and the sound sent his insides to quivering. He battled the urge to take her then and there, to let their naked bodies roll in the damp earth, get tangled in the vines and—"

"It's cool out."

He saw her rubbing her arms and quickly realized that like him she hadn't worn a jacket. He smiled a tight, restrained smile. Anything else would cause the erection to burst in his crotch. "Then let's go to my place where I can warm you. But that's not all I plan to do to you tonight, Chardonnay."

Her incredible gray eyes gazed deeply at him when she asked in a soft, sexy voice, "What else do you plan to do to me?"

She had a right to ask. She had a right to know. "Taste every single inch of you. Let my fingers stroke you. Let my body make love to you in all kinds of ways and various positions."

He took a step closer to her. "Will you let me do all those things to you again?"

"Yes."

Pleased she hadn't hesitated with her answer, he dipped his head and tasted her lips, savoring his own special brand of Chardonnay. He lifted his mouth, deciding he needed to take her to a place more private before he lost control. The last thing he wanted was for her mother to come upon them like he had on her earlier.

"When you leave my bed tonight I want you to be totally and thoroughly convinced that I am the only man you'll ever want and need." And then he swung her up into his arms and began walking back toward his villa.

He had gotten halfway there and couldn't go anymore. The feel of her in his arms, the way her breasts were pressed against chest, the scent of her in his nostrils, the way she had tucked her hands beneath his shirt to keep them warm, all of them increased his sexual craze. He couldn't move another inch without the threat of his aroused body exploding then and there.

Inhaling deeply, he placed her on her feet. She gazed at him for a moment and then as if understanding what he couldn't put into words, she took his hand and said, "Come with me. I want to show you something."

She led him through a thicket of low-hanging branches, parting several grapevines that blocked their way, to guide him to a grassy path. There at the end of it was a glass enclosed summerhouse, sitting amidst vines, ferns, a cluster of oak trees and palms. She glanced at his expression. He didn't even try to hide his smile.

"Gramps had it built years ago for my grandmother, a place where she could get away, sew, read and rest. She hasn't used it much over the years. It's climate controlled and should be nice and warm inside," she said, opening the door. He followed her inside and then she locked it behind them. It was nice and warm on the inside and the window blinds assured complete privacy.

After she turned on a lamp, he glanced around but only for a second. His gaze immediately returned to her when he saw the frown bunching her brow. "What is it?" he asked.

"Um, nothing, I guess. It's just that no one ever comes out here but me to read and take a nap on occasion. However, it seems the bedcovers have been changed since the last time I was here."

Spencer had an idea who had changed the bedcovers but kept his thoughts to himself. "Does it matter?"

She met his gaze and shook her head. "No. Nothing matters but this moment. With you."

Something tugged deep inside of him. He could not deny the sensation even if he wanted to. Even if he didn't fully understand it. He opened his arms to her and she took the few steps to walk into them. Instinctively she lifted her head and at the same time he lowered his, covering her lips.

A ferocious ache overtook him and he whispered words against her lips, not sure what he was saying and at the moment not caring. The only thing that mattered to him was the ravenous desire running rampant through his entire body. She arched against him and his senses went into overdrive.

Like a man with no control, he stepped back and

tugged her blouse over her head. The moment he saw her braless, he closed his hand over her breasts, reveling in their shape, their firmness and how right they felt in his hands. He then leaned down and kissed them, satisfying his hungry need to taste her.

But he soon discovered it wasn't enough for him.

He dropped to his knees in front of her and tugged her skirt down her thighs and almost swallowed his tongue when he stared her feminine mound smack in the face. She hadn't worn panties.

He leaned forward to do his own taste test as his nose nuzzled the curls at the apex of her thighs, taking in her scent, letting his nostrils absorb her aroma just seconds before his tongue thrust deep inside her while grabbing hold of her bottom, pulling her closer to the fit of his mouth. He became lost in heavenly bliss while his tongue stroked, caressed and probed, refusing to let up or let go. He heard her moans, felt the torture on his shoulders when her fingernails dug into them, but he refused to release her from his grip.

This was his Chardonnay and he intended to enjoy it to the fullest. Even when he felt her body explode beneath his mouth he held tight, needing to fully taste the very essence of her.

It was only after the last tremor had left her body that he drew back from the intimate kiss. He glanced up at her, met the dazed gray of her eyes and a smile curved his mouth as he licked his lips. "Best Chardonnay I've ever had the pleasure of tasting," he whispered before standing and sweeping her naked body off her feet and into his arms.

He carried her over to the daybed and placed her on

it and then quickly began removing his clothes. It had started raining again, a downpour that beat against the rooftop and glass walls. The air seemed to thicken with the fragrance of flowers, grapes and sex. He inhaled it. He licked his lips and could still taste it. He was suddenly filled with a sexual rush, a need to mate to an extreme he never thought possible. He wanted her. Damn, how he wanted her.

He moved back toward the bed. Instead of wrapping her arms around his neck like he assumed she would do, she grabbed hold of his shaft and stroked the head of his erection with soft fingers. In his already sexually glazed mind that was the last thing he needed but exactly what he wanted. Her touch was eliciting sounds from his throat, and he felt himself weaken, giving in to the demands of his body. The demands of her hands.

He felt her touch all the way to his bones, felt himself harden even more beneath her fingertips. She mentally fractured any thoughts he had, igniting a fuse within him that could explode any minute. And when she pushed him back on the bed and took him into her mouth, he clenched his jaw to keep from hollering. He gripped the bedcovers as her mouth began ravaging him, sapping him of any strength while at the same time seizing the air in his lungs. Sensations swamped him and he gave himself up to them, and to her.

Good God! What was she doing to him? He had to stop her before he was stripped of everything within him. A deep moan escaped his lips when he shifted and pushed her on her back, locking his thighs over hers, trapping her beneath him. Before she could mutter a single word of protest, he entered her and they both released moans of pleasure at the same time, just seconds before they began spiraling out of control.

He reached under her and lifted her hips as he thrust in and out of her, and with each stroke she arched her body to meet him, creating a sensuous blend of perfect harmony.

"Incredible," he murmured, just seconds before dipping his head to her mouth, laving her lips with his tongue from corner to corner before inserting his tongue into her mouth. Below he felt her inner muscles clench him, milk him, attempt to pull everything out him, and she succeeded.

"Chardonnay!"

His body seemed to explode in tiny pieces as his seed spilled deep inside her, overflowing within her and over-whelming him. Never before had he given so much to any woman and with no regrets and no restraints. That thought became logged in his brain but he refused to dwell on it now. The only thing he wanted to think about was how he felt inside her and how his body was still throbbing from the effects of the most intense orgasm he'd ever experienced.

Their gazes connected and he felt like he was sinking in quicksand. He clung to her, afraid if he let go that would be the end of it…of them.

As he pulled her shaking body closer to him, more sensations shot through him and at that moment, he couldn't fathom a life without the woman in his arms.

Donnay came awake to discover Spencer gazing down at her. She blinked, wondering how long she'd slept. The last thing she remembered was coming apart in his arms while he was buried deep inside of her, feeling the heated essence of him shooting to all parts of her.

"I have something for you," he whispered huskily.

His words made her study his features. "What?"

"This."

And then she felt him slip something onto her finger, and she knew what it was. Her engagement ring. The huge diamond shone brightly in the moonlight and Donnay's breath caught. It was exquisite, the most beautiful ring she'd ever seen.

Not knowing what to say, she sank against him instead and he pulled her into his arms and held her. She knew that loving Spencer when he didn't love her back wouldn't always be easy. He was a hard man, a man who'd been hurt by love. It would be up to her to go about repairing his heart mainly because she believed in the very essence of her soul that it was a heart worthy of fixing.

"It's beautiful, Spencer," she finally said. "Simply beautiful. Thank you."

"You're welcome." Then he said, "The rain has stopped. Are you ready to get dressed and go to my place?"

She looked at him. Her heart was assured that although he didn't love her, he definitely wanted her. "Yes," she said, wrapping her arms around his neck. "I'm ready."

# Ten

Spencer stood at the window in his bedroom and glanced out. It had been four days since he'd told his mother about his wedding plans and his phone was still ringing. His cousin Delaney had even called him all the way from her home in the Middle East to congratulate him.

He leaned against the windowsill, thinking the last few days had been sheer bliss. Chardonnay seemed to have accepted the way things would be between them and no longer fought the idea that in less than two weeks they would be getting married.

And their relationship had definitely improved. They were now an engaged couple and instinctively acted the part. They had begun sharing breakfast and dinner each day, would take walks together in the afternoon while he brought her up-to-date on that day's work activities, and at night they shared a bed. He no longer had to seduce her to do so. Each night she would come to him automatically, as though she knew her place was beside him in bed, and a part of him felt that it was.

Last night they had attended a wine-tasting gala in downtown Napa, Taste Napa Downtown. The outfit Chardonnay had worn had been both professional and seductive. and he had felt proud to be the man at her side. When they'd entered the ballroom where the event had been held, heads had turned and more than one person had commented that they made a striking couple.

On that thought he lowered his head as a deep sensation settled in his gut, one he'd tried ignoring over the past few days. Whenever he was with Chardonnay, whether in bed or out, he felt like a different person, a man on top of the world. A man who was starting to live for the first time. To appreciate the finer things in life. A man who was looking forward to his future.

A man who was in love.

His breath paused in his throat. Falling in love was something he never intended to happen to him, but it had. He rubbed his hand over his face, accepting what his heart had been trying to tell him lately, but what he had ignored until now.

Months ago, if anyone would have suggested that he'd give his heart to any woman, he would have laughed in their face, knowing such a thing wasn't possible. But he was living proof that it was possible.

He glanced out the window again when he heard the equipment plowing the earth to cultivate additional land for grapes to be planted in the spring. He was anticipating a good harvest in the coming year and was anticipating becoming a father in that time as well. But more than anything he wanted to be a good husband to Char-donnay, and he hoped that in time she would get over the circumstances of their marriage and accept the fact they were together and build on that.

Her grandfather had got out of the hospital a few days ago and Spencer found he was spending time with the older man as well. Daniel's health was improving and he'd been extremely happy to come home and discover his plans and dreams for the winery were coming true. To avoid tiring the older man out, the architect Spencer had hired was meeting with Daniel a couple of hours a day to make sure the plans being drawn were exactly the way Chardonnay's grandfather had envisioned them.

Spencer turned when he heard his phone ring, inter-rupting his thoughts. He moved away from the window and walked over to the desk to pick it up. "Yes?"

"Something interesting has developed that I think you should know about."

Spencer arched a brow at the serious sound of his attorney's voice. "And what is that, Stuart?"

"Over a million dollars was deposited into the Russell Vineyards bank account this morning."

Spencer's body stiffened as his mind began whirling with questions. He took a breath. "There has to be a mistake."

"No mistake, Spence."

"Then how did it get there? Who made the deposit?"

"It was a transfer that I was able to trace from a Korean bank. An international account in the name of BOSS."

Spencer lifted a brow. "Boss?"

"Yes."

He stared at the floor as various things ran through

his mind. He didn't want to consider any of them but knew that he had to. "Find out who owns the account and even more importantly, why they would have deposited that money into the Russells' account?"

"All right. You don't think that Chardonnay Russell borrowed the money elsewhere, even though she knew you'd agreed to front the financing for the expansion, do you?"

He inhaled sharply. That was a possibility he didn't want to consider. Over the past weeks he had let his guard down and had done something he swore he wouldn't after what Lynette Marie had done to him, and that was to begin trusting another woman. Not to mention fall in love.

He had to admit that his mind hadn't been on a lot lately, other than making love to her. A dark suspicion leaped to life inside of him. Had she used his moment of weakness to keep him occupied so he wouldn't find out what she was doing behind his back until it was too late?

"Spence?"

His attorney's voice made him aware he hadn't answered his question. "I'm not sure what's going on, Stuart, but I want you to find out."

"I will and in the meantime, be careful how you handle your business."

Spencer knew Stuart's meaning and as he clicked off the phone a part of him thought that his attorney's advice may have come a little too late.

A few hours later, Spencer snapped closed his luggage and moved away from the bed. Stuart hadn't returned his call. That meant the information they wanted was hard to get, which was usually the case involving international accounts. Why would anyone place that much money into the Russells' account unless someone had negotiated a deal elsewhere? And since Chardonnay was the one handling the family's business, he could only assume it had been her.

Doubt and suspicions he didn't want to feel were eating at him, and he couldn't forget the moment he'd received the coroner's report on Lynette Marie. Betrayal of the worst kind had wretched his insides and as much as he was trying not to let it happen, he was beginning to feel the same way now.

He walked over to the window and looked out at the hills and valleys. Disgust and anger ate at him. Although the circumstances were different, the results were the same. He had allowed another woman to betray him. And this time the pain cut deeper because he loved her.

From the beginning she had alluded that in the end, he would regret ever coming up with the idea for the two of them to marry. He had merely brushed her comment aside as insignificant. But Chardonnay Russell had played him for a fool. She had weaved her deceitful web around him, first in the physical sense and then in an emotional sense. Each and every time they'd made love it had weakened him, had turned him into putty in her hands to the extent that all he'd thought about over the past week—besides marrying her—was pleasing her, making her happy, trying to show her that a lifetime with him wouldn't be so damn awful.

And all the time he'd been working hard doing that, she had been undermining him, setting him up for failure and intentionally messing with his heart.

He turned away from the window when he heard the sound of the key turning in the lock downstairs. It would be Chardonnay. Before she'd left his bed early that morning she'd agreed to return a little before noon to give him a tour of the section of the winery he hadn't yet seen, and to introduce him to all the employees.

He turned back to the window when he heard her footsteps coming up the stairs. Anger consumed him to a degree he hadn't thought possible and it would have definitely been to her benefit if he could have left and returned to Sausalito without seeing her. In his present state of mind, he would have preferred it.

He turned when she opened the door and when his gaze touched hers he felt a hardening deep in his chest. At the same time a sensation of pain surrounded his heart.

"I told you I would be back," she said, smiling and stepping into the room, closing the door behind her.

When he didn't say anything but just stared at her, her gaze shifted to the bed where she saw his packed luggage. He watched as her smile faded. "You have to go away on business?"

He inhaled deeply, not in the mood to play her games, although she evidently assumed he was gullible enough to do so. He moved away from the window and went to stand before her. "Yes, I'm leaving but it's not on business. I'm leaving for good and won't be coming back."

She shook her head as if she hadn't heard him correctly. "But what about the wedding?"

His heart hardened even more when he said, "There won't be a wedding. You would be the last woman I'd marry."

If her reaction was anything to go by, it seemed that

his words had immediately knocked the breath out of her body, sent an invisible slap across her face. She placed a hand over her heart and her eyes widened in shocked disbelief. "Why? I don't understand. What happened?"

Her pretense angered him even more. "Let's cut the bull, Chardonnay, shall we? How long did you think it would be before I found out?"

A confused look appeared on her face. "Found out what?"

Spencer shook his head and laughed, not believing she had the nerve to ask him that. Even now she was standing in front of him with a puzzled expression, as if she had no clue what he was talking about, but he knew otherwise.

"I have to hand it to you. You are one hell of an actress. What did you do to get the money, Chardonnay? Are you sleeping with him like you're sleeping with me?" He watched color drain from her face. Guilt, he thought.

"I don't know what you're talking about," she said in a low, strained voice, shaking her head as if to deny his words.

"Don't you?" he said angrily, his tone bitter. "You want me to believe you have no idea who deposited a million dollars into the winery account this morning?"

"What! A million dollars? You're wrong. There must be a mistake."

He chuckled. "Oh, yes, there's a mistake all right, and it was made the day I set eyes on you."

"No, Spencer, listen to me. There has to be a mistake." She reached out as if to make a plea and he grabbed her wrist firmly in his hand and hauled her tightly against his chest.

His stony gaze met hers. "You played me for a fool, Chardonnay. You never intended to marry me and have my children. You had a plan B all along, didn't you?"

"No, that's not true. How could you think I could be so dishonest and calculating? How could—"

"Enough! I don't want to hear anything you have to say." He released her hand and moved around her and grabbed his luggage off the bed. He headed for the door, paused and then swung around to look at her again. "Tell your grandfather that I will continue to pay those men to clear the additional twenty acres like I promised him I would. I will also take care of any and all expenses associated with any surgery he might have, because deep down I don't believe he knew just what kind of games you were playing, just what a deceitful person you are. And," he said, pausing briefly, "if you're already pregnant with my child then rest assured you haven't seen the last of me. And if you aren't, then I hope to God I never see you again."

He turned around and without looking back again, he left.

"Donnay! What's wrong?" Ruth shot to her feet the moment Donnay entered the house.

Donnay had been hoping her mother had left to go to the winery's gift shop that she supervised and wouldn't see her this way. She hurriedly wiped the tears from her eyes as she moved toward the stairs. None of what Spencer had accused her of made sense. How could he have thought she had deceived him? Although she had called the bank and they had confirmed the million-dollar deposit, she had no idea who had done it, or why.

"Donnay?"

She met her mother's worried gaze and said in a low, shaky voice, "I'm fine, Mom."

"Then why are you crying?"

It took Donnay awhile to compose herself before saying, "Spencer has called off the wedding. He thinks I've deceived him."

Ruth looked stunned. "Deceived him? Why would he think that?"

Donnay tried to still her shaking hands as she wiped another tear from her eye. She was angry and upset. "He thinks I never intended to marry him because I was getting the money I needed to save the winery from someone else. He even suggested I was sleeping with someone else to get it."

"How could he suggest something so despicable?"

"Because someone deposited a million dollars into the winery bank account and I—"

Donnay stopped talking upon her mother's sharp intake of breath. She studied her mother's features. Ruth Russell was flushing guiltily. Something wasn't right and Donnay played her hunch by asking, "Mom, do you know where that money came from? I checked with the bank and it's actually there."

Ruth stared back at her daughter and slowly nodded. "Yes, I know where it came from. He said he was going to do it but I asked him not to, because I believed that everything with you and Spence would work out just fine."

Donnay was having a hard time keeping up with what her mother was saying. She placed a hand on her arm. "He? Who is *he*, Mom?"

Ruth drew in a ragged breath and then she said, "Your father."

Stunned, Donnay could only stare at her mother. Her mind tried denying what her ears had just heard. There had to be a mistake. But something pushed her to ask for clarification purposes. "My father?"

"Yes. I told him about the outlandish proposal Spencer had made to you and Chad said that he—"

"Whoa. Back up a minute, Mom. I'm trying to follow you here but I'm having a hard time. Are you saying you've seen my father? Actually talked to him?"

Ruth nodded again. "Yes, he called a few weeks ago and said he was in the area and wanted to see me."

"In the area?"

"Yes. He was in San Francisco on business and decided to rent a car and come to the valley. He wasn't sure if I was still living here, or if over the years I had married and moved away."

Donnay inhaled. "I guess you got around to telling him about me," she said quietly.

Ruth nodded. "Yes. At first he wasn't happy about having a daughter he'd never known about, was cheated out of knowing. But then I explained to him how those letters came back. I'd even kept them and showed them to him so he'd know that I had tried contacting him."

"So," Donnay said slowly, "what has he been doing all these years? Is he married? Does he have any other children?"

Ruth shook her head. "He's a widower. His wife of fifteen years died five years ago and they never had any children. He retired from the army and went into business for himself; some sort of international electronic corporation that has done well over the years. And now that he knows about you, he wants to meet you, Chardonnay."

Ruth smiled slightly. "You should have seen him that first night after I told him about you. He was ready to come here and claim you immediately, but I convinced him to wait until I felt the time was right. Besides, he and I needed to talk, to find out what has been happening in our lives over the years. When I told him about the winery's problems, and how you were willing to sacrifice your happiness to marry a man you didn't love just to save the winery, he offered to pay off the debt. He said he would put the money into our account as soon as it could be transferred. I asked him not to, but like you he's stubborn and has this protective instinct and he did it anyway. I'm sorry if doing so has caused friction between you and Spencer."

Donnay shook her head after hearing her mother's explanation. "It doesn't matter. Our marriage would have been doomed from the start, Mom. This shows just how little he trusted me, and a marriage not based on faith and trust is no marriage at all. I could have survived without love but I have to know that Spencer has faith in me and trusts me. Without it, a relationship couldn't last."

A small smile touched her lips as the picture became clear in her mind. "So, is my father the *old friend* you've been spending a lot of time with lately?"

Ruth actually blushed. "Yes, and he is very anxious to meet you."

"And I'm anxious to meet him as well." Donnay turned to go up the stairs then, but Ruth's voice held her back.

"He loves you, you know."

"Who, Mom?"

"Spencer."

Donnay chuckled to hold back fresh tears. "No, he never loved me, Mom. Our marriage was going to be a business deal. I told you that."

"Yes, but I have my own eyes, Donnay. That might have been his intent but it didn't last. That night he came for dinner, he couldn't keep his eyes off you. You might not have noticed but your grandmother and I certainly did. Spencer Westmoreland loves you."

Donnay glanced down at her left hand. She had removed her engagement ring and she held it, clenched tightly in her fist. She then looked back up at her mother. "No, Mom, he doesn't love me, but you know what's really sad and probably pathetic? I fell in love with him and was actually looking forward to being his wife and the mother of his children."

Knowing she couldn't hold back her tears much longer, she said, "I think I'll go into town. I need to get away for a while." Then without saying anything else, she raced up the stairs.

Spencer tensed visibly when the phone rang. A part of him knew it had to be Stuart. He placed his wineglass on the table and picked up the house phone.

Arriving home to Sausalito had been a welcome relief. He had spent the past couple of hours opening up windows and blinds to enjoy the view of the Bay from his living-room window. To keep busy he had immediately begun work on another business deal, one that would involve his cousins and brothers. His cousin Clint had retired as a Texas Ranger and was using the ranch he had inherited from his uncle to set up a business much like the one Durango and McKinnon had established.

He picked up the phone. "Yes?"

"I got the information you wanted, Spence."

Spencer remained silent for a moment then said. "All right. Who put that money into the Russell's account?"

"A man by the name of Chad Timberlain."

Spencer racked his mind trying to recall where he'd heard that name before. It suddenly hit him at the same time he heard a knock at his door. He felt a hard tug on his insides at the thought that he might have jumped to the wrong conclusions about Chardonnay.

"Look, Stuart, I'll need to get back to you. I think I know what might be going on, but I'll have to verify it and call you back."

He hung up the phone and headed for the door, wondering who would be visiting him since no one knew he had returned to Sausalito. He snatched opened the door to find a tall, muscular, fifty-something-year-old man standing there.

Spencer inhaled slowly. Although the two of them had never met, he recognized the man's profile as the one he'd seen that night on the path, just seconds before he had taken Ruth Russell into his arms.

"Chad Timberlain?" Spencer caught the man by surprise in asking.

The older man frowned coolly. "Yes."

Spencer stepped aside. "Come in. I really wasn't expecting you, since I just figured things out. But I'm sure you're here because you feel that the two of us need to talk."

The older man gave him a look that indicated the two of them needed to do more than merely exchange words and Spencer understood. If he was in Timberlain's place, he'd do the same thing. "And we need to come to an understanding," Spencer decided to add.

The man's features relaxed somewhat as he stepped over the threshold, and Spencer exhaled as he closed the door behind him.

"So, as you can see," Spencer said sometime later to Chad Timberlain, as they sat in his living room finishing off glasses of Russell wine, "I assumed Chardonnay knew about the money that had been placed in the winery's account.

"Even when she told you she didn't know anything about it?" Chad asked, his gaze boring into Spencer. After the two of them began talking, the older man's manner appeared calm and relaxed. But the more Spencer outlined just what his and Chardonnay's relationship was, the more the conversation between them became somewhat strained. Although Timberlain hadn't been involved in his daughter's life before now, he felt that was neither here nor there since he intended to become involved. Starting here.

There was only one answer Spencer could give and it was one he wasn't really proud of. "Yes, even when she denied my allegations."

The man's gaze hardened under Spencer's direct stare. "I felt compelled to place that money into the account because I couldn't stand there and let you railroad my daughter into marrying you."

After hearing his account of his relationship with

Chardonnay—minus, of course the intimate part—he didn't find her father's attitude the least bit unreasonable. "Yes, sir. I understand and I can also appreciate that."

The man nodded. "So what are you going to do to rectify the situation? Ruth feels that you love Chardonnay and what happened was a grave mistake on your part."

Spencer swallowed. Grave was too mild a word. He couldn't see her ever forgiving him. He had asked her to believe in him and trust him, yet he hadn't done the same for her. He met her father's intense gaze. "I do love your daughter and will be the first to admit I was wrong. If she never speaks to me again I will understand."

He then leaned forward. "But because I love her, I'm going to fight for her and hope that she finds it in her heart to give me another chance. It's no longer about what I can do for the winery, it's about us—Chardonnay and me."

A smile touched the corners of Chad Timberlain's lips. "I've yet to officially meet my daughter, in fact I plan to do so tonight. From what Ruth tells me she can be pretty stubborn at times, so you won't have an easy job."

No one had to tell Spencer about Chardonnay's stubbornness. He was very much aware of it. "I know, but I'm going to die trying," he said, and he meant every word.

Donnay glanced at her reflection in the mirror as she tried to ignore the butterflies in her stomach. She would be meeting her father for the first time tonight. Her heart was already filled with love for him. Without having met her, he had come to her aid by putting that money into the winery account and proving that he would be a father who would always be there for his daughter.

She had hoped that getting caught up in meeting her father would eliminate thoughts of Spencer from her mind. Tomorrow was soon enough to be faced with the task of canceling everything. She would have to call the florist, the caterer and the printer. She wondered if he had told his family yet and if he had, what reason he had given them for calling off the wedding. No doubt he had convinced them—like he was convinced—that she was someone who couldn't be trusted.

She glanced at the clock on the wall. It was nearing six o'clock. Tonight her family would be hosting a small dinner party to celebrate her grandfather's homecoming, as well as her father's entrance back into their lives. Her mother had confided in her earlier that she and Chad Timberlain were doing some serious dating. Donnay was happy knowing there was a chance her mother might be able to recapture the love she had lost over twenty-seven years ago.

She heard a knock on her bedroom door. Thinking it was her mother or grandmother, she said, "Come in."

Donnay turned to see the door open and instead of her mother or grandmother, her breath caught when Spencer walked in. Fierce emotions welled up in her throat when she remembered his harsh words, his accusations. He had asked her to believe in him when he had no intention of ever believing in her. "What are you doing here, Spencer? What do you want?" she asked in an angry tone.

He moved into the room so quickly that she hadn't been given time to blink. When she did, he was standing there, right in front of her. His voice was gentle yet husky when he spoke. "I'm here to apologize for all the things

I said. And as far as what I want…what I want Chardonnay, is you."

All it took was one look at Chardonnay's features to know his apology hadn't softened her any. Anger lined her gray eyes and she was standing stiff, with her hands balled into fists. He noticed that she had removed his ring.

"You accused me of those god-awful things. You played judge and jury. You didn't trust me. You—"

He reached out and tried touching her hand, the one that no longer wore his ring, and she angrily snatched it back. "No! You even accused me of betraying you with another man. How could you think so low of me?"

Spencer saw the tears in her eyes and a deep lump formed in his throat. He had hurt her. He had caused her pain and more than anything he wanted to make it right. "I love you, Chardonnay," he said in a low voice, straight from the heart. "I never meant to fall in love with you but I did. I'm the one who got caught up in all my scheming and manipulative tactics. I have been betrayed before. A few years ago, when my fiancée was killed, I discovered she was pregnant by another man. I made a promise to myself then that although I still wanted a wife and children, there would be no love. But you proved me wrong because you demanded my love without even realizing you were doing it. And when I found out about the money in your account, I felt used and betrayed because I realized you no longer had anything to gain from our marriage and that in essence, you no longer needed me…but I had begun needing you."

Donnay inhaled deeply. Spencer's words from earlier that day had been cruel, unjustified and angry. But now she understood why he had been so quick to judge her falsely. His former fiancée had gotten pregnant by someone else? She couldn't imagine a woman wanting to have any man's baby but his. Even now she was hoping that she was already pregnant.

She saw the strain and pain on Spencer's face. He had admitted that he loved her, which definitely came as a surprise. And she believed him because confessing his love to a woman couldn't be easy for him. And she loved him, too. She loved him with all her heart.

"If I accept your apology, and believe what you say about loving me, what do you expect of me?" she asked in a soft voice.

He placed both hands in the pockets of his pants as he stood gazing at her. "I expect—I would hope that you will take me back, give me another chance to prove just how wrong I've been and to make things right. I would want us to go ahead with our wedding and become husband and wife, but I'll let you set the date. If you prefer waiting until after the holidays then that's fine. I will no longer rush you into anything."

He sighed deeply then continued. "And I would want you to give me a chance to love you in such a way that you would want to love me back. " A smile curved his lips when he added honestly. "I will make it almost impossible for you not to do so. And if you're not pregnant already, then I'll let you decide when we'll have children. I won't make it a priority. I want to spend time with you and love you the way you rightly deserve without any limitations or stipulations imposed."

Donnay didn't say anything for a while and then she tilted her head and studied him. She saw the strain lines across his forehead, the tension that had tightened around his lips. But it was his eyes that brought it all home. They were dark, intense and filled with love...for her. "And what if I were to say that I already love you, that I had fallen in love with you weeks ago?" she asked in a tight voice, fighting back a sob that threatened to close her throat. "What if I were to say that, Spencer?"

He took a step closer to her. "Then I would ask you to give me an opportunity to make you never regret loving me, never regret giving me another chance. Never regret becoming my wife and the mother of my children. Will you?"

She slowly nodded. "Yes."

Happiness spread across his features and he removed his hands from his pockets and reached out for her. This time she didn't deny him and willingly went into his open arms. He held her tightly to him, as if he never intended to let her go, and then he tilted up her chin and captured her mouth with his, glorying in the taste of his own personal brand of Chardonnay.

The moment his tongue took hold of hers, sensations rippled through him, pleasure seeped into his bones and desire filled his entire being. If her family didn't have a number of dinner guests downstairs he would be tempted to lock the door and stay in this bedroom with her forever. Besides, her father would not let him do such a thing. The man had given him twenty minutes before he'd threatened to come up and rescue his daughter, if need be. The only need was the one Spencer felt in his crotch.

"I want to make love to you," he whispered against her moist lips.

"And I want you to make love to me."

He smiled. "Later tonight? At the villa?"

She grinned. "Yes, later tonight. At the villa."

Although he wanted to keep her in her bedroom a little longer, moments later Spencer found himself escorting Chardonnay down the stairs. In just the nick of time, he figured, because standing on the bottom step was her father, waiting on them. Spencer held her hand, the one that once again was wearing his ring.

Spencer stopped in the middle of the staircase and turned to Chardonnay. "This first meeting should be your time with him. Go down to your father."

She smiled when Spencer released her hand, and continued walking alone down the stairs. A grin of pure happiness covered Chad Timberlain's face and he opened his arms up to the daughter he only recently discovered he had. Automatically, she returned the affection by walking straight into his waiting arms.

"Dad," she whispered while he held her tight. Chardonnay glanced across the room and saw her mother standing with her grandparents, tears in their eyes. Tonight was very special. The father she'd never met had come to claim his daughter, and the man she had fallen in love with loved her back.

She felt utterly and truly happy.

Later that night, Donnay lay wrapped up in Spencer's arms. After an intense lovemaking session, they had talked. Since he hadn't called his family to cancel the wedding plans, and she hadn't cancelled the florist, caterer or printer, they decided to still get married the week before Christmas. Besides, each and every time they made love they ran the risk of starting a family, which was something the both of them decided they still wanted to do.

Donnay smiled, thinking about what he'd told her earlier. "I can't believe my father actually came to see you."

"Well, he did and he wanted to let me know in no uncertain terms that he would not tolerate me taking advantage of his daughter."

"He's really special. To think he put all that money into my bank account to help out."

Her father had explained after retiring from the military, he and three guys who'd served under him in the army had formed an international electronic company called BOSS and it was doing extremely well. He had assured her that giving her that much money had not affected the company's bottom line.

Chad was semiretired and the first of the year he planned to step down as CEO and turn over the day-to-day operation of the company to the three competent men whom he considered surrogate sons. Donnay would get to meet them at her wedding.

"So when do you think your mom and Chad will marry?" Spencer asked her.

Donnay's smile deepened. "Before Valentine's Day. I can't imagine them waiting longer than that. And trust me when I say that this time, she has no qualms leaving here and traveling with Dad, although she'll wait until after Gramps's surgery, of course. She's satisfied that you and I have decided to make our home here and we'll keep an eye on my grandparents. Mom deserves to finally spend time with the man she loves and to be happy."

"You deserve to be happy as well. I love you," he whispered close to her ear.

She smiled at him. "And I love you, too."

She snuggled deeper into the arms she had once believed were incapable of loving anyone, especially her. He had proven her wrong, and every time she looked into his eyes, she saw the truth reflected in their dark depths. He was a man who, she had discovered, not only had a lot of forbidden passion, but also had a lot of hidden talents. She couldn't help wondering where he got some of his smooth moves and creative positions when they made love.

"Ready again?"

She chuckled as she turned in his arms. She couldn't say he hadn't warned her about his inexhaustible energy. Reaching up, she placed her arms around his neck. "For you, Spencer Westmoreland, I'll always be ready."

# Epilogue

Spencer stood beside Reggie, the youngest of his brothers, who was still a bachelor and who was standing as his best man. Spencer watched his beautiful bride walk down the aisle to him on her father's arm. He thought Chardonnay was a stunning vision in white. The top of her gown fitted tightly to the waist and then flared out in a thousand ruffles.

All the love he never thought possible was flowing through him at that moment and he definitely couldn't wait for their wedding night. After spending the night in their villa, they would be flying out in the morning for Paris where they would spend two weeks.

"You sure you want to do this?" Reggie asked, leaning over to whisper in his ear.

Spencer grinned, not taking his gaze off Chardonnay. "Hell, yes."

His brother Jared, standing close by as a groomsman, poked him in the ribs, reminding him of the preacher who was within earshot. That didn't bother Spencer. On this day, his wedding day, nothing would bother him.

When Chardonnay reached his side and gave him her hand, he took it and lifted it up to his lips and kissed it. What the hell, he thought. He could definitely do better than that. Then he pulled her into his arms and kissed her lips. She returned his kiss in kind, until a few guests cleared their throats, reminding the couple of their presence.

Spencer pulled back and met the minister's frown. "You're supposed to wait until after I pronounce you husband and wife," the pastor scolded them in a low voice, trying to keep the smile off his face.

Spencer gave the minister a mischievous grin. "I know, sir. I'm sorry. I got carried away."

And then the wedding ceremony began.

When it ended, the minister presented the couple as husband and wife, and Spencer kissed his bride all over again.

\* \* \* \* \*

# FREE!

## 2 Stories
### and a surprise gift!

We would like to take this opportunity to thank you for reading this Mills & Boon® book by offering you the chance to take another specially selected 2-in-1 volume from the Desire™ 2-in-1 series absolutely FREE! We're also making this offer to introduce you to the benefits of the Mills & Boon® Book Club™—

★ FREE home delivery
★ FREE monthly Newsletter
★ Books available before they're in the shops
★ FREE gifts and competitions
★ Exclusive Book Club offers

Accepting this FREE book and gift places you under no obligation to buy, you may cancel at any time, even after receiving your free shipment. Simply complete your details below and return the entire page to the address below. You don't even need a stamp!

**YES!** Please send me 2 free Desire stories in a 2-in-1 volume and a surprise gift. I understand that unless you hear from me, I will receive 2 superb new 2-in-1 titles every month for just £5.25 each, postage and packing free. I am under no obligation to purchase any book and may cancel my subscription at any time. The free book and gift will be mine to keep in any case.

D9ZEF

Ms/Mrs/Miss/Mr ..................................Initials.................................
**BLOCK CAPITALS PLEASE**
Surname .................................................................................................
Address..................................................................................................
..............................................................................................................
...................................................Postcode ......................................

**Send this whole page to:**
**UK: FREEPOST CN81, Croydon, CR9 3WZ**